The Warrior

JUDITH E. FRENCH

LEISURE BOOKS  NEW YORK CITY

For Gary, my warrior,
who has never failed me.

A LEISURE BOOK®

December 2005

Published by

Dorchester Publishing Co., Inc.
200 Madison Avenue
New York, NY 10016

ISBN 0-8439-5395-0

The name "Leisure Books" and the stylized "L" with design are trademarks of Dorchester Publishing Co., Inc.

Printed in the United States of America.

Visit us on the web at www.dorchesterpub.com.

The Warrior

Long, long ago, beyond the misty space
Of twice a thousand years,
In Erin old, there dwelt a mighty race. . . .
                                        —D'Arcy McGee

The Western Coast of Ireland

"Faster, Kiara! Faster!" The boy squealed and clapped
chubby hands as the raven-haired girl kneeling in the
bow of the curragh thrust her paddle deep into the
foaming water. The hide boat bounced and skimmed
over the waves, sending salt spray flying amid the
splashing of tiny iridescent fish and the ghostly cries of
sleek seals riding the silvery tide.

Wind ripped the leather ties from Kiara's hair, sending her hair streaming behind her. A rising wave
caught the small craft and spun it hard to the left, but
she paddled with all her strength, regaining her course
with the third stroke. She shouted in triumph as the
boat shot neatly between two jagged stone pillars toward a patch of glittering sand on the sheltered side of
the island.

For an enchanted moment in time the curragh
glided over clear blue-green water, granting Kiara
glimpses of fallen columns and giant stone heads car-

1

peted in strands of waving sea grass. Then the bottom rose sharply and the hull grated against coarse gravel. Kiara leaped over the side and tugged the boat onto the beach, high enough so that the rising tide would not sweep it away.

Seals, in muted hues of gray, brown, and silver, lifted their heads and stared with huge, mournful eyes, but only a few cows and their pups slipped away into the sea. The rest lay sunning themselves on the sand, watching boldly as the children flopped down on the beach and tore open a bundle of bread and cheese. Between bursts of laughter and excited whispers, Kiara and the boy devoured the food to the last crumb, washing it down with the contents of a leather bottle of honey-sweetened freshwater.

"Is there any more?" Cian asked, brushing a lock of thick yellow hair out of his eyes. "I'm still hungry."

Despite his sturdy limbs and height, Cian's sweet voice still bore the lisp of babyhood. The music warmed his sister's heart and made her smile. "You're always hungry," she teased. "If we find enough mussels, I'll build a fire and we'll steam them here on the beach. Will that satisfy you?"

"Yes! Yes!" Cian leaped to his feet and danced on the wet sand. "Mussels! Mussels! I could eat a curragh full of mussels."

"Not so loud," she admonished. "You'll frighten the seals."

"No, I won't. They know we haven't come to hunt them." He paused and wrinkled his freckled nose. "I wish I'd saved some cheese for them."

She giggled. "They don't eat cheese."

"Well, if I ate raw fish and crabs all day, I'd like a bit of cheese." His gaze fell on a tiny gray seal pup. "Will it let me get close enough to—"

"Hush!" Kiara cried as she caught sight of two

2

strangers emerging from the fog at the edge of a jagged outcrop of rock. "Get down!" She shoved him hard onto his belly and dragged him behind a rock.

"What—" he protested.

"Shh," she whispered. "Outlanders. You can't let them see you. Hide! Don't come out, no matter what."

She peered cautiously around the edge of the stone. The men wore foreign clothing and their hair was cut differently from the style of any tribe she had ever seen.

Icy fear spilled down Kiara's spine as she scrambled over the boulders away from the beach. Her grandmother had warned her of sea raiders who struck without warning—looting isolated settlements, killing men, and carrying away women and children.

Startled by Kiara's sudden movement, the seals grunted and fled en masse toward the breaking surf, panic-stricken pups trailing behind them. From the corner of her eye, she saw her brother dart from his hiding place into a crevice in the granite rock. She screamed and ran in the opposite direction, praying that her ruse would give Cian time to squeeze into the half-submerged cave before the men caught sight of him; the flight of the seals ought to cover his tracks in the sand.

A crumbling boulder blocked her path. Waves crashed against it, sending spray and foam high into the air. If she dove into the water, the force of the tide would carry her back onto the beach.

Catcalls and shouts came from behind her. With no other way out, Kiara attacked the forty-foot wall of rock, clawing her way up the sheer face, digging the toes of her leather boots into minute hollows and finding fingerholds in the mossy, slick surface. She pressed her face into the cold stone as her hands cramped and her muscles ached.

A stone bounced off the rock beside her head. Kiara

flinched, and one foot slipped. She could hear the blood pounding in her head above the crash of the surf.

Pain shot up her fingers as two nails snapped off. Still, Kiara clung to the rock and kept climbing. Breathlessly, she thrust one hand up and grasped the thin branch of a wind-twisted sapling. She heaved herself over the edge of the rim onto her belly and lay there for long seconds, eyes closed, sucking in great mouthfuls of air.

A harsh male voice grated words she couldn't understand.

Kiara opened her eyes and stifled a cry of anguish. A pair of large filthy feet wrapped in strange rope sandals loomed inches from her face. The man's toenails were blackened and jagged, his scarred legs covered with dark hair.

She rolled and sprang up, prepared to leap from the cliff onto the jagged rocks below. But as she dashed for the edge, a net settled over her head and shoulders. She felt herself jerked off her feet, and her head slammed against the ground. A hand closed around her wrist. She screamed and bit down until she tasted blood. The sandaled foot smashed into her ribs. She kicked and fought against her attacker. And then something heavy struck the back of her head. For long seconds lights pinwheeled behind her eyes, and she felt as though she were sinking deep, deep into a black sea.

And then she felt nothing at all.

Chapter 1

Fist clenched, Ptolemy swept the alabaster chalice from the low table, and the gem-encrusted cup fell and shattered. Bloodred wine spread across the marble amid the shards of the ruined vessel. A goblet that could have purchased the services of a company of Nubian archers for two years, he thought wryly as he glared at his most vexing wife. "I have made my decision, woman. You and your daughter will abide by it."

Artakama, daughter of one pharaoh and royal wife to another, reached for an olive, tasted it, and spit it out. "These are not fit for a camel," she admonished the serving girl who knelt at her side. She motioned languidly with graceful fingers. "Out, all of you." The only indication that she was angry with him was the rustle of the gold and ivory beads at the ends of her multiple braids, an obsidian curtain of real hair, an oddity among Egyptian noblewomen. He suspected

5

the blue-black sheen was aided by cosmetics. After all, Artakama was close to forty. But still very desirable, he admitted reluctantly, and one of the most beautiful and dangerous women it had ever been his fortune to bed.

The maids and eunuchs knew their mistress too well to mistake Artakama's soft murmur for weakness. They fled the queen's bedchamber, leaving husband and wife alone, except for the musicians playing behind a linen screen painted with vivid scenes of Egyptian gods and goddesses engaged in heroic acts of procreation beneath a star-studded sky.

Artakama raised thick lashes rimmed in kohl and clapped once. Lute, harp, and lyre players vanished, leaving the last notes drifting on the incense-laden air. "You have decided, my lord?" she purred. "You, the bastard son of a Macedonian bandit, dare to suggest that our daughter wed the whelp of a barbarian whore?"

"Careful, my dear. One day you will go too far."

"As will you." She rose to her feet, diaphanous linen gown clinging to her slim, sensual body, her dark gaze smoldering with barely contained fury.

How he adored her when she was like this. Just watching her move made his loins throb with lust. He wondered if he had the energy for another night romp. Artakama's fire was the spice that had held them together all these years while lesser wives and mistresses came and went without raising the dust of Alexandria.

"Have you forgotten how you claimed the throne of Egypt?" she said. "Through me and my bloodline—a royal legacy that stretches back to the gods themselves. Mereret carries that blood in her veins. Better you give her to the lowest Egyptian offal carrier than to that sheep-rutting Bactrian nephew of yours."

Ptolemy's chest tightened and pain shot up his neck to lodge in the back of his head. Damn her. How could she stir his loins and make him want to choke her at the same time? He was no longer in the prime of his youth. The weight of office plagued him, taking a toll on his physical body. His gut would plague him tonight, and he might suffer another headache. Yet he could not back down. Artakama despised weakness.

"Enough," he ordered as he reached for another chalice of wine, a match to the broken cup that rested on a second table. "Another word and I'll have you—"

"Will you strip me naked and lash me with a rhinoceros whip in full view of the palace guard? Have me thrown to the holy crocodiles?"

"I'll have to think of something more original. I fear you'd enjoy those endeavors too much. You are such an admirer of pain."

Her kohl-painted eyes flashed warning. "Take care, Great Bull of Amon. This is still Egypt. The evil wind of the desert can bring death to even a god-king in the darkest hours of the night."

Ptolemy leaped to his feet, crossed the distance between them, and seized her arm in a sinewy grip. "Do you dare—"

"My lord." She dropped to her knees, giving him a view of high, firm breasts and the perfumed nape of a shapely neck, before looking up at him through thick, black lashes. Her lips parted and he glimpsed small white teeth and the tip of a scarlet tongue. "Have pity on a worthless woman. Mereret is my only child. It would break my heart to part with her. Besides, lord, have I ever done anything contrary to your best interests?"

"Or your own?" Roughly, he caressed her throat and the swell of one oiled breast. His loins pulsed with lust. "I can never decide if you are a viper or a cat, Artakama."

She leaned close and ran exploring fingers slowly up one leg to linger on his inner thigh. "Both have sharp teeth when they are threatened." She pressed warm lips against the front of his gold-encrusted linen kilt, and he inhaled sharply.

"Come to bed, wife. We can argue in the morning."

She arched her back and shook off his hand as she caressed the royal jewels and kingly staff. "As always, Pharaoh's wish is my command," she whispered.

Ptolemy groaned and tangled his fingers in her thick, blue-black hair. "I won't change my mind. Mereret will marry my nephew Alexander."

Ptolemy's head ached, and the weight of the double crown of Egypt cut furrows into his brow as he surveyed the great reception hall of the New Palace. He shifted on the lion throne, vainly attempting to ease the cramp in his left buttock. Perhaps his brother had been right; the proper place for a king was leading his troops into battle and not sitting a golden throne while eunuchs read endless scrolls detailing the price of wheat flour, onions, and olive oil.

The smaller throne to his left was empty. It was close to high noon, but no one would catch Artakama abroad so early. Like the creature of self-indulgence she was, she would sleep away most of the day, to arise languid and sloe-eyed hours from now. She would revel in her own sensuous pleasures, contenting herself with her bath, adorning her face and body with jewels, perfumed oils, very little clothing, and plotting . . . always plotting.

He wished his Greek wife followed the same routine, with the exception of the intrigue. Gray-haired Berenice sat rigidly to his right, stout body swaddled in the folds of a wool chiton and a ridiculous cone-shaped woolen hat balanced on her round head. With her numerous facial warts and pale eyes that never ceased to flicker nervously back and forth as though she were watching for tasty flies, she reminded him of a great toad.

At Berenice's feet, her darling son 'Toly perched on a scarlet cushion and gobbled one sugared date after another. The crown prince, Ptolemy II, was a plump boy as sheep-faced and colorless as his mother. The king shuddered to think of 'Toly becoming pharaoh after him. If things were different, the little prig would not have been his first choice as heir to the Egyptian empire.

The grand vizier cleared his throat loudly.

Ptolemy glanced at him. The man expected some response, but what? If he nodded, would he be agreeing to commit fifty thousand fallahin for the next twenty years to build another sphinx with his head and the body of a giraffe, or did they want him to abdicate his throne in favor of the Princess Mereret's horse master?

The vizier shuffled one narrow foot and made a vain attempt to suck in his potbelly. What? What was it? Ptolemy wondered. What did the damnable little bastard want?

A sudden clatter at the far end of the great audience chamber drew Ptolemy's attention. Three hundred pairs of eyes fixed on the cause—a guard had dropped his shield in surprise at a new arrival in the hall.

By the base of a massive pillar near the Isis Gate, Prince Paris flashed a grin as he dropped to one knee. The hapless guard threw himself belly-down and pressed his face into the mosaic-tiled floor. Berenice gasped. The vizier muttered angrily; his aide's eyes widened. The eyes of the court turned back to Ptolemy in expectation.

Ptolemy waved his left hand in a languid gesture of dismissal and nodded slightly. Any sudden movement might tilt the heavy crown on his head and send it bouncing across the dais. If that happened, the priests would proclaim the incident a dire omen, which would doubtless necessitate the ritual sacrifice of dozens of sacred black bulls and a revered crocodile or two, plus untold bribes, to calm the superstitious fears of his subjects.

At the visible proof of Pharaoh's mercy, the mood in the huge audience chamber lightened. Ptolemy motioned to his chamberlain, who wiggled a finger at an underling. In less time than it would take him to piss, a priest had lifted the massive crown from the royal head and replaced it with a coronet of golden laurel leaves. The leaves poked into his scalp and looked ridiculous, but this circlet was much less cumbersome.

In the ensuing lull, Paris had maneuvered through the throngs of supplicants, ambassadors, and noblemen to kneel at the base of the dais. It was all Ptolemy could do to maintain his stoic godlike expression. His heart swelled with pride at the sight of this beloved son who had been away at the wars far too long. Paris's skin was bronzed from the wind and sun, his body lean and hardened, his intelligent gray eyes bright with vigor. Here was a son to match the immortals, a prince fit to wear the crown of Egypt . . . if only he hadn't been born a bastard to a Persian mother. Ptolemy sighed with regret and extended his hand in welcome.

Paris unbuckled his sword belt, passed it to a lieutenant, and came forward to kneel and kiss the great ring of Pharaoh. "Father," he murmured. "I've missed you."

"And I you," Ptolemy replied so low that not even Berenice could make out his words. "Success?"

"Your enemies have scattered, their armies defeated, and order has been restored to the province." Paris grinned. "Not to mention the slaves and booty I bring you. Your Majesty has only to agree to the vizier's request, and the good fellow will proclaim a day of national celebration to honor Pharaoh's great victory."

Ptolemy rose, raised his son to his feet, and embraced him. The hall echoed with a silence so complete that Pharaoh supposed that had it been closer to the hour, he might have heard the great water clock in the columned passageway click. Then the assemblage burst into thunderous cheers and applause. Ptolemy glanced at the vizier. "This audience is at an end," he said. "We would hear the news of our success at once." As an afterthought, he glanced at Berenice. "Well?"

Flushing, she rose and followed as he and Paris passed through the curtains behind the throne. 'Toly, mouth and chin sticky with sugar, trailed behind, clinging to her hand and whining as usual.

In the corridor, beyond prying eyes, Ptolemy hastily dismissed both queen and annoying child and hurried through the maze of hallways, across a walled garden, and down a flight of steps beside his favorite son. There, in Pharaoh's private quarters, Ptolemy shed the silly laurel-wreath crown and settled onto a low divan while servants hurried to bring refreshments.

"How I've missed you," Ptolemy said. "If I'd guessed how tedious being king would be, I'd have remained a general."

Paris's eyes twinkled as he accepted a cup of beer from a slave girl. "Wasn't it the pharaoh Achthoes II who said, 'Royalty is a good profession'?"

"Perhaps he was right. I've suffered greater hardships as a soldier." The king glanced at Paris's drink and lifted an eyebrow in jest. "When did you develop a taste for beer?"

"I'll admit I shared enough of it with my men in the field. If you recall, I was never much for spirits. Besides, soldiers love the common touch in their commander."

" 'The soldier-prince.' Yes, I've heard it in the streets. You take after my brother. Alexander never missed a

11

chance to be one with his troops. It paid off well enough. They would hurl themselves into Hades's blackest pit for him. Once, during an assault on an Indian city, I saw him throw himself over the wall into the enemy's midst. His soldiers didn't hesitate. They followed him—some of them literally clawing at the gates with their bare hands. Alexander survived, of course. He always survived. But I can remember being shocked. Not that he would attempt the impossible—that was Alexander—but that otherwise rational officers and infantrymen would lose all sense of self-preservation to follow him into a hopeless conflict." Ptolemy shrugged. "I've never possessed that ability. My soldiers fight for me because I pay them well and they know what the punishment will be if they don't, but they've never loved me more than their own skins."

"They call him 'the Great One' now, don't they? But his whole military career lasted . . . what? Ten years, at most? You've proved the better king, Father, and the better general. His empire collapsed on his death. Yours will endure as long as the pyramids."

"Kind of you to say it, but I wonder."

"No, it's true. Look at what you've done here in Alexandria. Athens is a merchant's cattle fair compared to this city. Our library alone . . ." Paris shrugged. "There's no comparison. Greece's time is done. The future belongs to the great naval powers, to Egypt above all."

"Well said. I see you've become a diplomat as well as a warrior." Ptolemy wished again that he could name this son heir. But it was not to be. 'Toly carried the "right" bloodline, and he must be pharaoh . . . if he lived to sit the throne. Too many of the royal children had perished in infanthood. Ptolemy sipped his wine thoughtfully and then asked, "How did the new chariots perform? Did the leather-bound wheels—" The

12

king broke off in midsentence as familiar shouts invaded his sitting room.

"I don't care! I will see my father!"

Ptolemy's brow wrinkled in displeasure. Of all his daughters, Mereret was the most beautiful and the most troublesome. Like her mother, she was prone to dramatic displays of emotion. He'd hoped that this confrontation could be put off for a few days.

"Princess." Paris murmured a greeting to his half sister as she burst past the protesting servants and stormed into the room, tore off her court wig, and threw it at their father's feet.

"What is this?" Ptolemy demanded. He'd known she'd come running as soon as Artakama told her of her coming nuptials, but he forced himself to be harsh with her. "Is this the way you've been taught to behave in the presence of a god-king?"

Mereret dropped to her knees, ripped away an exquisite gold-and-ruby collar, and continued shrieking as beads scattered and bounced across the tile floor. Her eyes were red and swollen from weeping, and the kohl eye paint around them was streaked and running down her cheeks. "You can't do this to me, Father!" she sobbed. "You can't ask me to marry a barbarian and leave Alexandria forever!"

"Pharaoh does not ask permission of a daughter. He commands. For the love I bear you, I have arranged your marriage. To a king, I might remind you."

Mereret refused to be cowed. She shredded the bodice of her transparent linen gown, exposing her breasts and leaving the prints of her long nails in her flesh. "I won't! You can't make me! My beauty will wither if I cannot bathe in the sacred Nile. My heart will break if you send me away from you. And when I die . . . when I die, my soul will die with me. If I am not embalmed in the manner of every Egyptian princess before me, I am condemned to perish without hope of rebirth among the gods."

"Stop it, Mereret. You're behaving like a spoiled child." Ptolemy flushed. He would never grow used to this Egyptian disregard for nudity. It was shameful for his daughter to confront him with her womanly attributes. "For Hera's sake, girl, cover yourself!"

"What do you care? You're giving me to a savage who lives in a hide tent and smells of goat!"

Paris turned his back to both of them and retreated to a balcony that overlooked an artificial lake. Ptolemy wished that he could do the same without looking as though he were too cowardly to control his own daughter.

"I'll enter Isis's service and live a life of celibacy rather than wed—" Mereret wailed.

"Calm yourself!" Ptolemy picked up the pitcher of beer and dashed it into his daughter's face.

She gasped, choked, and began to cry in earnest, her shoulders heaving with emotion as she sobbed. The king motioned to Mereret's ladies, who hovered in the doorway like a flock of frightened doves.

"The princess is unwell," Pharaoh called. "Take her to her bed and summon her physician."

"Father!" Mereret cried. "Have mercy on me. If you have the slightest affection for—"

"Take her now!" Ptolemy followed his son onto the balcony as the women fluttered around his protesting daughter and swept her from the chamber. "Welcome home, Paris," he said. "As you can see, little here has changed."

Paris shrugged and fixed his gaze on a grove of palm trees on the far side of the lake. "I take it that not everyone is in favor of this wedding between Prince Alexander and the princess Mereret."

"King Alexander," Ptolemy corrected.

"According to my sources, Roxanne still sits the throne of Bactria and Sogdiana . . . she and her consort, Kayan."

"Yes, but that's only a formality. My informant on her high council assures me that she will pass the crown to Alexander when he marries. I wonder if he's ready to be king."

"He's old enough. He's only a year younger than I am."

"I know the whelp's age. You forget. I was in Babylon the day my nephew was born."

"The Great One's son."

"Men claim he is. But who can know for certain? There are witnesses who claim Alexander the fourth died in prison when he was a young child."

"His mother survived. If she did, why not the son?"

Ptolemy's mouth firmed. "I deal in reality. Whether or not this Alexander is my nephew and heir to my brother's kingdom isn't important. What is important is that the Bactrians and Sogdians accept him as Roxanne's son. He will assume the crown of the Twin Kingdoms. He will control their magnificent cavalry, their trade routes, and their wealth. Thus, marriage between Mereret and the lad is a wise match."

"You think to gain influence through the alliance."

Ptolemy nodded. "We've wasted too many resources fighting them. And a legitimate heir might rule both Egypt and the Twin Kingdoms."

"How would that be possible? If Mereret goes to Bactria—"

"Who said anything about my daughter leaving Alexandria?"

Paris's eyes narrowed in confusion. "But everyone assumes that she will go with her bridegroom to his country."

"Am I responsible for what others assume? I am

pharaoh. All that matters is my will. Once the prince is wed, we may convince him that his best interests lie here in the midst of true civilization."

"You think he will be that easily swayed from returning to assume his throne? I haven't seen him since I was child, but I remember Yuri . . . Alexander," Paris corrected. "I remember him as strong-willed."

"The two of you were close. But it has been many years since you've laid eyes on each other. My nephew will not be the man his father was. Remember, he has been raised by a doting mother."

Paris met his gaze evenly. "She's a formidable foe. And she's unpredictable. Can you trust her to keep her word?"

"Don't underestimate me. I've dealt with the woman before. I think I know best how to handle Roxanne."

Chapter 2

Bactria

"You don't know Ptolemy." Roxanne grasped her son's arm and felt his muscles tighten in stubborn opposition. Alexander was taller than she, two hand spans taller than his namesake, broad in the shoulders, and as hard as the snowcapped granite peaks rising around them.

"You know him well, don't you, Mother?"

The thrust went deep, and she winced. The time she'd spent in Alexandria as Ptolemy's friend and lover was something that Alexander had never fully understood or forgiven her for, but she never wasted energy on regrets. *What was* could not be changed; *what could be* was what mattered. She'd never shrunk from confrontation with any man. She wouldn't start with her own son.

"Ptolemy can't be trusted," she said in a reasonable tone. "This could be a trap. He might want to lure you to Egypt to—"

"To be rid of me once and for all?" Alexander shrugged, his demeanor softening toward her as he flashed a boyish grin. It was his father's smile, a smile that had disarmed as many opponents as his sword, especially among the fairer sex.

In spite of herself, Roxanne's heart swelled with love. She knew Alexander's faults and weaknesses all too well, knew them as she had known those of his legendary father. Her son was headstrong and bold, too bold for a crown prince with the responsibility of a kingdom resting on his shoulders. He was absolutely fearless; she had seen him throw himself into combat against overwhelming numbers and win by sheer force of will and luck.

Her son had inherited both intelligence and athletic ability. He was a master swordsman who never ceased honing his skill. He rode like a Scythian, wrestled like a Tartar, played games of chance like a merchant of Chin, and pursued the opposite sex with the single-mindedness of a mountain ram.

"You've seen Egypt," she reminded him. "Ptolemy's might has only grown in the last two decades. And he never forgets. You stand between him and the prize."

"Ptolemy's past his prime. The Twin Kingdoms are stronger than they've been since my sire invaded Persia. Kayan defeated the Egyptian army when I was twelve, and again when I was sixteen. Ptolemy invaded a third time nine years ago."

Roxanne's eyes narrowed. "He would have repeated the attempt two summers ago if Antigonus hadn't betrayed him by picking a fight with his own allies. What is your point?"

"Each time Ptolemy sent his armies, our cavalry drove him back across our borders."

"What if he joins forces with Antigonus again? Or he makes a pact with one of the kings on the Tigris?"

Alexander scoffed. "That's not going to happen. Ptolemy has stolen too much land for them to trust him."

"Proving his past history of deceit and trickery. Why should we trust him if they won't?"

"Mother, you're thinking like a woman. Ptolemy knows we're a power to be reckoned with. He has a quiverful of daughters. Why shouldn't he want me for a son-in-law? Can you think of a better way to seal the peace between our countries? You're always talking about the benefits of trade. What better market than Egypt? This will be a good alliance."

Kayan knelt and thrust a gnarled log into the central fire pit. Sap hissed and snapped, catching Roxanne's attention, and she glanced at her husband.

Despite his age, nearly two score and ten, Kayan's long hair was still thick and dark, with only a few silver threads. The years had chiseled his features, honing the high cheekbones, proud nose, and square chin, making him even comelier in Roxanne's eyes than he had been as a young man. What strength the passing years had stolen from his graceful body had been more than compensated for by experience. Kayan's fame as a master horseman and warrior was legendary, and his mind matched his physique.

A shower of glowing sparks flew up. Roxanne watched as a draft caught them, swirling them through the open smoke hole at the top of the round hide-walled yurt. Above, the endless stars winked in the blue-black sky, brilliant pinpoints in the velvet curtain of night.

"There's much wisdom in what your mother says," Kayan pronounced. "I'm against this political marriage, Alexander. Egypt has nothing that we want."

Alexander's blue-gray eyes took on a steely hue in the firelight, a hint of the stubbornness he'd inherited

19

from his Greek father. Roxanne folded her arms over her embroidered sheepskin vest. "It's the girl, isn't it? You've taken a fancy to Mereret's likeness."

A painted sculpture of the Egyptian princess's head and upper torso had accompanied Ptolemy's invitation to wed his daughter. The piece was magnificent, portraying a striking young woman with classical features, large liquid eyes as dark as Ahriman's heart, and a mouth so sensual that men would risk their lives to taste it.

"You must admit, Pharaoh's daughter has attributes that you don't usually see in royal women," Kayan said. "Most have the features of a goat and the brains of an onion. Present company excluded, of course." He dusted off his hands and settled, legs crossed, on a blanket beside the fire, where he resumed the task he'd started after the evening meal—braiding a horse-hair halter.

"You're no help," Roxanne chided her husband affectionately. "The Egyptian girl appears curvy, and you always were a breast man."

A smile played over Kayan's thin lips, but he didn't answer. Kayan rarely spoke when he felt the answer was evident.

She turned her attention back to her son. "Marriage should be more than sexual attraction. We know nothing of the girl, other than her parents. If she's anything like Artakama, Ormazd help the man who weds her. She's a cobra in human form."

"If rumor is true, Ptolemy was more than my sire's friend and companion—he is his half brother. That makes the king of Egypt my uncle."

"And the girl your first cousin. I am no Greek. I don't approve of marriages so close within the family."

"Says the woman who married her cousin?" Alexander pointed out.

"My father was second cousin to your grandfather,

20

Prince Oxyartes," Kayan put in. "Hardly the same degree of kinship that you're considering."

"We breed horses closer." Alexander squatted beside his stepfather and poked at the fire with a stick. "I've seen none born with two heads."

"You're not a horse," Roxanne reminded him. "Although you are equally as stubborn. And I would hope you'd choose a wife with as much thought as you put into mating that Siddhartha of yours."

"If she doesn't suit me, I can always marry a second time. Our faith does not forbid a man's having more than one wife. I might make a better husband that way."

"One woman's been enough for me," Kayan said. "Sometimes more than enough."

Alexander raised a hand in mock protest. "No more, I beg you. This conversation is taking a turn to an area I'd rather not visit. What you and my mother do behind closed doors is scandal enough in the palace. You'd think the two of you would remember your age and position and leave the sexual adventures to the younger generation."

"That's your youth speaking," Kayan replied with a grin. "Your mother and I have something rare, something you would do well to search for before settling for the first pretty princess who's offered on a silver plate."

"I'll admit I share my father's excesses when it comes to the pleasures of women, but the chance to marry into the royal house of Egypt doesn't come along every day. Uncle Ptolemy is a crafty statesman, perhaps a better king than most would admit."

"A spider," Roxanne said. Her throat constricted. Forbidding Alexander to marry Ptolemy's daughter was useless. Her son was twenty and seven, well past the age of manhood, and once he'd fixed his mind on a goal, he was impossible to reason with. She had no fears about his insight or his courage. He'd proved his skill in battle and at the council table. But she was not certain that he was ready to match wits with the wily Ptolemy just yet.

Alexander chuckled. "The daughter of a cobra and a spider; she should never be dull. Haven't you been after me to take a wife and give you grandchildren?"

"Yes, I have. But someone suitable. A woman of our own people, one who understands you. Someone who will make you happy. I just want you to know the kind of marriage I've known with Kayan."

"Not what you had with my sire?"

"I've never denied I loved Alexander, but he was a Greek conqueror. The circumstances didn't make for a peaceful household, and at times we didn't like each other very much."

"That's putting it mildly, from what I've heard. I'd never have a wife like you, Mother. You know that I love you dearly, but if we weren't mother and son, one of us would have to kill the other one."

"I can see that trying to talk sense into you is impossible. You've already made up your mind." Roxanne walked swiftly to the door, pushed back the hide covering, and stepped out into the cold night air, where she could compose herself . . . before she said words that couldn't be taken back. She inhaled deeply, willing herself to accept what she couldn't change.

Her son was a man, and men didn't always think with their heads. Come to think of it . . . neither did women.

Across the high meadow, fires glowed from the hearts of other yurts. Roxanne could smell the sweet smoke and hear the contented stirring of the horse herd. The shadowy form of her mare, Yasmin, moved in the darkness, the black silk of her thick coat standing out against the snow. Beyond her, Roxanne could make out the shapes of two more horses, Kayan's tall gelding and Alexander's stallion, Siddhartha.

Her disagreement with her son about this proposed marriage aside, it was good to be here at the edge of the great steppes with the two men she loved most in the world. But now the trade agreement had been made with one of the largest tribes of the Rus horse people, and the excuse for leaving her capital was over. State affairs would not permit her to remain here. She must return to the palace, her daughters, and the daily demands of a queen—a duty that would not lessen anytime soon if her son was determined to go to Egypt and bring back his foreign bride.

As usual, the Twin Kingdoms of Bactria and Sogdiana were threatened by the armies of Greece, the warlords of Chin, the petty kings of India, and the barbarian tribes of the steppes. For six months there had been no battles, other than the disastrous collapse of the peace talks with the Budin and Auchat Scythians and her son's near assassination.

Doubtless Kayan would want to lead an expedition to punish the Budin tribe's betrayal and take revenge for Alexander's lost companions. Ignoring the insult would only invite further attacks on outlying Bactrian farms and trade routes. As much as she hated seeing either her husband or her son ride into danger, she knew that such was the price of freedom. The armies of the Twin Kingdoms must always be ready to defend her borders.

Since she had assumed her father's throne, her husband's strong sword arm had kept their enemies at bay until her son had grown strong enough to take his place as crown prince and warrior. Now Kayan and Alexander fought side by side, leaving her to do what a woman did best: improve the lot of her people by encouraging commerce, supporting the education and health of children and families, succoring the arts, and assuring equal justice for all—regardless of race or station in life.

Ancient trade roads from east and west sprang from windblown tracks where bandits reigned to safe, well-traveled caravan routes that fed the growing demand of Samarkand and Markia, and a half dozen fledgling cities. Sleepy towns grew to commercial centers of art and commerce as the jewelers, potters, weavers, and craftsmen of far-flung nations had flooded into the Twin Kingdoms.

Agriculture flourished. Assured of a profit, farmers repaired the irrigation systems, planted fields of grain, orchards and vineyards, reaping bountiful harvests. Herds of cattle, sheep, camels, and the finest horses in the civilized world grew fat on the rich grass of Roxanne's homeland. . . .

"Ptolemy is our enemy," she said softly.

Kayan came up behind her and slipped strong arms around her waist. "You're right, but so is Alexander. It's time he was king. And with the crown comes the weight of making decisions."

"And if he's wrong? Ptolemy will murder him. What's to be gained by this alliance?"

Her husband nuzzled her hair. "We cannot fight the whole world for him. All along, since the day you placed him in my arms and told me to bring him home, we've had one goal: to make him ready for this responsibility. He's older than you were when you took the throne. And he's male. The army will follow him into fire. Our job is done."

"Is it? Is a mother's job ever done?"

"Maybe not, but if she's wise, a good mother will

know when to let her son become a man. He loves you, Roxanne. But in many ways, he's his father's child."

Abruptly she turned in the circle of his arms and gripped his vest. "He's your son! Who rocked him to sleep when he was afraid of the dark? Who taught him to ride and wield a sword? Who has he called Father since he could first form the word?"

"The son of my heart, not of my loins. I raised him, but he carries the blood of the conqueror. He has the Greek fire in him, my love. And if you don't stand back, it will consume you."

Ten days later, on a starless and cloudy night, Alexander stood on the balcony of his palace bedchamber and stared west into the misty blackness. Spring had turned the valley meadows from winter brown to a verdant carpet of green. He couldn't see the knee-high grass, but he could smell it, as sweet as any woman's perfume. He could imagine the herds of horses, blacks, duns, bays, and chestnuts, cropping the rich pastureland, long-legged foals tottering after their mothers on slender, unsteady legs, and battle-scarred stallions snorting and jealously sniffing the wind for any scent of rivals.

What would his bride think of this rough-hewn fortress, carved a thousand years ago from living rock . . . this land of soaring mountains, breathtaking waterfalls, and emerald valleys? How could she—the daughter of a god-king—come to love and know a people who cherished their independence and would die rather than bend a knee to a tyrant? Was his mother right? Would he be happier choosing a wife from his own kingdom—a woman who could ride like a steppe nomad, shoot a bow like an Amazon, and find joy in skimming down a boulder-strewn river in a skin boat at flood time?

" 'Zander?"

Pythia's husky voice drew him back from his reverie. He turned to her and smiled. "What are you doing out here, little dove? It's cold." Pythia's silver-blond hair fell to her hips, almost covering a darker nest of curls at the apex of her thighs.

She fingered the ornate gold-and-ruby necklace he'd given her when he returned from the treaty expedition. One bloodred gem the size and shape of a sparrow's egg hung between her ample breasts. "I woke and you weren't there," she murmured huskily. She held out a beringed hand, beseeching him to return to their bed.

"You're insatiable," he said. His smile widened. Giving up Pythia and her twin, Pylia, would be one of the most regrettable aspects of becoming a married man.

"What are the two of you doing out here?" Pylia appeared behind Pythia.

The two were identical, from the color of their hair to their generous hips, narrow waists, and pouting, bee-stung lips. He would not have been able to tell them apart if it were not for the tattoo of a hooded cobra that coiled around Pythia's right leg from slender ankle to shapely thigh. No such tattoo adorned Pylia. Her lascivious nature simmered beneath smooth and unblemished skin, needing only the slightest spark to ignite her carnal appetites.

Pylia was clad only in his latest gift, a silver filigree hip belt, strung with dangling lengths of priceless black pearls. "My bed is cold without you, my lord. Unless you are weary . . ."

". . . of our charms," Pythia finished. "Or perhaps the stories of your strength are greatly . . ."

Alexander groaned. "Come, my doves, and I will show you whether what they say is truth or fiction." He seized Pylia and threw her, giggling, over one

26

shoulder. Her sister squealed and fled through the doorway into the bedchamber.

A low, circular bed, heaped with cushions, stood in the center of the room. At one end, a fire blazed on a hearth large enough to roast an ox. It was a man's room, evidenced by the weapons hung on one wall and the bare, utilitarian furnishings. Simple, but not crude, the straight-back chairs were made of teak and ivory, fashioned after the Egyptian style. The largest wall, unbroken by doors or windows, boasted a tapestry of scarlet Chin silk showing a map of the civilized world, complete with seas, deserts, rivers, and mountain ranges as well as cities and major trade routes.

Alexander deposited Pylia onto the bed and advanced on her squealing twin. Pythia dodged behind a chair and made a halfhearted feint for the door leading to the inner corridor. Alexander lunged for her.

Abruptly the door swung open wide enough to admit a massive furry black head. Two glowing eyes caught the firelight. Pythia's cry became a shriek, soon drowned in the roar of the leopard.

"Down!" Alexander shouted.

Neither cat nor woman obeyed. Pythia spun and fled toward the balcony. Pylia's screams echoed her sister's. The leopard covered the distance between the door and Pythia in an instant, catching her neatly between front paws and throwing her to the rug. Alexander snatched a sword from the wall.

"Banu!" A pigtailed sprite in a green leather hunting tunic and trousers darted into the chamber, a quiver of arrows bouncing against her back. "No!"

Pythia's wails of terror rose from beneath the leopard.

"Bad cat!" The small archer ducked under Alexander's upraised arm and threw herself onto the animal.

Grabbing the silver-studded collar, she tugged as hard as she could. "Banu! Stop it! Come on!"

"Put down that sword!" The dark-haired child glared at Alexander. "It's not Banu's fault. She shouldn't have run. Banu thought it was a game. Didn't you, sweetie?"

The leopard stopped licking Pythia's tear-streaked face and grinned, revealing a mouthful of gleaming white teeth. The girl pulled at the cat's collar. "Get off."

Alexander knelt on the rug, shoved the panther aside, and took hold of the struggling and shrieking Pythia. "Stop; it's all right," he soothed. "You're not hurt." He lifted her, still screaming, to her feet. Limp, her legs folded under her, and she started to slide back onto the floor.

Banu yawned and emitted a lazy growl. Pythia's eyes widened and then went out of focus as she lost consciousness. Cursing, Alexander caught her as she fell.

"Stop that!" the seven-year-old scolded. "You know what Mama said about using that kind of talk in front of—"

Alexander's blue-gray eyes blazed. "What are you doing here in the middle of the night, Ava? And why didn't you leave that . . . that—"

"Banu goes where I go." She drew herself up to her full height. "You'll be leaving tomorrow. I knew I wouldn't get a chance to talk sense to you." Ava put her hands over her ears and grimaced at Pylia. "Can't you make her be quiet? Banu doesn't like all that noise."

"Take your leopard and go to bed, little sister. I'll deal with you in the morning."

"Nope. You're just saying that to get rid of me. Tomorrow you'll be too busy to talk to me."

He dropped the limp woman onto the bed beside Pythia, snatched up a blanket, and wrapped it around his loins. "You've no business here. It's not decent. I'm not even dressed."

"Your night flowers don't seem to care," Ava replied. She straddled the leopard and hugged it. "And Mama will be mad at you for letting me in here when you were doing nasty stuff with them."

Alexander felt torn between wanting to turn the child over his knee and laughing. He glanced at the twins. Pylia had recovered enough to start sniffing and burrowing into her sister's arms. Pythia began to curse Ava, Banu, and him, including his ancestors back to and including his Amazon great-grandmother.

He waved at the two women. "Go. I'll come later."

"The brat's right," Pythia cried. "Tomorrow you'll have forgotten all about us. You promised me a house in Samarkand, and I won't go until—"

"Out!" he bellowed.

"Yellow-haired bastard," Pylia managed between sobs. "Go! See if I care! You—"

Alexander took one step toward the bed, and both women leaped up and ran from the room. Crossing his arms over his chest, he turned back to Ava and scowled. "As for you—"

"I like the snake tattoo. Will you ask Father if I can—"

"I will not." He crossed the room, turned his back, and thrust his legs into a pair of knee-length Persian trousers. "You know better than to come in here unannounced. And you know better than to come when I'm . . ." He hesitated, wondering how much she did know. She was wise for seven, but still so much a child. "When I'm entertaining," he finished, feeling foolish.

Ava giggled. "I'd say they were entertaining you."

"Where is your nurse? She should be whipped for letting you out of your room. It's not safe for a royal princess to wander about at this hour of—"

"Who's going to hurt me? I'm not the crown prince." She settled into one of the Egyptian chairs and drew her knees up. Her small feet were bare. "First comes you, then Shahi, then me. Everybody has to die without issue before I get to be queen. And Mama keeps saying that she wants another baby. That's disgusting."

"What would-be queen runs around with a quiver of arrows, shoeless, with no bow?"

"I wanted to show you my arrows. They're too small. And the arrowheads are rounded. How can I hunt bears with bird points? Father is completely unreasonable."

"I asked you about the bow," he reminded her.

"I think . . . I think it's in the stables," she admitted. Small spots of scarlet glowed on her tanned cheeks. "I fell off Tirdad's pony this afternoon, and my bow . . . sort of . . . it sort of broke. I thought maybe you might . . ." She glanced at the array of bows on his wall.

"You want one of mine?"

Dark braids gleamed as she nodded solemnly. "Mine was a baby's bow. I want a real one, one that will kill an elephant."

He stifled a burst of amusement by clearing his throat. "You think you're old enough to hunt elephants?"

"Not wild ones." Ava grimaced. "I mean, I know we don't have elephants here, but if the Indian warlords come, if there's an invasion while you're away in Egypt marrying that stupid princess, I could help Father fight. Indians ride elephants, don't they? Mama said that she used to ride elephants, and once tigers attacked and her elephant ran away. So if one comes here, or lots of them, I need a real bow."

"I can see that," he replied. He took down a laminated horn bow, made in the Scythian style, and handed it to his sister. "See if you can pull that."

Ava leaped off her chair, took the bow, and tried mightily to draw back the string. Her face reddened

30

and she gritted her teeth, but the size and strength of the bow were beyond a grown woman's ability, let alone a small child's. "Not quite," she admitted finally. "But I could practice."

"You do that," he said. "The bow is yours. I make a gift of it to you. Practice every day, and when I come home from Egypt I'll bring you a woman's bow. It won't hurt for you to have two."

"Really?" Ava's dark eyes sparkled with delight. "You will?"

"It's a promise." He knelt and opened his arms. She ran into his embrace. "You be good while I'm gone, pigeon. Take care of Mama and your big sister."

"Shahi?" She wrinkled her nose. "You know she never listens to me. Nobody does."

"No, and I suppose Kayan hasn't spoiled you rotten."

Ava giggled. "Maybe Papa does a little. Shahi says so. But I still wish you wouldn't go. Mama says that it's dangerous. What if you don't come back? Who will be king if you don't come back?"

"Then you or Shahi will be queen."

"She doesn't want to marry. She's says she's going to be a priestess."

"Then it will have to be you, brat."

"No. I'd rather be a great general, like Father, and go to war. Being queen is boring. Mama says it's your turn to rule, and I'm not letting you get out of it."

"All right, all right," he agreed with a sigh. "If you insist. But first I've got to go and get Princess Mereret. I'll marry her and bring her home, and you'll have a new sister."

"I'd rather have a lion cub."

"Between us, so would Mother."

Chapter 3

Cheering throngs of merchants, peasants, housewives, toddlers, artisans, mariners, slaves, and scholars jockeyed for position along the streets of Alexandria. The holiday crowd chattered, laughed, quaffed cups of free beer, and snacked on Pharaoh's bounty of dates, bread, and onions as petty thieves enriched their purses and enterprising pleasure girls did a thriving business in the narrow alleys just off the main thoroughfare.

Hundreds of gaily costumed musicians, dancers, snake charmers, animal trainers, and magicians followed the stately procession of priests and priestesses representing the multitude of gods and goddesses worshiped within the city walls. Temple schoolboys, released from their lessons, carried bright sacks on their backs and tossed rag dolls, wooden pull toys, and balls to the watching children.

Amid swirls of incense and the blare of trumpets, chained leopards, tame monkeys, baby elephants, sleek hunting dogs, sacred bulls, giraffes, goats, and eight different species of antelope with circlets of flowers around their graceful necks paraded down the wide avenue that led from Ptolemy's unfinished lighthouse on the Island of Pharos to the center of Alexandria.

Next, imposing war elephants with gilded tusks and toenails lumbered two abreast down Hephaestion Way. Each brightly garbed animal carried a mahout and a bevy of beautiful temple girls throwing sweets, strings of beads, and coins from flower-draped howdahs. Behind the elephants rolled horse-drawn chariots bearing archers of Pharaoh's own guard, marching companies of heavily armored Greek hoplites, and hundreds of sinewy sailors, their curved swords, boarding pikes, and silver armbands glittering in the hot Egyptian sun.

For hours, the inhabitants of the city gazed wide-eyed at the assembled proof of Pharaoh's might: Nubian archers, Greek cavalry, veiled Persian infantrymen, and exotic Indian mercenaries. So numerous were the combined forces of Egypt that it was not until late afternoon that Alexandria's nobility, seated under awnings on the steps of the great library, caught sight of the foreign bridegroom's delegation.

"Look! Look, there," a pretty Egyptian slave girl cried from her post behind her mistress. "See! They're coming! The barbarian prince is coming."

"Where?" Kiara demanded. "I don't see—" She caught her breath as the first line of horsemen trotted into view. "Oh . . . they're magnificent." A rainbow of prancing horses poured forward down the wide street, proud necks arched, flowing manes and tails fluttering in the hot wind off the desert.

"Yes, they are magnificent," Tutu agreed. "And the animals are lovely, too."

Kiara rolled her eyes. "Can you think of nothing but—"

"Who could think otherwise? Look at the barbarians!" Tutu's kohl-rimmed eyes narrowed suggestively as she moistened her lower lip with the tip of a dainty pink tongue. "I wouldn't mind being the night's entertainment for any of them. And especially . . . Oh, look at that one! In the center on the big white horse. Now there's a tasty morsel."

Kiara shaded her eyes with her hand and studied the fierce, yellow-haired warrior in the golden cuirass and ornate Macedonian helmet.

"Well?" Tutu challenged. "You can't find fault with him. By Bastet's breath, he must be the prince. Why wasn't I born Pharaoh's daughter?"

"Because you were born a slut," Kiara retorted. "I see an arrogant, muscle-bound savage without the brains to find his way out of a beer jar."

"Who cares if he picks his nose with his dagger? Don't tell me that you can look at that face, those arms, and not wish to share joy with him? He's probably hung like a stallion. Either you're blind or a liar." Tutu giggled. "Mmm-hmm. Oh, yes, I would love to see what he has under those . . . those . . . What is it he's wearing?"

"Trousers," Kiara replied. "In the Persian fashion."

"Trousers are loose. The leg coverings he's wearing are skintight. And they aren't made of linen or wool."

"Leather," Kiara said. "Doeskin, probably. Deer or antelope."

"Wish I were a deer."

Alexander's companions were no more than two hundred strong, but the young Bactrian and Sogdian noblemen represented the bravest soldiers, the finest riders, and the most skilled swordsmen and archers of the Twin Kingdoms. Each chosen bachelor was a hardened soldier in the prime of his years, fluent in language, poetry, and the arts—and single. Following his father's example, it had been Alexander's wish that as many of his followers take foreign wives as could be matched with suitable brides. That way, the prince had concluded, his princess would not pine for women of her own culture, and a lasting friendship between Egypt and his own land might be sealed.

As the first column reached the royal box, Ptolemy stood, smiled, and extended his arms. "Welcome, nephew. Our heart warms to see you again."

"And mine, Uncle." Alexander removed his helmet, placed his fist over his heart, and nodded. Ptolemy had grown a little stouter, a little grayer, but the intelligent eyes, the firm mouth, and the proud Macedonian nose remained as he remembered from childhood. "On behalf of my soldiers and my family, I thank you and your subjects for receiving us with such friendship," he said. "My mother, Queen Roxanne, sends her dearest wish that you remain in good health."

Alexander's gaze flicked past Ptolemy, over his three wives and the household guards to rest on the face of the beautiful, dark-haired princess who could only be Princess Mereret. A rush of excitement filled his chest, making it hard to breathe. She was more beautiful, more desirable than his dreams.

"Siddhartha," he murmured softly, kneeing the stallion, "down." In response, the horse dipped his head and went down on one knee, causing a wave of applause from the noble ladies.

Alexander smiled and met his uncle's eyes. "You sent a likeness of your daughter, her royal highness the princess Mereret, with your offer of marriage. But neither your ambassadors nor the statue did her justice. She is truly the jewel of the Nile, and her image was but a pale reflection of her true beauty."

Ptolemy chuckled. "I see you have inherited both my

brother's appreciation for the ladies and his skill at honeyed speech." His courtiers and noblemen laughed, but Mereret inclined her head modestly and concealed her face behind a feathered fan. Her ladies giggled and cast bold glances at Alexander and his companions.

You were wrong, Mother, Alexander thought. *Mereret was meant to be mine. All this time I've been waiting for her.*

"Come," Ptolemy said. "You must be weary after your long journey. My servants will show you to your chambers. When night falls, you must come to Queen Artakama's palace. There it is our wish that you and your men be honored with a feast."

"Will your daughter be there?" Alexander demanded.

Ptolemy stood. "Yes, my eager bridegroom. The princess Mereret will be at her mother's side."

"Then we will come most gratefully," Alexander agreed. Once more he glanced at his intended, and this time she favored him with a faint smile. "Although I would gladly have ridden twice the distance for a word from the lady's sweet lips."

Alexander stood hip-deep in the bathing pool while Nubian slave girls scrubbed his body with sweet-scented soap and sluiced clean water through his freshly washed hair. He'd made no protest when a bevy of them had led him into the water, but when he'd tried to speak to them in his scanty Egyptian, they'd only giggled behind their hands and whispered to one another.

"It's no use," a male voice said from behind him. "Whatever they do speak, it's a dialect I've never learned, and I'm fluent in four African tongues."

Alexander turned to see a black-wigged Egyptian

36

nobleman standing by the archway that led to an enclosed garden. For a few seconds he stared, stunned by the stranger's resemblance to the brother he'd not seen in twenty years. But surely this bejeweled and linen-kilted court fop couldn't be—

The newcomer laughed. "You've grown up, Yuri. Did you expect me to remain nine years old?"

"Val?" He shook off the attendants' clinging hands and climbed out of the bath. "Val! By Apollo's foreskin, can that be you hiding under that bearskin hat?"

"This is the finest goat hair, I'll have you know." Val grinned and pulled off the braided wig, revealing close-cropped fair curls underneath. "And I'm Paris here. Prince Paris."

Alexander threw his arms around him and hugged him tight. "Brother . . ." His voice cracked. "How I've missed you."

Paris returned the embrace, then stepped back. "I'm still taller," he said. "But not by much."

"Taller," Alexander agreed, "but I outweigh you by a few stone." He couldn't keep from grinning as he studied Val. His first glance had been hasty; he'd nearly missed the faint scar on his brother's chin and the corded muscles on his forearms. "I see you've put Kayan's early teaching to good use—unless it was us you were fighting."

Val shook his head. "No. Syria, Carthage, Persia, even India, but I haven't led troops over the borders of the Twin Kingdoms."

Alexander swallowed, attempting to gain control of his emotions. A girl handed him a towel, and he wrapped it absently around his midsection. "I'd hoped . . . We didn't know if you were dead or alive."

"Alive, so far. Trying my best to remain that way."

"And a prince of Egypt as well as Sogdiana?"

"That was a courtesy title. Here I'm Pharaoh's son. Bastard or not, that makes me royal and worthy of the title."

"All these years . . . Kayan's mourned you . . . and Mother. I think she missed you almost as much as I did."

Val averted his eyes, and his posture stiffened almost imperceptibly. "A wonder, since they traded me so easily to save their own skins."

"It wasn't like that."

"No? Kayan traded me to my father for free passage. How else would you interpret his actions?"

"You were badly wounded. You needed more medical attention than Mother could give you. She was afraid you'd bleed to death if—"

Val shook his head. "That was a long time ago, little brother. It's best forgotten. I'm grateful to Kayan for fostering me when I was a child, but I belong here with my real father. Ptolemy is a great king, maybe the greatest the world has ever seen."

"Other than Alexander, you mean?"

"He's created an empire, gathered the greatest thinkers of the age, founded universities, and made Alexandria the envy of every other city. Your father was a different kind of king, a general and a conqueror. But years from now, when we're dust, who will history remember? Another great warrior or the man who united Greek art and kingship with the wealth of Egypt?"

"You thought differently when we were children," Alexander reminded him. "You wanted nothing more than to be a soldier—that and Kayan's son."

Val folded his arms over his chest. "Let's not squabble. What Kayan and your mother did or didn't do isn't your fault. You aren't responsible, and nothing changes the way I feel about you." He extended his hand. "Brothers?"

Alexander gripped it firmly. "Brothers. And soon to be united by my marriage to your sister."

"Half sister, the beautiful Princess Mereret." He waved Alexander to a divan beside a low table laden with fruit, bread, wine, and steaming slices of beef. "Come, let us take a drink together and talk of old times."

Alexander sat across from him and accepted the silver goblet of dark red wine that one of the Nubian girls handed him. He took a sip. "Not bad."

"Shouldn't be. It's Etruscan. They're damned fine vintners as well as pirates." Val reached for a bunch of grapes. "Eat. The prayers at tonight's dinner will be so long that you'll be starving before the food's actually served."

"Tell me about Mereret. What's she like? Does she ride? What are her interests? Can she speak Greek?"

"There's not much I can say about her. I've been on campaign for five of the last seven years. I've seen her, of course, but her mother, Queen Artakama, isn't particularly fond of me. Princes are as scarce as talking dogs in Egypt. My younger half brothers are either stillborn or they die from illness or some unforeseen accident before they're old enough to walk. There's young Ptolemy the second—'Toly, as he's known in the family—but he's a rarity and as likely to eat himself to death as not. Whiny little creature, hardly a brother to boast of, even if he is Father's official heir."

"You were going to tell me about my bride," Alexander reminded him. "The beautiful Mereret."

Val popped a grape into his mouth and chewed. "I really don't know her well. She's clever, healthy as her mother—I don't know that either of them has ever been ill. It's custom for royal children to be educated together, and I know she shared some of the same tutors I had, so she's not stupid. But Artakama kept her secluded, and there's a nine-year gap in our ages. By the time Mereret was old enough to attend court dinners and official celebrations, I was in military training."

Alexander sensed there was more Val wasn't telling him. "You disapprove of this marriage?"

Val drained his wineglass and motioned to a servant. "Bring a pitcher of beer and suitable drinking cups." He glanced back at Alexander. "You come from very different worlds. I'm not certain that sharing a bed can bridge that gap. You might be happier with some Bactrian Amazon."

"Is she being forced into this match?"

Val grimaced. "Not forced, exactly. Princesses rarely have the option of choosing their husbands. But it did come as a shock to her. I think she'd expected to marry a Greek or possibly an Egyptian."

"I'll win her over. Women like me."

"Do they?" He chuckled. "I suppose they do. I heard of that pretty speech you gave this afternoon. The court ladies are all aflutter."

"I was serious."

"I don't know if anyone has warned you, but Egyptian noblewomen dress quite suggestively. And they are nothing if not forward. You'll doubtless receive what could be construed as invitations from many, married and unmarried. Usually they don't expect to be taken seriously. The unmarried Greek women won't be at public events, so that won't be a problem. But, just so you know, knowledge of an Egyptian princess before the official ceremony is as great a crime as it would be in Athens. Little sister may invite you to her chambers, but make certain there are suitable chaperones. Even for a crown prince, I suspect that deflowering the bride beforehand might end badly. Something about the offender having his offending parts crushed by a

40

two-ton statue of the goddess Taweret before being fed to the holy crocodiles."

"Ouch. Sounds uncomfortable," Alexander said. "And the other ladies? Are their invitations as dangerous to accept?"

Val shook his head. "You're shameless. Who would have guessed that little Yuri would turn out so? Seeking my sister's hand in marriage and all the while lusting after her ladies-in-waiting?" His grin widened. "No, such mischief is generally overlooked, so long as a jealous husband doesn't catch you. Egyptian women have far too much freedom, if you ask me."

"And you, brother? Have you taken a wife?"

"Not me. I take comfort where I can find it. But I've never met a woman yet whom I wanted to be faithful to. There are too many stars in the night to be content with the light of just one."

"We've been months in the saddle. My men possess as great an appetite for earthly pleasures as any others. Will Pharaoh provide suitable—"

"You'd hardly expect Father to concern himself with such mundane affairs, but there are eunuchs . . . eunuchs everywhere. I'm sure one of them has been assigned to see that your companions are suitably serviced. I'll make certain." Val rose to his feet.

Not Val, Alexander realized. This was no longer the boy who'd been his best friend, who'd known the deepest secrets of his heart, but a stranger named Paris. "I'm afraid I won't be at the feast tonight, but we'll get together tomorrow or the next day. Perhaps my lieutenant can arrange a lion hunt in the desert."

"I'd like that." Alexander stood and clasped Paris's hand again.

"Good. And if there's anything you need or want"— the Egyptian prince gestured to a shaven-headed man waiting patiently in the doorway—"Hector will attend to it. He's a rascal who would sell his own mother for profit, but he will serve you well, and he won't steal more than you can afford to lose."

Hector, a slight, middle-aged official garbed in the Greek fashion in a short fine wool chiton and draped himation, bowed respectfully. "Prince Alexander, I offer you my humble services, and bring a welcoming gift from her royal highness, the princess Mereret."

"Tomorrow," Prince Paris repeated before striding purposefully out of the room. "And don't get too drunk tonight. Father's wine is very expensive and very potent."

"I'll try not to." Alexander turned his attention to Hector again. "I, too, have a gift for my bride-to-be. It's with my baggage train, but as soon as my things arrive, perhaps you could deliver—" He stopped and stared at the young woman who emerged from the shadowy corridor.

She, too, was dressed in the Greek style, in a simple white linen tunic bordered with a pattern of green lotus blossoms that left her shoulders and arms bare. Her dark hair was held away from her oval face by a silver diadem and fell in glossy curls to the small of her back. She was young and fair of complexion, with the most unusual eyes—eyes as green as new spring grass and flecked with bits of glowing amber. Luminous, huge, and thickly lashed, they held such depths that for seconds he was speechless, unable to do more than gaze at her.

"This is Kiara of the Misty Isles," Hector said matter-of-factly. "The princess has commanded that Kiara is yours without reservation so long as you have use of her. She has been trained in the arts of pleasure. You may do with her whatever you please, even unto her death."

42

Chapter 4

Drapes rustled, bare feet pattered on the tile floor, and bracelets jingled as the Nubian bath girls vanished through a narrow doorway, leaving Alexander alone with the green-eyed woman. Muted notes from a five-stringed harp drifted from the garden, but the lady before him made no sound at all. He found himself listening for the faint sounds of her breath, but she was as silent as the ivory fresco of *Marsh Geese Taking Flight* on the wall behind her.

Oddly, Alexander found himself torn between eagerness to possess this alluring plaything and surprise that his betrothed had sent her. He assumed this woman must be a professional courtesan, accustomed to easing the physical needs of guests. Yet she didn't have the appearance of a whore, even an expensive one. He could find no hint of the brittle gaiety that prostitutes, male or female, acquired in the pursuit of their career.

Still the green-eyed woman said nothing. She stood,

almost within arm's reach, slender hands clasped, back straight, eyes downcast, all innocence and composure. Mentally, Alexander searched for what it was about her that disturbed him. Her fragility? No, she was small but sturdy, her feet high-arched and strong, her creamy skin flushed with health and vigor.

Like his father before him, he had always been fond of the opposite sex. And he'd never agreed with the prevailing opinion that—because they had been created weaker than men—they were less intelligent or incapable of courage and self-sacrifice. He knew all too well that women were a different species from men, more cunning, more apt to act on emotion than reason, but capable of using their feminine wiles and attributes as skillfully as any seasoned warrior wielded his bow or sword.

Instinct warned him that Kiara was as dangerous as any Egyptian viper. Just being in the same room with her excited him. He'd long ago lost count of the beautiful women he'd dallied with, but he found this one so sensual, so ripe and fresh, as to be almost irresistible.

Despite her deferential stance, Kiara was far from subservient. He read pride in the firm set of her mouth, in her body posture, and . . . something else . . . something intangible. This night-blooming flower radiated a sense of suppressed emotional strength, almost as if she, rather than he, held the power in their meeting. Another, less observant man might not have recognized it, but he had grown from boyhood to warrior in the care of a queen among queens. Indeed, his mother and his two sisters possessed the same essence that this barefoot pleasure girl radiated.

The notion that a pleasure wench might share qualities with the hereditary queen of the Twin Kingdoms was impossible. He must be wearier from his trek across Persia and the sea voyage from Tyre than he'd realized. Eager to break the spell she had cast upon him, Alexander said, "You are Kiara of the Misty Isles?"

"Some call me that," she answered in slightly accented but musical Greek.

Her soft voice touched a chord deep inside him, and he felt a rush of tenderness toward her. "And you know who I am?" he asked without condescension.

"Yes, lord. My mistress told me that you are the crown prince of Sogdiana and Bactria, son of Queen Roxanne and the King Alexander whom men call 'great.'"

She seemed to fix her gaze on an invisible object hovering a few inches above the floor and remained completely motionless. He saw in her no acceptance of their relative social positions, but rather . . . amusement.

He stiffened. "I am a stranger to Egyptian customs," he said brusquely. "In my homeland, these matters are more discreet. It isn't the practice for a bride to send a bedmate to her bridegroom."

Kiara's thick, dark lashes fluttered and she looked up. Her countenance remained neutral, almost solemn, but the sea-green eyes danced with light. "You wonder if you have understood correctly? If I am part of some deception . . . some trick to discredit you before the princess Mereret and her father, the pharaoh, the Great Bull of Egypt?"

Her voice dragged him deeper into confusion. This was no common slave; she was too intelligent, too well-spoken. He wondered if she were a woman of rank, perhaps even a priestess of some Egyptian cult, serving her pagan goddess by offering up her body. Alexander's throat tightened as he studied Kiara from

45

the tips of her carmine painted toenails to the crown of her shining head. Rays of sunlight pouring through the garden archway revealed gleaming highlights of chestnut in the glorious weight of her long, dark brown hair.

She wore no jewelry but a single pair of dangling copper-and-faience earrings that echoed the pattern of green lotus blossoms in the hem of her linen tunic, a finely woven garment so transparent that it left little of her feminine charms to the imagination.

He could well believe that Kiara had been chosen for her profession because of her lush body and intriguing face. Her waist was small, her hips in perfect balance with her firm, full breasts. Her legs and thighs were shapely; the dark triangle below her flat belly and the faint scent of apple blossoms that lingered in the air around her were cause enough to resurrect the shrunken staff of a dead man.

"Do you find me pleasing?" she asked, as if reading his mind.

"Very." His reply was harsher than he intended.

"My lady did not know what type of refreshment you would prefer. If I do not satisfy, she will send another. Perhaps a boy?"

"No." His palms felt hot, and he ran his hands through his damp hair to cool them. "No boys. I am not a man to—"

"A goat?" she offered helpfully.

"No goats!" he roared. "No animals, no wildfowl, and certainly no boys."

"My mistress meant no offense, Prince Alexander. She only wondered . . . because of your father. Rumors said that the king—"

"Rumors spread by his enemies. Lies."

"Of course," she agreed. "As you say, gossip whispered by those who would taint his memory."

"Exactly."

A hint of amusement teased the corners of Kiara's mouth. Her lips were full and ripe, naturally pink, promising a depth of passion. Her teeth were straight and white, her pretty nose and cheeks lightly dusted with freckles.

But always he found himself drawn back as though by magic to her intense emerald eyes, eyes framed by dark, dainty brows and a high forehead. She was no child, but a full woman, yet still glowing with an impression of youthful fertility.

"I find you acceptable. More than acceptable. Very beautiful, but I have no need of your services. Not today, not on the eve of meeting my intended," he lied. He had need, a physical need that he'd not fed since that plump plum of a Syrian girl in Tyre, an urgent need that was making itself more evident with every passing minute.

Quickly, before she found reason to laugh aloud at him, he tried to fix his mind on something disgusting, an image so repulsive that his rising interest in this woman would deflate. Poisoned water. Dead sheep. Dead sheep with maggots crawling on them. Crows tearing at the glazed eyes.

But the fragmented picture he created dissolved, to be replaced by a woman's eyes . . . eyes as green and mysterious as the sea . . . as green as a mountain meadow in springtime. . . .

She undid one tie at the shoulder of her chiton and let the material fall, revealing a perfectly shaped, rosy-tipped breast.

His breath caught in his throat as heat seared his loins.

Kiara unfastened the other ribbon and the tunic pooled at her ankles. With a groan, he crushed her against him, buried his face in those soft breasts, inhaling an intriguing scent of wild violets and pine. She turned her face away, and let her head fall back so that the length of her hair brushed his bare hip, and he swept her up into his arms.

Kiara closed her eyes as the blond barbarian swept away the heaped cushions and threw her roughly onto the low, Greek-style bed. He was strong, this prince. His hands were the hard hands of a swordsman, his lean body coiled with taut muscle, but she sensed control in his passion. His strange blue-gray eyes had glittered like fiery opals, but she had sensed only healthy appetite in his gaze, not cruelty. She was not afraid of him . . . not yet.

Her flesh responded to his, making it hard to remember the role she must play. His big hands roamed over her breasts; his warm lips and tongue teased until her nipples grew firm and sensitive. He was all over her, touching, tasting, caressing, wrapping his long horseman's legs around hers, enfolding her so tightly against his broad, hairless chest that she could feel the thud of his heart. And she responded as she had been taught—the little moans, the love bites, the molding of her curves to his.

He was big as well as lusty. His phallus was thick, and long, and pulsing, of a size to cause jealousy in other men, but as beautifully made as the rest of him. And he was magnificent, all bronzed and glowing, as though Apollo or even Poseidon had fathered him, making him only half-mortal.

She could feel Prince Alexander's heat, hear the deep shudder of his breathing, and imagine the hot, reckless excitement in those jeweled eyes. Yet, despite his intense arousal, his obvious readiness to mate, he seemed in no hurry to enter her and spill his seed. Instead he continued to stroke and caress her, to run his lean fingers over her skin and coax the embers of her suppressed passion.

She tried to fight as she had always done . . . to think of the sea . . . of the island of the seals and the soaring flight of seabirds. Always, she could will her mind away from this place and time to a happier one. She was not immune to the pleasures that a man and woman could share, especially when her chosen partner was as attractive as this one, but she rarely allowed herself to partake of them while completing an assignment. She told herself that only her body was his to use; her spirit was beyond his reach . . . beyond the grasp of any man.

The thought that she had never been given to a dignitary as appealing as this one crossed her mind, and she brushed it away. She could not allow herself to think about the clean, virile scent of his hair and skin, to feel the exquisite sensation of his warm breath on her belly, or the texture of his fingers as they stroked her inner thigh. Forgetting, even for the space of a few moments, could be deadly.

To this man she was no more than an object, a sensual toy that could be tossed aside or broken at will. If he was one who took gratification in causing pain, he would, and she must summon the courage to suffer any torture without crying out and without resistance. Survival demanded constant vigil, spirited compliance, and wit. And no woman could ensure all those defenses if she permitted herself to enjoy that which belonged only to her master.

But it was sometimes almost beyond human endurance. . . .

She quivered, thrilling to the waves of hot, tingling desire that washed over her. His tongue . . . Oh, sweet breath of Isis! What was he doing with his tongue?

Gooseflesh rose on her arms and bare breasts. Her stomach knotted with tension.

Deeper . . . He was murmuring words that she must not hear . . . could not listen to . . . lies that would only deceive and destroy . . . gossamer ribbons that could bring her downfall.

"Beautiful Kiara. Kiara of the sea-green eyes . . ."

Her pulse quickened. Her heart thudded against her rib cage, and her chest grew tight. The aching grew with each flick of his tongue. Breathlessly, she knotted her fingers in his thick, yellow curls, and raised her hips to meet his sweet invasion.

What was he doing? What did he want from her? She was offering everything . . . what more could he extract from her body?

She burned . . . was consumed by his will. Tendrils of his hair tickled her thighs. How long could she suffer this bittersweet anguish without dissolving into . . . into what?

His calloused palms massaged her buttocks. His hot, wet, thrusting tongue probed ever deeper with slow, sweetly tantalizing strokes. His lips . . . his mouth . . .

A low groan of frustration escaped her clenched teeth. She tugged at his shoulders, tilted her hips in invitation, only to be rewarded by a low, sensual chuckle. The gossamer ribbons tightened, ensnaring her in a web of confusion.

"Do you want this?" he asked, capturing her hand and folding it around his engorged phallus. "Shall I fill you with it? Open your eyes, Kiara. See what I have for you."

But she couldn't . . . wouldn't. She was weak . . . too weak to deny that he had crushed her defenses . . . that he had defeated her utterly and completely so that she could not hold back the tears of frustration.

"Tell me what you want! Spread your legs wide, and I'll give you what you know you want."

She did. She wanted him as she had never wanted a man. She wanted him with all the pent-up lust and longing of a wild leopard screaming for sexual release. But this savage prince had asked for what she would not give.

"Look at me, Kiara! Open your eyes and look at me."

She would not. If he held her hand in an open flame, she would not beg him to quench her madness. Yet she would die if she could not find release . . . die as surely as the heat of his sweat-sheened body permeated hers.

He laughed. "So be it. But you've only yourself to blame." He pressed her back against the bed. Every muscle cried out for her to fight, but her will was stronger. She lay panting, heavy limbed, waiting for him to claim what was his to take, and unable to stop the seepage of tears that spilled down her cheeks.

His touch was gentle, almost featherlight, erotic. She felt her cheeks and throat flush with hot blood. *Hurry,* she wanted to shout. *Do it. Just do it.* But she held her breath and did not utter a sound.

He lowered his face between her legs and kissed her and she was lost. Billowing tremors of pleasure rocked her, spiraling through her with a greater intensity than she had dreamed possible, shattering the last fragments of her composure.

"Yes, yes," he murmured. "Feel it, feel it, sweet, fly with it." He rose on his knees and stretched out beside her, gathering her to him and sliding the swollen tip of his tumescence against her leg until he gave a mighty gasp and found his own release.

Later, he rose and drew her with him into the pool to bathe away the proof of their mischief. Although he tried, he could not get her to meet his gaze, and her reluctance both perplexed and amused him. "Come, little bird. You can't be shy with me now. Neither of us

51

lost by the encounter. And I could tell that I'm not the first man with whom you've shared pleasure. Can you give some indication that I'm not the worst you've spent an hour with?"

Obediently she raised her chin and gave him an entertainer's smile. "You were magnificent, lord. The best."

He wanted more—expected more. Hoped for the truth. "We played together," he answered. "We didn't . . ." He used a coarse term, one that he'd used a thousand times in the barracks among his troops.

She flushed, and he felt a tinge of shame. Guilt made him sharp with her. "You may return to your mistress and give her my thanks. Tell her that I found you more than adequate."

For the first time Alexander saw her composure falter as fear flashed in her eyes, followed by glistening moisture.

"No, please. I cannot. If you send me back, she will not believe that I fulfilled her command. I will be beaten . . . or worse."

Suspicion reared in his mind. He stared at her, wondering if she was lying. But if she was, why? Could she have been sent to spy on him? Or was she the assassin his mother had warned him of? "If I can't send you back, what am I supposed to do with you?"

"Keep me here, your highness. Let me attend to your needs. I will be no trouble, and if you wish . . . ease, you have only to call me to your bed."

This is wrong, he thought, *all wrong.* He glared at her. "Why? I am to take a royal bride within days. Why should I trouble myself with another woman?"

She stepped back. Her mouth grew firm, and her chin went up. "No reason." Her beautiful green eyes darkened. Once again, he had the odd sensation of being in the presence of a queen. "If it is your command that I leave you, I—"

He swore a foul oath. "Stay if it pleases you. It's no great matter to me. Just keep your hands off my helmet and shield. My squire will tend to those. And don't touch my bow or quiver. The arrowheads are honed to a razor's edge."

She inclined her head, waded out of the water, and took a fresh towel to offer him. Shrugging off her assistance, he dressed, ran his fingers through his hair, and strapped on his sword belt.

"You may not enter Pharaoh's presence wearing weapons," Kiara said.

"He'll have to make an exception in my case. And I expect him to extend his invitation to include my officers. I will not insult them by attending this welcome feast without them."

She dried herself quickly, retrieved her tunic from the floor, and put it on. She left a trail of small wet footprints from the pool to the center of the room. Scarlet smudges still showed on her high cheekbones, giving Alexander the impression that he'd insulted her.

She was high-strung, petulant. He should have guessed. The pretty ones often were, whether blooded mares or women. He'd waste no more effort placating her. She was a pleasure girl, no more and no less. "Send a servant to fetch my belongings and my squire. His name is Jahan, and he will be in the stables with my horse."

"As you will, lord."

She inclined her head respectfully, but he wasn't deceived by her pretense of obedience. She was up to something.

"Let us understand something between us," he said. "I am not by nature a cruel man. Harming women or children is repugnant to me, but I am no fool. Betray me and I will slay you as swiftly as I would a poisonous snake. Do you understand, Kiara of the Misty Isles?"

"I hear you, lord," she answered softly.

"I know you hear me, wench. But do you understand me?" He caught her chin between his fingers and raised it so that he could look into those inscrutable green eyes. "Do you believe me?"

"I swear to you, I will not. I pledge my honor that I will give faithful service and true service."

He grunted. "Good."

"Until the vows are taken between you and my mistress."

"And then what?" he demanded. "You'll slip poison in my wine? Put a viper in my bed?"

She smiled up at him with the innocence of a child. "Why, then, great prince, then my usefulness to you is over and my mission will be discharged."

"Why doesn't that reassure me?" He released her, and felt a sharp ache of regret when he saw the marks of his fingers on her fair skin.

She stood waiting.

"Well? I gave you an order, didn't I? Send for Jahan at once. And when he arrives, see that he has refreshment. Treat him with the respect that you would give me."

"In all ways, lord?"

Irritation flared in his chest. "Stupid jade. Respect, not sexual service. He's quite capable of bathing himself and too well mannered to take what belongs to me."

"Lord?" Kiara's lashes fluttered in confusion.

"You. You are mine. You knew perfectly well what I meant."

She dropped gracefully to her knees. "Forgive me, prince, for my foolish error. As you say, I am but a stupid servant, and I feared to—"

"Don't even try it," he said, grasping her hands and lifting her to her feet. "You're far from stupid. I didn't ask for you, but now that you're here, I'll deal with you. So long as you serve me, you'll not give your favors to another man. And there's no need to bow and scrape with me. It is not the custom of my homeland. Is that clear?"

"Utterly," she replied. A faint smile played over her lips. "I am yours in all things."

Chapter 5

Oblivious to the cries of her ladies, Roxanne dropped the gold-and-silver coronet set with rubies that she'd intended as a gift for her new daughter-in-law and dashed out of her private reception chamber. She raced down the great curving stone stairway with the life-size marble stallions, through a lower private passage, and down another narrow set of stairs to the ground level of the palace. Without pausing to catch her breath, she ran past the guards at the massive bronze doors, across a tiled and pillared hall, through the ceremonial entrance where the elite Bactrian archers stood watch, and around a startled delegation of merchants from beyond the Ganges River. Roxanne was three-quarters of the distance across the outer courtyard when Kayan appeared in the open gateway with their nineteen-year-old daughter, Shahi, in his arms.

Roxanne stopped short. Her knees were weak, her heart pounding. Waves of panic swept over her. "Is she . . . ?" she called, trying to hide the terror in her voice.

"She's fine," Kayan said. "Just a nasty bump on the head."

"My arm hurts," Shahi said, "but I can walk. Put me down, Father."

Ignoring her protests, Kayan crossed to where Roxanne stood. Several of Shahi's companions followed. One of the girls had obviously been weeping. Another's face was so ashen that it seemed carved of marble.

Roxanne swallowed. Her mouth was so dry that it was almost impossible to speak. "You're all right? Really? They told me that—"

"That she was dead," Kayan finished. "A boy said the same thing. I was training a new falcon just beyond the outer wall. They were wrong. She's well enough, although I wager she'll have two black eyes by tomorrow."

A crowd was gathering around them. Stable hands, noblemen, and soldiers stood side by side with a cook, a blacksmith, and a dairymaid carrying buckets of milk, all anxiously staring at the royal family.

Ignoring everyone else, Roxanne took her daughter's face in her hands, brushed aside a lock of silky dark hair, and examined the rising swelling on Shahi's temple. "You were thrown, not kicked?"

Shahi nodded. Her eyes were full of pain, but she was breathing regularly, and she showed no sign of shock. "It was just a fall. Nothing to get yourself all in a fuss over. I must have been knocked unconscious, but I'm all right. Just a few bruises."

Roxanne glanced up into her husband's face. He was attempting to pretend otherwise, but she could see that he'd been as frightened as she. "Let me see that arm." She moved her fingers over Shahi's right wrist. The girl winced as Roxanne felt the grate of bone. "It's broken. Take her upstairs." She motioned to a soldier. "Bring the surgeon. Tell him to come at once."

Shahi shook her head. "Let me down. I can walk. I'm not a child." Her shaggy black dog, taller and broader than a newborn calf, nosed against her hand and whined anxiously. "It's all right, Bear," she reassured him. "I'm fine."

"The horse?" Roxanne asked. "Was it injured?"

Freny, the young woman who'd been weeping, touched her forehead in respect. She was tall and thin with a red birthmark that covered a portion of her left cheek. Freny was the only daughter of a highborn Sogdian general, and a favorite in the court, loved for her sweet nature and unfailing optimism. Roxanne knew that it would take more than a mere tumble to make Freny believe her best friend had been killed.

"The mare is fine, your majesty. One of the grooms caught her." Freny tossed a long dark pigtail over the shoulder of her red cloak. "A partridge flew up unexpectedly out of the tall grass and startled Mahin. That's why she reared."

"It's not Mahin's fault, Mother," Shahi said. "It was mine for not being more alert. Ava will never let me live this down."

"We thought she had been killed, your majesty," Freny admitted. "She lay there so still. We couldn't get her to wake."

"Yes, yes," the other girls chimed in.

Roxanne followed Kayan back into the palace and up to Shahi's chambers. The two of them tucked the injured girl into bed and sent servants for medical supplies and hot water. Shahi was already drowsy from the mug of fiery koumiss that Kayan had pressed into her good hand at the bottom of the stairs. Now he insisted that she drink another.

Two physicians entered the room, followed by attendants carrying their chests of herbs, medications, and instruments. Kayan explained the accident while Roxanne drew a stool close to the bed and talked quietly to Shahi.

"You're making too much of this, Mother. There's isn't any need. . . ." Her voice slurred with the effect of the potent alcohol.

"Shh, there's every need. You and your sister and brother are my heart. I could not go on living if I lost one of you."

Shahi managed a wan smile. "How is that possible? You tell Father that he's your heart all the time."

"And so he is. You are all my heart. I lost a husband and two children whom I cherished, and I'm too old to lose any more."

"Old, you aren't old," her daughter protested. "You're not even two score and five. You're not wrinkled. You have all of your teeth, and your hair isn't even gray."

"I am a crone with a stiff back and failing eyes," Roxanne said.

Shahi uttered a small sound of amusement. "You are such a liar. Who killed that wolf with a single arrow last spring?" She giggled. "From horseback—at a full gallop?"

"A lucky shot," Roxanne admitted. "Before I got old."

"You'll never be old. You'll remain the 'Little Star,' the most beautiful woman in all of Persia, long after I've turned into a toothless hag."

Roxanne stood and leaned over her and kissed the crown of Shahi's head. "You are your father's heart and soul as well, you and Ava. You must take better care of yourself."

Shahi's dark eyes narrowed. "You are hardly the person to tell me to take care—after some of the stories Father's told."

"Long ago, when the world was young and I was foolish," Roxanne said. She'd been only a little younger than Shahi when she'd been forced into marriage with the Macedonian Alexander and had followed him to the far ends of the earth. Pray God that her daughters would live much more ordinary lives . . . or as ordinary as any princess could expect.

"Shahi! I heard you fell off a horse and broke your neck!" Ava shouted.

Roxanne turned and caught her younger daughter in her arms. "Slow down, slow down. Your sister's fine. A bruise on her temple and a broken wrist. Her neck, as far as I can tell, is intact."

"You fell off Mahin?" Ava jeered. "You should let me train her to saddle." A black nose showed in the shadowy doorway, followed by a massive head. One of the physician's assistants squeaked in terror and shrank against the wall as Ava's leopard padded into the room. Shahi's dog raised his head and rumbled a warning at the cat. The big cat yawned and twitched its tail.

"Shh," Roxanne said, placing two fingers firmly over Ava's lips. The girl's hat was askew, one pigtail was undone, and her cheek and chin were smeared with dirt, as were her leather tunic and trousers. "The physicians need quiet to think. You may see Shahi for just a minute and then . . ." Roxanne cleared her throat to stifle a giggle. "Then you and your friend need to return to your own chambers. You, my small horse-woman, smell of the stables and are badly in need of a bath."

"Mother," Ava pleaded.

"You heard your mother," Kayan said. "Give Shahi a hug and then off with the two of you. You may join us later for a quiet supper."

Ava sighed. "No one ever lets me stay and see anything interesting."

60

"Your sister is about to have her wrist set and bandaged. It will hurt, and she may cry out. I don't think there's any need for you to witness it."

"Amen to that," Shahi agreed. She raised a hand to meet her sister's. "Go on, little one. You can come back later and read me . . . I mean read *to* me."

Ava made a face. "You smell like koumiss. Maybe you're so drunk you don't know that your neck's broken."

"Silly goose," Shahi replied. "I'm not, and even if I were, I'd know if my neck was broken. It . . ." She giggled. "It wouldn't hold my head on, would it?"

"All right." Ava blew her a kiss. "Later. But I get to choose the book. I've a new one that grandmother found in Samarkand. It's about Egypt and wrapping dead people in cloth so that they last a thousand years and come back to life."

"I can't wait," Shahi said.

The oldest physician approached the bed. "If you'd let me examine the arm, your highness."

"I suppose you must." She closed her eyes and lay back against a silk-covered bolster. "Do your worst." She gritted her teeth.

"I believe it's a simple break," Roxanne said.

"I agree," the doctor said after a moment or two. "We'll wrap and splint it. You'll feel better then, Princess Shahi. I'll have a soothing potion made to take away the pain."

Shahi opened her eyes and glanced at her father. "I won't cry," she promised him. "I'm not a coward."

"I know you're not," he said gruffly.

Roxanne moved gracefully to his side. "Let us wait on the balcony," she suggested. "We'll be only a short distance away if she needs us. I think it's better if we give her privacy."

Kayan looked back at his daughter. "If you want us, send one of the lads," he said.

Roxanne took his arm and they walked together through a smaller chamber and out onto a stone balcony filled with pots of blooming flowers and small trees. "She will be all right," she assured her husband. "You look worse than she does."

"A blow to the head can be fatal."

She nodded. She was still shaky herself from the scare, but she tried to calm him. "You are a doting father to your daughters."

"What else should I be?"

"You let them run wild. You were harder on the boys."

"Val and Yuri needed a firm hand."

"Not Yuri," she corrected. "You know how he hates to be called by that name now. Alexander. But if our girls are the best of daughters, you are the best of fathers. Even if you do let them get away with murder."

"Do I?" He slipped an arm around her waist and nuzzled her hair. "I waited a long time for them, and I will have them only a little while. Shahi will be off to her temple, and our Ava will be making some other man's life crazy."

"Not for a while, I hope. She's only seven. Did you plan to find her a husband this week?"

"Not until she's twenty and seven. Until then, she's ours."

"Spoken like the man I know and love." Roxanne slipped her arms around his neck and rose on tiptoe to kiss him. "You are very special to me," she whispered.

"And you to me." He hugged her. "Has my hair turned white? When they told me that Shahi had—"

"No, it looks dark enough to me. Except for this one." She tugged at a blue-black strand.

"Ouch. Torturer. She will heal well enough, won't she?"

"Yes, I'm sure of it." She stepped back out of his embrace, but kept tight hold on his hand. "There is something that I've been wanting to tell you, but it never seems the right time. I think it's now. I believe you could use good news."

"A courier came from Egypt?"

"No, no word from Alexander. Something else, something between us." She lifted his hand and placed it, palm flat, against her swelling belly.

He scowled. "What are you saying?"

She sighed. She'd been afraid he'd be difficult. "I'm saying that spring will bring more than a crop of new foals to the Twin Kingdoms. I'm with child, Kayan. I'm going to give you another daughter to spoil—or a son."

"No! I told you! You cannot have another—"

"Cannot? Cannot? I am. Whether you like it or not. I've missed my moon courses three times. My breasts are sore, and the waistband of my trousers is growing tight. I'm pregnant, and like it or not—you're going to be a father again."

"Not if I have anything to say about it!"

Salt tears stung her eyes, but she dashed them angrily away. "You don't," she flung back. "I want this baby, and I'm going to have it. With you or without you."

Alexander reclined on a divan next to Paris and waved away the servant with the wine pitcher. He had already imbibed far more than was his custom, and despite the unavoidable toasts, he felt the need to keep his head clear. A few of his officers were already in their cups, but the majority had followed his lead in drinking as sparingly as possible without offering insult to Pharaoh or his Egyptian queen. Both Queen

Berenice and her son, Prince Ptolemy, were absent from the hall.

All of Alexander's company had been invited, but only three of his companions were among the exalted seated around the half dozen tables here on the raised dais. The rest of the Bactrians and Sogdians were scattered among the Greek and Egyptian nobles, military officers, and foreign dignitaries throughout the huge banquet hall.

Queen Artakama, the sultry mother of the bride-to-be, drank steadily but appeared no less sober than when the banquet had begun three hours earlier. Ptolemy, in contrast, ate little and only touched his lips to his wine goblet with each new toast.

"And what he drinks is greatly watered," Paris had whispered. "My father believes in moderation in all things."

Alexander noticed that his uncle's food and drink were brought in separately and assumed that Ptolemy's caution was due to fear of poisoning. Alexander had never worried about what he ate or drank. Death would come to all men and women in time, and his would arrive when it suited the good God and not a day before. Still, it was a matter to give further thought—that Pharaoh, master of one of the mightiest empires in the civilized world, might be afraid of his own subjects.

The Nubian entertainers were followed by a troop of female Indian acrobats and dozens of nubile Egyptian slave girls carrying silver trays of meat and flatbread and wearing cones of perfumed wax on their heads. The Indians were scantily clad, but the Egyptian serving maids wore nothing but elaborately curled black wigs, and silver chains around their slender hips. Their golden bodies were oiled, their body hair shaven, and their eyes painted so that they looked as identical as the line of gazelles engraved on the nearest column.

The vast reception chamber boasted whitewashed walls and brightly patterned mosaic-tile flooring. Most walls were decorated with stylized images of Egyptian gods and goddesses in some act of creation, but several realistic murals depicted intricate scenes of the Nile and rural life. Painted columns reared high overhead to vanish into darkness. Fountains bubbled beneath wide skylights open to velvet-black heavens strewn with thousands of glittering stars. The soft notes of Egyptian harp and flute music were foreign to Alexander's ear but not unpleasant, and the air was sweet with the scents of perfumed oils and incense.

"Better than a Scythian feast?" Paris asked. "Not a slab of raw horsemeat in sight."

Alexander laughed. "You remember those, do you, brother? I wonder if all this soft living has spoiled you." He refused delicate slices of gazelle and a highly spiced dish of eels and dolphin, choosing instead a bunch of purple grapes. He tore off one grape and popped it into his mouth. When he bit down, he found the fruit bursting with sweet juice.

"I forget nothing." Paris drained another cup of wine and held it out for a boy to refill. The prince's pleasant expression almost, but not quite, countered his cynical reply.

Alexander was troubled by the change in this man who'd spent his childhood in the Twin Kingdoms as Kayan's adopted son. The three of them had shared hardships and danger as well as days that for Alexander were as dear as any he could remember. Val—*Paris,* he corrected himself mentally—had been the most important person in his early life, after their father. And he knew that Paris had loved Kayan, and later Roxanne, as deeply as he had. Part of his reason for accepting Ptolemy's offer had been to come to Egypt, to find his lost brother, and to bring Val home.

Fulfilling that wish seemed difficult now at best. The years of living with Ptolemy had changed Paris, perhaps irrevocably.

There was a stir at the far corner of the hall, and the person Alexander had been waiting for all evening entered, accompanied by an entourage that he supposed must be her handmaidens and ladies-in-waiting. He rose to his feet and offered his princess a warm smile. She seemed not to notice, but sat erect, eyes straight ahead, in her carrying chair, as muscular Egyptians, clad only in small linen kilts and sandals, delivered her to her mother's side.

Ptolemy lifted his cup. "Welcome," he said to his daughter. His voice was pleasant, full of authority without being overly loud or strident. "Nephew, here is your bride. Is she not the flower of the Nile?"

"More beautiful than sunrise," he replied.

Neither Mereret nor her mother gave any indication that Alexander had spoken. The bearers lowered the chair, and an official hurried to offer his hand to help her step down.

Alexander's pulse quickened. Mereret's white linen tunic was no less sheer than that of the green-eyed courtesan waiting in his room, or the queen's. Wide bracelets of gold weighed down her slender wrists; a multilayered collar of gold cowrie shells, carnelian, and opals glittered around her throat, and her ears dripped icicles of diamonds and silver. But the magnificent display of jewels did not detract from the exotic allure of the woman he'd come to claim as his own. Below her necklace, Mereret's small breasts were clearly visible; her nipples, her woman's mound, and the soles of her feet were rouged with henna. Her legs, though not as long as Kiara's, were shapely. The princess's face was as haunting as he had remembered from his brief glimpse of her on their first meeting. A mixture of Greek and Egyptian, her features were finely drawn, her eyes large and black, painted in green and kohl, and her lips tinted a brilliant scarlet. Her complexion was somewhat darker than Ptolemy's and appeared to be dusted with gold. Alexander felt his loins stir as he imagined what a tasty delight she would prove in his bed.

Yet his Egyptian princess had yet to acknowledge him. The thought pricked at his pride, and he could not let it go. "Princess," he said, "have you no word for your beloved?"

For a second he thought she would ignore him; then she glanced sideways at her mother. The queen nodded, and her painted lips turned up in approval. Mereret lowered her head, only a little, and then shyly looked up at him and bestowed a smile so enticing that the hall shook with laughter and roars of approval.

Alexander turned to Paris and grinned.

"Careful, little brother," he murmured. "The Nile is swift and deep, and more than one stranger has been swept to his death by the currents."

Alexander motioned for more wine and lifted the goblet in salute. "To my bride," he said, "the future queen of the Twin Kingdoms."

"To the bride," his companions echoed. Bactrians, Sogdians, Greeks, and Egyptians alike raised their cups and drank deep.

Greek players replaced the dancers, and after them came three snake charmers who climbed ropes and vanished before the eyes of the audience. Princess Mereret did not glance his way again, but Alexander was satisfied. Whatever pressure his uncle had put upon her to bring about the marriage, his betrothed was not unwilling. State weddings were not expected to be love matches, but physical attraction between bride and groom made the political union smoother.

Roaring tigers came next, accompanied by dancers from Chin and more musicians. Alexander was able to exchange a few words with his uncle, but the entertainment and the sheer number of guests made it next to impossible to carry on a conversation.

The tables groaned as servants continued to carry in trays of olives, cheese, stewed vegetables, all manner of exotic fruits, honeyed cakes, bread, and sweets, accompanied by yet more wine and bowls of yeasty Egyptian beer. Alexander wearied of the loud noise and unending courses of food, but knew that leaving before his host and hostess would be an insult of the worst kind.

Finally, two hours before dawn, Ptolemy rose, bade Alexander and the others good night, and departed with his family. Paris leaned close. "Don't forget our hunting expedition, Alexander. Unless you're a late sleeper."

"I'll be ready," Alexander assured him.

"Good. I'll send a boy to fetch you at first light. There's a small village on the edge of the desert that has been plagued by a rogue lion. The beast has been preying on the fellahin's goats, but recently it's become bolder. Three days ago it killed an old man." Paris motioned toward a doorway. "Follow me. I'll have someone show you a shortcut back to your chambers."

"I need to speak to my captain first."

"Bring him with you in the morning, if he likes hunting lion. Choose three of your men. We'll keep the party small. More and we'll lessen the chance of making a kill."

Alexander nodded and clasped Paris's hand. "Until tomorrow, brother. I look forward to it."

"And I as well." Paris motioned to a servant. "Remain with Prince Alexander and escort him back to his own quarters when he is ready."

The young man, a reed-thin eunuch with round, intelligent eyes and a shaven head, made an obeisance. "As you wish, lord," he murmured.

A quarter of an hour later, after he'd consulted with his companions, Alexander followed the young eunuch through the maze of corridors. The passageways intersected with many smaller halls, courtyards, and rooms, so that Alexander lost all sense of direction. He was about to question his guide when suddenly the man stopped and bowed low.

"Here, your highness." The man indicated a door that looked exactly like the last fifty.

Alexander pushed it open to find, not his guest quarters, but a small, walled garden with a central fountain. "What . . . ?" He turned to find that the eunuch had vanished as completely as the snake charmers, although, he was certain, the servant had not climbed a rope or made himself invisible.

Alexander put his hand on his sword and listened. He heard nothing but water bubbling from the fountain, a musical flow from a bronze dolphin's open mouth into a massive oyster shell of rose quartz. These desert people seemed obsessed with fountains; he'd seen at least one in every room of the palace in this desert kingdom. The humid night air smelled of jasmine and myrrh.

"Don't be afraid," a sultry female voice called from the semidarkness. "Come in. I've been waiting for you." Her Greek was cultured and without the slightest accent.

A slender figure moved from the shadows of a tree. "Mereret?"

A heady wave of musk enveloped him as the princess extended a small, hennaed hand.

Chapter 6

Ptolemy lowered himself onto the bed, oblivious to the musician playing the lyre or the oiled and gyrating dancers wearing nothing but masks of heron feathers, and watched as Artakama performed the steps of an ancient Egyptian fertility rite. The room was thick with smoke and hot from the charcoal braziers that surrounded the queen's sleeping couch. A tray of dried mushrooms lay on the floor beside him, but he needed no drugs to stir his loins for this woman who had been his wife for so many years . . . *his* but never truly possessed.

Artakama wore nothing but a feathered mask, and a hip belt formed of living, writhing snakes. Her skin gleamed with honey; her taut nipples, the soles of her feet, and the shaven glory at the apex of her thighs bore erotic patterns in henna. Ptolemy wanted her as fiercely as if she were an untouched virgin, a desert whirlwind that he had never bedded . . . never devoured until he was satiated and sore.

He sipped from the cup of dark, sweet wine and felt

his veins pulse with liquid heat. A flute wailed from a shadowy alcove to be followed by the urgent throb of a goatskin drum. He drank again, and a single bead of liquid spilled down his chin. Guilt teased at the corners of his mind. Had Egypt spoiled him, as his brother Alexander had once taunted? Had he come to conquer Alexandria, only to be utterly swallowed up and transformed into a pleasure-sated oriental potentate? Was Artakama a well-earned reward or punishment?

He worked hard for his people, he assured himself. Hadn't Alexander drowned himself in wine and women? Hadn't he defied the world by taking a barbarian princess as his wife because he lusted after her? What had Alexander done to compare with the civilization he—Ptolemy—had created here in Alexandria? What ruler didn't deserve some small portion of relaxation for himself? How was his Artakama any worse than his brother's sword-wielding Roxanne?

From somewhere, the heron dancers had been joined by three naked males in jackal masks. The men obviously were meant to represent Egypt; one's skin was fair as a northern Greek, another red-brown as nutmeg, and the third as black as ebony. Each performer was a magnificent specimen, sleek and muscled, all in full sexual arousal. Never missing the beat of the primeval rhythm, the jackals pursued the herons, who fled and were caught, struggled free to scatter with shrill wails of alarm, and finally were captured again. Flames leaped high in the darkness as the jackals flung their prizes down and performed a variety of original and physically demanding feats of passion that seemed well received by their feminine partners.

Still, Ptolemy could not tear his gaze from Artakama as she moved in and out of the living tableau, thrust hips and breasts nearly within his grasp, and spun away before he could seize her. Sweat beaded on his face and dampened his hands; his swollen phallus pulsed with exquisite pain. He could wait no longer, yet the wait made her coming surrender all the sweeter. "Artakama," he groaned, extending a hand to her.

She melted to the floor and inched toward him as her serpents slithered away under the raised bed. When she was close enough to touch, she turned away and pressed her face to the tile, exposing her firm, heart-shaped buttocks and more . . . much more.

Ptolemy looked down at his right hand and the thin leather whip that had materialized there. The whip seemed to possess a life of its own. He raised it and brought the length slashing down over Artakama's sweet flesh. Once. Twice.

Catlike, she rolled away and came up on hands and knees just out of reach. "More?"

"Yes." His reply was dragged from the deepest pit of his gut.

"Promise me that you will not send her away."

Lust turned to fury. "You dare to—"

"He is like his father. He will defeat you—steal what is yours. Even now he ruts with your daughter like a drunken Scythian."

Ptolemy lunged from the bed, catching her by one ankle, dragging her squirming across the floor, pinning her against the tile, driving into her wet center.

She laughed, wrapping her legs around him, arching her back and taking him deep inside. "He will steal your crown," she hissed as she dug her nails into his naked back. "Your precious 'Toly will lie in the House of the Dead while Alexander's son snatches the crown of Egypt from Pharaoh's head."

"No! No!" he cried, hammering into her. "He will not!" Need drove him. Her scent filled his head, intoxicating him, driving him close to the knife edge of madness—giving him strength and virility to equal a god's.

"How men will laugh," she panted into his ear. "Your seed will vanish from the earth while his . . . your brother's son . . ."

He silenced her lying mouth with his, thrusting his tongue between her sharp teeth and pounding faster, harder, drowning her poison with his hot gush of seed.

And yet later, when he lay spent and limp on the bed with Artakama curled beside him, he could not forget her words. Words of warning . . . or a means to her own desires? He did not know, and, not knowing, he could not sleep for wondering if he were truly pharaoh or if all his dreams were empty posturing and this woman, this daughter of Egypt, truly ruled here.

Mereret fed Alexander another grape. He caught her wrist, turned it, and pressed his lips to the underside of her elbow. She sighed and made no effort to pull away as he trailed kisses to her bare shoulder.

"You are not as ugly as I thought you might be," she admitted, placing fingertips on his lips.

Alexander sat up. "You were told that I was ugly?"

"My half brother, Prince Paris, said that you were small, with scabby knees."

"I've grown."

"In all ways?" She took his calloused right hand and examined the palm. "You have hard hands for a prince."

"I'm a swordsman."

She traced the creases across his index and middle fingers. "And a chariot driver?"

He used his free hand to touch her cheek.

She smiled. "You are very forward. Do you have any idea what my father will do to you if he finds you here?"

"Some. It would be unpleasant, I imagine. So why did you invite me here?"

"Who says I did?" She smiled. "Not chariots, then. A horseman?"

"Yes. My country is too rugged to make use of chariots. There are few roads, and the valleys are often rock-strewn. We fight from horseback or on foot."

"Yours is a poor country, then?"

"Far from it." He brushed the pad of his thumb across her lower lip. It was fuller than her upper one, giving her a sensual look that he found appealing. "For hundreds of years—perhaps thousands—our people have built aqueducts and underground canals to bring water from the mountains to our fields. Orchards flourish. Wheat grows tall and fat. Our horses and cattle are the finest to be found anywhere."

Her long lashes fluttered. "I have never concerned myself with agriculture. I have other more important duties. Mine is the blood of pharaohs, going back for thousands of years."

He caught her lip between thumb and forefinger. "I can match your royal lineage. I am descended not only from the kings of the Twin Kingdoms for millennia, but from the rulers of Greece and Macedonia on my father's side."

She shrugged. "My father was born Greek, but now, through his marriage to my mother, he has become Egyptian and immortal. You cannot compare the rulers of a mountain horse culture to the god-kings of the Nile."

He smiled at her. "I can and do."

She pushed away his hand and sniffed. "You found the woman I sent to you repulsive?"

"On the contrary." He leaned forward and kissed her. Her mouth curved to his. She tasted of licorice. He slipped an arm around her shoulders.

Mereret ducked her head. "I know that you didn't

74

partake of her favors. Do your tastes lie elsewhere?" She moistened her lips with the tip of her tongue.

His interest quickened. He wished he hadn't drunk so much. She was clever, this little Egyptian princess. Ptolemy's daughter . . . She might possess his cunning. Yet . . .

She released his hand.

He let it fall to rest on her knee. Only a thin wisp of linen separated him from her skin. "Why did you bring me here?" he demanded.

She took his hand between both of hers and lifted it to cup her breast. "I wanted to see whether you were a man or a eunuch."

His fingers tightened on her nipple. He swallowed as the bud ripened at his touch. "You wished to know if I feared your father?" He caressed her until she sighed with pleasure, then lowered his head and kissed the hennaed swelling through the transparent tunic.

Mereret groaned. "You must think me a harlot," she murmured softly. "But I am not." She wiggled forward until she was on his lap and slid her arms around his neck. "Not only you would die," she said, "but so would I." She kissed him, thrusting her small, pointed tongue deep into his mouth.

Breathing harder, he moved his hands over her, exploring soft curves and warm, sensual flesh. They kissed again, and he felt the effects of the strong wine as his reason warred with desire to have what was already promised to him.

Mereret moved her hips over his erection, and her pliant heat was almost more than mortal flesh could stand. He tore the tunic from her shoulder and sought her breast with his mouth. She moaned as he drew the nipple between his lips and suckled. She pushed her skirt higher and rocked over his straining tumescence.

The crash of crockery brought Alexander to his senses. He leaped to his feet, dumping Mereret unceremoniously onto the floor, and whipped out his sword.

A figure dashed from the darkness. Alexander raised his weapon, prepared to deliver a killing blow.

"Please!" a woman cried. "Hear me! The palace guard is coming. You must get away."

"Bitch!" Mereret scrambled to her feet. "How dare you invade—"

Kiara struck Alexander with a clenched fist. "You will die if they find you here!"

He glanced from her to Mereret. "Is there another way—"

Mereret pointed. "There! She will show you." She picked up a tiny metal hammer and struck a brass gong on the low table. "Hurry, fools. My women will be here in seconds." She scowled at Kiara. "I will not forget this."

"Come!" Kiara grabbed Alexander's hand and tugged. "Follow me, quickly."

The tramp of soldiers came from the corridor he'd used earlier. "Open!" an authoritative voice shouted. "Open in the name of . . ."

Alexander didn't hear the rest. He ran hand in hand with the green-eyed woman through the fruit trees and into another courtyard. She pressed on a section of wall and a doorway opened. "Through here," she whispered.

"If you betray me, you die," he said, touching his sword hilt.

"If I betray you, she will kill me."

The passage was completely without light and so narrow that he brushed the walls with his shoulders. His chest felt tight. He hated the feeling of being hemmed in. It was hot, and the air here was thick and stale.

"Make no sound," Kiara warned.

A sticky substance brushed his face, and something scurried down the back of his neck. He gritted his teeth, determined not to let her know how much he hated this place. "Where are—" he began.

"Shh."

Shouts filtered through the walls. Kiara stopped so quickly that he bumped into her. He jerked back and his head struck an overhead beam.

More shouting. Someone screamed. A door slammed.

Kiara took hold of his hand. "There is a sharp left turn," she said. "Very tight."

The thought that she might be leading him deeper and deeper into the bowels of earth, that the walls would grow closer together until he was stuck, made his gut knot. It was harder and harder to breathe.

"I swear, wench, if you get me—"

"Just a little farther." She threaded her fingers through his. "Trust me."

"Why should I?"

For a moment she didn't reply. Then she uttered what could have been a small sound of amusement. "You're right; you should trust no one in this palace. Least of all Pharaoh."

"Why? Do you know something? Is this a plot to murder me?" His mouth tasted of ashes. Had he left his high country of clean mountains and open grassy plains to end his life here in his uncle's city? Had his mother been right?

"Make no sound."

He smelled oil and onions. And baking bread. They must be near the kitchens. He jerked her back and pressed his lips to her ear. "Unless you want to feel the point of my sword, you'll tell me where we are."

77

"You're hurting me."

He released her.

"Here," she whispered. "There should be a lever. I can't . . . Reach up, over my head."

Getting his arm up was harder than finding the wooden handle. "I've got it."

"Pull."

He took a deep breath and did as she said. There was a loud grating sound, and light poured through a trapdoor directly ahead. Kiara slid down and out into a wider hall. When he let go of the handle, the opening began to close.

"Wait, I'll hold it open for you," she said.

An instant later he was scrambling to his feet beside her. He glanced up and down the passageway. Oil lamps hung at regular intervals, but the corridor was too plainly decorated to be anything other than a service hall.

"We must hurry," Kiara said. "Soon it will be light." She turned a corner and led him through a storage area filled with clay jars large enough to hold a grown man. The space smelled of flour and mouse droppings. That room led into another that held oil jars and open bins of onions. Minutes later they exited a final doorway into an outside courtyard.

"Be quiet," she warned. "There are guards beyond that gate." Keeping in the shadow of the high wall, she led him through a metal gate to a vegetable garden. "There's a ladder there, on the side of the building," she said. "We can use it to go over the wall."

"We're leaving the palace?"

"Of course." She folded her arms over her chest. "I'm taking you to Prince Paris. Your squire said that you were going hunting with him this morning. If you are with the prince, no one will suspect you of making mischief with Pharaoh's daughter."

"We did nothing wrong."

"So you say, lord."

"You are impudent, woman."

"And you are ungrateful. If the guards had found you with Princess Mercret, they would have skewered you first and asked questions later."

"Why did you help me?" he asked as he moved the ladder to a place she indicated against a wall where bean vines grew thickly.

"I was to serve you and to report any wrongdoing to the chamberlain. If you broke the law and shamed Pharaoh with his daughter, I would have been held responsible. I would have faced torture and death. Why should I to die for a man's mischief—even a prince?"

"So you didn't risk your life for me?"

"No."

"You're an honest whore, at least." He threaded his fingers through her hair and tilted her face up. "Betray me, Kiara, and you'll die. I promise you that." He lowered his head and kissed her. "Remember that," he murmured.

"Must men, even princes, always think with their ballocks?" She squirmed free and wiped her mouth with the back of her hand.

"Am I so distasteful to you?"

"I meant no disrespect, lord. But why is it that you think I would welcome your kiss when you just threatened my life?"

"It was a reminder, nothing more."

"Then I remind you that you would be food for the royal crocodiles if I hadn't led you out through the wall passage. You would do well to remember that."

His eyes narrowed. She did not know her place, this woman. He found her disturbing, as prickly as the yellow flowers that grew high on the mountain slopes: sweet-smelling and lovely to look out, but possessing sharp thorns. "You were but following your mistress's order."

"No, I did not. She wanted me to lead you through the garden to the court of the reflecting pool. That garden has only one entrance. If we'd gone there and the guards pursued us, we would have been trapped."

"We found a way over this wall," he reminded her.

"This is a servant's area. A princess wouldn't know where to find a ladder or if one existed. Without it . . ." She shrugged. "Even you, Prince, could not scale this wall unaided."

"We're wasting time. You steady the ladder. I'll go up first. If it's clear, you follow."

"No." She shook her head. "If anyone sees me, I can easily say that I'm sneaking out to meet a lover. Slaves do it all the time. No guard would go to the trouble of reporting a servant. It would only cost him time and explanations to his sergeant."

"You think of everything, don't you, little Kiara? You must think you are very clever."

"I try to be." She scampered up the ladder to the top of the wall. "All right. Come." When he reached the walkway, she said, "Now, push the ladder away from the wall."

The ladder thudded into the rows of vegetables. "Won't someone notice that it's not where we found it?"

"Yes, the gardener's boy will be blamed. He's lazier than a hippopotamus. He steals the queen's onions and trades them for beer. A beating will do him good."

"What makes you so certain that Paris will welcome me to his quarters, if you can get us there without being caught?"

"Because he won't be there. He rarely sleeps in Pharaoh's palace. He prefers to be in the barracks with his troops. We can sleep in his bed until dawn. Then I will take you to meet him."

"But he was to send a servant to my quarters. My own men are going there."

"I'll send a message to your squire to bring your comrades to the stables. You drank heavily at the feast. Likely so did he. A misunderstanding is easier to pass off than a Bactrian in the arms of the princess royal."

"I see scheming comes easily to you."

"One who makes a wrong move in Queen Artakama's games does not live to play another day."

Chapter 7

"This is wrong, Roxanne," Kayan shouted as he drew his horse up alongside her mare. "You know it's wrong. Your life isn't your own to throw away at will. It belongs to the Twin Kingdoms and to me."

She turned her head away and stared at the mountain peaks. Winter would soon be on them. Fierce winds would sweep down through the passes, and snow would carpet the valleys where the pride of Bactria now grazed. The greens and browns and blacks of her beloved country would be shrouded in white.

Winter was for laughter and making love, for reading and study. She had always loved this time of rest and gatherings, of crackling fires, and good food and drink shared with friends and family, of sharing stories and counting the blessings that they had survived another year. Poets would sing the ancient sagas, priests would preach the holy word of the Wise God, and children would learn the old dances and games. Marriages were arranged in winter, new trade routes mapped out, land bought and sold, and plans drawn up for building new irrigation canals and planting orchards.

The long and bitter winter was not a time for a wife to be at odds with her husband.

She looked back at Kayan, and she was almost overcome with emotion. "I've loved you since I was seven years old," she said to him. "It breaks my heart to see you so unhappy."

"Then end this pregnancy before it's too late."

"You wanted Shahi. And you love both your daughters. How can you ask me to kill your unborn child? It could be a son. You, of all men, deserve a son."

"A pox on sons!" His features hardened.

No wonder his enemies fear him, Roxanne thought, suppressing a shiver. If any man was ever a warrior born, it was this beloved husband of hers. Both her husbands, she mused, both Kayan and Alexander were the mighty warriors that bards sang of, the legends that grew with each telling until the mortal soldier could not be found in the fog of myth. Her sons were cut from the same mold. Had she been blessed or cursed to love such men?

But they had their faults, the natural failings of the male species. For one, they were rarely rational. They thought flinging themselves onto a field of battle where any lucky fool might skewer them with a pitchfork or a pike was good fun. Men boasted of such deeds, and the greater the odds against success, the more they seemed to enjoy it. Blood held no terror for them. They found the discomfort of sleeping on wet, rocky ground, or marching for weeks across a waterless wasteland exciting, and they enjoyed nothing so much as drinking koumiss or wine until they lost all sense of dignity and woke the next day with empty pockets, a mouth that tasted like sheep dung, and a headache the size of an Indian elephant. Men thought all danger to themselves was insignificant, yet they fled at the sight of a few drops of menstrual blood or the sounds of childbirth.

"I will not die having this baby," she said with more patience than she felt.

"Won't you? You came close to it with Shahi, and again with Ava."

He did not mention the child they had lost. They rarely spoke of that loss; the pain was still too fresh, even though years had passed since a summer fever had taken the life of their small daughter. Neither did he mention Val, the son he'd adopted and raised as his own . . . the boy she'd come to love so much . . . and lost to Ptolemy, perhaps forever.

As if reading her mind, Kayan continued. "I have two sons, Alexander and Val. I need no more."

"We don't know if either of them is alive or if they will ever come back from Egypt."

He touched her mittened hand. "Now I know you're unwell. You've never talked like that. Why would you fear that Alexander won't come safely home with his new bride?"

"Because I know Ptolemy. Because I know how far it is from our borders to the Nile, and I know what dangers lie between." She yanked her mare's head right and moved away from Kayan, but he was as good a horseman as she. He urged his stallion close enough that Roxanne's leg brushed his.

"You think I don't remember the desert, the weeks of dusty plains, the mountains? I was there with you."

"Greeks prowl our borders like hungry wolf packs. Syrian bandits. Hostile Berbers. Persian warlords and generals greedy to seize what is ours. Alexander is heir to Bactria and Sogdiana, a rich prize for any thief.

Some would murder him for the price of his boots, let alone his horses and gold."

Kayan nodded. "True enough. So why do you fear Ptolemy most of all?"

"His daughter would not be my first choice for a daughter-in-law. Still, she will be queen here, and I will be queen mother."

"Now we come to it," Kayan scoffed. "You're jealous. Alexander must marry. He must have heirs to rule the Twin Kingdoms. But you have done your duty. You've given your kingdom a son and two daughters. You need risk your life in childbed no more."

It was a long speech for her husband, and she had no good answer. Instead, she dug her heels into the black mare's sides in an attempt to end the conversation. But he was too quick. He seized one of her mare's reins. "Let me go," she said brusquely.

"Never."

She raised her gaze to meet his, and her anger melted. Grief shone in Kayan's fierce eyes, grief and the closest thing that she would ever see to fear. He was the rock whose strength had sustained her all her life—the man who'd crossed half the world to defy Pharaoh and steal her from his royal bed.

"Do this for me, Roxanne."

She shook her head. "I could no more snuff out this life than I could take a knife and cut out Ava's heart or put an arrow through my Shahi. I love you, Kayan, but I love this child too. This baby is as much a part of you as it is of me. And I will guard him as I would you or Alexander."

"If you were the prince you wish to be, you would think of the daughters you already have. If Alexander doesn't return, Shahi must be heir. And she isn't ready, not for a long time. By the prophet's beard! Shahi's too softhearted and womanly to rule. Ava would make a better queen, and she's only seven."

"Nearly eight. And do not mistake Shahi's gentle soul for weakness. She has much of your mother in her. Shahi will be strong when strength is needed."

"She says she will never marry."

"I'd rather see her commit her life to God's temple than lead troops into battle, as Ava insists she will."

"You did."

Roxanne sighed. "I did, and I would again if it was necessary, but the woman in me wants to keep my children safe."

"As I want to keep you safe."

"I will not die. I promise you that," she said. "I feel that this one is a boy. You remember, I knew that Shahi was a girl."

"Your promises are as empty as your reason. I only remained in your bed because you assured me that you would not quicken with child—you said you took the herbs that your physicians gave you. But you lied to me. You didn't use them. You wanted this child, and you deceived me to have it."

"Yes, I did. When Alexander told me that he was going to Egypt, I was afraid that I'd never see him again. And I didn't want to leave the burden of the Twin Kingdoms to Shahi or Ava, or to you alone. I wanted this last chance to give you a son before I grow too old."

"You wanted another baby."

"Yes." She nodded. "I did. My children are all growing up. Even little Ava acts as though she doesn't need me. I wanted the feel of a babe nursing at my breasts again."

"You admit you made the decision selfishly, knowing how I felt?"

"Yes," she said. "I knew you'd be angry, but I

thought that you'd forgive me. And once our son or daughter is born, we could share the joy."

He shook his head. "You've always gone your own way, done what you wanted, regardless of what I said. Since you've made this decision, live with it. I can't. I'm going to winter with Harder and his troops on the edge of the steppes. The Greeks don't make war in winter, but the Scythians do. Harder can use me there to help turn back the raiding parties."

She looked at him in disbelief. "You'd leave me? Leave Shahi and Ava?"

"You left me when you made this decision alone. Shahi is happy in her temple. And I'm taking Ava with me. If she wants to be a warrior, it's time she learned what she faces in the future. There will be danger enough to teach her caution, but not enough to keep you from sleeping at night."

She felt suddenly chilled. Without Kayan, the winter nights would be cold and dark and her bed lonely. "Don't go," she said. "Stay with me."

"Will you reconsider having this baby?"

Tears welled in her eyes. "I can't."

"And I can't stay and watch you sicken and die. Goodbye, wife. May Ahura Mazda, the Wise God, show you more mercy than I can." He slapped his leathers across the stallion's rump and the big bay leaped away. "Haah!" Kayan kicked the animal into a gallop.

Roxanne watched as his proud figure grew smaller in the distance and finally dwindled to a dark speck against the vastness of the mountain. "I would do anything for you," she whispered. "Anything . . . but not that. Not that." Shaken, she wiped away the tears and turned her mare back toward the citadel and the long wait ahead.

The chariot wheel bounced hard on a rock, and the reed vehicle tilted to one side. Alexander and the driver, Pepi, shifted their weight to keep from overturning, and the chariot righted itself and continued on at breakneck speed. Foam streaked from the horses' open mouths as Pepi shouted pet names at the animals and urged them faster with the crack of a whip that snapped over the heaving backs but never came within a handbreadth of touching their hides.

Alexander cursed the rocking motion of the chariot and the dust. The heat was nearly unbearable, and every inch of his exposed body was caked with dirt and sweat. Between the glare of the midday sun and the windblown sand, it was impossible to keep his eye on the fleeing lion in the distance.

"There! There!" Pepi cried, pointing at what might have been a yellow-brown outcropping of dried foliage. "We're gaining on him! Make ready!"

From the left, down the rock-strewn channel of an ancient riverbed, burst another team and chariot followed by a second. Once-white plumes and golden harness identified the owner of the lead horses, but the team behind was obscured by dust and could belong to any of a half dozen hunters.

"Prince Paris!" Pepi shouted, pointing at the nearest chariot. He cracked the whip again. "Run, you sweet whores of Memphis!" he exhorted his team. "Run, my darlings!"

Paris's driver was a stocky man with massive arms and shoulders, but stood hardly taller than an eight-year-old child. Alexander guessed that Pepi knew the man, because he took the trouble to make an obscene gesture to the opposing driver. "Son of a snakebitten vulture! Turd on the wheel of a shit cart! You think you can handle a team? My blind grandmother could outdrive you!"

Paris's team churned the red sand with their hooves,

racing downhill, sending up a cloud of dust that turned the day to twilight. The team of grays was fast, but Pepi had the lead and had no intention of letting the other chariot catch him.

"Make ready!" Pepi screamed. "See, the lion turns! He turns!"

Alexander notched an arrow and tried to take aim. The light chariot swayed from side to side, bounced, and slid sideways as Pepi attempted to outmaneuver the lion. Paris's grays gained ground. The horses' heads were nearly level with the wheels of Alexander's chariot and coming hard.

Abruptly a yellow blur streaked from a house-size boulder directly in front of the two racing chariots. Pepi yanked the team hard to the right. "Lion!" he yelled. "Lion!"

Alexander had no chance to take the shot. He grabbed the side rail in a vain attempt to hold his balance, but one wheel wrenched and snapped. Spokes flew into the air and the chariot tilted. Alexander felt himself falling and threw up his arms to protect his head. He hit the ground and rolled as the team pulled the remains of the shattered chariot away.

Alexander opened his eyes, wiped away a smear of blood, and scrambled to his feet. Nothing seemed to be broken but the stump of the bow in his right hand. Choking from the dust, he threw it aside and drew his sword. Sand and dirt made his eyes stream with water. He could hear Pepi cursing, but where the driver was, Alexander couldn't tell.

A shadow materialized ahead and to his left in the swirling dust. He caught the rank scent of rotting meat before he heard the lion cough. The sound made the hair rise on the back of Alexander's neck, and he whirled to meet the cat's leap.

The beast's roar drowned out the world. As Alexander braced for the attack, a ribbon of fire seared along his ribs, midway between hip and shoulder. He barely had time to register the sensation of intense pain before the animal struck. He thrust the point of his sword through the lion's thick hide and into the throat. Blood poured over Alexander as claws tore into his shoulder and the weight of the animal threw him back onto the sand.

Alexander twisted, trying to avoid the snapping jaws and the thrashing hind legs that threatened to eviscerate him. Foul breath scalded his face, yet he held tightly to his sword hilt and forced the blade up into the lion's brainpan. In seconds it was over. By the time Pepi and Paris reached him, the cat was dead.

Pepi swore.

Paris heaved the carcass off. "How badly are you hurt?"

Alexander rolled over onto his stomach. For a moment he thought he was going to be sick, but the feeling passed and he got shakily to his feet. "I'm all right," he said. "Most of the blood is the lion's."

Paris shouted an order, and his driver came with a goatskin of water. Alexander swallowed a mouthful and then dumped another measure over his head.

"You look like you slept in a slaughterhouse," Paris said.

Alexander shook his head, wiped his face with the back of his arm, and looked down at his injuries. Four furrows in his left shoulder and chest leaked blood, but the wounds were not deep. His side hurt more. Alexander felt the edges of the slice and forced himself not to wince. A steady trail of blood dripped down his hip and leg. "I'm not certain . . ." he began, and then stopped as he saw the feathered shaft protruding from the sand a few yards away.

Pepi saw the arrow at almost the same time. For a heartbeat their gazes met, and the driver frowned and then dropped to one knee. "Great Bull of Egypt," he murmured.

Ptolemy approached. "It seems as though you had three close calls. You've your father's luck."

"Uncle." Alexander regarded him grimly. When had Ptolemy joined the hunt, and why? Paris had not mentioned that his father would be part of the group. "How is that?"

"It should be obvious," Ptolemy said. "You survived the chariot mishap, the lion, and Paris's arrow. Another inch, and the shaft meant to kill the lion would have finished you."

"It's not my arrow," Paris protested. "I couldn't see anything for the dust. By the time Hory got the horses turned—"

"Not your arrow?" Ptolemy said. "Let me see it. The markings should settle the question of whom it belongs to."

Paris's driver, Hori, returned with the arrow, prostrated himself, and offered the shaft. Paris jerked it from the man's small fingers.

"It's bare of any markings," Paris said.

Ptolemy shrugged. "Perhaps it was left by another hunter on an earlier trip."

"With my blood on it?" Alexander said.

"A mystery," Ptolemy said, "but there are many in Egypt. Perhaps Apollo wished to strike down the lion before it devoured you, and you stepped into the path."

"Perhaps." Alexander wondered which of them had taken the shot and what the real target had been. Had it been a hunting accident or an attempt on his life?

Paris stood over the fallen lion. "This isn't the beast we were pursuing. This animal is female, and she was in her prime."

"Then our hunt isn't over," Ptolemy said. "The old male is the man killer. But your father would be proud of you, nephew. Besting a grown lion with a sword is a feat to boast of. Let's get back to camp and have one of the women tend those scratches. A lion's claws carry fever and worse evils."

Alexander nodded, not trusting himself to speak.

"He can ride with me, highness," Paris offered. "I'll drive, and Pepi and Hori can wait here with the other horses until men come for them with other chariots. Prince Alexander's is ruined. Both wheels are shattered, and the basket's torn to shreds."

Alexander glanced at Pepi, wondering if the driver could tell him anything. He doubted it. "All right," he agreed. "I've had enough of hunting lions for one day."

Paris walked Alexander to a blue tent against a sheer wall of rock. "A slave is there to tend to your needs. I'll send a physician as soon as you've bathed. You may not feel like hunting with us tomorrow. Those wounds will stiffen."

"We'll see," Alexander said. He pushed aside the curtain and stepped inside.

Paris followed, still surprised that Alexander had been able to walk unaided this far. He supposed that all he wanted to do now was to find someplace to lie down before he fell down. "I'll send your men to you as soon as they return."

"Aiyee!" A woman appeared from the sleeping room at the back of the tent. She clapped her hands over her mouth to stifle her astonishment before remembering her place and dropping to her knees. "Forgive me, Prince. I saw the blood on the barbarian and thought—"

"The barbarian speaks Egyptian," Paris said. "This stupid girl is Tutu, brother. She is known more for her other charms than her wits, but she will do whatever you ask of her. Won't you, Tutu?"

"Yes, great Prince."

Alexander looked around. "I'd expected Kiara."

"Sorry. Doubtless the chamberlain who made the arrangements didn't think you had a preference. You'll enjoy Tutu so long as you don't allow her to prattle on. Isn't that true, girl?"

Tutu giggled.

"I'll check on you after the physician's seen you," Paris said. "He may want you to return to Alexandria."

"I'll hunt lion with you tomorrow."

"Don't be reckless. I've seen men sicken and die from far less serious wounds than you've received. And it would shame Pharaoh if his son-in-law died before the wedding."

"Yes, it would."

"Send Tutu if you need me for anything." He touched Alexander's uninjured shoulder and grinned. "You've become a mighty hunter, little brother. Mereret should appreciate the man she's getting for a husband. Few could face what you did and come out alive."

As he walked across the common ground to where his servants had erected his own tent, twilight had already fallen over the camp. At the horse lines, he could see that two chariots containing Alexander's Bactrians had arrived. One of the Egyptian charioteers was talking animatedly to a companion and pointing to Pharaoh's pavilion. They hadn't expected Ptolemy on this hunt. Neither had he. He wondered what had brought his father away from the duties and pleasures of his capital.

Paris ducked inside and his eyes widened with surprise. "Queen Artakama. You honor me."

She studied him. "I hear that Prince Alexander had a narrow escape today."

"You are well-informed."

She moved toward him, and he was struck again by just how beautiful she was—if one liked the type. She appeared far younger than she was; certainly she was much younger than his father.

"Mereret's heart would be broken if an accident befell her bridegroom. The desert is a dangerous place."

"Of what service can I be to you, highness?"

"There is no need for formality between us, Paris, not when we are alone. You remind me so much of your father, when I first laid eyes upon him . . . many years ago. The Great Bull was a virile man then."

"And remains so, I trust."

"Of course. That need not be stated. No mortal man may compare himself to a god-king. He has the strength of—"

"Ten bulls. Yes, I know, lady. What do you want of me?"

She stepped closer. "Have I so wronged you that you should speak to me so coldly? You are your father's pride, the hope of Egypt."

"My brother, Ptolemy, is the hope of Egypt. He is Queen Berenice's son. He will be pharaoh when my father joins the gods in the afterlife."

"If he lives to ascend the throne." She spread her hands gracefully. "Unfortunately, some say he is sickly."

"Speak plainly."

Artakama smiled, and Paris felt the chill desert air sweep through the tent. "Some things are better not spoken aloud," she said. "I only remind you of what you already know. If young Ptolemy dies, you will follow your illustrious father. You are well suited to be pharaoh after him."

"My blood is stained with that of my Persian mother."

"Fool. Must I lead you by the nose? Alexander must not have my Mereret. If he marries her, then his claim to the throne is greater than yours, perhaps even greater than Ptolemy's. It is that my husband wears the crown of Egypt through me. Get rid of Alexander and I will see that he gives you Mereret."

"My half sister?"

"I have seen you watching her. She can bring you Egypt."

Paris stiffened. "You're right, lady. Such things should not be said. As a child I considered Alexander a brother. Young 'Toly is surely my half brother. You expect me to wade through their blood to claim my father's throne?"

She laughed. "Think on it, Paris. Think of the joys to be found between Mereret's sweet thighs. Your mother may have been a Persian whore, but your father was a Greek. What Greek crown is not soaked with the blood of those who came before him? Consider carefully what course you will take. Will you remain a bastard supplicant, bowing for crumbs at Pharaoh's table, or will you grasp immortality for yourself? If you choose unwisely, it may be Alexander's son who seizes what you were afraid to reach for."

Chapter 8

A serving woman came into the room and whispered to the high priestess. She frowned and motioned to Shahi. "Your highness, the queen wishes to speak with you. Immediately."

Shahi nodded. The other novices glanced up curiously as she rose from her place on the bench, rolled the sacred text she'd been copying, and returned her papyrus, brush, ink, and unfinished manuscript to the wooden chest along the wall. Taking her scarlet cloak and mittens from a hook in the passageway, Shahi hurried outside to find her mother waiting for her in the entry courtyard. It was very cold, and a few flakes of snow were drifting down; wind had gathered folds of whiteness against the base of the center fountain. Roxanne's mare dribbled drops of water from her velvet-dark nose.

"Where's Ava?"

Shahi tugged on her sheepskin mittens and tied the cloak at her throat. "I thought you knew. She's gone with Father."

"Already? But I thought—"

"She rode out with the patrol as I was going to morning prayer. Really, Mother, she'll be fine. It will suit her, spending the winter with him on the borders. The Wise God knows the palace will be peaceful without her. It's disgraceful how you've both spoiled her. That leopard should be caged instead of allowed to wander around terrifying the dogs and the servants."

Roxanne's lips tightened. Daughters! Why were they so complicated? She should have known that Shahi would react this way to Kayan's fuss over the coming baby. "It doesn't bother you that he's left us alone for months?"

Shahi shrugged. "Hardly alone. The palace is filled to overflowing with relatives, court officials, ambassadors, and their families. And what can you expect? You knew he didn't want you to have another baby. And with good reason. You came close to death when Ava was born. You may be a queen, Mother, but even you can't always have your own way without paying the price."

"You think I should abort this child?" She felt like slapping her daughter. At Shahi's age, Roxanne had given birth, been widowed, and had to struggle to survive, while this girl's life had been sheltered. Shahi had never known hardship or the loss of anyone she loved with all her heart. "I should have known better than to come to you. There's never been any doubt who your favorite parent is."

"You see, you're doing it again." Shahi rolled her eyes. "Pregnancy has already clouded your reason. You know I love you. I just want what's best for you, for all of us. I'll admit that Papa—Father," she corrected herself, "has always been easier for me to understand. And you're wrong if you think I want to see you end the pregnancy. Not now, now that it's . . . that you're already with child. But it was wrong for you to allow it to happen. It wasn't an accident. You did it deliberately."

"How do you know this?"

"Mother, please. Servants talk; you know they talk. If you never replenish your birth-control herbs . . ." Shahi folded her slender arms over her chest and scowled. "It's not as though you and Father are practicing abstinence. The two of you are too old to carry on like . . . like newlyweds. It's common knowledge that you do it like rabbits. It's embarrassing. Where is your sense of decorum?"

"Like rabbits?" Roxanne laughed. "I love your father, and he loves me. Sex is a natural part of a good marriage. I've never pretended that I didn't take joy in our bed." She chuckled. "What do people say about us?"

"I wouldn't repeat it."

"You, my dear daughter, are a prude. Perhaps the temple *is* the place for you. For if you ever met a man who made you go all shivery when he looked at you—the way your father does me—if touching his hands or hearing his voice made your bones turn to butter—"

"No more! Please. This is a temple and I'm a holy novice." Crimson smudges tinted Shahi's cheeks, and her beautiful eyes, so like Kayan's, widened in dismay. "Why can't either of you understand? I don't want to meet a man. I have a calling to serve God."

"There's more than one way to serve God," she reminded Shahi.

"Ava can give you grandchildren, and doubtless Alexander already has dozens of woods colts scattered around the kingdom. You know how he is with women. He's warmed more beds than you've—" She broke off. "I'm sorry, Mother, that wasn't—"

"Never apologize for telling the truth. Most men are enamored with casual sex, until they take a wife."

"But I don't want to be a wife. I don't want to worry about a husband riding off into battles and getting killed. I don't want to worry that I'll grow gray-haired or fat and he'll find a younger and prettier woman. And, frankly, I find the whole physical process of intercourse distasteful—not to mention childbed."

Roxanne tried not to show her amusement. "Have you ever—"

"Mother! I'm a Sogdian princess. How can you ask if I am a virgin?"

"Daughter, daughter, where have I gone wrong? There's nothing unclean about sex between two people who love each other. Do you think that the Wise God would have created us with the potential to enjoy physical love if he didn't approve of it?"

Shahi's face paled. "That's blasphemy."

"That's truth."

"I won't argue with you. I must get back to my class. I have to finish copying that text this afternoon. I'll be spending the night here, so don't hold the evening meal for me. We're tending the sacred fires tonight and offering prayers for Father's safety."

"And your sister's, I hope." Roxanne leaned down and kissed Shahi's cheek. She was very beautiful, this young woman she and Kayan had created, but very stubborn. Whether Shahi had it in her to live a life of celibacy as a holy priestess or simply hadn't met the right man, Roxanne didn't know, but she sensed an untapped well of passion beneath Shahi's proper demeanor.

The girl was bright and brave and loving, but so different from her own fiery nature that sometimes she wondered how she had given birth to her. *Oh, my precious darling,* Roxanne thought, *if ever you kick over the traces, thrones will topple and the heavens will echo with the clap of thunder.*

"I have to go, Mother."

"So go." She kissed her again. "Tell the high priestess that I beg her forgiveness for disturbing her class and that I will send her a hundredweight of the best papyrus and five measures of Tibetan ink to make up for it."

"We're short of gold leaf."

"And a casket of gold leaf," Roxanne agreed. "You will make a pauper of me. I've already spent a fortune on saddles and Greek fire for your brother. Not to mention the Indian horses."

"You have no trouble finding coin for war. You shouldn't begrudge the temple."

"Pray that you are never queen, my girl. Temples and priestesses are important, but the security of our kingdom must come first. Without a strong army, your temple will be smoldering ashes and your novices body slaves to some foreign conqueror."

"Perhaps, but if Alexander's marriage brings peace, there may be no need for war or for soldiers."

"May that day come," Roxanne intoned piously, but she doubted that it would ever come to pass this side of heaven.

Alexander woke in the night. Something had disturbed his sleep, other than the naked girl curled beside him. He'd not been in the mood for sex, but with Pepi and three of his companions stretched out on the floor of his tent, there'd been no place for her but his bed. Normally, he would have found her a pleasant diversion, but this night he'd found himself longing for the elusive scent of wild violets and pine. Besides, his skin burned with fever, and blood was slowly seeping through the bandages around his midsection.

He was thirsty, but that wasn't what had awakened him. He held his breath and listened. A pebble struck the side of the tent over his head. When a second one followed the first, he stifled a groan and rose from the straw mattress.

Tutu touched his arm. "You wish something, master?" Her voice was heavy with sleep. "A urine vessel? I will—"

He swore softly. "I can still stagger outside," he answered. "Stay where you are."

"I can fetch the—"

"On my deathbed, I'll not piss in a pot like an old woman," he grumbled. Strapping on his sword, he braced himself against a post and took a deep breath. He was dizzy, and his wounds burned as though the physician had dressed them with live coals. "Don't argue with me, girl. I'm just going outside to relieve myself."

"The second lion may be lurking nearby."

"Any lion with a lick of sense is leagues from here." The brace of lean hunting dogs would have caught the scent and bayed an alarm, but he didn't need to trouble himself to explain that to a slave woman. Unsteadily, he pushed through to the outer space and stepped over his sleeping comrades.

Hermes sat cross-legged by the door, a naked sword across his lap. Born of a Macedonian father and a Sogdian mother, Hermes had spent his life proving that he was a true son of the Twin Kingdoms. No enemy would cross the threshold while he drew breath, and few swordsmen could best him on horseback or on foot. Alexander was one of the few, and the feat had cemented their friendship.

Hermes leaped to his feet. "Something wrong?"

"No, just need to take a piss. Get some sleep, why don't you? I'm awake, and the camp is quiet."

"You lost a wineskin of blood before that physician got you sewed up. I'll watch. Best you get your rest and tumble that pretty Egyptian piece another day."

Alexander answered with a good-natured obscenity and pushed aside the door flap. The night air was cool on his fevered skin, and the heavens were pierced with brilliant stars. The same sky as at home, he thought, and yet not. Maybe the Egyptian goddess Nut did stretch her naked body over the Nile here. In this ancient land of mysteries, anything was possible.

He straightened, waited, and then rested his hand on his sword hilt. The moonlight filtered among the tents and horse lines, distorting and illuminating the waiting chariots and the cliff faces, making the sand beneath his feet glow with silvery radiance.

"Here, brother," Paris called.

Alexander's hand went to his sword.

"Easy," Paris said. "It's me. I was coming to see how you were."

"I've been better."

"Are you strong enough to walk a little?" He motioned. "I'd like to talk to you where there's no chance we'll be overheard."

"Yes. It was too hot inside. And I needed to take a piss."

"Don't let me stop you."

"What did you want to talk about?" Alexander asked. He kept his voice low, so as not to rouse guards or hounds.

"Women. Hunting. Lions. What else do princes concern themselves with?"

Alexander felt as though someone had turned a herd of horses loose in his head. Every step was agony, but he joined Paris, and together they walked away past the camp guards and into a dark gully. When they were several hundred yards from the outer perimeter, Paris halted.

"If you've brought me out here to challenge me to a

boxing match, I'm betting on you," Alexander said. He turned his back to Paris and relieved himself.

"You're too trusting. It's a good spot for an ambush."

"Not you, Val. My right arm would betray me before you."

"We're not children anymore. I'm Egyptian and I go by the name my father gave me, Paris. You are—or were—the enemy. Politics is a dangerous game. It may be that you're in over your head."

"She still weeps for you, you know," Alexander said. "Mother. She counts you as her lost sheep and made me promise to bring you back with me. She's a stubborn woman. Once she claims a person as her own, she never gives up."

"We're cousins, not brothers. And Greeks have never shied from murdering closer kin for gain. Bactria and Sogdiana are rich prizes. Whoever holds you, holds them."

Alexander laughed. "I'm not so easily held. Although someone came close with that arrow."

"Not mine. If I kill you, you'll see me coming."

"If not you, who? My driver or yours? Ptolemy or someone else?"

"Have you wondered why my father might want to wed you to my sister?"

"Trade routes. A partner he can trust in an uneasy world. Marriages have ended more than one feud."

"A Greek or an Indian match would make more sense," Paris said. "He might even have pledged her to the emperor of Chin."

"All right. Why me?"

"You're Alexander's son."

"Part of me, but Kayan raised me. He's the man I think of as my father."

"Nothing changes the fact that you are the heir of

the one men call great. As the son of that Alexander, you could get greedy, want to claim Egypt."

"Or Ptolemy might want my homeland. Men call him the spider for good reason."

"Yet you think you are a match for him?"

"You're against the marriage?"

"I am. Better you'd never come here, or that you gather your horsemen and leave Egypt in your dust."

"So you think your father lured me here with the promise of marrying his daughter just to put an arrow through me when I was otherwise occupied?"

"Maybe it was an accident."

"An accident with an unmarked arrow? When no one would admit to taking the shot? Who else besides Ptolemy should I beware of?"

"What matter? You could die here, little brother, and leave the Twin Kingdoms to a woman."

Alexander chuckled. "Have you forgotten my mother so much that you could dismiss her so easily? She's more than a match for Ptolemy. And she has Kayan."

"He's not as young as he once was."

"Who is? But a few gray hairs hardly make him a doddering ancient. He may be a little slower, but he's smarter. I'd not care to face him, sword against sword."

"He taught me well," Paris admitted. "I had only good memories of our childhood and of him—until I learned that his love was based on deception, that he'd stolen another man's son and held him for ransom."

"Lies."

"I didn't bring you here to argue. Remember who you are and who I am. I only wanted to warn you."

"But you never said who else would profit from my death."

"Does it matter?"

Alexander nodded. "To me it does." The sand was coarse and chill under his bare feet. He thought of scorpions and wished he'd taken the time to strap on a pair of sandals.

"All right. Start with my stepmothers. Queen Artakama has never favored giving Mereret to you. And my father's Greek wife, Queen Berenice, would see any male connected to Ptolemy by blood in his grave. Except for her darling son. She means to set 'Toly on the throne, whether he's fit to rule or not. And sooner, rather than later. She and my father have hated each other for years. If 'Toly inherits the crown, she rules through him."

"Who else?" Far off, a jackal yelped, a lonely cry soon echoed by another. "I want names."

"Father's generals, the priests of Amun-Re and of Anubis." Paris spread his hands, palms up. "It's Egypt. Everyone wants you dead."

"Including you?"

"I haven't decided yet."

"While you're making up your mind, I have a favor to ask." Alexander hesitated. "The green-eyed woman, Kiara. I fancy her. Make certain she comes to no harm."

"I can add the bride herself to the list if you take too much interest in a slave girl."

"It's not like that."

Paris snorted in amusement. "You like her for her mind."

"No. But I owe her. I'd hate to see her punished for something that wasn't her fault. Besides, it was Mereret who sent her to me."

"Maybe. Maybe not. Nothing in Alexandria is ever what it seems. Not even me."

"I was promised Pharaoh's daughter, and I have no intention of leaving Egypt without her."

"Still as stubborn as you were as a child. Don't say I didn't warn you, and don't blame me if this all ends badly."

"Consider me warned." He laid a hand on Paris's shoulder. "I hear you've made a fine general. We could use you at home. Kayan and Mother would welcome you with open arms. As I would."

Paris stiffened and stepped back. "You don't listen, do you? I am a prince of Egypt, son of Pharaoh. In the Twin Kingdoms I would always be the enemy's son, standing in your shadow."

"You were Kayan's son before you were Ptolemy's. No matter what your father's told you, you were close to death when Mother let Ptolemy take you. She let you go so that you'd have a chance to live. No other reason."

"Lucky for them that it was me and not you who was so badly wounded," Paris said coldly.

"I was there. I saw everything. I saw Kayan's anguish at having to leave you."

"A long time ago."

"And you live in the present."

"And my future."

"Fool. What future will you have when your brother, Ptolemy, comes to the throne? You'll be the unwanted bastard son of a Persian woman, a general with an army behind you and enough real power to make you a threat to a boy-king."

"You're twisting things to suit your own purpose," Paris flung back.

"Am I? You have no claim to my throne, brother. I want you by my side because I love you. I've never stopped loving you."

"As your father loved Hephaestion?"

Alexander swore. "If you can't tell the difference between a brother's love and a carnal one, then Ptolemy has changed you from the boy I knew."

106

"Go home, back to your mountains and your steppes. Go before someone kills you—or I do." Paris turned abruptly away and strode into the night.

"If you can," Alexander shouted after him.

He stood there for a long time, willing his anger to dissipate, trying to fight past emotion to cold reason. He'd come looking for a brother and found a stranger, a man who might be his enemy. It made no sense that he and the boy he'd known as Val should ever come to blows or talk of distrust and envy. Egypt had poisoned Paris, but whether the potion was fatal remained to be seen. Slowly Alexander started walking back toward camp.

He'd gone no more than half the distance when he caught the scent of a woman's perfume on the air. He stopped and listened. Seconds later he heard the unmistakable rustle of a garment and the crunch of sand beneath a light foot.

"Who's there?"

A familiar squeak.

"Tutu?"

"Yes, master. It's me. Someone wishes to speak to you."

"Who?"

"I cannot say, lord."

He seized her arm and drew her close. "You will say, Tutu. Who wants to talk to me?"

She gasped. "You're hurting my arm. Please, I'm only a slave. I must—"

"I'll break it off and bash you over the head with the bloody stump if you don't answer my question."

"The queen, lord. Queen Artakama."

Chapter 9

"Queen Artakama." Alexander glanced around the interior of the pavilion. Larger than Ptolemy's hunting quarters, the tent was so luxurious that had he been led here blindfolded, he would have believed he was in a palace. Silk lined the walls, and thick carpets covered the floor. Light came from crystal oil lamps suspended from a web of golden ropes. In one corner of the room, a blind musician coaxed sweet notes from a silver harp.

"I heard that you had been injured by the lion. I see that your wounds are not as severe as I had been led to believe." Artakama, looking barely older than her daughter in this soft lighting, reclined on a striped lounge heaped with pillows. At her feet glowed a charcoal brazier, and behind her stood two enormous Nubian guards clad in the colors of her household guard and carrying war axes.

"Come, Prince Alexander, this is a hunting camp. We do not stand on ceremony here. Sit." Her voice flowed like warm honey as she waved him to a seat on the other side of the brazier. "You may speak freely without fear of consequence."

He glanced at the ebony faces of the guards as he lowered himself painfully into the chair. So expressionless were they, the two might have been carved of black marble. "Why have you asked me here?" He smoothed the folds of the simple Egyptian kilt that Tutu had wrapped around him before she'd led him here.

Artakama smiled and stroked the white cat stretched at her side. "They are all deaf and mute."

"A deaf musician," he said. "Unusual."

"He was not always deaf."

"It's late. What do you want of me?" He wondered where Ptolemy was and if he knew that his wife had summoned her soon-to-be-son-in-law to her private quarters.

"The court of Alexandria is different from anything you have ever known." The white cat raised its flat head and stared at him with slitted blue eyes; it was very thin and wore a collar that glittered with precious stones. "It will be helpful for you to have friends," Artakama continued.

If the queen had worn little at his welcoming feast, here she wore less. Her linen tunic hid none of her charms. Her breasts were high and firm, the nipples rouged with henna. Her hair was blue-black, very straight, and smelled of myrrh. It was the same scent he had noticed on Tutu when she'd stopped him outside the camp.

"You opposed the match," he said. "Why offer friendship now?"

"I see strength in you, barbarian. You may be more useful to me than one who would see you dead." Artakama's teeth were small and even; her eyes were rimmed in black kohl, her mouth rouged as red as blood.

"Pharaoh?"

"You're bold, son of the great Alexander. I like that in a man. Mereret will like that. She is like a young date palm, waiting for someone to appreciate her value and help her grow to what she can be. Many men desire her. Prince Paris is such a man. He pretends otherwise, but I have seen his eyes when he watches her."

"What do you want me to do?"

"Kill Paris before he kills you. He is the seed of a plot to seize Mereret and Ptolemy's crown."

"Is this something you know or only suspect?"

"Does it matter? Paris hates you, and he will stop at nothing to destroy anyone who keeps him from becoming pharaoh after the Great Bull goes to join the gods."

"Prince Paris is not the heir. Young Ptolemy is. What of him?"

"A sickly child. None of Berenice's other brats lived. Why should this one?"

"You must know that Paris and I were raised as brothers. If I did kill him, how would it benefit you?"

She lowered her head and nuzzled the cat. The animal began to purr and to knead a pillow, extending and retracting the claws on both front paws. "I was born daughter and granddaughter to pharaohs," the queen said. "I am the wife of the greatest pharaoh that Egypt has known for centuries, perhaps a millennium. Ptolemy came to power through me, and I have remained faithful to him. So long as he draws breath, I will do all that I can to protect and support him."

He must have revealed some of his doubt in his expression, because the queen smiled.

"It surprises you that a woman can be faithful to her husband?"

"Love between a man and wife is rare, rarer still among the great."

"Who spoke of love? Had I been born a man, I

would have been crowned a living god. I am my husband's vessel, his helpmate in all things, and I will do what I must to ensure his well-being."

"And you believe that murdering his favorite son is to his advantage?"

Artakama lifted her hand, and one of the guards placed a glass goblet between her fingers. "You are bold, and your speech is harsh."

"I'm a soldier. Plain talk comes easier to me than subtleties."

"Yes, a simple soldier with simple needs. Or perhaps that is the illusion you wish to present." She sipped daintily at the dark liquid contents. "Will you take refreshment?"

He shook his head. "No."

"You're wise. How do you know that I won't slip you poison in the wine?" She tilted her head and laughed. "It's a joke, barbarian, a joke. Even if I wished to be rid of you, I'd hardly do it so obviously. Poison in a corpse is easily detected. The Great Bull would never forgive me."

"If you want Paris dead, why not have your own people do it? You are queen here."

"He has bewitched you as he has my daughter. Paris hides an evil heart behind his handsome face and charming smile. He is one who has the art of saying what people want to hear and making them believe it is truth."

"I've seen nothing but good in him."

Her beautiful jet-black eyes narrowed. "Perhaps it is too late for you, then. If you were as wise as you are brave, you would know that evil hides in the hearts of all men."

"And women?"

Her scarlet lips twitched in what was almost a smile. "And in women. Our religion teaches us that the forces of good and evil fight for possession of every soul. Often the difference can be measured in the weight of a feather."

"Yes," he agreed. "In my country we follow the teaching of Zoroaster. The prophet teaches that the Wise God, Ahura Mazda, is in constant conflict with Ahriman, who rules over a kingdom of lies."

"So you do understand. If Paris were my son and his heart was filled with treason, I could strike him down."

"You could kill your own son?"

"As you say, I am a queen, and those whom the gods have set over men must make difficult choices. But Paris is my husband's child, and if I were to harm him, it might be said that my breast burned with jealousy because I could not give Ptolemy a son. Ptolemy would never forgive me when he found out, and he *would* learn the truth in time. They say there are a thousand secrets in Alexandria . . . and no secrets." She leaned forward so that the bodice of her tunic barely constrained her breasts.

Alexander swallowed. His mouth was dry, his head pounding. His skin felt as though he had been standing naked in the Nile sun for hours. "I will consider what you have told me," he said, "but now I should retire to my tent. Dawn will come soon, and with it another hunt."

"Yes, another hunt, but what will the quarry be? Kill Paris, Alexander. Kill him and bury his body in the desert where no one will ever find it."

"If I do that, if he lies in an unmarked grave, his soul will be lost to eternal torment. Isn't that so?"

She shrugged. "Better his than yours. But if you will not hear good advice when it is given to you, watch carefully. Turn your back to none, and listen for the arrow that will send you to judgment. It is time, Prince, to forget emotion, to use reason. The gods favor the bold. The timid fall and are trampled underfoot."

Alexander rose. "Thank you for your advice, lady."

She smiled at him. "Treat my daughter as she deserves and give her strong sons. That will be thanks enough for me."

"That I can promise you. As my wife, she will be queen of the Twin Kingdoms. As long as she keeps our marriage vows and gives me the support you claim to give my uncle, I will pledge my life to protect and care for her."

"What is this of pledges?" Ptolemy called from the doorway. "And what brings you here at this hour to my wife's tent?"

His tone was hearty, but Alexander did not mistake the question for idle curiosity. His uncle wore a short linen chiton and red leather sandals. His hair was tousled, but his eyes were clear. He had not been sleeping, and he had come armed to Artakama's pavilion with a sword and a short spear.

"Do you look for your missing lion here, husband?" the queen asked. She rose and went to Ptolemy's side. "I sent for your nephew so that we could talk—away from the ears of the court. I wanted to learn exactly what kind of man you had chosen for my daughter."

"And have you?" Ptolemy asked.

"I'm afraid not," she replied softly. "He is much like you, son of Horus. He hides his thoughts well."

"Then he is wise beyond his years." Ptolemy smiled. "Has she convinced you to refuse my daughter's hand, nephew? To tuck your tail between your legs and flee back home?"

"Not yet," Alexander said.

"Good. I hoped you'd not be easily discouraged. The

priests tell me that the most fortunate alignment of the planets for a royal wedding will occur in ten days. Will that suit you?"

"Yes."

"Take care, Alexander," Ptolemy said. "I don't know where the arrow came from that nearly took your life, but I don't believe it was meant for the lion. Watch your back and trust no one."

"Not even you, Uncle?"

Ptolemy chuckled. "Perhaps not. Especially not, if you pay heed to my loving wife. She believes that I am the worst of scoundrels."

"Never trust a Greek," Artakama said. "And a Greek husband even less."

"Is that true?" Alexander asked.

"That, my boy, you'll have to decide for yourself," Ptolemy answered. "For this is Egypt, where nothing is what it appears."

Prince Paris waited until Alexander left the queen's pavilion and crossed to his own tent before he emerged from the shadows and entered his stepmother's quarters. Ptolemy's back was to the door. He'd wrestled Artakama down on the divan, ripped away the linen covering her breasts, and was engaged in active foreplay when his wife gave a sharp intake of breath.

"What are you doing here?" she demanded, making no effort to cover her nakedness.

Ptolemy turned toward the door and scowled. "Have you no decency, to invade the queen's tent at this hour?" He pushed down his chiton and stepped in front of Artakama, blocking Paris's view.

"It seems no one sleeps this night," he answered. "Queen Artakama." Paris inclined his head in mock salute. "I'm surprised you're not holding a camel race or a slave auction in here, what with all the coming and going."

"Say what you've come to say and get out," the queen said. "The Great Bull and I have unfinished business."

"Which of you tried to have Alexander killed?"

Ptolemy scoffed. "I was about to ask the same question."

"It wasn't I." The queen sat up and adjusted the shreds of her tunic.

"Father?"

"Why would I want him dead? I'm the one who asked him here—who offered the princess Mereret to him in marriage."

"Send him back. Make any excuse, but get rid of him. Alive. There are at least three more suitable men that you could choose."

"So I suggested to Pharaoh," Artakama murmured. "But now it is too late. She must marry the barbarian, and soon."

Ptolemy fixed her with a questioning gaze.

"Mereret's moon time has come and gone without her red tide. Even now, she swells with child."

"Nonsense," Ptolemy snapped. "He's been here only three days. How could he possibly have—"

"Pharaoh's daughter does not lie. And this Alexander is the son of a god, is he not? Everyone accepts that the great Alexander was the son of Apollo." She shrugged. "Gods do not need mortal time. Likely the child will be born in far less time than—"

"You bitch!" Ptolemy backhanded her hard enough to knock her off balance. She half fell from the divan. Neither Nubian guard stirred so much as a muscle. For all Paris knew, they might have been blind as well as deaf. "What have you done? Who is the father of her unborn child?"

Artakama laughed. Blood seeped from her split lip, and she licked it with an expression of satisfaction. "Ask your bastard son. He has more to gain from this than anyone."

"If you need to ask me if I slept with my half sister, nothing I could say would convince you otherwise."

"Would you expect him to admit it?" she asked. "If I were you, and if I valued Berenice's weakling son, I'd find a quiver of physicians for him. I hear he is accident-prone."

Ptolemy struck at her again, but this time she dodged the blow and crept over to wrap her hands around his bare leg. "I am but the bearer of the news, great Horus in the nest. Although you could wed Mereret to the young Ptolemy and prevent either Alexander or Paris from claiming her babe and thus the throne."

"Berenice's son is my heir," Ptolemy roared. "I have no need to marry him to your whelp to claim the crown. I am Pharaoh."

"Forgive me, lord," she whispered.

Her voice sent a chill down Paris's spine. "I never sought to steal my brother's claim to your throne," he said. "I'm a general, nothing more. I serve you and Egypt."

"Where have I heard that before?" Artakama said. "One is a simple soldier, the other a poor general with no ambition."

"Quiet, woman," Ptolemy said.

"Like father, like son." Artakama pressed her cheek against Ptolemy's calf. "Remember, husband, you were once a general to the great Alexander, but fortune favored you and you rose to godhead."

Ptolemy sank onto the divan. "Was Alexander intimate with Mereret, or is this more of your plotting and lies?"

"The palace servants know they were alone together.

Mereret admitted it to me," Artakama insisted. "She refused to say if they had consummated the betrothal."

"Servants' gossip," Ptolemy grumbled.

"What the lowest slave prattles of, the nobility soon know. And from there all Alexandria will hear of it within the space of a single day." She fondled his thigh. "Whoever the true father of Mereret's unborn child may be, Egypt will see him as the grandson of the great Alexander."

"So you no longer need the heir to the Twin Kingdoms," Paris said. "Let Mereret and Alexander go through with the wedding, if it is your will, Father, and then send him home. If you keep Mereret, you control the child."

"A good plan," Artakama agreed. "So long as my daughter remains in Alexandria, Zeus can be the father of her child, for all I care."

"A babe who, if male, may wear the throne of Egypt as well as Bactria," Ptolemy mused.

Paris nodded. "If anything happens to Alexander, you will be blamed, Father. It will stain your reputation as a great king and cause unease among your allies."

Ptolemy looked thoughtful. "If we return Roxanne's brat, it will soothe relations between us, and I may yet gain the new spice routes. And if my beloved daughter is with child, no sane monarch would expect me to send her on a perilous journey that could well last six months and endanger the life of her coming babe. I like it. You have more of the statesman in you than I suspected, Paris. So be it. We will go through with the state wedding, wait for the duration of two full moons, and then announce the joyous news of Mereret's fertility."

"And then you will send Alexander back to his mountain kingdom unharmed?" Paris asked.

"It is the best way. I'd thought to keep him here,

where I could watch him, but he can do less damage beyond the Euphrates."

"I have your word?"

"And if our daughter should miscarry the child?" Artakama demanded. "What then?"

"She will deliver a strong male infant," Ptolemy said. "Providing at least one healthy boy is born alive in Alexandria, we will have Alexander's heir."

Artakama laughed. "You are wise, my husband. But even you need rest this night. Didn't you say you hunt the man-eater tomorrow?" She rose and took his hand. "My bed is near, Great Bull, nearer and more comfortable than your own."

Ptolemy motioned with his chin. "Leave us, Paris. We will follow the lion's trail at daybreak whether Alexander is fit to ride or not."

Alexander did not appear at dawn. When a quarter of an hour passed, Paris went to the tent and found him awake, but hardly fit for a hunt. Tutu shook her head and looked worried. Alexander's eyes glittered with fever, and the flesh around the injuries caused by the lion's claws was tight and swollen.

"Bring me wine," Alexander ordered. His voice sounded hoarse and dry. "Unwatered wine will see me on my feet and ready to draw a bow."

"The physician said that you were not to leave your bed," one of Alexander's captains said. Paris thought he was the man called Hermes. "We'll stay with him, Prince."

Alexander cursed. "You're determined to make an old woman of me, aren't you? Take Hermes in my place, then, to protect you and my uncle from the lion's jaws."

The tall Sogdian knelt beside Alexander and looked at the wounds. "I've seen enough of lion hunts in this cursed desert."

"You're a poor liar. Go. I'll bide here with this sweet wench and think of you in the dirt and heat."

Hori's oversize head peered though the tent flap. "Prince Paris. Pharaoh waits."

Paris glanced back at Alexander. "Would that I could stay with you as well, but—"

"Go, brother. I'll be fine."

"What physician came to see him?" Paris demanded of Hermes. "Queen Artakama's doctor or the same man who sewed him up?"

"The same," Hermes replied. "He seemed to know what he was about. Alex was bleeding like a slaughtered ox last night."

"The queen's physician isn't here," Hori said. "She came with only a small party. For her," he added, loud enough for only Paris to hear.

"Take good care of him," Paris instructed Tutu. "I hold you responsible."

"Yes, lord," she said. "The physician said that the fever will burn out the evil spirits in the wounds. He said he would worry if the fever turned in instead of out."

"I'll leave some of my men here with yours," Paris said. "If you don't feel better by evening, I'll insist that Pharaoh send you back to Alexandria to the palace surgeons."

"Will you get out of here?" Alexander said. "It's bad enough to be laid low by a few scratches without you all carrying on so. I've a wedding in ten days. Give me a few hours' sleep and I'll not disappoint the bride."

"I'll bring you the skin," Paris said. "Or at least the tail."

"I'll hold you to it, brother."

Hori tugged at his arm. "Pharaoh is not known for his patience, Prince."

"Very well." Paris nodded. "I'll be back by nightfall, with or without the lion." He left the tent and he and

Hermes followed Hori back to where the chariots waited. He pointed to the team next to his. "Pepi will drive for you," he said to the Sogdian.

"You promised to leave men to stand watch over Prince Alexander," Hermes reminded him.

"I will." Paris gave the orders to one of his lieutenants. "Six of my best men are to stay with the Bactrians and their prince. See that he comes to no harm in my absence." He glanced across the dusty common area to the place where the queen's pavilion stood. All was quiet. No servants stirred nor guards stood outside.

"Do we hunt today or not?" Ptolemy bellowed. He stood ready in his chariot, looking for all the world like a man who'd slept the night away in a soft bed instead of spending part of it carousing with his charioteer and the rest with his most gracious queen.

The huntsmen loosed the hounds and they burst free. Pharaoh's charioteer cracked his whip over his team and they broke into a trot. Hori fell in behind, with Pepi and the others strung out in single file.

Paris braced himself and took hold of the railing with one hand. The day promised to be fair and the chase a good one. He grinned. "I will bring you that tail, little Yuri," he murmured half to himself. "And I'll fill the skin with silver coins as a wedding gift."

Chapter 10

Ptolemy's chariot driver was Ubaid, an Egyptian born of a Nubian slave mother and a Syrian soldier. Skilled with horses as well as bow and sword, Ubaid could track a man or a lion over bare rock, and he had served his pharaoh faithfully for fifteen years. Ptolemy had spent untold hours standing shoulder-to-shoulder with this silent man and knew him better than he knew his own son 'Toly.

Thus when Ptolemy gave an order, he could count on Ubaid to carry it out. Early on, they had turned off from the spoor that the hounds were following, leaving behind Paris, Alexander's captain, Hermes, and two other chariots of hunters. They struck across the desert to a sinkhole where Ubaid suspected an old lion might hide. Naturally, Pharaoh was not alone and unprotected. A half dozen chariots raced after him, all carrying noblemen and soldiers loyal to the throne.

Ptolemy had traveled perhaps two leagues in the jouncing, dusty chariot when he first heard the voice in his head . . . a voice he'd dreaded, but hadn't heard for nearly twenty years . . . the unmistakable voice of his dead brother, Alexander.

"You venture into dangerous ground. Didn't I warn you before?"

Ptolemy stared at Ubaid. The driver hadn't spoken. Ptolemy knew that Ubaid hadn't spoken. He glanced around him, knowing the search was useless. It was a two-man chariot. No one else could be there.

Alexander the Great was calling to him from the grave. Again.

Ptolemy struck Ubaid sharply on the shoulder with his fist. "What did you say?" he demanded. He knew that it wasn't Ubaid who'd spoken, but to admit otherwise was to accept the truth: the specter of Alexander had returned to plague him.

The driver's eyes widened in surprise. "Nothing, Lord of the Two Lands."

"You spoke. I heard you," Ptolemy insisted. "Repeat yourself."

"No, Great Bull. I said nothing."

Laughter, bright and familiar, rang in the shadows of Ptolemy's head. "Leave me be!" Ptolemy said.

Ubaid turned his full attention to his team, but the corded veins on the tops of his hands and the tightness of his lips left no doubt that he felt his master was behaving irrationally.

"Your hair grows thin. Perhaps it is the weight of your crown. My crown, which you wear on your unworthy head."

"Stop!" Ptolemy ordered.

Ubaid reined in the horses. The other chariots behind them slowed and circled before stopping.

"What is it?" a nobleman cried. "Have you found fresh spoor?"

In the distance the blue hills wavered. The sun was hot, the wind that blew off the empty wasteland hotter.

122

For as far as Ptolemy could see, there were no trees, no grass, and no boulders where a ghost might hide. Ignoring Ubaid's puzzled expression, Ptolemy leaped down from the vehicle and strode quickly out of the driver's earshot.

"Ptolemy. I know you hear me."

"Why? Why do you return after all these years?" Ptolemy placed both hands over his ears. "What do you want of me? I built you a tomb greater than any other mortal has ever possessed. Bulls are sacrificed on your birthday and the anniversary of your death. I've made your city into one of the wonders of the world. Why do you haunt me?"

"Why do you threaten that which is mine?"

Something shimmered and took form not a spear's length away, something beautiful and terrible, and Ptolemy's bowels knotted. He dropped to his knees, clutching his belly and rocking to and fro. "What do you want?"

The something, which could have been a mirage or could have been the outline of a Macedonian warrior carrying sword and shield, flashed gold in the sun and then vanished into a whirlwind of sand as quickly as it had come.

Tears formed in Ptolemy's eyes. He could hear the shouts of his soldiers, the pounding of horses' hooves and chariot wheels on the hard-packed sand, but they seemed more alien than the words echoing in his head.

"Didn't I warn you before?"

Ptolemy leaned over and vomited. Nothing came up but green bile, yet he choked and coughed and retched again.

"My lord!" Ubaid yanked up the team and flung himself from the chariot. "You are ill!" He turned and called to the rest. "Come quickly! Pharaoh is stricken!"

Cursing, Ptolemy forced himself to his feet and wiped his mouth with the back of his hand. "We return to camp," he rasped. "At once."

Alexander stirred. His mouth was dry; his skin felt like old parchment. His head throbbed with a dull ache.

"Good morning," the woman beside him said.

His eyes felt weighted down with lead. He didn't have the strength to raise his head from the mattress. He groaned.

"Are you thirsty?"

He forced his eyes to open. Mereret lay beside him under the same linen covering. He blinked. "What . . . Where am I?" He closed his eyes again and smelled incense and some kind of soup. Suddenly he was ravenously hungry.

"You must wake, my prince."

"Mereret?" He opened his eyes again. There was no mistake. His betrothed was curled in the circle of his arm. Her shoulders and breasts were bare, and he could feel the heat of her thigh and leg next to his. "Where am I?" Confused, he looked around, certain that he had never been in this room before. "Not the hunting camp," he said. Images flashed in his mind. A rocking litter. Bare rock. The sun scorching the moisture from his body . . .

"Hardly." She leaned close and kissed his cheek. "You've been here five days. Don't you remember? You're in my mother's palace. In my bedchamber. Does it look like a tent?"

"No." He started to shake his head, but the effort was too much. He dropped his head to the wooden rest and winced. Egyptian sleeping habits didn't suit him. "I was hunting lion." His voice rasped unnaturally in his head, so dry and hoarse it might have been that of a withered mummy.

"So I heard, husband. Prince Paris told me of your bravery. All the court is talking of it."

"Husband? We're not . . . Our wedding is . . ."

"Five days off. But you needed me. You were close to death, and who but your bride should lend you her strength?"

He swallowed, wanting wine or water, wanting the soup, but not wanting to ask. "I don't understand."

Female twitters.

He looked toward the source and saw a familiar face among the covey of plump and naked serving maids standing at the foot of the bed. "Tutu. You were with me in the desert," he said.

The slave girl nodded. "Your fever rose. Pharaoh feared for your life. He ordered you brought here."

"Where I could care for you," Mereret said. "Everyone knows that a weak *ka* can be aided by a strong one. By sleeping next to you, I could lend you my spirit." She waved to Tutu. "Water for Prince Alexander. Drink slowly, song of my heart. When we first gave you water, it made you sick."

He sipped, thinking it was the best thing he'd ever tasted. "More."

Mereret shook her head. "Later. The physicians were adamant."

"What's that I smell?"

"Goose broth. Do you think you could keep some down?"

"Give me the whole bird. I'll eat it raw."

The girls twittered again. Mereret smiled at him, threw back the sheet, and rose from the bed. She was naked from brow to painted toes. Any other time he would have enjoyed the sight. Now the bowl of soup and the spoon to eat it were more important.

"My uncle knows I'm here?" He wasn't certain he'd heard her correctly.

"The Great Bull, pharaoh of two lands, and son of Horus has given his blessing to our union. We will have the wedding ceremony, but in his eyes, we are man and wife already."

"Why?" Artakama raged. "Why can't you see what a danger he is? You will live to regret this."

Ptolemy rose from her bed and wrapped a long linen kilt around his waist. "I thought we were in agreement on the matter of my nephew. I will send him home once Mereret's pregnancy is made public."

"He is like his father. He will never be satisfied with his Twin Kingdoms of sheep dung and skinny horses when his wife carries the blood of pharaohs. I looked into his eyes, and I tell you that he desires all that is yours—all that should be 'Toly's."

"You mean you looked into his eyes and saw that he won't bend to your will. Therefore he must be disposed of." Ptolemy reached for a jug of wine. He filled a glass chalice to the rim and drank half in one gulp. "I don't have time to listen to your scheming. They have completed another section of the lighthouse, and I have to be there for Poseidon's priests to give the blessing."

"Think of your heir. Will he be strong enough to face the son of the great Alexander?"

"You are as bad as Berenice. I hear it from her by day and you by night. I will live for many years yet, perhaps enough years to father many more sons. Perhaps even to see a son of Mereret and Alexander named my heir instead of 'Toly."

"Alexander plots with Paris." She ran fingers through her tangled hair. "Why else would your bastard plead with you to send Alexander away rather than kill him? The two of them were raised together. They are a danger to Egypt. And if you want to put a fine point on it, your brother's son has a better claim on Egypt than you do. I have thought more on our plan. It is not enough to send him away. Alexander must die."

"Enough. Can't you see that my head is hurting?" Ptolemy rubbed the nape of his neck. The old headache was back. Light hurt his eyes, and he saw colored sparks when he closed them. The slightest sound seemed magnified twenty times. He sighed. The sun would be very bright on the island where his magnificent lighthouse rose from a bed of stone blocks. The pain in his head would be excruciating. He wished that he'd slept alone last night, so that he could rise in quiet, but his fear was too strong. The mirage in the desert was still too fresh in his mind.

Had he heard the ghost of his brother or had it been the onset of this headache? More than one man had seen things that weren't there in the midst of the desert. Seen or heard? He hadn't actually seen Alexander. It could all be his imagination. It must be. Years had passed without the nightmare coming back to haunt him. Better to listen to Artakama's tirade than that ghoulish laughter. Alexander had never haunted him when he was with his Egyptian wife. Perhaps she was more terrible than any ghost. He smiled. Even she had her purposes. And he could not deny that Artakama was wiser than her years. She was right about Alexander.

"Go to your daughter's chambers," he said abruptly. "Take your ladies with you, not the slaves but the wives of the nobility. Go unannounced so that all see what man lies in the princess's bed. We want no doubt as to the father of her child."

"I hear you, my lord, and I will do as you say." She smiled back at him and unwound the snake from around her neck. The serpent slithered across the bed and sought the cool shadows beneath the bed frame.

"Now tell me," he insisted. "Who did steal her honor?"

Artakama yawned and stretched. "She is your child. She has as much taste for the pleasures of life as you."

"Who is the man?"

"Who plucked the royal lotus or who fathered the child?"

Ptolemy felt his last scrap of patience draining away. "No riddles this morning, Artakama. I'd as soon part that pretty head of yours from your neck as not."

"Mereret has shared her bed since her first moon's blood. With men, with women, with both."

"But you know who got her with child."

"Is it important? You yourself said that the child is undoubtedly that of Prince Alexander."

"Maybe I won't kill you. Maybe I'll just cut off your nose. In a veil you would still be appealing to me, just not to—"

"He's no one, a eunuch."

Ptolemy scoffed. "A eunuch has fathered my first grandchild? A miracle. Proof that the gods do love me."

She sighed. "All eunuchs are not created equal. Sometimes bribes are made and whole men manage to infiltrate the palace."

"Does he have a name, this superior eunuch?"

"He did." She smiled at him. "But he will need it no more. A tragic accident. He drowned in my bath."

"A pity." Ptolemy eyed her, wondering if she was telling the truth or another lie. "And Mereret? Was she devastated by this loss?"

"No. She had already tired of him."

"Why should I believe you?"

She chuckled. "So suspicious. One would almost think you had been born a pharaoh's son. The eunuch is dead because it cost me nothing to dispose of him. And had he lived, someone would have had to pay him to 'forget' his nights in Mereret's bed."

Ptolemy nodded. "It's what I would have done. Yes,

128

it was the right thing. If you had not been born a woman, you would have made a king."

She yawned again, daintily covering her mouth with her fingers. "Is there anything more, Great Bull?"

"No." He shook his head. "I'll leave you to your sleep." He would take the underground tunnel to his own palace, bathe, and dress there for the Poseidon blessing. He paused halfway to the door. "Do as I say," he ordered. "When we meet for the evening meal, I want whispers to have already spread through the palace about Alexander and Mereret. No one will dare to mention it to me."

"They would not, would they?" She smiled.

Four of Ptolemy's private household guard walked a dozen paces in front of him as he descended into the cool, stale air of the underground passageway. Four followed a respectful distance behind. Wall lamps every two spear-lengths lit the brick floor. There were no cross corridors, no rooms where an assassin might hide. Here Pharaoh was as safe as he had ever been in his mother's womb—if that could be called safe.

Ptolemy's thoughts were on his morning meal and the cool bath that awaited him in his chambers. He had not been exactly truthful with Artakama when he'd led her to believe that the ceremony at the lighthouse would be this morning. Actually it was not scheduled until three hours past noon. He would have time to work on his memoirs, perhaps even read the translation of the scrolls about a new type of metal being used in Chin for weapons. The emperor had sent a knife as a gift, and the blade was said to cut through bronze like—

The sword stroke came without warning. Ptolemy heard the hiss as the honed edge missed his neck by a finger's width. Gasping, he jerked back.

A scream caught in Ptolemy's throat as his attacker

loomed up and blocked his way. Ptolemy tried to shout for his guards, tried to run, but his muscles froze. Unable to draw breath or utter a sound, he stared in horror at the golden-haired specter in front of him.

Alexander of Macedon stood a sword's thrust away—illuminated by an unholy light brighter than the dawn. No wispy spirit, this was a man of flesh, muscle, and bone, clad in battle helmet, cuirass, and purple cloak of the companion cavalry. Alexander's beautiful face was unmarked by death's kiss, and his gray eyes blazed with fury.

"I warned you."

"I've not harmed him." Ptolemy's words tumbled out as fear churned in his gut.

"Kill my son and I will wipe your city from the face of the earth. Your seed will wither and crabs will devour your bowels, bite by bite."

"No! I haven't . . . He's recovering from his wounds. He's to marry my daughter in three days."

"My name will be remembered for ten times a thousand years, but take his life and I promise you that yours will be forgotten. I will torch your libraries and churn the sea to devour your puny monuments."

"You're not real," Ptolemy protested.

"Real enough to drag you into the grave with me, brother."

Ptolemy's scream burst from his throat. He felt that he was falling into a black abyss.

Seconds or minutes passed. When he opened his eyes, a trembling guard was peering into his face. Another held a lamp.

"Great Bull. Are you hurt? Shall we send for a physician?"

"Did you see . . ." Ptolemy began, and then trailed off. What had they seen? Was he clairvoyant or had he lost his wits? Would he soon be crawling on the floor and drooling into his bread bowl?"

"You fell, son of Horus. We thought you might have struck your head. . . ."

Ptolemy's head, oddly enough, was clear. The pain had receded. His reasoning seemed whole. Could it be that no one else had seen or heard what he thought he had? "Was there a light?"

"Take the light away, fool," the guard said to his comrade. "It shines in his eyes."

Ptolemy pushed the man away and rose to his feet. He was a little giddy, but otherwise seemed none the worse for the terrifying incident. "Proceed," he ordered. "It's nothing. I caught my sandal on a crack and fell."

The guard stared at him a fraction of an instant too long. "Are you deaf?" Ptolemy asked. "Lead on. Or must I put another in your place?"

"No, Great Bull," the guard said hastily. "No, lord." He gestured to the others. "Continue."

"And you will repeat nothing that happened here," Ptolemy warned, "or you will have no tongues to ever repeat anything again."

"Yes, son of Horus," the man said. "I saw nothing. I heard nothing."

Ptolemy swore. "Then why are we standing here?" His heart raced as he followed the soldiers down the passageway. He gazed into the dark recesses of the arched ceiling, searching for what he hoped wasn't there. Had never been there. Could never be there.

But it had. His brother had reached from the grave once more to foil his plans.

Kill my son and I will wipe your city from the face of the earth, Alexander had said. So what now? Allow the conqueror's son to steal his throne? Or find a way to outsmart them both?

Chapter 11

Alexander's wedding procession was three times as large and twice as elaborate as the one that had welcomed him into the city of Alexandria. Besieged by the cheers of the crowds, he rode through the streets of the city, standing beside Ptolemy in a golden chariot, followed by his own cavalrymen and half of the Egyptian army. Of his bride or of Paris, Alexander had seen nothing. He'd not spoken to Paris since the day he awakened from his fever in Mereret's apartments.

"You're making a mistake," Paris had warned in the few moments that they'd been alone without the princess or her servants within earshot. "I have heard whispers in the palace. Take my advice and leave while your head is still attached to your shoulders."

"Why are you so against this marriage?"

"Because it will be your death."

"Is that a warning or a threat?"

"Take it as you will." Scowling, Paris had stalked from the room, leaving Alexander more perplexed and disappointed than ever. His strength seemed slow in returning, but the pain of losing his brother hurt far more than that of his weakened body.

He wondered if Paris had ever loved him as he'd believed, or if he himself had lived in a child's fantasy. Maybe those who advised him to reject marriage to Ptolemy's daughter were right; maybe he was in over his head here in Egypt. But the years and distance that had separated them had never altered his love for Val, and he would have willingly laid down his life for him.

If Paris had been a disappointment, Mereret had been a pleasant surprise. To his relief, she'd made no effort to consummate their union. In his weakened condition, Alexander was afraid that even if he managed to sustain an erection, he'd not have done his best. And the way to a wife's heart was not to show oneself an inadequate lover two days before the wedding.

Try as he might, Alexander could find no fault in his princess during his recovery. He'd rarely been sick enough to remain in bed once the sun came up, and he readily acknowledged that he was a poor patient. Mereret had shown great forbearance and good humor, catering to his every whim, remaining by his side whenever the physicians attended his wounds, and ignoring his bad temper. She'd supervised her ladies when they'd bathed him and tempted his appetite with sweet fruit juices, broth, eggs, and other food suitable for a man who'd been close to death. Mereret possessed the discretion to amuse him when he wished for company and to give him peace when he wearied of women's chatter.

Twice, Ptolemy had come to speak with him. The second time his uncle had suggested that he and Mereret might wish to remain in Alexandria for a few months, just until they were comfortable together and she'd learned enough of his language to communicate with those who did not speak Greek or Egyptian.

"As your wife, my daughter will be yours to command," Ptolemy had assured him. "But it will ease an old man's heart if you are tender toward her. We have spoiled her, Artakama and I, but she is the only one of our children to survive infancy, and she is dear to us."

Alexander made no promises, but he could see the wisdom in his uncle's suggestion. Mereret's attempts at Parsi were endearing, and although he found her accent delightful, it was difficult not to laugh. He hoped that her language skills would improve, but it was a small thing if they didn't. His bride was bright and funny and charming, every inch a daughter of pharaohs. She was young, but he sensed in her the potential to be a great asset to his kingship. Despite her exotic appearance and sensual body, she possessed a sharp mind and a strong will. She'd not bore him in a week, as many beautiful women did, and despite his mother's predictions of disaster, he was more than satisfied in the match.

In one matter only did Mereret disturb him. On the second day, he'd asked Mereret what had happened to the green-eyed Kiara. His bride-to-be had looked slightly puzzled before shrugging prettily. "There are many slave girls in my mother's palace. Would you like one? You can have your pick if you wish to take pleasure with them. There is a fair-skinned girl with flaxen hair and blue eyes from the far north, an Etruscan dancer who is said to be double-jointed, identical twins from Cathay, and an acrobat from Crete. All are very popular with the nobility. Prince Paris favors the Etruscan wench. Or"—she motioned to Tutu—"you may have her. The Great Bull, my father, will give us a palace after the wedding. You may have as many concubines as you like."

"It's not important," he'd lied. "I only thought Kiara

must be a favorite of yours, since you sent her to me. I wondered where she was."

Mereret had motioned to Tutu and asked her to inquire as to the woman's whereabouts, but nothing had come of it. He did not ask again. Whether his betrothed was telling the truth or was having an attack of jealousy, he couldn't tell, but he thought that the best course was to drop the subject. He hoped Kiara had come to no harm. She'd helped him, and somehow she intrigued him too.

He could have reminded Mereret that the slave had been a gift, and technically belonged to him already, but he felt that to make a fuss would be to ensure that the girl ended up picking onions in some muddy field or chopping them in the kitchen. As people kept reminding him, this was Egypt. Here they had their own customs.

As to whether or not he would remain in Alexandria or depart at once for home, Alexander hadn't decided. There were ancient monuments in Egypt that he hadn't had an opportunity to see. He wanted to explore the wonders of this desert land, to visit the Temples of Karnak and Luxor, to climb the great pyramids, and wander through the crooked streets of Memphis. He wished to journey down the Nile and hunt crocodile from a boat, perhaps venture as far as the mighty cataracts of which his tutors had spoken.

Yet he knew that he could not stay away from the Two Kingdoms for long. His family and his country depended on him. Invasion had been a constant threat since he was a child, and he was too old to expect Kayan and his mother to fight his battles. As king he had to shoulder the responsibilities they had carried so long. But today was his wedding day and he need make no decisions. Tonight he would taste the mysteries of Egypt; tomorrow would be time enough to decide.

Alexander flexed his shoulder. The stitches in his side pulled, but the arrow wound was healing. He would carry scars from his encounter with the lion, but his ability to shoot a bow or wield a sword would not be compromised. The incident would make a great story to share with his friends around a roaring fire, and the mysterious arrow shot would only add to the telling.

The wedding procession filed up one grand avenue and down another. It was clear to Alexander that his uncle had made great improvements to the city in the past twenty years. And although Alexander had never seen Athens, he doubted it was more beautiful.

Proudly, Ptolemy pointed out temples and universities, libraries and edifices built to carry out the day-to-day running of the country and his uncle's far-flung empire. It was not until well after the sun reached its highest point that the charioteer drew his team to a halt at the steps of Alexander's tomb. At Pharaoh's order, children came forth with their arms full of flowers and fruit and laid them on the steps of the monument.

"Later, we will return here so that you can enter the tomb to pay your respects to your father," Ptolemy said.

A high priest came out, surrounded by a flock of lesser servants of Apollo, and gave a short speech on the immortality of Alexander the Great while Ptolemy watched solemnly. Once the eulogy was complete, Ptolemy raised one outstretched palm in salute.

The hundred onlookers went wild with approval as Ptolemy's charioteer urged the horses slowly around the great square three times before taking the wide thoroughfare back to the Avenue of the Gods.

"We're almost there," Ptolemy said, leaning close to Alexander so that he could be heard above the tumult. "Mereret and her mother are devotees of Isis, and they wished the ceremony to be held there. I don't know about you, nephew, but I'll be glad to get out of this midday sun."

Alexander had never seen so many people gathered together in one place. Children danced in front of the pharaoh's chariot, strewing heads of wheat and flowers on the street, which someone had scrubbed as clean and white as the day the paving stones had been hewed from the quarry. The noise was overwhelming, pressing on Alexander from every side, so that he felt it hard to think or even to breathe.

The chariot rolled slowly past magnificent structures dedicated to Zeus, to Apollo, to Osiris, and to Hera before finally coming to rest at the foot of marble steps leading up to the Temple of Isis. Pharaoh raised his hand, and all fell silent. The only sound was the jingle of the chariot horses' harness and the soft shuffling of their hooves. It was so hot that sweat ran down Alexander's face, soaked his tunic, and turned his bronze armor to an oven.

Ptolemy and Alexander ascended the wide marble steps to the bronze doors, which Ptolemy struck three times with his flail. Alexander assumed that someone inside the temple was striking a bell at the same time, because each touch of Pharaoh's flail produced a loud resonant bong that could be heard for blocks.

Slowly the doors swung open and the two passed through into the cool interior. The doors closed behind them, drowning out the noise of the crowd. Inside, the thick, still air pulsed with the scent of cedar, myrrh, and cinnamon. Alexander had the impression of row after row of columns with priestesses garbed all in white, standing in shadows on either side of the high, carved pillars. He heard water flowing, and the sound of a single flute. The reed instrument played high and sweet, a melody old beyond time yet eternal.

His pulse quickened.

"I bring the bridegroom," Ptolemy proclaimed. "Deliver to him that which has been promised, even unto the beginning of the world." He smiled at Alexander. "I can go no farther. You must proceed alone." Muted drums and low chants from the throats of many women joined the wail of the flute.

A veiled female, too tall to be Mereret, glided forward. Her throat and wrists were heavy with jewelry, her ankles weighed down with gold and precious gems. Alexander caught the unmistakable scent of sandalwood. "Come," the woman intoned in a haunting voice. The light was too dim to tell if she was young or old. She held out a strip of scarlet silk.

"You must be blindfolded to pass through the goddess's holy of holies," his uncle explained. "Only women may look upon Isis's inner sanctum. They won't even let me catch a peek."

Reluctantly Alexander allowed the priestess to tie the sash around his head, shutting out both sound and light. He felt many women's soft hands upon him, tugging, guiding him forward into the interior of the temple. He stiffened, knotting his fists in frustration. It was not in his nature to allow anyone to confine him.

His first instinct was to protest this pagan ritual. His uncle was pure Macedonian. How could they expect him to endure such indignity to marry Ptolemy's daughter?

"Just a little way," a woman whispered. "She awaits your coming."

"Prince Alexander," Mereret called. "My lord. Why have you come to this holy place?"

"To claim you as wife."

"Enter the womb of Isis," the high priestess said. "Enter, barbarian, and be consumed by her sacred fire."

Alarmed, Alexander jerked away the blindfold, caught the flash of torchlight in the blackness, and fell heavily as a ceremonial ax slammed into the back of his skull.

Paris heard the shouts and the clash of swords as the Memphis heavy infantry, marching just ahead of his troops, turned the corner onto the Avenue of the Gods. Jerking the reins from his driver's hands, Paris cracked the whip over his team's back and forced his chariot through the ranks of soldiers.

Startled by the sudden appearance of a war chariot in the midst of their formation, some men leaped aside, while others not so agile tangled their long spears and cursed. Soldiers spilled into the crowd, causing a confrontation between a group of drunken sailors and the infantrymen.

"Make way!" Hori bellowed. "Make way for the prince! Make way, you lame sons of poxed baboons!" Twisting, the dwarf thrust his broad fist in the air and swore at Paris's battalion behind them. "What are you waiting for? Do you follow your prince? Come, you sons of dogs! You half-witted arrow fodder! Are you men or skulking vermin?"

Howling their battle cry, Paris's soldiers tore after him. Men and women scattered as chariot after chariot of screaming Greek mercenaries poured through the opening that their prince had punched through the lines of heavy infantry.

As his team galloped past the great Temple of Zeus, Paris saw pandemonium ahead of him. Pharaoh's soldiers had surrounded Alexander's cavalry. Outnumbered ten to one and hemmed in by hostile bystanders, the horsemen of the Twin Kingdoms had backed their horses into a tight circle and were using swords and shields to hold off the crack Alexandrian archers. A third of Alexander's countrymen were already down, dead or dying, their blood pooling in the street.

"Cease fire! Cease fire!" Paris lashed his team through the outer circle of Ptolemy's troops, placing himself between the Egyptians and the foreigners. "Have you gone mad?"

Arrows continued to fly from both sides until Paris's charioteers caught up and circled the besieged Sogdians and Bactrians to form a living barrier between the two forces. An Egyptian officer took aim at Hermes, but the shaft missed and sliced across the withers of one of Paris's horses. The gray horse reared in the traces and snorted as a scarlet stain spread over his shining coat.

Enraged, Hori notched an arrow in his own bowstring and shot Ptolemy's man through the throat. The Egyptian clutched the shaft and toppled over as cries of shock and anger rumbled through the troops.

"Fall back!" Paris commanded. "Fall back or I'll cut you down to a man!"

Stunned silence settled over the street. Paris leaped down from his chariot, pushed through the Egyptian archers, and raced up the steps of Isis's temple. Ptolemy, accompanied by members of his household guard and followed by the princess Mereret, the high priestess, and a dozen of her priestesses, walked onto the wide columned veranda. Paris noticed that Mereret was smiling.

"Where's Alexander?" Paris said. "What have you done with him?"

"This is none of your affair," Ptolemy snapped.

"Is he dead?"

His father fixed him with a stare so malevolent that Paris felt the force of the blow. "Take your battalion back to their barracks. At once."

Bile rose in Paris's throat. He swallowed. "This was supposed to be his wedding day."

"I gave you an order," his father said.

"He's your own brother's son. Is this Macedonian honor?"

An officer of the guard advanced on Paris with drawn sword, but Paris stood his ground. "I want to know what you've done to him."

"I owe you no explanation," Ptolemy said. "Without me, you're not a prince. You're just one more nameless bastard."

"Where is he?"

"Follow my commands or receive the punishment of any traitor."

Paris saluted. "I hear and obey, Great Bull of Egypt." He hurried down the steps and crossed to where Hermes sat astride a wild-eyed sorrel gelding. Near him, Paris recognized a younger man, Jahan, whom Alexander had pointed out as his squire. Jahan was bleeding from wounds in his left thigh and right hand.

Hermes held a naked sword across his horse's withers. The man's dark eyes were filled with fury, his muscles tense. "Where is Prince Alexander?" he demanded.

Paris shook his head. "It's too late. Tell your men to lower their weapons."

"Go swive yourself!"

"Trust me. I'm not your enemy."

"Why should we?"

"Because you've got no choice." Paris motioned to his troopers. "Disarm the barbarians and escort them to our barracks! Pharaoh's command!" He glanced back at Hermes. "It's your only chance."

Reluctantly Hermes passed the order to his comrades. "Gather the wounded and the dead."

"Leave your dead," Paris said.

"We have never left the field without a man," Jahan shouted. He flashed Paris a look as if daring him to try to stop them, but Paris only nodded.

"Hurry!"

"Move out!" Hori shouted. "Chariots on either side of the street. Prisoners in the middle."

Paris swung up into the saddle of one of the riderless animals and reined close to Hermes. He tugged a ring Ptolemy had given him off his finger. "Go ahead of us to the harbor," Paris ordered. "There are three warships ready to set sail for the waters off Carthage on tomorrow's tide. Tell the highest commanding deck officer you can find that Pharaoh has changed his mind."

The dwarf's eyes narrowed.

"Tell him that this is a direct command from the Great Bull himself. He is to prepare to take on passengers. Order him to summon whatever crews he can find, but to keep his mission a secret on pain of death. Do you understand, Hori?"

"Yes, my prince."

"Then go as fast as you can to the barracks. Get my weapons and whatever personal belongings you possess. Move the leather chest under my bunk. There is a loose tile. Beneath it you will find a metal box. Bring it. If anyone tries to stop you, don't hesitate to kill him."

"We aren't coming back, are we?"

"When I reach the harbor, you'll be free to come or stay. If you have—"

"I am your man. To the River Styx and back."

In less time than it had taken for Paris to realize that Ptolemy had murdered his brother, Paris's chariots and Alexander's remaining cavalry were retracing their path down the Avenue of the Gods. At the first intersection, Paris directed the battalion to turn off onto Canopic Street. There he stationed fifty charioteers and commanded them to overturn their vehicles and use any means short of combat to delay pursuers.

Each time he came to a crossroad, Paris repeated the order until they reached the docks. There, he ordered the Sogdians and Bactrians to dismount and board the small craft waiting to take them on board the warships.

"You expect us to leave our horses?" Jahan demanded. "We have raised them since they were foals. They are our brothers."

Hermes cursed him. "Fool! Would you trade your life and the lives of your comrades for a horse?"

"I'm not afraid to die," the angry squire flung back.

"It takes more courage to live than to die heedlessly," a Bactrian nobleman admonished him.

Cheeks crimson with shame, the youth swung down and pressed his face against his bay's velvet-black nose. "I won't forget you, Adar," he murmured to the animal.

Paris grabbed the horse's reins. "They need help with the wounded," he said brusquely. "I'll see your horse has a good master." He gestured to one of his officers. "Lycus! Here. Take him."

The Greek captain's mouth gaped.

"See that the horses are apportioned out to good men," Paris commanded. "I'm leaving Alexandria."

"My duty is with you," Lycus answered.

"You have a wife and a son. Your duty is to your king. I take only a few men with me. None who have families."

Of the three vessels, only two captains were present. Most of the crewmen had been given leave for the holiday, but enough sailors were pressed into service to man the ships. Within an hour, Alexander's soldiers and a hundred and fifty of Paris's men were safely aboard. The seamen on the first two ships had already pulled anchors and hoisted sails when Hori's chariot thundered down the street to the wharf.

"Wait!" Paris shouted.

"We almost left without you," Paris said as the little man reined in at the water's edge. "You'd have been a rich man."

"Promises," Hori muttered. He tossed Paris a shield and horn bow. "What are you standing there for?" the dwarf roared at a hapless Egyptian sailor. "Bend your back, you dog's spittle. Get Prince Paris's belongings into that boat!"

Later, as wind filled the sails and their vessel slipped past the harbor entrance, Hermes approached Paris and asked, "Why?"

Paris could give no answer. As grief washed over him, he clenched his teeth and stared silently at his father's unfinished lighthouse. Alexander was dead. He could do nothing more than lead his brother's companions home.

Home . . . It had been years since he'd thought of the Twin Kingdoms as home. He wondered if his future there was as hollow as the promise of Pharaoh.

Chapter 12

In the wild borderlands between Bactria and the steppes, Ava crouched low under the spreading branches of a tree and waited, heart pounding. *He's dead,* she thought. *He's dead. I know it.* A single tear trailed down her cheek and she brushed it away with the back of a sheepskin mitten. "Oh, Papa," she whispered. "It wasn't supposed to be like this."

A hundred yards away her horse snorted, and Ava jumped so hard that she bit the inside of her cheek. The sound meant that Kai smelled other horses or strangers. The black gelding would never show alarm at the approach of animals or people he knew.

Sucking gingerly at the slice in the side of her mouth, Ava pushed aside a feathery bough and peered out. She couldn't see Kai because he was tied in a narrow gully hidden by a brush-covered hillock. *Leave your horse and hide until I get back,* her father had ordered. *Keep a distance between you and Kai, so that if he's discovered by enemy scouts, you may not be.*

That had been hours ago. Ava squinted up at the

145

sky. The gray clouds hung low and threatening, heavy with moisture. The temperature had been dropping since noon, and that could only mean snow. Until today, riding off to spend the winter on the frontier with her father had been an adventure. Now Ava wished she were home in the southern palace. By this time of the day, she'd be finished with her daily lessons, exchanging secrets with her friends, and practicing archery or training her new hawk. Ava missed her mother, even missed her annoying sister. Worse, far worse than anything she could imagine, something terrible might have happened to Papa.

The thought that she could lose her father was almost too terrible to conceive. Kayan was a prince, a mighty warrior, tall and strong, more clever than any Scythian. Twice in her life she could remember Papa being wounded in battle. His injuries had been only slight, and he'd recovered quickly. She'd always believed that he was immune to death or serious harm. Surely the Wise God must realize how much his country needed him—how much she needed him.

They'd spent last night with the patrol in a walled fort in the shelter of She Bear Mountain. The commander's wife, Gulrukh, had been overwhelmed to have their reigning prince and his daughter ride through the gate, but the plump, ruddy-cheeked woman had quickly gotten over her shock and had proved a wonderful hostess. Gulrukh had fussed over her, stuffed them all with her delicious stew and hot bread flavored with honey and herbs, and even let Ava hold her four-month-old baby, an adorable little dumpling with puckered lips and huge brown eyes. Ava had slept in a soft feather quilt near the fire with two of Gulrukh's giggling girls, and had awakened this morning to the smells of raisin cakes and hot porridge.

Trouble had not come until she and Papa and the

soldiers had ridden for perhaps an hour and come upon a burning farmstead. Bandits had left two men and their dogs dead and an old man severely wounded. The grandfather had told them that Scythian raiders had struck just after sunrise. The bandits had stolen four horses and some sheep and cattle, and carried off two women and a five-year-old girl.

Her father had known from the horses' tracks how many Scythians there were and which pass the bandits would be most likely to use to return to the steppes. He had to go after the thieves and rescue the kidnapped women, but he hadn't wanted to take her with him into danger.

"It's too far for you to ride back alone to the fort," he'd said. From the expression on his face, Ava could tell that he wished he'd left her at home with her mother. They had twenty troopers, all seasoned warriors, more than enough to fight the raiding party, but too few to divide. Kayan had kept her with him until they neared the Scythians, and then had left her hidden here while he closed in on them.

But something had gone wrong. Papa had promised he'd be back in an hour, two at most. Noon had come and gone. The afternoon was passing. What would she do when it got dark? Where would she take shelter? And if she built a fire to keep warm—which she was perfectly capable of doing—the fire would protect her from wolves but not from men. Flames could be seen from a long way off, and the glow would reveal her location to anyone with less than honorable intentions.

What she needed to find was a safe spot to hide until morning, perhaps a cave or grove of trees where the wind wouldn't reach her nor the fire be too evident. Then, if Papa still hadn't returned, she could ride back to the fort. But it would be wrong to go now. A lot of things could have made him late. Maybe the Scythians had fled, left the stolen animals and their captives, and her father had decided to take them home before meeting up with her. Or the bandits might be holed up in the rocks so that Papa and his soldiers had to wait until it was dark to sneak up and surprise them.

Or the Scythians might have doubled back and ambushed the patrol. . . .

Ava shivered and rubbed her arms. Her embroidered coat was warm, but the wind had teeth. It cut through the leather and sheep's wool and made the ground under her as cold as a tomb. She stood and stamped her feet on the frozen earth. Spooky tombs weren't the best thing to think about, not if she and Kai had to spend the night alone in a creepy cave with spiders and who knew what else.

What if something had happened to Papa? What if he wasn't coming back? She couldn't just sit here until she turned into an icicle. With a sigh she rose to her feet, looked around, and saw nothing different from what she'd seen for the past hour. Her eyes ached. A light dusting of snow covered the ground, and the white glare hurt her eyes. She stretched, rolled her shoulders, and listened. Far overhead, a steppe eagle shrieked, but there was no whinny of horses, no male laughter, and no familiar shouts.

What had Kai heard? She hoped there wasn't a wolf skulking nearby. Or a bear . . . She had a bow and a knife, but she hadn't gotten strong enough to pull the man's bow that Alexander had given her. She was a good shot, but she didn't think she could kill a bear with a child's weapon. Resolved, Ava trudged back to where she'd left the gelding tied to a gnarled root. The snow was churned under Kai's feet, proving that it had been too long to leave him tied. The horse was probably as cold and stiff as she was.

Once, when she was little—no more than six—she

and Papa had come upon a flock of sheep frozen in the snow. Their eyes had been open, glazed and staring. She'd had nightmares about those creepy sheep for a long time. If she and Kai spent the night in the open, someone might discover them the same way, if the wolves didn't find them first.

She untied Kai, slipped her foot into the iron stirrup, and grabbed a handful of shaggy mane to help her scramble up into the saddle. She knew that the black gelding was big for her, much bigger than her dapple gray at home, but Kai's longer legs made it easier for the animal to keep up with the men's mounts. If she was going to spend the winter on the frontier, she couldn't ride a pony.

Ava wondered what to do about leaving a sign for her father, so that if he did arrive after she left, he'd know she hadn't panicked. But leaving something for him to find meant leaving a trail for an enemy to discover—provided there were still Scythians roaming inside the border. If it didn't snow, Papa could track her, but if the weather worsened . . . Making decisions was hard. Maybe her mother was right; maybe she did have a lot to learn to be a good general.

Ava was worried about her mother too. She knew that Papa and Mama had argued about the coming baby. Papa was afraid that having the child might kill her. Ava didn't think so. Her mother was strong, too strong to die from having a baby. Women had babies all the time. The nice commander's wife had nine children.

If the Scythians had killed her father . . . if they had . . . that loss might kill her mother. She might just lie down and never get up. Women did that in the old stories, just died of broken hearts when their lovers went away to war and never came back. Mama had taken it hard when Alexander had ridden off to claim his Egyptian bride, but she hadn't shed any tears. She never cried. Even Papa said that she was a strong woman. So worrying about her and the new baby was probably foolish. Ava had to think of what her mother would do if she were in a situation like this. Her mother was brave. Spending the night in a dark cave with spiders, even tigers or bears, would be easy for her.

But it was not so easy when you were only seven. Almost eight, she reminded herself. Almost eight and taller than the boys her age. Too big to be afraid of being alone—especially since she was a princess of the Twin Kingdoms. Her great-grandmother had been an Amazon. She'd have to remind herself of that when it started to get dark.

Ava found the shelter she was searching for just as the afternoon light was fading. The hole in the mountain wasn't much of a cave, but it had a rock overhang and solid stone on three sides. She'd almost missed it, but Kai had smelled the spring trickling out of a crack in the rocks only a few yards from the cave opening. A natural stone basin small enough to jump across held ice and a skim of liquid that hadn't yet frozen. There was just enough water to satisfy Kai and to fill Ava's goatskin bottle. The water was so cold that it made Ava's teeth ache, but it was sweet and refreshing. She drank and drank until her belly hurt.

The cave was high enough for Kai. If Ava tethered the horse at the back of the space, there was still room enough for her to roll up in her bearskin and to build a fire between her and the outside. They'd be warm and cozy. There was plenty of deadwood in the trees in front of the cave. Ashes on the floor proved that other people had camped here in the past. It was a good spot, and Papa would be proud of her for locating it.

It did take longer to start the fire than she'd expected. Most of the small tinder was damp, and she'd had to use her fire bow until blisters rose on the palms of her hands. It was with a cry of relief that she finally saw the first wisps of smoke, and—at last—tiny blue tongues of flame. She fed the twigs slowly, just as Mama had taught her, and in time she had a small but decent fire. She dragged in a branch too heavy to carry and banked her fire against that. Once the eight-inch log started to glow, it would burn all night and keep the wolves at bay.

Ava fed Kai a few handfuls of grain from her saddlebag and took out food for her own supper. Her eyes felt heavy, and although she was hungry, she kept nodding off. Any fears she had of being alone were soon lost in an overwhelming fatigue. She fell asleep with her uneaten bread and dried meat still in her hands.

She didn't know how long she'd slept. It was still dark, and flakes of snow were swirling though the cave opening and sizzling on the fire when she heard the unmistakable sounds of men and horses coming through the trees. She leaped up, still only half-awake, and dashed out into the icy night. "Papa!" she called. "Papa! I'm here!"

A shadowy figure laughed, dropped to his knees, and held out his big arms. It was too black to see her hand in front of her face, but Ava didn't hesitate. Crying out with joy, she leaped into the arms of the Scythian bandit.

Roxanne woke, certain that she'd heard Ava call her name. She sat bolt upright in the huge bed, waiting to see Kayan's broad shoulders fill the doorway, expecting a rush of dogs and a squealing seven-year-old hurling herself into the bed.

Nothing.

The room was icy; the central fire had burned low. "Kayan? Ava?" Roxanne called.

"My lady?" A maid stirred on her pallet. "Is anything wrong?"

"Did you hear voices? I thought perhaps . . ." Roxanne trailed off. Had she been dreaming? She pushed back the furs and crawled to the edge of the raised platform bed. The stone floor was too cold to walk barefoot on it, but she did anyway.

She walked through the antechamber to the shutters that closed off the balcony in winter. Pushing them open, she was nearly toppled by a blast of wind and frozen rain. Shivering, she shielded her eyes from the storm and gazed down onto the courtyard below.

No torches. No running servants. No laughter.

Kayan hadn't come home to her.

"My lady!" The maid settled a fur robe around Roxanne's shoulders. "You should not be out of bed, let alone standing in the cold. Are you ill? Has the bleeding started again?"

Roxanne shook her head. "No, no, I'm fine." But it was a lie. Although the pains that had troubled her over the past week hadn't returned, and there had been no show of blood for days, she wasn't fine. Her heart ached for Kayan and little Ava. And she couldn't shake the ominous shadow that hovered over her.

Something was wrong. Her husband or daughter had been hurt. Hurt or . . . She swallowed, trying to dissolve the lump that filled her throat. "Build up the fire," she said to the woman. "It's freezing in here." That was a lie as well. It wasn't her bedchamber that was cold; her icy dread was within.

"How did he die?" Kiara demanded. "Who murdered him?"

Tutu dropped the Greek sandal she was stitching and leaned close to whisper to her friend. "Everyone says that it was the great goddess Isis. They say Prince

GET UP TO 4 FREE BOOKS!

You can have the best romance delivered to your door for less than what you'd pay in a bookstore or online. Sign up for one of our book clubs today, and we'll send you **FREE* BOOKS** just for trying it out...with no obligation to buy, ever!

HISTORICAL ROMANCE BOOK CLUB

Travel from the Scottish Highlands to the American West, the decadent ballrooms of Regency England to Viking ships. Your shipments will include authors such as CONNIE MASON, SANDRA HILL, CASSIE EDWARDS, JENNIFER ASHLEY, LEIGH GREENWOOD, and many, many more.

LOVE SPELL BOOK CLUB

Bring a little magic into your life with the romances of Love Spell—fun contemporaries, paranormals, time-travels, futuristics, and more. Your shipments will include authors such as LYNSAY SANDS, CJ BARRY, COLLEEN THOMPSON, NINA BANGS, MARJORIE LIU and more.

As a book club member you also receive the following special benefits:

- **30% OFF all orders through our website & telecenter!**
- **Exclusive access to special discounts!**
- **Convenient home delivery and 10 day examination period to return any books you don't want to keep.**

There is no minimum number of books to buy, and you may cancel membership at any time. See back to sign up!

*Please include $2.00 for shipping and handling.

YES! ☐

Sign me up for the **Historical Romance Book Club** and send my TWO FREE BOOKS! If I choose to stay in the club, I will pay only $8.50* each month, a savings of $5.48!

YES! ☐

Sign me up for the **Love Spell Book Club** and send my TWO FREE BOOKS! If I choose to stay in the club, I will pay only $8.50* each month, a savings of $5.48!

NAME: _____

ADDRESS: _____

_____

TELEPHONE: _____

E-MAIL: _____

☐ **I WANT TO PAY BY CREDIT CARD.**

☐ VISA   ☐ MasterCard   ☐ DISCOVER

ACCOUNT #: _____

EXPIRATION DATE: _____

SIGNATURE: _____

Send this card along with $2.00 shipping & handling for each club you wish to join, to:

**Romance Book Clubs
20 Academy Street
Norwalk, CT 06850-4032**

Or fax (must include credit card information!) to: 610.995.9274. You can also sign up online at www.dorchesterpub.com.

*Plus $2.00 for shipping. Offer open to residents of the U.S. and Canada only. Canadian residents please call 1.800.481.9191 for pricing information.

If under 18, a parent or guardian must sign. Terms, prices and conditions subject to change. Subscription subject to acceptance. Dorchester Publishing reserves the right to reject any order or cancel any subscription.

JOIN NOW!

Alexander committed blasphemy in the inner sanctum and Iris burned him to a crisp."

"I don't believe that," Kiara said, folding the princess's linen shift and placing it carefully in a carved cedar box. The two were in one of the service rooms that lay between Artakama's laundry and the passageway that led to Mereret's apartments. "He was paying honor to Isis in having her bless his wedding. Why would he insult a goddess in her temple?"

"Princess Mereret told one of the eunuchs that the barbarian was arrogant, that he made improper advances to one of the priestesses."

"Even if he did, why did Pharaoh's archers attack Prince Alexander's cavalrymen? Surely they weren't guilty of blasphemy. They weren't even in the temple."

Tutu shrugged, picked up the silver lace, knotted the thread, and bit off the loose end. "There, that should hold." She placed the repaired sandal beside its mate. They were dainty, with delicate braided laces. Once she returned them to the princess's chambers, she would string precious stones on the cross ties. The penalty for removing jewels from the royal apartments was public whipping, and none of Mereret's slaves would dare to do so. "You needn't glare at me," Tutu scolded. "Look at the trouble he got you in. But I, for one, had nothing against him. He was . . ." She rolled her eyes suggestively. "He was a magnificent man. His spear was—"

"Spare me," Kiara said. She turned her back to Tutu and shook out another garment. Her vision blurred as moisture pooled in her eyes. Disappointment washed over her. It was her own fault. It was too late for hope. She was trapped here; she was a slave, and she'd remain a slave until she lured some guest into making her his concubine or died of old age. She'd been a fool to think that the barbarian might be a way out of Egypt.

"You were with him. Can you deny that he was hung like—"

"Be quiet, or I'll slap you silly," Kiara threatened. "Do you think of nothing but the size of a man's shaft?"

"No." Tutu grinned. "I think of how skilled he is with it. I've slept with small men who could put the giants to shame, but the barbarian wasn't one of those. He wanted to please me."

"Then perhaps he left you something to remember him by."

"No. No chance of that." The Egyptian girl fanned herself. "It's hot in here, isn't it?" She sighed. "Our mistress may be with child, but not me. He pulled it out before he spilled his seed."

Kiara shook out another of the princess's tunics and began to fold the multiple pleats in the material. "Are you certain that Prince Alexander is the father?"

"Shh! Are you mad? You could get your tongue cut off talking like that." She peeked around the corner. "Someone's coming." Tutu grabbed up one of the sandals and pretended to fix a strap.

"What's taking you lazy sluts so long?" Hekhummut dropped a basket of royal laundry in front of Kiara.

She nodded, but said nothing. Hekhummut was a slim, effeminate eunuch with an elaborate wig and artfully painted eyes. Her dislike of the man was returned. He hadn't made any attempt to hide the fact that he was pleased she was in disfavor with the princess and had been assigned demeaning tasks.

"Her highness says that you should have returned with her dresses an hour ago." He folded his arms over his thin chest. "Kiara, she wants you to fetch licorice root from the kitchen."

Kiara's eyes widened. "Licorice root?"

"You heard me." Heckummut smirked. "She has cramps."

"Not the onset of her moon's courses?" Tutu said. "She shouldn't—"

Hekhummut flicked aside the covering on the basket, revealing bloodstained clouts. "I believe I know the red tide when I see it, even in royalty."

Tutu gasped and covered her mouth with her fingertips. "The princess has suffered a miscarriage," she murmured.

Hekhummut sniffed. "If you say so. If she was ever pregnant in the first place. She hardly had time, considering how long her bridegroom had been in Alexandria."

"You were at the temple, weren't you?" Kiara asked. "Did you see what happened?"

"What I saw or didn't see is none of your affair, bitch. What's wrong? Didn't the two of you get enough of him?"

Kiara picked up the basket of dirty linen. "I'll take these to the laundry."

Hekhummut shook his head. "The princess was quite specific. She said she wanted you to fetch the licorice, and then you are to wash her clouts. Personally."

Kiara inclined her head in the slightest acknowledgment of submission. "Yes, Hekhummut. Whatever you say."

He smiled. "That's better. Curb your tongue and show the proper respect, and I may even suggest that you be part of the funeral procession."

"Procession?" Tutu asked. "They will give Prince Alexander the proper funeral rites? But he will be ninety days in the House of the Dead, preparing the body."

"What body?" Hekhummut chuckled. "Isis consumed

155

him in fire, remember?" He spread his hands, palms up. "She wasn't very efficient. The goddess, I mean. I saw his body being carried into the tunnels under the temple. Whatever's left, they're ferrying it across the Nile tomorrow."

"Tomorrow?" Tutu's mouth gaped. "But there's been no time for the priests—"

"He's a barbarian," Hekhummut replied sarcastically. "There will be no afterlife for him, so they will bury him as he is."

"But his body will decay," Tutu protested. "He will rot and his *ka* will—"

"Will rot with him, I suppose," Hekhummut finished. "And if you aren't careful, you may come to the same end. Her majesty's entire staff will be part of the entourage. Wouldn't it just be awful if she decided to seal the two of you up in the tomb with him? So that he wouldn't be all alone when the scarab beetles begin to devour his stinking corpse."

Chapter 13

Alexander awoke in darkness. *No, not dark,* he thought, *this is absolute blackness.* His muscles were stiff, as though he'd lain without moving for a long time. The surface beneath him was hard. Tentatively he felt with the fingers of his left hand. Stone. He tried to sit up, but he was so dizzy that he gave up after the second attempt.

He listened. Silence as deep as the black void around him. He wondered if this was death. No Kingdom of the Lie, no monsters tearing his flesh from his bones, no icy stretches of nothingness. Utter and complete lack of sound.

Fear skittered like ants beneath the surface of his skin. He drew a deep breath and forced himself to a sitting position. His head throbbed. He touched the tender swelling at the back of his skull and felt crystals of dried blood on his fingertips.

Where was he? Nausea gripped him. He leaned over and retched, but little came up. He felt hollow inside.

For an instant he considered the possibility that whatever injury he had suffered had left him sightless.

Blind.

What future could there be for a blind king? Bitter amusement grated from his raw throat. He might as well have asked, What future could there be for a dead man? But was he blind? Priests had told him that the wicked would suffer through eternity for their foul deeds on earth. If he had died, been judged by the Wise God, Ahura Mazda, and been consigned to Ahriman's domain, why was it only his head and stomach that hurt? Shouldn't the soles of his feet and the palms of his hands be rotting?

What was the last thing he remembered? Images swirled through his mind. A flute. He could remember a flute. And a man. Ptolemy. His uncle. A procession. Glaring sun on the sand. No, not the sand, the streets of Alexandria. Sand, definitely sand . . . and the unmistakable outline of three huge stone triangles that blotted out the sky.

His wedding day. Steps. He definitely remembered walking up marble steps. And the sound of water, not a fountain. He could remember the scents of a large body of river. Sounds . . . crowds cheering and, oddest of all, the rhythmic chant of galley slaves, those men chained to their oars and condemned to row until they drew their last breath.

Alexander retched again. His mouth tasted as bitter as death. Maybe he was dead. Any moment Ahriman or his legions of demons would come to lead him to the torture fields. But the cold stone slab under him had the feel of reality. And he was thirsty. Parched. His lips were cracked, his tongue swollen.

An image lingered in the far corner of his mind. Something hard was prying his mouth open. Not something . . . someone. Hands pinning his shoulders down. A cold rim against his mouth and bitter liquid burning a path down his throat. Poison? Had he been poisoned?

Too many questions and no answers. He felt for the floor with his right foot. Nothing. He rolled onto his stomach and lowered himself down, reaching. When he could find no bottom, he pushed off and dropped, expecting to tumble, perhaps forever, in this thick, clinging blackness.

A solid floor waited below. Too weak to stand, Alexander slammed forward and landed on his hands and knees. He felt the surface and found more stone. He reached back to find what he'd been lying on and encountered a wall carved with Egyptian symbols. Hawk. Ankh. Writing. He skimmed his scraped fingertips across the broad surface. He could speak the language of the Egyptians well enough, but his knowledge of their writing wasn't good enough to translate this inscription in the dark.

Alexander found the end of the structure, rounded the corner, then paced off the distance of the rectangle—roughly five feet by ten. He persevered, searching the surface of the way until he returned to the hawk followed by the ankh. Then he rested his back against the stone and slid down to the floor.

The truth dawned with the clarity of sunrise. This was a tomb. And, dead or not, he had been buried.

Ptolemy and Artakama reclined on facing couches on the top deck of the queen's barge. A purple-fringed awning shielded the royal party from the direct rays of the sun. The side curtains were white linen, transparent enough so that the passengers could watch the banks of the Nile slide by and those on the shore could catch glimpses of their god-king and his chief Egyptian wife. Harp music drifted from the main deck below in an attempt to muffle the song-chants of the slaves who manned the great oars. But the outpouring of human misery could not be drowned any more than the perfumed oils on Ptolemy's skin could overpower the earthy scents of the tilled fields, marsh, and the river teeming with fish.

"Admit it," Ptolemy said, looking up and tossing aside a scroll containing blueprints for an extension to his library. "Leaving him there was a stroke of genius. I'm well rid of my brother's brat without staining my hands with his blood, and I can claim the Twin Kingdoms as the rightful inheritance of my grandson, Alexander's heir."

"It was genius." Artakama nibbled at a sweetened date. "If you are judged by Osiris himself, you are innocent of murder. Or . . ." She licked the last drop of honey from her index finger. "Innocent of your nephew's death, at least."

He regarded her for several moments before reaching for his wine cup. He inhaled and savored the aroma. He was quite fond of his peppery wine; it had come from a small holding near Corinth. He must remind his steward to order more of it for his personal consumption. "Mereret conducted herself with dignity during the ordeal," he said. "I'm pleased with her."

"She will be glad to hear it. Poor child, to be widowed so young." Artakama smiled. "What will become of her?"

"After Alexander's son is born and acknowledged, I will marry her to young 'Toly. That will assure her place on the throne when we are gone and will make up for his weakness of character."

"What if the child is female?"

Ptolemy shook his head. "No, a girl will not do. He must be male to contest the rights of Roxanne's daughters. A boy, blond, half-Greek, and light-eyed, so that there can be no doubt as to his parentage."

"Pharaoh is god on earth. Surely you can intercede with holy Taweret, goddess of childbirth, to insure the sex of your grandson."

He scoffed. "If I could do that, my dear, do you think my palace would be filled with worthless girl children? I would have a legion of sons, so that I wouldn't have to concern myself with protecting Toly's succession."

"Then I shall add my prayers to yours."

"And that will ensure that Mereret delivers a healthy boy?"

She reached for another date. "Of course, my lord. You have my word on it."

"Excellent. I knew that I could depend on you."

"Always."

He smiled at her. "We really suit each other very well, Artakama. A pity you never gave me a son."

She inclined her head. "Sons are greatly overrated. They rarely live up to a father's expectations. Daughters who carry the blood of the pharaohs are more valuable. They tend to survive infancy, make fewer enemies, and never quarrel with their sires."

He wondered what Artakama was plotting now, and if it was in his best interest. "I would take it amiss if anything happened to 'Toly."

She blinked. Her eyes were very dark. Whenever he looked into them, he had the feeling that she knew secrets she would never share. Perhaps it was why she still fascinated him after so many years together.

"Why tell me this, husband? Have I not always supported you and yours?"

She was good, very, very good. But the expression of shocked innocence smacked of falsehood. "I'm serious," he warned. "You have the best of all worlds. You do as you please, and you have my power to enforce your own. But if 'Toly should come to harm, if he should be bitten by a mosquito and fall ill or if he should accidentally step into the path of a chariot—if he suffers the slightest hurt, I will hold you and yours accountable."

"Yes, my lord." She smiled guilelessly and handed him a bunch of dewy purple grapes, large and bursting with flavor. "I shall pray for 'Toly's health every day . . . as I pray for yours."

"Good." He drained the last drop of wine. "It's what I love best about you, my dear. You are a woman of intelligence and reason."

"Mother!" Mereret called from the deck below. "Mother, I must speak with you."

"Come, daughter," Ptolemy called. "Join us."

Mereret pushed through the curtains and dropped onto her mother's couch. She wore a linen kilt, gilded sandals, and more pearls than he would have believed she could carry and still walk upright. Her belly, he noticed, was flat and taut. "I am most annoyed," she cried. "One of my slaves is gone. She was with us when we left the pyramid, and now she is missing."

"You've lost a maid?" Ptolemy asked. "Don't upset yourself. This is a stressful time for you, what with losing your husband so soon after your wedding ceremony. I'm certain the wench will turn up. Likely as not, she's below in the galley, stuffing her mouth with my delicacies."

"No," Mereret replied. "I've ordered the barge searched. The fool has run away. She was with us just before we boarded but no one has seen her since."

"Nonsense," Artakama chided. "Where would she go? There is nothing but desert and the village for the guardians. There's nowhere to hide. Any of the guards or their families would turn her in for the reward. She could not be stupid enough to wander off into the desert."

"She would be. She is nothing but a troublemaker. May she die of thirst and be devoured by jackals! The crazy slut. She favored him. My bridegroom. It would have served her right if we'd shut her up with his corpse."

Artakama glanced at Ptolemy questioningly. He shook his head. He didn't mind if his wife knew that his nephew had been still alive when the stone blocks were cemented in place. But Mereret was young, and he didn't know if she was as cunning as her mother. She might repeat what should never be suggested. His brother's son had been struck dead by the goddess Isis at the temple, and that was the end of it. "I'll give you another slave," he soothed.

"Wise, my husband," Artakama said, "For her maids have seen too much, and maids chatter."

Ptolemy nodded. His wife was right. Mereret's servants would have to die, and so would all those who'd entered the pyramid with Alexander. But not his precious daughter. "Do nothing to harm your health, Mereret," he reminded her. "That is a precious child you carry beneath your heart. He holds the key to the Twin Kingdoms."

"Thank you, Father." Mereret dabbed at her eyes. "I shall try to remember to take better care of myself."

"Daughter?" He fixed her with an intent gaze. "Are you certain that you are with child?"

She averted her eyes for an instant before meeting his. "Is it your will that I carry Prince Alexander's son?"

"It is," he said, glancing back at Artakama. Her smooth expression told him what he had suspected all along: Mereret had not been pregnant, or had been and had slipped the child.

Mereret smiled at him and reached for a grape. "With your blessing, my son will be a great consolation to me in my grief and a credit to you."

Artakama knelt on the rug, took his hand, and pressed it against her cheek. "Your will in all things, immortal pharaoh of the Two Lands."

He nodded. Perhaps it was better this way, he thought. His brother's ghost could not haunt him, he was rid of Alexander, and the fair-haired, male infant that Artakama would provide and pass off as Mereret's, eight months from now, would ensure the continuation of his dynasty.

"Say that you are not angry with us," Artakama begged.

Ptolemy chuckled, leaned over, and kissed the crown of his wife's head. "We understand each other," he murmured. "I have what I want, and you have your daughter." He smiled at Mereret. She really was very beautiful and very young. In time, she might be more enticing than her mother.

Shivering, Kiara leaned against the rough stone of the pyramid and prayed for courage. The desert was cold and she was lightly dressed. A keening night wind drove grains of sand like needles against her bare skin, skin already blistered by sun and scoured by sand. Far off, a jackal or some crazed spirit cackled an eerie laugh. Closer, an animal grunted and snuffled in the darkness. A village cur, she told herself, a mangy dog made of flesh and bone, not the materialization of a nightmare.

Her heart hammered; each breath was a conscious effort. For the hundredth time, she wondered if she'd committed suicide by this foolhardy attempt. Prince Alexander had been alive when they'd laid his drugged body on top of the stone crypt of a long-dead princess. She'd heard him groan and seen his chest rising and falling as he sucked in the fetid air. They had not sealed him in the king's chamber or even the grand gallery. Instead, the soldiers had carried him to a small antechamber, the final resting place of the little daughter of one of the great pharaoh's foreign wives, a child dead for so many years that her coffin must contain only beads and dust.

Kiara, Tutu, and ten of Princess Mereret's slave girls had followed the royal procession from the landing place of the royal barge to the pyramid closest to the Sphinx, the half-lion, half-man that guarded the tombs of the old ones. Ptolemy and Queen Artakama had not entered the tomb; they'd waited outside under a canopy while the priests, Pharaoh's eunuch, and a score of Greek household guards had escorted Princess Mereret and her ladies inside.

The torchlit procession had entered the Sphinx through a hidden doorway that led to a series of chambers and finally to a passageway beneath the pyramid. The corridor was so low that the Athenians carrying Prince Alexander's litter had to bow their heads as the tunnel twisted and turned back on itself like a labyrinth.

There were false hallways running off the true path. Kiara had heard the chief eunuch telling Princess Mereret that her women must not wander; some passages had deep pits that opened abruptly in the floor; some grew smaller and smaller until even a child couldn't squeeze through, while a few contained poisoned spikes, set into the mortar when the pyramid was built. Kiara supposed that the poison might have dissipated over the years, but she couldn't be certain. The air in the tunnel was stifling, still and heavy as death, but worse than the air quality was the absolute silence.

Tutu and the rest of Mereret's waiting women had been near hysteria, weeping bitterly as they skittered along, afraid that the princess meant to entomb them with the hapless bridegroom. Mereret had laughed and taunted them, seeming to enjoy the afternoon's entertainment. "It's a fit ending, is it not?" the princess had asked. "For a hill savage who thought to claim the hand of Pharaoh's daughter?"

Kiara hadn't shared the other girls' fear. Death had long since ceased to hold terror for her. Even now, on the evening of the third day since her escape, her anxiety was not at the thought of dying but that she might fail.

Long ago, when she was a young child, Kiara had watched her beloved mother Taillte pass from this life into the next on the morning of Cian's birth. Her mother's courage had not wavered, though blood had rushed out of her body with the infant, soaking the bedclothes and sheets and running onto the floor. "Dying is not hard," she'd murmured to Kiara with her last breath. "Living is what tests the soul." Try as she might, Kiara could no longer remember her mother's face, only the rays of sunlight coming through the window and gleaming on the strands of her red-gold hair.

Kiara took a deep breath and pushed away the memories of her mother. She could not linger in the past; she would lose heart and lack the strength to do what she must. Besides, if the guard did not return with a torch and a container of water, Kiara knew that she had no chance. If Sethos betrayed her for the reward paid for runaway slaves, all was lost. Everything rested on the honor of an uneducated man born to the clan of Guardians of the Dead, whom she had known only briefly.

Sethos risked more than she did. If she were caught,

she would die; if he were caught, he and all his family would be buried alive—not in a stone tomb, but in the sand. "We will be forced to dig a pit twice as deep as a man's height," Sethos had told her. "Soldiers will smash our legs and arms with axes, and we will be cast into the hole. Then Pharaoh's men will heap sand on us until the last infant's scream has been muffled forever by the desert."

Kiara wondered if the evil she had committed in begging Sethos's help was greater than that of allowing Prince Alexander to die slowly in the crypt. Perhaps it was, but maybe they wouldn't be caught. It was possible that she could retrace her steps and lead the prince from his silent prison.

If he wasn't already dead . . .

And even if he was alive, would she be able to lead them both safely back along the true route out of the chambers beneath the Sphinx? Sturdy Sethos of the one ear and mutilated hand had absolutely refused to set foot inside the pyramid.

"The pyramid is protected by a powerful curse," he told her. "You are a foreigner and a slave." He shrugged shoulders burned black by the relentless sun. "I would be struck deaf, dumb, and blind, and my *ba* would be forever cursed to be ripped apart by vultures, day after day into eternity. No, I cannot enter. No bribe on earth could tempt me—not even Pharaoh's double crown."

If she were Sethos, she would have been afraid, too.

The jackal-ghost howled again. Gooseflesh rose on her arms. If she had to die, she could think of many ways less painful than being ripped apart by the teeth of a beast, living or spirit. She hugged herself and drew her knees up close to her body.

Why hadn't she done what Tutu and the others had

done—walked away out of the crypt into the light? They had followed their mistress onto the royal barge and back to the palace. How many slaves would trade their lot in life for hers? Why couldn't she be content with what she had?

The horse fell on the second day. Kayan felt him stumble, and he kicked his feet free of the stirrups and jumped before the stallion went down. Kayan rolled and scrambled up. Shirzad lay on his side, neck and belly streaked with sweat, nostrils flared, eyes bloodshot with exhaustion. Veins bulged out on the horse's neck as he flailed his head in a vain attempt to rise.

"Koo, koo," Kayan murmured. He crouched beside the big chestnut, stroking his throat and head and feeling the front legs for broken bones. When he could find so sign of permanent damage, Kayan unfastened the saddle and slipped it off. Using the blanket, he rubbed Shirzad's shaggy hide until his winter coat stood up in small, clumpy tufts. Kayan tried to coax the horse to his feet, but Shirzad only groaned and lay stretched on the dry earth.

"Poor boy, I've misused you, haven't I?" Kayan stood, shielded his eyes, and scanned the horizon. Nothing. As far as he could see, there was nothing between him and the distant line of blue mountains but a sea of waving grass. He'd outridden his troop just after nightfall. They would follow; he could depend on it, but he didn't know how many hours he was ahead of them.

He cursed his impatience. Riding as though the devils of Ahriman pursued him had gained him little. The Scythian war party was still somewhere ahead, and Ava, his precious treasure—if she were still alive—was with them. He should have waited, should have stopped to rest his horse, and should never have left Ava alone while he pursued the bandits. He'd believed she'd be safer there, but the first band had joined up with a second, and the running fight had taken them hours and miles from where his little daughter waited.

Waited in vain for him to come . . . waited until the jackals discovered her hiding place . . .

"No!" He knotted both fists, dropped to his knees, and pounded against the frozen ground until his knuckles bled. "I should never have taken her from her mother's side!"

Despair settled onto his shoulders as he imagined the terrible ways that a helpless child could die at the hands of Scythians. Scum of the earth! Flesh-eating savages! Ava could be buried alive, raped, or butchered and left for the vultures. She might be dragged back to the main camp and offered up as a sacrifice to Papai, their bloodthirsty god of war. He could hear her weeping, hear her calling, *Papa! Papa! Help me!*

He'd failed her. It was his job to protect his wife and his children, and he'd failed them all.

Why? Because Roxanne had refused to abort their unborn babe? Had he lost Ava because of his own stubbornness and refusal to forgive his wife's desire to give him a son? Was this his punishment for loving too much? For being so afraid of losing the woman he loved more than his god that he would order her to destroy the babe created of their blood and bone?

Rage seeped away as Kayan collapsed, sagging forward until his head touched the cold earth. If he had been judged by the Wise God and found wanting, so be it. He would gladly pay for his sin. "A life for a life," he grated. "But mine. Mine, do you hear! Not Ava's!"

Tears clouded his eyes as he got to his feet. "I'll get her back," he swore. "If I have to follow her out of this world and into the next. I will get her back! And if . . . if the worst has happened, I'll not rest until Scythian blood runs like a river across these accursed steppes."

A snort and a shove yanked him back from the brink of madness. He turned to see Shirzad standing behind him, nudging him and nickering anxiously. The chestnut was trembling, his legs wobbly, but he was up and his breathing rasped deep and regular.

"All right, all right." Kayan embraced the horse's head and kissed the white patch on his forehead. Taking hold of the dangling leathers, he began to slowly walk the animal in a large circle. "Easy, now, easy, boy."

Shirzad limped. His right front hoof was cracked, but otherwise the fall seemed to have done the horse no harm. He was just tired, bone tired. "Good boy."

Kayan found the water bag on the discarded saddle, opening the mouth wide enough to allow the stallion to thrust his muzzle in and drink. "Slowly," Kayan said. "Slowly. Not too much." From another skin, he removed handfuls of dry bread mixed with berries and fed it to Shirzad.

When the stallion's coat had dried enough so that he wouldn't take a chill and stiffen up, Kayan removed the bridle and turned him loose. "You'll have to find your own way home," he said. "Keep a sharp eye out for wolves, and watch for thin ice crossing the rivers."

Giving Shirzad a final embrace, Kayan slapped the reins across the horse's rump. "Go home!" he shouted. He turned with moisture glistening in his eyes, gathered his weapons and the saddle blanket, and set off on foot, following the trail that the raiding party had left in the grass.

Chapter 14

Alexander made his way around the four walls of the tomb for the twentieth time . . . or was it the fiftieth? His fingertips were raw from running them over the stone blocks, and the dust made him cough until he choked up what little fluid remained in his body. For a time he'd wondered if he might lose all reason and end his life howling like a trapped jackal, but then a sense of acceptance settled over him.

All men faced death. Sometimes the veiled rider on the black horse was kind, and for others his face was terrible. Alexander didn't want to die. He had too much to accomplish, too many promises to fulfill. But what mattered most to a man was not the dying but how he met his end—with courage or cowardice.

Most of all, Alexander was reluctant to face final judgment as a fool. Better to have a multitude of sins to atone for. Not that he didn't; he was no holy man or mystic. The deaths of many good men weighed on his soul. A few of those lives he regretted taking, but given the chance, he would make the same decisions.

He had not used his time on earth wisely, and he regretted the waste. He was twenty-seven. His sire had conquered the known world from Greece to India before he died at thirty-one. And what had Alexander done to equal his father's deeds? He'd not won his kingdom with his sword; he would have been handed his crown by his mother and Kayan. He'd leave grieving parents and a country divided, defended by an aging prince and the brave daughters of an ancient race of Amazons. He'd been too arrogant to heed his mother's warning or that of Paris. He'd been certain he could outwit Ptolemy and win the hand of the Egyptian princess, but the old fox had had the last laugh.

Hunger gnawed at Alexander's belly, and thirst plagued him more than the Stygian darkness. He'd never been afraid of the dark. The two things he feared most were being trapped in a confined area and disappointing those he loved most. Those fears tormented him now.

He still had his weapons: a sword, a knife, his bow, and a quiver of arrows. Small use when there was no enemy to fight. Had it been Ptolemy's final joke, to bury him in a king's tomb with rings on his fingers, armbands, and a collar studded with precious gems? At least, he thought they were real stones. Daylight might reveal paste gems and base metal instead of gold, but Alexander doubted it. Ptolemy might be many things, but he doubted if his uncle were tight-fisted, even with the dead.

If he'd been conscious when he'd been brought here, then he'd have some idea where the tomb entrance was. He didn't know if he was aboveground or below, but he had the feeling of some great mass pressing down on him. If he couldn't find the entrance, nothing else would matter. He wished he'd made love to the green-eyed woman. He wished he'd gone back to hug his mother one last time before he rode out. He wished . . .

"Have you given up?" an amused male voice asked.

Alexander reeled. "Who's there?"

Silence.

He inhaled sharply. This was no trick of his mind. He felt in the dark space around him. Whoever had spoken had been standing within arm's length. "Who is it?" he demanded. "Identify yourself."

The voice had been that of young man in his prime, an educated man. And he'd spoken in Greek. Not simply Greek, Alexander corrected himself, courtly Greek with an unmistakable Macedonian accent.

"Are you one of Ptolemy's guards?" Alexander peered into the black void. "If you've come to finish the job . . ."

Laughter. Faint. And a spark of light near the stone coffin. Alexander blinked and shielded his eyes. A glittering ball no larger than the pad of a man's thumb hovered there. Alexander's breath lodged in his throat as the light grew larger and brighter. He found the hilt of his sword and drew it from the sheath at his waist.

"Come then," he shouted as a frisson of energy sizzled from his fingertips to the soles of his feet. "Show your face, demon!" He charged, piercing unearthly light with the point of his blade and then drawing the sword back to deliver a slashing overhand blow.

The light shattered into a thousand tiny grains of iridescence, showering him like falling stars. Again the laughter came, not mocking, but affectionate. *"A wise man once told me that the gods favor those who risk all. Tell your mother that. And tell her that I'll never stop waiting. She was the greatest prize I never conquered. . . ."*

Alexander swung again. The stars blinked out, one

by one, and the air in the tomb seemed to grow less heavy. "Who are you?" he called again, but there was no answer. Swearing softly, he sheathed his sword.

For the better part of an hour he crouched, listening and watching. And then, once again, he began methodically to trace the cracks around the stones that made up the four walls.

Ava closed her eyes and crouched low with her hands over her head, shielding herself from the blows. Loud curses flew from the woman's mouth in a spray of spittle. The boy laughed and kicked Ava hard. It hurt, but she refused to cry. Instead she rocked back and forth and began to mouth the words to a song she'd heard Mama's Scythian stable boy sing when he was sad.

> *I am the arrow shot from a bow,*
> *I am the wind across the steppes,*
> *I am the cold star burning bright,*
> *I am the horse beneath the warrior,*
> *I am the favored wolf child of Papai."*

Then something strange happened. The woman called Api broke off her tirade and stopped hitting her. Ava didn't know what to do, so she began the song again. The boy muttered. She didn't know his name, didn't want to. She couldn't understand his heavily accented words, but he sounded confused, almost afraid.

"Aiyee!" Api cried.

Another woman moaned.

Ava kept singing. Jumping into the Scythian's arms when she'd expected her father had been bad. The long day's riding without anything to eat but half-raw horsemeat and sour water was worse. Her captor, Ish, the man she soon realized was the leader of the raiding party, terrified her, but other than a few slaps and kicks, he'd not hurt her.

At first Ish had bound her wrists with strips of leather and made her run beside his horse. Later, when she couldn't keep up, he'd put her on a spare horse and tied her ankles together under the animal's belly. At night he'd slipped a loop around her neck and tied it to his wrist so that she couldn't move without his knowing. If she hadn't known a few words of Scythian, she was certain he would have killed her. The man had no patience. If she didn't do what he said immediately, he'd hit her or yank her by the hair.

Her captor was a little man, compared to her father, but very strong and hairy. Ish was what Shahi would call swarthy, but Ava couldn't tell if he was really dark-skinned or if he was just dirty. In her time among the Scythians, she'd never seen anyone bathe. Ish wore a gold disk earring in one ear, a colorless leather cap pulled down over his greasy, braided hair, and leather pants that smelled worse than the palace midden. His soft boots had once been red but were so stained and dirty that you could hardly see the pattern of horses stitched in the leather. She hated his boots because the pointed toes turned up and really hurt when he kicked her.

There had been other prisoners, two women. At night the Scythians would take turns with them. Ava covered her ears so she couldn't hear their cries. When the women died, Ava had been afraid that the men would do the same to her, but Ish wouldn't allow anyone to touch her. She obeyed him, but she hadn't said a word to him or to any of them. She prayed to the Wise God that her father was alive and well and that he would come with his soldiers and kill these bad people.

The days melted one into another. She'd thought

175

they would never stop riding, but finally they'd reached the camp. She'd seen Scythians before, but never so many in one place. There were two huge herds of horses and another of cattle. She couldn't count the wagons because they weren't arranged in any order, just scattered on both sides of the muddy river. Ish had given her to Api, and Ava understood when he'd said the word *slave,* but whether she was Ish's slave or his woman's, she didn't know.

Api had taken one look at her and started shouting. She'd torn off Ava's heavy coat, punched and kicked her and tied her by the neck to one of the high wheels of their wagon-houses. It had rained that night, and Ava was so cold that she couldn't sleep. Ish had come back to the wagon staggering with drink and had yelled at his wife. Soon after, Api had thrown a skin blanket over the edge of the wagon. The covering had holes in it and smelled nasty. Fleas and lice crawled in her hair, but Ava had been freezing. She'd kicked aside the dogs, wrapped herself in the filthy covering, and endured the night.

This morning, Api, a short, dirty woman with bad breath and greasy hair, had untied her, grabbed her by one pigtail, and led her to the river. "Water," she shouted, as though Ava were stupid or deaf. "Water . . . carry . . . you!" It sounded like "water crazy," but the motions Api was making seemed to mean that Ava should bring water to the wagon.

It wasn't as easy as it sounded. The banks were muddy and the current swift. If it had been summer, she might have considered jumping in and trying to escape, but the water was too cold. Her heavy clothing would pull her down, and she could never remain in the river long enough to get away without freezing to death.

She'd dipped up a bucket full of water and carried it through the obstacles of hostile people, mean dogs, and unruly horses to Api's wagon, but before she could give it to the woman, the boy had run out and kicked the bucket over. Api stuck her head out of the wagon, saw the spilled water, and started screaming. And that was when Ava had curled up and begun the stable boy's wolf song.

People began to gather around them. Ava fell silent. Api continued to mutter, and Ava heard the word *demon* and something about fire. She opened one eye, just a slit, and saw Ish striding through the knot of on-lookers. He asked Api a question. Her answer was too garbled for Ava to understand, but then Ish slapped her. The woman scrambled up into her wagon-tent and threw Ava's embroidered coat into the mud.

Ava got to her feet, picked up the coat, and with as much dignity as she could muster, put it on. Ish shouted at her. She raised her head so that her gaze met his. She didn't glare at him, tried not to look frightened, tried not to show any emotion at all.

"Come with me," he said.

Grabbing her coat sleeve, he pulled her along through the wagons. Dogs barked, jeering boys ran after them, curious round faces peered from wagons as they passed. Ava had to half run to keep up with Ish's bowlegged stride. They kept going until they reached a large rounded tent.

This wagon-house was on wheels too, but it was much bigger and more brightly colored than the other huts. Several men sat cross-legged on the ground, gambling beside a pole. Attached to the top of the pole were three horsetails, and on the top, a stuffed bear head. Ish spoke to the men. Ava knew he was talking about her and the song, but she couldn't follow everything he was saying.

Ish shoved her down, pointed to the ground. "Stay. This." He climbed into the wagon.

Ava folded her arms and squatted on her heels. It

was as muddy here as in the rest of the camp, and she didn't want to get her trousers any wetter than they were already. Her fleabites itched, but she wasn't going to scratch them here in view of half the camp, so she tried not to think about them. She smelled cooking meat, and her stomach growled. She'd drunk her fill at the river, but she was hungry. She couldn't remember when she'd last eaten.

Several women passed in and out of the house, one carrying a baby in a sling. They were younger and prettier than Api, but although their long hair was secured with silver pins and they wore gold jewelry, they still smelled of horse pee. A pregnant woman strolled by leading a light-haired boy, no more than four or five. His boots were green and he wore a tiny knife on a thong around his neck. The boy was chewing a round of flat-bread. He stopped, stared at Ava, and took another bite.

The mother looked at Ava for a moment, then removed another piece of bread from her pocket and held it out. Ava hesitated. "Take it," the woman said. "Eat. Good." She said more, but the rest didn't matter.

Ava took the bread and nodded her thanks. She knew the words for *thank you* but she wasn't willing to let her enemy know that she understood the language. The bread was coarse and unsweetened, but she devoured it to the last crumb and licked her fingers.

After a long time, Ish came out of the wagon with two other men. One of them had a gray beard; his skin was the color of tanned leather, and his dark eyes were nearly hidden in wrinkles. He wore clothing much like Ish's, but had a green stone on a necklace. He motioned for her to stand and turn around.

Ava did as he wanted. She kept her eyes down and tried not to show how afraid she was.

"Do it again," Ish urged. "Sing the song you sang before."

178

Ava gritted her teeth.

Ish gave her a shove. "Sing!"

The third man shook his head. He stepped between them and crouched. He was a giant with cold blue eyes, a shaved head except for a braided scalp lock that hung nearly to his waist, and a long yellow mustache and stringy beard. He'd twisted the mustache into curling horns like those on a bull and waxed them so that they stood out on either side of his mouth. A knotted scar ran from his left temple, dividing one eyebrow and slicing across his lumpy nose. The blue-eyed man wore a different style of leather clothing, higher boots with tassels that didn't curl up at the toes, and a curved saber in a wolfskin sheath.

"Sing," he ordered in a low, raspy voice.

Ava took a deep breath, sang the song once from beginning to end, and then clamped her lips together. She didn't like this blue-eyed man; despite being younger and cleaner than the other two, he made chills run up and down her spine. She wished she were back under Api's wagon, even if the dogs did growl at her. She had to pee, her bites were itching fiercely, and she was afraid that she was going to cry.

The stranger tribesman held up three fingers.

Ish shook his head. "Ten horses."

"Six."

"Nine."

"Seven and an ox."

Ish nodded, and the two clasped their right hands together. Ava looked from one to the other uncertainly.

"Go with him," Ish said. When she didn't move, Ish said, "She doesn't understand."

"She understands, all right," the stranger said. He slapped himself on the chest and pointed at her. "Targitaos," he repeated. "You belong to Targitaos."

Ava closed her eyes. She'd been sold for seven

horses and an ox. And if this scary Scythian took her away from Ish's camp, how would her father know where to look for her?

Kiara smelled the Egyptian before she caught sight of the bobbing torch. Still, it was all she could do not to cry out as the flickering light distorted his features. "Sethos?"

"Who else would be fool enough to come out here after dark? This place is haunted by the spirits of the dead." He flattened himself against the stone and tried to shelter the flame from the wind. "There is this one and another, unlit. You must make them last or you'll never find your way out."

"Yes." She nodded.

He leaned the empty torch against the wall and groped at her breast. "I'm risking much for you. You should—"

"No." She slapped his hand away. "You've already been paid."

He grabbed a handful of her hair, pulled her face close to his, and ground his mouth against hers. His breath stank, and her gorge rose as he tried to force his foul tongue between her teeth.

"No," she repeated. "We had a bargain. Where's my water?"

"I could still turn you in."

"Not without killing me. I'll tell the others you kidnapped me, held me against my will."

"No one would believe you, slut."

"Are you certain of that, Sethos? I'm a valuable slave. My princess might believe me and order you thrown to the crocodiles."

"You'd be punished too."

"I'd be beaten. You'd be dinner."

He shoved a sloshing water bag at her. "Go on, then.

You'll end up as dead as he is. Once the spirits claim a soul, they never release it."

"Then you'd best run back to your bed, hadn't you, Sethos?" she said as she slipped the strap on the bag over her shoulder. "Before they decide they want you, as well."

"I should leave you here."

"Lead me to the door!"

Cursing, he turned and walked along the edge of the monument for about twenty feet, then felt along the wall. When a hidden slab opened, he stood aside and made the two-fingered sign of protection against a witch. "Your death is not on my head," he said.

"Nor yours on mine." She ducked inside, clutching the burning torch and the unlit spare. Sethos didn't follow her.

Kiara closed the door, turned, and paused to get her bearings. Her heart was beating like a drum; her ears still rang from the sound of the wind. She took a swallow of the water. It was warm and muddy, but she needed to drink to keep up her strength. What she had to do was so difficult, and she didn't know if Sethos would change his mind and have guards waiting for her when she came out.

If she came out . . .

With a murmured prayer to the Lord of Heaven she entered the archway and proceeded down the first flight of steps. The torch burned steadily, casting a yellow circle of light in the darkness. The passageway smelled of dust. She hoped that the first torch would last long enough to reach the inner crypt where Prince Alexander was trapped. She hoped that he'd still be alive when she reached him.

She hoped.

Chapter 15

Ava glanced over her shoulder at the camp as she rode away on horseback with Targitaos and his followers. She wasn't sorry to be seeing the last of the murdering Ish or ill-tempered Api, but every step taken her feel farther and farther from home and her family. Ish had been a hard man, but he had protected her. Targitaos might be as terrible as he looked. Even if she was the great-granddaughter of an Amazon princess, she couldn't help feeling small, alone, and afraid.

There were about two dozen men in the group, all Scythians, but dressed in the slightly different style of clothing and boots that Targitaos wore. Most of the warriors had blue tattoos on their faces and hands and carried double-curved bows and longer arrows than Ish's raiding party. The saddles on their horses had higher pommels and stirrups woven of willow. Ava counted six women and several children in the party, including Jun, the kind-faced woman who'd given her bread, and her little boy. None of the women carried weapons, other than short eating knives, and all were young.

Jun and her red-cheeked son were obviously of high status, because they were mounted on a fine dun horse with an elaborate saddle and blanket. The saddle was fashioned of elegant red leather, decorated with bells and red and green silk tassels. The dun's bridle and harness bore tiny griffins and leopards fashioned of thin beaten gold.

Ava wondered if Jun was Targitaos's wife, but couldn't ask without revealing that she spoke the language. Her mother had told her that anything you knew that your enemy didn't could be used against him. Ava thought she needed all the help she could get. And besides, her barnyard Scythian was poor. She would sound stupid if she tried to speak it.

Ava didn't like the horse they'd put her on. The raw-boned bay had a short, stubby tail, one walleye, and a mean disposition. His gait was hard, nothing like the sweet trot of her horse, Kai. She wished she had the black gelding now, but Kai was somewhere back in her mountains. Ish had captured Kai in the cave where she'd spent the night alone, but the horse had chewed through his tether the first night on the steppes and made good his escape.

One of Targitaos's men had tied her wrists together in front of her. A lead line ran from the shaggy bay's bridle to the neck of another horse ridden by a moon-faced girl with small eyes and red tattooed dots from the center of her bottom lip down her chin and throat. Ava guessed the woman was close to Shahi's age and just as difficult. The tattooed girl never smiled at anyone but a warrior with a scarred mouth and finger bones knotted in his greasy hair, and she never glanced at Ava, even though they rode side by side for hours.

Clad in her own coat and attached mittens, Ava was warmer than she had been under Api's wagon, but close to tears with worry. Her father could track her from the borders to the big camp, but with so many people and so many horses, he would never know where Targitaos had taken her.

The steppes were vast and scattered with tribes of nomads: Scythians, Cimmerians, Samations, Avars, and Huns. To the north, in the cold lands, people told stories of half men, half wolves known as Rusk. They said that the Rusk kept slaves and drained their blood for food as the Scythians did their animals. What if Targitaos sold her to a Rusk? Or even a Mongol?

They would keep trading her from one savage tribe to another until she reached the lands of ice, where she'd freeze to death. A thousand years from now, if someone went there looking for her, they'd find her, a lifeless statue with eyes as empty as the sheep that had died in the blizzard.

Ava wondered if she should tell Jun that she was the daughter of Queen Roxanne and Prince Kayan of the Twin Kingdoms. If they knew she was a princess, would they try to sell her back to her parents, or would her royal status put her in still greater danger? She looked back again, wishing that she could still see the mountains . . . wishing that this were a bad dream and she would wake up and everything would be all right, but all she saw was endless grass and sky.

As the afternoon wore on, the dry air became colder, and the mingled scents of horses, trampled grass, and leather became tinged with the unmistakable smell of an approaching storm. Snow was coming. It was early in the season, but she'd never been this far out on the steppes before. Here, there were no mountains to challenge the winds, and the gales swept down from the north without mercy. First Ava's hands and then her feet grew numb, and by the time Targitaos called a halt for the evening, her teeth were chattering from the cold.

One of the women took hold of Ava's horse and motioned for her to dismount. She obeyed, but when she slid to the ground, her feet had pins and needles and it hurt to walk. Jun called out to her. Ava hurried over and quickly became part of the team assembling the round, skin-covered shelters, building a fire, and preparing food for the men.

The two communal tents went up just as the sun slipped below the horizon. Ava found that the dialect this tribe spoke was closer to what she'd learned from the stable boy at home. As they worked, the women talked and laughed among themselves, but no one spoke directly to her, other than to point out something that they wanted her to do. Ava noticed that Jun was referred to as "Lady" and shown great respect by the others, and the women fussed with one another as to who would get to hold her son.

When the meat was cooked, or what passed for cooked among the Scythians, the women served first Targitaos and then the other men. Dinner was soured mare's milk, rancid cheese, and horseflesh that had been tenderized beneath the women's saddles. Ava was hungry, but her stomach turned over at the smell. She knew she had to eat, if she could, and she hoped that Lady Jun still had some of the coarse bread packed away. None of the women were eating yet; they all stood back and waited for some man to call for something.

Jun unpacked a beautiful ivory-colored bowl set in gold filigree with golden stags circling the rim and filled it with strong-smelling liquid that Ava supposed must be something like koumiss. One by one, the men drank from the container and passed it on. When the cup was empty, Targitaos held it out to Jun. She took it and gestured for Ava to bring her the goatskin bag so that she could refill the ceremonial bowl. Taking care not to spill any of the fermented spirits, Ava carefully untied the mouth, lifted the bag, and fixed her attention on the ivory-and-gold container. With a shock, she realized what Jun held in her hands. With a whimper, Ava took a step back, stumbled, and fell.

"Clumsy brat!" a man shouted.

Ava uttered a small cry of distress as she fumbled to keep the contents of the goatskin from spilling. Salt tears stung her eyes, and she felt as though she were going to be sick.

"Stupid!" accused a woman as she snatched the goatskin from Ava's hands. She kicked at her, but Ava dodged the blow.

A warrior rose to his feet, raising a clenched fist.

"No!" Targitaos said. "She is promised."

Ava clapped a hand over her mouth. She swallowed, trying not to gag. She wanted to run, but there was no place to go. She couldn't tear her gaze from the hideous bowl. The cup inside the golden shell wasn't ivory; it was bone.

The Scythians were drinking from a human skull.

"Sssh, sssh," Jun soothed, slipping an arm around her. "It's all right, girl. Nothing harmed." She hugged her, then swiftly filled the bowl and passed it back to Targitaos.

"The slave needs a good beating," said the man who'd called her stupid. He said more, using words she didn't know, but Ava could guess that they were words her mother wouldn't want her using in mixed company.

"Touch her and feel the point of my saber," Targitaos warned. "She is marked for Pata."

Ava backed as far away from the fire pit as she could get.

"He means her for Pata," one woman whispered to another.

"She's too young. He likes . . ." Her companion cupped her breasts.

"Look how tall she is. She'll ripen by spring."

Jun silenced the women with a finger to her lips. "Hush, you chattering geese. You'll terrify the girl. A bride must not shed tears. It is unlucky."

Ava understood the word *bride.* Did they think to marry her off to this Pata? A lump rose in her throat. She wanted to shout at them all, to tell them that she was tall for her age, that she was only eight and wouldn't get her moon blood for years. But who would believe her?

Jun thrust her little boy into Ava's arms. "Here, Opoin, hold Ku so that he does not fall into the fire. Do you hear?"

Ava stared at her.

Jun pressed the boy into Ava's lap and motioned for her to feed him. "Are you hungry, Ku?"

"Yes, Ma," Ku said.

Someone handed Ava a bloody piece of horsemeat. Jun bit off a piece, chewed it, and placed it in the child's open mouth. "See, you must chew it for him," Jun said. "Eat," she said, gesturing to her mouth and then Ku's. "Feed him."

Ava swallowed hard. The boy had teeth. Why couldn't he chew his own disgusting meat?

Jun patted Ava on the head. "Be a good girl, Opoin. Don't cry. Everything will be all right."

Will it? Ava buried her face in the child's hair. Her shoulders trembled, but she wouldn't let them see her cry. She had to find a way to escape. She couldn't be a slave or a bride. She was a Bactrian princess, and she was going home.

Storms swept the Mediterranean, driving Paris's ships ahead of Ptolemy's fleet of pursuers and finally becalming them within sight of land south of Samaria. The prince ordered the two captains to ferry Alexander's soldiers and those men of his who wished to leave Pharaoh's service. As he'd promised, Paris left the commanders and crews unharmed. Before he boarded the last dory he had the sails slashed, so that the vessels could not sail as far as Gaza, Samaria, or Tyre and spread word of the prince's treason.

Many of the worst wounded had perished during the voyage, so that Paris's company was burdened with only a few injured men as they began their march to Ptolemy's citadel in Samaria. Once, he had commanded thousands of Egypt's finest; now Paris led a band of less than three hundred: Bactrian, Sogdian, Egyptian, and Greek mercenaries. They could seek no quarter in Ptolemy's empire or among the Greek-held territories. Paris knew that their only hope lay inside the boundaries of the Twin Kingdoms, and there, he might find cold welcome from his foster father, Kayan, and Queen Roxanne.

"It's not too late for you to go back," Hermes said. "You are your father's only grown son. Ptolemy will be angry, but he will forgive you."

"Maybe," Paris said, "but I can't forgive him. His hands are stained with my brother's blood." He glanced at Hori. "What of you? You're too fine a charioteer to be blamed for my sins. Can you turn your back on Egypt forever?"

The dwarf laughed. "By the staff of Amon, do you think I would leave you to the mercy of these pretty boys? I hear the mountain women are fierce, with breasts like ripe apples."

"And claws like leopards," Hermes warned. "Our women choose their own lovers. And they like big men."

"Who says I'm not a giant?" Hori roared, making a crude gesture. "I'm hung like a Memphis bull."

Paris raised his hands in mock surrender. "As you wish, old friend. I'll not deny that it would seem strange riding into battle with someone else at my back."

"Riding? Riding?" Hori demanded. "All I've done since you left Alexandria is puke over the side of a boat and tramp in dust that would choke a camel. You promised me a proper chariot."

Paris grinned. "I did, and a chariot you shall have. I'm still Ptolemy's son and a royal prince until the first ship touches at Samaria. Like as not, I can still requisition horses, supplies, and chariots at the outpost."

"For what reason?" Hermes asked.

"To make an advance expedition to the Twin Kingdoms. Surely you've guessed Pharaoh's plan. With the crown prince dead, Sogdiana and Bactria are ruled by a woman without sons. What better time for Egypt to declare war?"

The torch sputtered, and Kiara's heart skipped a beat. Sweat trickled down the back of her neck, and she had to force herself to take normal, shallow breaths. She hadn't remembered it taking this long to reach the burial chamber of the little Egyptian princess. If she'd taken a wrong turn . . . if she'd lost her way . . .

The headache that had started at the back of her skull and worked its way forward was now raging. The walls were definitely getting closer together, and the ceiling was lower. The passage shouldn't be so narrow. Not here. It had grown larger when the funeral procession had neared the grand gallery. She must have made a mistake at the last intersection.

"God of sea and sky, help me," she whispered. "Lord of rainbow and earth, see your daughter. Guide my steps, creator of all things." Shivers passed through her as she turned and hurried back the way she had come. The torch was definitely flickering. If it went out, she'd have no way to make another light. She would be lost in these stone corridors . . . lost forever.

She retraced her path, deliberately halting. But which aisle had she come down? *Think. Think. Which way did the priests go?* "Fool," she cried, and her voice echoed and reechoed down the stone halls until gooseflesh rose on her skin. "Look for the footprints in the dust." She bent down and examined the floor. The path to the left clearly showed the passage of many feet, not the right hall, which she had chosen.

"Nothing to be afraid of," she murmured softly, hoping not to hear the ghostly echoes again. "I'm almost there. Almost there."

The small circle of light from her smoking torch dimmed and then went out. Kiara stifled a wail. For the space of a dozen heartbeats, she crouched, frozen, not knowing what to do as the ghosts of the dead crowded in around her and fingers of icy fear skimmed her throat.

Then she brought the dead torch close to her lips and blew. A spark flared. Patiently she fed the infant flame on fresh fuel from the second torch, until finally, when her palms were damp with fear, the brand caught, illuminating the passageway.

She made her way back to the crossing and laid the dead torch in the center of the hall so that the base pointed toward the way out. Turning, she walked swiftly. Right, left, left again. There. She gasped in relief as the grand gallery opened in front of her.

In less time than it would have taken to rig a fishing pole, bait a hook, and cast it into the sea, she was at the entrance to the small antechamber. Fresh mortar marked with Ptolemy's seal covered the door. She pressed her face to the stone and called out, "Alexander!" When she heard only the rush of blood in her own head, she shouted again, "Alexander!"

"Damn you, you cursed harpy! Get back to the underworld where you belong!"

Triumph made her giddy, and she laughed. She propped the torch up against the wall, pulled the handpick from the rope at her waist, and swung it at the seal with all her might.

Alexander swore.

Still laughing like a madwoman, Kiara hacked at the new mortar until it crumbled away, leaving a window large enough to thrust her hand through. She didn't. "Prince Alexander, do you want to get out of there, or have you gone stark raving mad?"

She grabbed the torch again and lifted it to reveal him peering through at her.

"Kiara? What the—"

"No time for explanations," she said. "I've only one torch. Do you want to get out, or would you rather die in there?"

"Out."

"Good. But there is a price to pay."

"Ransom?"

She swore. All men were fools and the world better without them—if they weren't necessary for the obvious reasons. "I don't want your gold," she answered patiently, as though to a dull child.

"Then what?"

"I need you."

191

"I'm listening."

"I want you to take me home, back to my own people."

"All right. Give me whatever you're using to chop through the door."

She took a step back. "Not so fast. You agree to my demands?"

"Get me out of here; then we'll talk terms."

"Not on your life."

"Yes, whatever you want. Give me the chisel and—"

She lifted a handful of the crumbling mortar and threw it across the hole. Alexander choked and sputtered, then cursed foully.

"You stupid bitch. What was that for?" he managed, spitting gravel and sand. "I said I'd do what you wanted."

"You didn't mean a word of it." She rested the torch against the door and scraped up handfuls of stone chips. "Sit in there and rot!"

"Kiara! No, what are you doing?"

She hesitated. "My home is a long way."

"No, I mean, yes. It doesn't matter. I'll return to the Twin Kingdoms, take you with me, and once I—"

"No! Now! Not tomorrow. Not next year. You will swear on your mother's life to take me back to my own country today. You will cut your wrist and you will swear an oath of blood to return me to my land at once. Or I will leave you there."

"What makes you think I can be trusted to keep such a promise, if I make it?" His tone was different now, serious, honest.

"I know men, Alexander. Good men, bad men. I look into their eyes, and I know what lies in their hearts. Most you cannot trust. But you are different. Spoiled barbarian princeling or not, you are a man of your word. What you swear, you will do."

"I swear then."

She took a deep breath. "You give me your word of honor, on your mother's life and immortal soul, that you will escort me back to my own people. And we will leave this day?"

"Yes."

"Say it." Dust made her eyes sting and water, thickened her throat so that her voice came out weakly. "Say the words as I said them," she insisted. "And the blood. I want to see blood."

"Fierce little thing, aren't you?" He made a sound that was almost amusement. And then he repeated the promise she demanded.

"Just one question," he said, when she passed the pick through the opening to him. "Where exactly is your home? Where do you want me to take you? India? China?"

"I thought you knew," she said, clawing at the stone from her side of the door. "I am Kiara of the Seven Shields. My home lies in the Northern Sea, in the Misty Isles. You're taking me across the ocean to Eire."

Chapter 16

The Indian physician Dhumavarna felt Roxanne's throat and abdomen, inspected a sample of her urine, and studied the color of her blood. He asked her to breathe on a holy black stone blessed by the prophet Zoroaster and to drink water that had melted from snow high in the Blue Mountains. He burned incense, prayed with her, and meditated in complete silence for a day and a night. When he had completed his examination, Dhumavarna summoned the princess Shahi and the dowager princess Soraya to the queen's private bedchamber to hear his diagnosis.

Roxanne settled back against the heaped pillows and glanced nervously around the room. Oil lamps gleamed from the walls, illuminating the star map set in colored mosaic tiles on the high, concave ceiling, a work of art similar to but more detailed than the one in her bedroom in the ancient palace at Sogdiana Rock. Her father and stepmother had planned these apartments for her during the seven years she was a prisoner in Macedonia. Seeing the rooms completed when they didn't know if she would ever come home was an act of faith and love. Whenever she considered the serene beauty here, her heart warmed with love for them both.

This room, dominated by the oversize round bed hung with embroidered silk draperies, was unique in all the world. Her father had spared no expense, bringing the finest carpets, silk, furnishings, gems, marble, and artisans from India, China, Greece, and Crete to create a sanctuary for his only daughter.

Columns carved to look like the trunks of massive trees sprang from the marble floor in the four corners of the spacious room and spread their branches and leaves overhead. One wall displayed a twenty-two-foot stucco mural of mountains and lush valleys. At the center, a real spring bubbled from a sheet of living rock, forming a miniature waterfall. The water drained into a crystal pool set with brightly colored fish crafted of precious stones and large enough for two to bathe. The sitting area in front of the spring was defined by a brightly colored Persian carpet reputed to be centuries old. Couches and cushioned chairs and stools clustered around a marble table with a charcoal stove built into the base. Here, away from the formal bustle of the great court hall on the second floor, she, Kayan, and the children often dined together privately or gathered after the evening meal to exchange news of the day.

The rest of her apartments were equally as lovely. Carpets, tiger-skin rugs, gleaming wooden tables and chests were scattered across the wide expanse of the room. The wall across from the mural held her personal library; niches chiseled in the rock from floor to ceiling were filled with scrolls, manuscripts, royal seals, and writing materials. An antechamber off the main area boasted a heated floor, a water closet, and a dressing area where her clothing and jewels were stored in cedar chests.

JUDITH E. FRENCH

Roxanne massaged the back of her neck to ease the stiffness. She loved these apartments where her daughters had been born and, the Wise God willing, Kayan's son would be as well, but it was not in her nature to remain confined. She felt the need to be out riding, hunting, visiting her military outposts. She had never been forced to stay in bed when she was carrying a child, but she was no longer young, and she had never worried over her pregnancies as she had this one. She was still spotting blood, not a great deal, but enough to make her fear for the babe's welfare.

"Where is that infuriating physician?" she demanded, unable to remain patient any longer.

"I am here, your highness," Dhumavarna said from the archway. Smiling, the old man placed his palms together, steepled his fingers, and touched his temple. He was very old, with piercing black eyes, long gray hair, a thin face, and skin as wrinkled as a raisin. Roxanne echoed his movements, solemnly bowing her head and offering a silent prayer. "Peace to you, lady," he murmured.

Dhumavarna was as immaculate as always, dressed in a spotless white robe, fur hat, and vest. Soft russet boots with pointed toes were his only vanity. He smelled of cloves and cinnamon, and she suspected that he had indulged in a honey cake on his way up to her bedchamber.

"Peace to you, magus," she said. The old man wasn't Persian, but if he didn't merit the title of wise one, who did? Dhumavarna had studied the art of healing in his native India, in Babylon, and in Memphis, and had traveled as far as the roof of the world before coming to be a part of her father's household. She suspected that Dhumavarna had forgotten more about medicine than most doctors would ever know.

"Well? How am I to have peace until I know what

196

you've found?" she said. "Enough of smoke and mystery. Tell me something good. I know this baby is alive. He kicks more strongly than any of my other children."

Dhumavarna's mouth grew firm, and Roxanne slipped her hands beneath the blue silk coverlet and tightened her fingers into fists. *Say something that I want to hear,* she prayed as a chill sense of unease passed through her. "Please, master, sit," she urged, waving to the bed.

Compassion radiated from his gaze, and Roxanne felt her hopes sink. *Something is wrong with this pregnancy,* she thought. *I'm going to lose this baby, and I've driven Kayan and Ava away for nothing.* She bit the inside of her cheek and tried not to reveal her fear.

Soraya rose from her chair and came to the bed as well. "Is the queen's condition serious? What must we do for her?" She found Roxanne's hand and squeezed it.

The older woman's presence lent her strength. Soraya had been Roxanne's foster mother and confidante long before she'd married Oxyartes to become her stepmother.

Footfalls from the hall proclaimed Shahi's arrival. Her daughter rushed in, red-cheeked and excited, threw off her snow-covered cloak, and hurried to the bed. "Sorry I'm late, Mother, Grandmother. I know, I know, I always say that. But they called me from prayer and—"

"It's all right," Roxanne said. "You're here now." She patted the space beside her on the bed. Shahi was in her formal novice's scarlet robe and head covering, and Roxanne couldn't help thinking how much she looked like her father.

"Well?" Shahi clasped Roxanne's other hand.

Beautiful and ever impatient, Roxanne thought. Of all her children, Shahi had been the one most difficult to understand. She knew that Shahi loved her, but they always seemed to be at odds. Perversely, Roxanne wished that the physician hadn't summoned Shahi from the temple. If something was wrong, her daughter would blame her for getting pregnant in the first place, and if it was nothing, Shahi would be piqued for being called from her studies.

"It pains me to bring you unease," Dhumavarna said softly.

"We have never been untruthful with one another," she reminded him.

"Yes." He looked directly into Roxanne's eyes.

"I know this child is strong," she repeated.

He nodded, closed his eyes, and began to speak in a deep monotone. "It's true that your child possesses an old soul and is meant for great deeds. But clouds obscure the vision. I feel strength and courage, in both the mother and child, but there is danger in the passageway. There are twists and turns, and if the wrong path is chosen, dark forces will prevail." He shook his head.

"What should I do, magus?" Roxanne tried to keep her voice from cracking. "I would protect my child at any cost."

"Even to your own life?" Dhumavarna asked.

"No!" Shahi protested. "No, Mother. You can't." She looked at the physician. "My mother's life is more important. She is the heart of the Twin Kingdoms, not this unborn baby. You have to save her."

"The choice is not mine to make," the old man said. "And it may be that my eyes do not see as clearly as once they did."

"Tell me what I must do to deliver this child safely," Roxanne insisted.

Dhumavarna sighed. "I will pray for a solution, but the outcome is uncertain. I can only give you the advice that any good midwife would offer."

"Yes," Soraya said. "And that is?"

"The queen must rest as much as possible; yet she

must walk for a little while each day out in the walled garden."

"The council," Roxanne said. "Can I meet with the council and my generals? Prince Kayan is in the north. I must consult with those who guard our borders from invaders." She glanced at the leather wall map and then back at Dhumavarna. "Even now there are rumors of another Greek invasion as soon as the snow melts."

The physician considered. "The princess Shahi can relay messages from the council and deliver your commands. If Prince Alexander does not return from King Ptolemy's court, Princess Shahi will someday assume the throne. You must rely on her."

"I'll do whatever Mother asks," Shahi said, "but I've been trained in the temple. I know little about military—"

"You will learn, lady. The queen must care for herself and for her children."

Shahi nodded. "I will ask the high priestess—"

"You must tell her," Dhumavarna corrected. "You were not born a shepherd's daughter. Great gifts have been given to you, and much is expected. A princess must learn to give orders, not take them." He turned his attention back to Roxanne. "You are to drink only fresh water and broth made from fowl. I will direct the kitchen what to prepare for you. No sweets but a little honey, eggs, vegetables, and lean meat."

Roxanne laughed. "You never touch meat, esteemed Dhumavarna. How can you order me to eat it?"

"I was not born queen of the Twin Kingdoms or a woman." He chuckled. "Eat your cooked flesh of goats, sheep, and oxen, lady. The creator will not condemn you for it."

"Am I to stay penned up in this room?"

"You may study, so long as you sleep well. You may

have friends and your daughter to cosset you. And you will walk every day, as I ordered."

"I think you would have made a good king if you had been born to it," she said.

"King or beggar, a man—or a woman—must bear this life's burdens so that he may gain reward in the next one."

"But you will continue to pray for me," Roxanne urged him, "and you will tell me if these clouds pass and you can see clearly."

"I will," he promised. "May the gods grant that you be safely delivered of a healthy infant."

"I have been troubled," she admitted, "by dreams. I worry about my husband and all my children."

"For that I can offer no medicine," Dhumavarna pronounced. "For women are born to worry about those that they love. It is their nature and a part of the creator's plan."

Alexander savored the tepid liquid from the goatskin bag. Strength returned with each drop he let slide down his throat, but he knew better than to drink too much too soon. If he quenched his terrible thirst, his stomach would revolt. He would vomit and the lifegiving fluid would be lost. Without water, he would weaken and die, and only the Wise God knew when they could find more—provided they ever made it out of this black hole.

"Hurry, we must hurry," the green-eyed woman insisted. "The torch will not last. I had only two to begin with, and I was forced to light the second before I reached you."

The days he'd spent in the tomb without food or water had taken their toll. And whatever drug or poison Ptolemy's servants had given him had made him slow of wit and clumsy. The entire plot was so bizarre that it passed all reason.

If his uncle wanted him dead, why hadn't the ax parted his head from his body? And why hadn't Ptolemy's soldiers finished him off once he was unconscious? Why bury him alive? And why had this slave girl risked her life for his?

It galled him to allow a woman to lead him, especially when they might face danger. He knew nothing of these passageways, but her warnings of tunnels that led nowhere, pits, and traps seemed believable. What wasn't believable was her tale of coming from some far-off Misty Isles, or that she would trade a life of comparative ease as a palace servant for the dangers of a journey with little chance of survival.

"Let me take you with me to Bactria," he offered, handing her back what was left of the water. "No one there will know what occupation you held in Alexandria. I'll give you a dowry and find you a good husband. Or, if you prefer, I'll reward you handsomely, and you can open your own shop or house of—"

"Of prostitution?" She scowled. "What makes you think I want a husband? Or that I'd wish to spend my life giving strange men sexual thrills?"

He bit back the quick retort that rose to his lips. She was as prickly as a desert thorn, this pretty little pleasure girl. "A woman must do something. If she is not a wife, then she must have some skill to support herself," he said, wondering why—when she seemed of normal intelligence—he should have to explain something that should have been as plain as the fingers on his hand. "I'll not cheat you of your reward, but even a woman of means needs a plan. You must be a merchant, a jeweler, or a farmer. Otherwise, in time, the gold will slip through your fingers and you'll end up destitute."

"I told you, I don't want your money. I want to go home. And I'm not such a fool as to think I can cut off my hair, disguise myself as a boy, and hire myself out as a sailor on a trading vessel bound for the northern sea."

"No," he agreed. "You'd not pass as a lad, but even if you could, boys are in as much danger of becoming sexual toys at sea as women."

"No doubt you've had experience with— Watch your head! That beam overhead is studded with metal spikes! Keep your eyes open if you want to get out of here. I've no wish to have you kill yourself, after going to such trouble to save you."

Alexander ducked. The air here was bad. The torch sputtered, and bits of oil-soaked reed sparked onto his arm, burning his skin. "Ouch." He brushed at the debris. "Had experience with what?"

"With boys. You're Greek, aren't you?"

"Half. Not Greek, but Macedonian, and I do not favor boys. I am a man for the softer sex, as you should suspect." He settled a hand familiarly on her shoulder.

She shook it off and whirled to face him. "Don't do that!"

He stopped short. The torch cast grotesque shadows on the stone wall, and he had the oddest sensation that someone other than Kiara was watching him. "Don't do what?" he asked her.

"Touch me."

"Touch you?" He wondered if she were entirely sound of mind. "If you recall, I did more than touch you in my apartments at the palace, and you seemed to like—"

She struck his chest with the palm of her hand. "That was before. Now everything is changed. I'm not a whore. You must forget what happened in Alexandria. Until we reach my island, we must travel together, eat together, sleep together. Together, but apart—not as a couple. Without being intimate."

He scoffed. "You expect me to take you halfway across the world and not touch you?"

"There are touches and touches." She shook her head impatiently. "You're not a fool. You know what I mean. I'm not your night's entertainment or your concubine. We are . . ." She seemed to search for the word. "We are companions. Partners."

He chuckled. "Partners?"

"Yes. I have paid you to protect me, to take me where I want to go. Nothing more. We are equals. And I will not be . . . be used. If you have a man's need, find comfort in your own hand or with someone else."

"You've reformed."

Her green eyes glittered. "I have more skills than you know, barbarian. If I have been trained to give pleasure, I've also learned to give pain. Betray my trust, try to break our bargain, and I will not hesitate to make you sorrier than you ever imagined."

"Is that a threat?"

"It is a promise." She turned and plunged ahead.

He caught up with her. "Wait. I am grateful to you. I don't want to argue."

"We must hurry. The torch will go out."

"Do you have any idea how difficult it will be for the two of us—alone—to reach your homeland? Years ago, when I was a boy, my foster father led my mother, my brother, and me out of Egypt across the desert. But we had supplies, soldiers waiting. You and I have nothing. We'll have to follow the Nile to the sea, buy passage on a ship."

She glanced back at him, and a lock of her hair fell across her face. "How we reach Eire is up to you. My part of the bargain is to get you out of here alive."

"This was your idea?" he pressed. "Yours alone? How did you bribe the guards?"

"Don't ask stupid questions."

"Do you forget who it is you're addressing, girl? I'm the crown prince of—"

"Of vultures and dung beetles if I don't save your skin."

"Are you a thief?" he persisted. "What did you use to pay—"

"I am a woman," she replied flatly. "I do what I must."

It was all he could do not to recoil. The thought that she had bought her way into the tomb with her body was repellent. It shouldn't have mattered. She was a hetaera, nothing more than a high-priced whore. She was accustomed to servicing strangers. But not common grave guards. And not for him.

Shame and a sudden tenderness for her made him uncertain. His throat tightened, and he tried to cover his discomfort with a brusque question. "And you insist you have no one working with you? My brother Paris didn't—"

"Prince Paris fled the city with what was left of your company."

He grabbed her arm and spun her around. "What do you mean?" Guilt rushed over him as he realized that he hadn't thought of his men. "Tell me what happened to them."

Her explanation was short and brutal. "Ptolemy's archers shot them down in the street outside the temple of Isis at the same time you were struck down inside. I know only what was repeated in Mereret's chambers, servants' gossip. They said that many of your Bactrians died, but not all. Prince Paris took those that lived prisoner. I don't know what happened to them. He seized ships in the harbor and escaped before Pharaoh could stop him."

Escaped, Alexander wondered, or led an expedition to seize the throne of the Twin Kingdoms in Ptolemy's name? And what of his men? Cold anger swept over him. Had Paris been a part of the plot to bury him alive? What had Paris done with the brave men who'd followed him to Egypt? Were they imprisoned? Executed? Or did Paris intend to use them for his own purposes? "What did they say of who was responsible for my betrayal?"

She shrugged. "Pharaoh? Queen Artakama? Mereret herself, who can say? It is Egypt. If you had the power of a god, you might not get an answer—or you might get many answers. All I know is that Paris left the city by ship. And Mereret is not with child."

"Not by me she's not."

"She claimed otherwise. Queen Artakama says that you were struck down by Isis after the wedding ceremony, and that your widow—her daughter—carries your child. But that's a lie. Mereret had her courses. I saw the bloody clouts."

"So I am to be a father?"

"Officially, yes. Poor man, never to see your son and heir. You're dead, you know."

"I'm dead?"

"I told you. You were destroyed by the goddess Isis. She was angered by your attempt to use the princess Mereret to seize the throne of Pharaoh."

"What?" He shook his head. "What madness is that?"

"It is what all Alexandria will believe, all Egypt." She motioned to him. "We cannot stay here arguing of such things. What is done is done, and we must get as far as we can before the torch is used up."

"What then?"

"Then I depend on my memory," she said. "And we pray."

Chapter 17

Kiara stopped again when she reached an intersection of tunnels. The walls and ceiling here were higher, plastered, and covered with hieroglyphics. She closed her eyes, seeing the maze of corridors in her mind, working out the pathway they must take once the light failed.

The women in her family had been blessed with the gift of remembering. As a young child, her mother and grandmother had encouraged that talent when they'd trained her to recite the line of O'Ryans running back through the mists of time to the hero-king who found refuge on Eire's shore when the sea swallowed Atlantis. Kiara's earliest memory was of sitting in her grandmother's lap and listening to her sing the history of the Seven Shields. Each line spun a glittering thread, and when woven together they formed the magical tapestry of who her people were and what they had endured in the green lands entrusted to them by the creator. If she let herself, Kiara could hear that voice now, enfolding her in an embrace of love and hope.

She swallowed, blinking back tears. Dwelling on her

lost loved ones was of no help to her here in this accursed tomb of rock and mortar. She must remain focused. It shamed her to think that she'd neglected the
lessons she'd been taught. She'd not used her gift of
memory in years, no more than was necessary to make
her day-to-day life easier.

Sometimes the difference between a painful ordeal
and merely a tedious experience was a simple matter of
remembering what pleased a particular master in food
or drink or sexual service. She'd never spoken of her
early training since she'd come to Egypt. No one had
ever asked her about her homeland, and she would not
have told them if they had. Hers was an island nation,
an ancient and sacred culture, as different from these
mainlanders as a soaring seabird was from a carrion fly.
The less the outer world knew of Eire, the better.

"Well?" Alexander urged, breaking through her
reverie.

"Ah . . . this way," she said, leading him on. She
hoped she hadn't made a mistake in choosing him.
Years of servitude had given her a rare insight into the
character of men, but they were dangerous creatures,
easily stirred into action by their baser instincts. This
half-breed Greek had the look of a warrior. She had
heard of his bravery in facing the lion. Her way home
would be long and perilous. Only a champion had a
chance of winning against the evils that lay between
her and Eire.

And she must get there. More was at stake than her
life . . . or even her freedom. Much more . . .

A feathery chill brushed the nape of her neck. She
grimaced at the metallic taste of fear in her mouth.
The air sizzled with energy. She caught her breath and
glanced back at the torch. The yellow flame held
steady, yet the hairs prickled on her arms. "Something
is—" she began.

"Wait!" Alexander yanked her back as the stone beneath her right foot gave way under her weight.

Kiara cried out as an entire section of the floor crumbled. A black shaft loomed in front of her. She scrambled to find a footing as Alexander dragged her after him. Stone rumbled and crashed. The noise was deafening. More and more of the tunnel pavement disintegrated, peeling away and tumbling into the shaft.

Blinded by dust, they ran until they came to the first junction of hallways. "There!" she shouted. "That way."

Alexander lunged to the left as a four-foot-long chunk of stone floor collapsed. Walls and ceiling blocks groaned. Painted images seemed to come alive. A jackal mouth gaped wide. Alexander flung her against a wall, sheltering her with his body as plaster rained around them. It was over in seconds. The boom of falling rock gave way to the hollow thud and rattle of settling mortar and then to silence.

"Are you all right?" he demanded, wrenching her around and staring into her face. His voice sounded overloud in the absolute silence.

She blinked, choking from the dust, her ears still ringing.

"You almost got us killed!"

"I didn't—"

"You said you knew the way!"

"I did." She pushed at him, her heart thudding so hard that she was certain he must hear it. "It was the way, my lord. I . . ." She stopped as anger washed away the years of subservience. "It was the right path," she insisted. "I don't know why the floor—"

Alexander swore as he released her and retrieved the fallen torch. "You made a mistake. Admit it and—"

"No. I wasn't wrong. Think!" She glared at him, and again he had the sense that she held herself with more dignity than any court whore would dare to. "You saw the footprints in the dust. You must have. It's the way they carried you in. The way I followed tonight. It's the only way out."

His shoulders stiffened. "If this is some trick to—"

"Listen to me, you great fool," she flung back. "I tell you, that is the way I came."

Alexander bit off a retort. "All right, all right, I believe you. We'll just have to find another—"

"There is no other!" Her eyes were streaming water from the dust, and her face was streaked with dirt. "I don't know why the floor caved in, but I do know that the priest said these corridors are filled with traps to foil would-be grave robbers."

"Maybe we can find another tunnel that runs parallel to the one that collapsed. Or—"

"The torch will go out. We'll be left in darkness. We can't find another path without light."

"Then we need fuel, wood, anything that will burn." He shoved the torch into her hands and ripped off the garment he'd been buried in.

"Roll the cloth tightly," she suggested, "so that it will last as long as possible." When he'd completed the task, she gave the torch to him and stripped away her own tunic. "Here, use this as well."

Alexander shook his head. "Not yet. There's hardly enough material there to bother with. It would burn in seconds."

"Then why did you let me—"

He grinned. "If I'm to see one last thing before the end, a naked woman would be high on my list." She replied in a language he wasn't familiar with before dropping the flimsy tunic over her head and jerking it into place. "Come," he said. "We don't have much time." He started down the narrow tunnel.

At first she didn't move, but then he heard the soft

tread of her sandaled feet behind him. "This tunnel leads up," she said.

"I'd noticed that, but what—" Alexander stopped abruptly and swore.

Ahead lay a man, or what had once been a man. Curled into a fetal position, withered arms and legs wrapped tightly around a broken canopic jar, mouth stretched wide in a silent scream, the would-be thief seemed more mummy than human. Dry air and time had turned his skin to leather. Worn-down teeth gleamed in the torchlight. Empty holes replaced eyes, and drying flesh had pulled away from his nails so that they seemed more like claws protruding from fingers and toes.

Kiara did not scream, but Alexander heard her small intake of breath. He stooped and picked up the lid of the canopic jar, discovering that it had been fashioned in the shape of a jackal's head. "What do you think killed him?" he asked.

"Thirst. Or fear."

He pulled off the dead man's reed sandals. "These will burn," he said. There was nothing else, not even a loincloth. The man's genitals had shrunk to brown nubs. He placed the jackal lid beside the fragments of the jar. "Let's go." He stepped over the corpse.

Kiara dropped to her knees.

"What are you doing?" he demanded. "We're not giving up."

She shook her head. "No, wait. I must do something." She closed her eyes and murmured in her strange tongue.

"What are you doing?"

"Praying for his soul, that his ghost might leave this place and—"

He grabbed her arm. "There's no time."

She pulled back with amazing strength for a woman. "I must," she said. She touched the mummy's forehead. "Be at peace." As she started to rise, she cried. "Wait. What's that under him?"

Alexander brushed aside the skeleton. It weighed no more than an empty water bladder. On the floor under the bones lay a wooden adze with a metal blade. As he picked up the shaft, the leather bindings crumbled to dust.

"Wood," Kiara said. "We can burn that."

"No," Alexander replied, "I was thinking more of using this as a tool, in case we need to cut our way . . ." He unwound the leather straps of his sandals and prepared to lash the blade back in place.

"Water," she said. "Soak the laces first." She offered him the precious water bag, still hanging around her neck on a braided rope. "If we can't find the passage out of here, the water won't do us any—" She gasped and snatched up a scrap of linen. "Hold the torch so I can see. I think it's a map of some kind."

"Excellent," Alexander said sarcastically. "If his map had been any good, he wouldn't be here, would he?"

Ignoring him, Kiara stared at the charcoal drawing. "We need to go back."

"Back?" He scoffed. "Back to where the floor collapsed under us?"

"When you pulled me back, we leaped to the left."

"You told me to go left," he reminded her.

"I did, but I was wrong. This shaft leads to a dead end. We were right . . . on the correct path when the floor gave way. Now we need to jump to the other side of the gap and take the right passageway."

"Jump over the hole?"

"Yes. How far is it? Six feet? Less? You're not afraid, are you?"

Afraid? His hackles rose. If she were a man . . . He gritted his teeth and led the way back to the junction. He knew he could make the leap, but he wasn't certain if he could do it with her in his arms. He was still weak from lack of food and water.

"I'll go first, and then you can throw me the torch," Kiara suggested.

"You'll jump this?" he asked, indicating the yawning pit that had devoured another foot of the corridor floor that they were standing on. "What if you don't make it?"

"Then I fall. You take the map. It shows that the passage ahead does turn back and crosses over the tunnel we were in—the one that gave way. When you reach that point, you lift the paving stones with the adze, drop down to the passage below, and—"

"You want us to take the same corridor that gave way? The one without a floor?"

"I'm hoping we'll break into the hall ahead of the fault, where the floor remains whole."

"What if the entire length has crumbled?"

She shrugged. "Do you have a better idea?"

"Climb on my back. This is too far for a woman. We'll do it together."

She shook her head and took two steps back. "No, you go first, if you like. I'll toss you the adze, and then I'll jump. I can do it. I know I can."

"Kiara!"

"No time to argue. Go!"

Swearing, he thrust the adze into her hands, took a running leap, and landed solidly on the far side, torch in hand. He propped the torch against the wall, came as close to the chasm as he dared, and held out his arms. "Your turn."

She threw the tool. He caught it and tossed it behind him as Kiara took a deep breath and retreated about ten feet. "Ready?"

"On three," he said. "One, two—"

She dashed down the corridor and lunged into space. She would have reached the far side if the last section of stone hadn't given way under her left foot. She stretched out her arms, and his fingers closed around her right wrist.

She slammed against the thickness of the walkway and hung from his hands. When he dragged her up, Kiara was trembling from head to toe, but she didn't utter a sound. He stepped back away from the edge and cradled her against his chest. She felt good against him. Warm and alive.

"Are you hurt?"

"No." Her voice was very small.

"We have to keep moving." He clasped her hand. "Can you carry the adze if I take the torch?"

She nodded.

"All right. Let's see how good that grave robber's map is."

They'd dislodged the first stone when the torch began to fail. Alexander cut the leather thongs holding the blade to the shaft of the tool and shoved it into Kiara's hands. By the time he'd pried loose the paving section, the wood was glowing. He enlarged the hole and lowered Kiara down.

Her feet didn't touch the bottom.

"Let go," she said.

"And if there's no floor?"

"Then we both die anyway."

He swore softly, wondering at her courage.

"Do it!" she cried.

He released her hands. Time seemed to stop as he waited to hear her scream. Instead there was a soft thud. "Are you—"

"I'm fine. It seems solid. Quickly. Come on," she urged as he passed the burning adze handle to her.

The hole was tight. He had to squirm his way through, and still the uneven rock dug gashes in his

213

chest, shoulders, and arms. He was bleeding from a half dozen spots when he landed beside her. "You should have saved some of those prayers for us," he said.

"I did." She took his hand again and they hurried on for the length of a child's bow shot before turning left, then straight, then left again.

The wood from the adze was dry and burned quickly. Alexander tried not to think of what it would be like in this passageway in the dark. "How much farther?" he asked after a quarter of an hour.

"Not far. Trust me."

"Right." And yet he did. Of all those he'd met since he'd arrived in Egypt, this pretty little whore was the only one he did trust.

"Here," she said, taking the stump of their makeshift torch from his hand.

"What are you—"

"Bend over. Watch your head. There's a low beam."

He ducked. A wooden upright grazed his left arm as he pushed through.

"Watch your eyes," she warned.

Light flared. Amazed, he stared around them. Kiara had lit an oil lamp. They were standing in a small room lined with tall jars and dusty furniture stacked shoulder high. The air was better here.

"We're in a chamber beneath the lion-man," she explained. "They call it the Sphinx. The statue has some religious significance, but it's so old, even the Egyptians don't remember why it's here. They believe it's holy, but the guards fear it. They say that ghosts walk here."

"We can reach the outside from here?"

She laughed. "Yes, you fool."

He grabbed her and kissed her.

"Stop that." She pushed hard against his chest.

He kissed her again.

She wiggled out of his arms. "Are you deaf? I said no!"

He began to chuckle and then to laugh, sidesplitting peals of glee.

"Have you lost your mind?" she demanded.

He shook his head, coughed, and gave a final chuckle. "Are you made of stone? By Zoroaster's beard, woman! Can't you see how funny this is? I was buried alive. I was as good as dead, and you appear out of nowhere." He swore. "I'm not sure yet if you're real or if you're a ghost."

"I'm real enough." She brushed cobwebs from her face. "And we can reach the outside from here easily enough."

"You weren't so sure an hour ago." He grinned. "If you'd looked as bad then as you do now, I'd have taken you for a demon." She was covered in dirt. Her braid had come loose, her tunic was shredded, and she was bleeding from both knees and an elbow.

Her scowl became a mischievous smile. "And you, my lord? You hardly look like the prince I first saw in the palace. In fact, you look more like a galley slave."

He looked down at his own bruised and naked body. In truth, he'd come through more than one battle looking better than he did now. "All the more reason to celebrate our good fortune. You're lucky, Kiara of the Seven Shields. Or I am. We both should have been dead twice over."

She folded her arms over her chest and motioned for him to stay where he was. "We're not out of this accursed place yet. I'll look to see if it's daylight. We'll have to wait until dark again, if it is. There is a village nearby where the guardians live. We can't get past them in daylight."

Alexander touched the hilt of his sword. "Don't bet on it."

"No," she said firmly. "You will harm no one here. I gave my word."

"To whom?"

"A man called Sethos."

"A guard. The man you bribed to let you in here?"

"I promised him that none would be hurt. If we're seen, we'll be killed. They have dogs. The sole purpose of these people is to guard the graves from robbers."

"What makes you think this Sethos won't betray you? He may be waiting outside. Ptolemy would pay a handsome reward to keep me from escaping."

"Sethos has already been rewarded. And he believes I'm dead inside the pyramid, as dead as you. He won't be waiting for us. And we will leave quietly by darkness."

"You forget who I am," Alexander said. "You're no longer in a position to give orders."

"Perhaps not," she said. "But I think you're smart enough to take good advice when you hear it. Why risk capture or raising the alarm, when our way is open? No one chases the dead."

"True, but I have scores to settle before we leave Egypt."

Her green eyes flashed with anger. "Then they will go unsettled. Kill all you want, barbarian. Let your blade run red with blood and end your life in this desert, but not before you keep your oath to me."

He turned away from her.

"On your mother's soul," she reminded him. "I have your word, Prince Alexander. Is it as worthless as that of Pharaoh?"

Ten days later they were in Memphis, where Kiara pried one of the jewels from Alexander's scabbard and sold it to a one-eyed merchant in a narrow shop behind a butcher's yard. The man cheated her, but she had expected that. Alexander's Egyptian was good, but he still spoke with a foreign accent, and she didn't want anyone asking questions about a Greek mercenary with a jewel to sell. Better that the fat merchant with the roving hands believe she was a thief.

Kiara rented a narrow room opening onto an alley near the harbor. The chamber had a single sleeping platform against one wall, two stools, and a tiny barred window. There was no place to cook and no heat, but the weather was mild. She purchased two blankets in the marketplace and bought their meals from the beer seller on the next street.

For a week Alexander rested from his ordeal and tried to persuade her to share his bed and go with him to his mountain kingdom. "My brother may try to steal my throne," he argued. "My parents will believe me dead."

She closed her ears to his pleas. Her family must have long given her up as lost. She would not release him from his promise, and she would not be intimate with him. Better to sleep on the floor alone than to yield and lose all her newfound dignity.

Kiara went out into the city twice a day to buy beer, bread, and meat while he remained hidden in the small room. Kiara purchased used clothing more suitable to their new circumstances, and she cut Alexander's hair close to his head and dyed it a dark brown. No matter how carefully she guarded their money, city living was expensive, and the small store of coins dwindled.

"I'll have to sell another stone to the merchant," she said on the seventh day after they had finished the evening meal.

Alexander scowled. "The coin would go farther if you could cook. I'm sick of onions and bread. I need meat."

"Stop whining. You would be eating dust if I'd not rescued you from your tomb. And I've never learned to cook."

217

"I thought all women knew how."

She laughed. "Then you never tasted my mother's honey cakes. They were so hard, we threw them to the crows. They pecked at them, but in the end the birds didn't like them either."

How her father had teased her mother about those cakes, Kiara thought. A lump rose in her throat as she wondered if her father still lived . . . if any of her family still survived. She had been away so long. Perhaps too long . . .

"You're set on this course?" Alexander asked. "To take passage on a boat out of Egypt?"

She glanced back at him. The short hair suited him, but not the color. She would have to take more of the dye with them if they were to keep his natural golden locks hidden. As it was, both women and men would notice him. He was very handsome and built like a god. A hawk among gulls, she mused, and as troublesome. She could not deny that she felt a strong sexual attraction to him, but she'd not allow desire to blind her to what she must do.

She wiped crumbs off the window ledge that served as both shelf and table in the bare room. "Must we go over this again? We will take a boat—any boat—to one of the larger trading ports. And there we will find a merchant who deals in the tin or gold trade. He will know what ships sail for Eire."

"And the reason I'll give for wanting to take a woman on such a dangerous voyage?" Alexander drained his beer cup and wiped the foam from his mouth with the back of his hand.

Light from the window gilded the shadow of beard on his cheek, and she stifled an impulse to feel the prick of his whiskers against her fingertips. She'd not forgotten the taste of his mouth or the feel of his strong hands on her body.

Kiara averted her eyes. "I don't know, my lord. That's for you to say. Claim to be a trader. Say anything. What use are you to me if you can't think of a good reason?"

"Strong words."

She stepped away from the window and lowered her voice. "But we must leave Egypt as quickly as possible. The baker knows I'm not Egyptian. And word will have spread that I live here with a man. Soon others will speculate whether or not we have something worth stealing."

"A thief who comes here will find the point of my sword in his teeth."

"Yes, yes, I know. You've boasted of your prowess enough."

"No boast, but truth."

She sighed. Men. They were all alike under their skins. "But Memphis is ruled by law. Any disturbance will be reported to the city guards. And neither of us can give the right answers to questions. We cannot risk it. We must leave here as soon as possible."

"I agree. I can't stay here cooped up in this clay box any longer. Even the deck of a ship would be better." He caught her hand. "But I'll sell the next jewel. Take what we have left and buy cloth. I'll garb myself as a Syrian."

She sighed. "It's risky."

"And hiding here isn't?"

She bit back a retort. If she pressed too hard, he might not honor his word at all.

"Once we have more money," Alexander continued, "I want you to cover yourself, hair to ankles." He smiled grimly. "You can be my concubine. You'll be easier to protect if your face and body are hidden. As you are, you're too much of a temptation."

"To you, or to our enemies?" she asked.

"Maybe a little of both."

Chapter 18

A world away on the great steppes, a woman's scream tore Ava from her fitful sleep. Fragments of dreams clouded her mind as she opened her eyes and stared around the goatskin hut. The yurt lay in semidarkness, the only light glowing feebly from a central fire pit.

"What was that?" Jun cried.

Targitaos flung off his wolfskin blankets and leaped to his feet. "Stay here," he ordered.

The night air was chill; wind whipped around the tent, and the frozen ground outside lay frosted in snow, but Ava didn't feel the cold. Warmth shimmered beneath her skin as dream images of home floated in her mind's eye. A roaring fire . . . her mother's face . . . her father's laughter . . . the feel of Banu's silky ears and soft fur . . . She could smell Mama's perfume . . . taste her grandmother's licorice candy.

"Watch the girl," Targitaos said. His voice was hard.

"She's sleeping."

"Don't let her out of your sight."

Ava could not see the Scythian prince's blue-tattooed face in the shadows, but she didn't need to. The sour odors of man-sweat and dried blood wafted over her as he passed her bedroll. She lay absolutely still, watching through slitted eyes as Targitaos ducked out through the flap of the yurt.

There were no wheels on the tent-huts of the Pestici, but the women transported these structures as easily as Api's tribe had moved their wagons. The willow framework snapped apart. Goatskins and rugs rolled. Targitaos's band of Scythians lingered at a campsite only as long as there was fresh grazing and water for their herds of livestock.

And although Jun was often kind to her, Ava trusted Targitaos even less than she had Ish. Each move took the Pestici farther east, away from her mountains, away from her family and her home. And perhaps each day's journey took her closer to Pata, the man Targitaos wanted her to marry.

Ava's mouth tasted of sour milk; curds, rancid butter, and mare's milk mixed with blood made up the greatest part of the Pestici diet. Her stomach revolted at such food, but it was either eat what was offered or starve, and Ava had no intention of allowing herself to sicken and die. She was going to steal a horse and escape. She was going home.

Several spots on her body itched fiercely. She supposed it was the fleas. If the horses here were stunted runts compared to the magnificent animals her own people raised, the fleas were monstrous. The last flea she'd dug out of her hair had been nearly the size of a blueberry. But she had another, more pressing complaint. The skinny ground squirrel's leg that she'd eaten last night had been nearly raw, and it sat uneasily in her stomach. She needed to find a private place to pee and to empty her bowels.

"Jun," she called. "I need to go out."

"Go back to sleep, Opoin," the woman said sleepily. "But I have to—"

"You heard Targitaos. Do you want him to beat you again? Do as you're told, child."

Ava's belly gurgled. She didn't think she could wait until daylight, but she knew better than to argue. Jun was more even-tempered than her husband, but she could be fierce when she was crossed. And she was quick. It was hard to avoid the back of Jun's hand when she was displeased.

Nearby, Ava could hear Ku noisily sucking his thumb in his sleep. Ku, Ava had learned, was Targitaos's only son. He'd had two older boys by another wife, but they had died of some sickness in the summer. The Scythians did not talk about their dead and never mentioned their names for fear of ghosts.

Ava could not say that she'd been treated any worse by the Pestici than any other girl child. Here, boys were favored. Boys ate first, were given the warmest clothing by the women, and were expected to lord it over their sisters. Only rarely had she seen a man pay any attention to his baby daughter, but they took their sons everywhere, carved them small bows and arrows, mounted them on their finest ponies, even gave them koumiss.

Small Ku was clearly the spoiled princeling of the camp. Old women chucked him under the chin, fed him choice bits of meat and bowls of tea filmed with butter, and clapped with glee at every sound that came out of his mouth.

Little girls seemed largely ignored, even by their mothers, and females her own age and older worked as hard as the women. They cooked, gutted animals, tanned hides, sewed clothing, shook out blankets, minded babies, and gathered dung for the fires. None of the other girls in the Pestici camp had befriended her, and her attempts at talking to them had been met with stony silence.

Outside, dogs began to bark and a horse whinnied anxiously. Jun got up, wrapped a blanket around her shoulders, and followed her husband outside. Ava rose cautiously, crept past where Ku was sleeping, and peeked outside. Snow was falling, and she could make out Jun's figure standing only a few feet from the entrance. She was talking to someone, but the wind caught her words and whirled them away into the bitter night.

Ava's belly cramped. She looked around the hut. The walls of the yurt were two thicknesses of skins reinforced by the strong, interlocking wooden frame and covered with brightly embroidered cloth. If she'd had time, she could have dug her way out under the bottom, but she needed to go out now. She'd have to risk getting past Jun without being seen.

Luckily she slept in her clothes. No one had taken her trousers or her boots, and she'd used her coat as a pillow. She tugged it on, stepped around the sleeping child, and pushed aside the heavy fur tent flap. A dog growled at her, but it didn't matter. All the camp curs were barking. Men were shouting, and women were calling out anxiously.

Jun never glanced back as Ava darted out, ran around the yurt, and dashed through the camp to an outcropping of bushes beside the river. She yanked down her trousers and sighed with relief. These clothes were all she had. If she soiled them, she'd have to wear them just the same, and the thought was disgusting. Relief settled over her as she readjusted her clothes and stood up.

She broke ice along the bank to wash her hands and scrub them clean with sand. The Scythians never bathed, so far as she could see, but Ava wasn't one of them and never would be. They could call her Opoin all they wanted. She was still Ava. She wouldn't wash her hair in mare's pee, and she'd stay clean if it killed her.

The frigid water made her fingers so numb that she could hardly feel them. Her sturdy boots were lined with lamb's wool, but the cold seeped up from the frozen ground through her soles and chilled her so that her teeth began to chatter. As she turned back toward the village, she smelled smoke.

Not cooking fires. Smoke!

Flames shot up from the far side of the camp. The gust carried the bawl of terrified animals. Hooves pounded the earth like a monstrous drum as the vast horse and cattle herds spooked. If they came this way, she would have to run or be crushed. Unless . . . Wild hope rose in Ava's chest. If she could leap onto the back of a pony, she might escape from the Pestici.

A woman screamed, high and shrill. Men on horseback charged through the camp uttering war cries. Falling stars arched over the camp. Not stars, Ava realized—fire arrows. Other yurts flared as the missiles found their targets.

Ava stood paralyzed, wondering what to do. Was this the chance to escape she'd been waiting for? On foot, without weapons or even a blanket, she wouldn't last the night on the steppes. But if she had food, blankets, a way to make a fire . . .

She knew she had to go back into the camp, take what she needed, and find a mount. It was what her mother would do if she were here. Mama was brave. She would expect Ava to be too. But she didn't feel brave. She was afraid.

Ava took a hesitant step and then another. The village was in a state of total chaos. No one would notice her, no matter what she did. A riderless horse galloped out of the darkness, eyes white with fear. Ava grabbed for the trailing rein, but missed. The horse reared and struck out at her with its forelegs, but she threw herself out of the animal's path and it bolted away and slid down the riverbank into the water.

Determined, she forced herself up and ran back toward Targitaos's yurt. An old woman and two boys dashed past her. Flaming sections of hide and wood from a burning tent rained around her. Shrieks of injured and dying Scythians mingled with the cries of dogs and horses, but Ava kept moving.

As Ava neared the yurt, she saw it was still there, but glowing with an orange light. She wanted to run. She was scared and she wanted her mother. She couldn't stop tears from forming in her eyes. They trickled down and froze on her cheeks. She dashed them away and began to run toward the house.

The yurt was on fire. Not far from the entranceway, Jun was struggling with a bearded stranger. Ava stumbled over a dead dog. She gave a small yelp as she fell facedown in the red snow. All around her was madness: horses running, women screaming, arrows flying.

A Pestici youth and a warrior rolled on the ground, wrestling and slashing at each other with knives. The attacker pinned the boy to the ground and was about to cut his throat when suddenly a feathered shaft sprouted from his back. He fell forward onto the Pestici.

Smoke and falling snow made it hard to see. Jun screamed. Her assailant had her down on the ground and was tearing at her clothes. From inside the yurt, she heard Ku howling in fright. Blood pounded in Ava's ears. She wanted to run away, but she couldn't leave the baby to burn. As she yanked aside the door flap, heat flashed over Ava's face. Closing her eyes, she threw herself through the entranceway.

Choking smoke rolled over her. She fell to her knees. Water streamed from her eyes. Ku shrieked.

Burning sparks showered around Ava. One struck her hand. With a yelp, she dove for Ku, threw the blanket over his head, and dragged him outside. Sobbing, the little boy clung to her. His clothes smoldered, and she pressed him into the snow to smother the sparks.

Sparks burned her hands and cheeks. She smelled the acrid stench of burning hair and realized that her own braid was on fire. She beat at it, then panicked as something black and heavy enveloped her and pinned her arms against her sides.

"Be still!" Jun cried, yanking away the blanket. "I'm only putting out the fire in your hair." The Scythian woman's eyes were as crazed as those of the horse that had almost run Ava down, and her mouth was swollen and streaked with blood. She thrust Ku into Ava's lap. "Keep him warm!" she shouted before turning away to aid a wounded woman.

Ava gulped cold air into her lungs. Ku was weeping, and she rocked him against her and murmured soothing sounds. The snow was still falling, but the burning yurts made the camp almost as bright as day. Ava saw the man who'd been hurting Jun sprawled on his back, his skull shattered.

Fighting continued all around her, but Ava could tell that the tide of battle had turned. The village warriors had rallied and were driving off the Auchat. Now the war cries were Pestici, and those fleeing for their lives were not women and children but the invaders. She had lost her one chance to escape.

Targitaos appeared on horseback and flung two dripping heads at his wife's feet. "Is the boy safe?" he demanded. Jun shouted back, assuring him that Ku was unharmed. "And Opoin?"

"I'm all right," Ava said. Her throat stung and it was painful to talk.

He nodded and without saying anything more dug

226

his heels into his horse's sides and galloped away. Jun helped the woman to her feet and led her over. "Share the blanket," she said to Ava.

The injured woman groaned and settled onto the ground beside Ava. Her broad face was smeared with blood. "He means to give this one to Papai?" she asked.

Jun shook her head. "Watch what you say. She understands more than she lets on."

The older woman grimaced. "She's too skinny. A bride of Papai should be ripe, not all eyes and bones."

"Targitaos says she will ripen," Jun replied. "Give her time. And Papai will find her big eyes beautiful."

Ava tried to make her face blank. She hated it when adults talked about her as though she weren't there. Her hands and face were sore, and Ku's squirming hurt them even more.

"Fatten her on mutton and mare's butter," the rude woman said.

"I will, Auntie. Watch her while I go and see if I can help the others."

"Tagi is dead, and your cousin Eir-mas. I saw Sakas running for the riverbank with her daughters."

"Eir-mas was close to her time to give birth to her first child," Jun replied. "Sometimes it is hard to accept the ways of Papai."

Ava stiffened.

"You lost your yurt. Both Eir-mas and her man are killed. You can move into her tent. It is not so large as yours, but it will keep the snow off your heads until the women can sew a new one." The old woman coughed. "So many dead. And winter just beginning."

"Jun!" a man shouted. "My wife needs you."

"I must go, Auntie Chabi," Jun said. "Guard my son and the girl." She darted off between the burning tents.

Ava waited until Ku stopped his fussing and lay quiet in her arms, and then she ventured a question in deliberately bad Scythian. "Who is Papai, lady?"

"Hush!" the woman scolded. "Don't show your ignorance." She glanced around as if she expected to see this Papai leaping out of the darkness. "Little fool! What heathens do you come from that you do not know the great god?"

"He is god?"

Chabi scowled at Ava. "Our god of war. Supreme over all other gods. Even a toddling babe knows that."

"Yes," Ku lisped. "Great Pata."

"Papai," Chabi corrected. "Only ignorant people call him Pata."

"Ma said it. She said, 'great Pata.' I heard her."

"Whether your foolish mother said it or not, children who do not want great Papai to bite off their heads when they sleep give him proper respect."

A bad sensation settled over Ava, but she asked the question anyway. "How does Papai get married?"

"You will see, girl." The woman cackled. "You will see."

"Get down," Kiara whispered. "On your face." She shoved Alexander. "Do you want to get us killed?" She threw herself down beside him on the deck.

The crew dropped the sail and hid their faces as Queen Artakama's barge slipped past the smaller boat. From the larger vessel came music and the sound of laughter. The barge dwarfed the small trading *Byblos*, and the wake set them to rocking.

Alexander cursed softly.

"Shh," Kiara warned.

"He's on that boat. I know he is."

"Who?" she whispered.

"My uncle. Ptolemy."

228

"What does it matter?"

Alexander started to raise his head and she yanked a lock of his hair. "No," she said. "Would you risk all our lives for a bold show of defiance? Do you think you could climb the side of the barge, sword in your teeth, like some pirate? The queen's guard would cut you down before you set foot on the deck. And we would die with you, all of us." She gripped his hand. "Let it go."

"You expect me to leave Egypt with—"

"With your head," Kiara finished. "You may be a prince, but you're flesh and bone. You can die as easily as any galley slave." She peered out of the corner of her eye at the rows of oars rising and falling in unison. The lines of rowers chained to their benches were invisible except for glimpses of sweaty bodies through the gaps in the hull. "Pharaoh and Queen Artakama are rarely together in the daytime," she said. "He's probably not on board."

"I'd be happy to choke the life out of Artakama—or my betrothed."

"Your widow?" Kiara's lips tightened. "Keep your voice down," she whispered. "These sailors speak at least a smattering of Greek. You're supposed to be a Syrian." She sat up. "It's all right. The royal barge has passed."

Alexander rose to his feet and stared at the wake of the queen's vessel. The captain of their small boat shouted orders to his men, and they swiftly raised the single sail. The canvas snapped and billowed in the hot breeze, and the *Byblos* leaped ahead. A naked boy on the bank waved, and when one of the grizzled crewmen waved back, the child danced and whooped with delight.

Kiara settled onto a coil of rope and watched as the brown tide of the mighty Nile carried them past a panorama of rich farmland, mud-walled villages, and orchards heavy with fruit. Farmers drove long-horned cattle and flocks of geese to market along the dusty road that snaked beside the river; housewives washed clothing, gossiped, and dipped endless jars of water. Children, their skin bronzed to a toasty brown, laughed and chased one another with carefree abandon.

As if reading her mind, Alexander said, "I find much in Egypt to admire. The peasants seem well fed and content. For a Macedonian, my uncle makes a good pharaoh."

"Yes," Kiara agreed. "He keeps a balance between the priests, the country folk, and the merchants, all the while retaining absolute power for himself."

"Too much power. In my country—Bactria and Sogdiana—the mountain people are more independent. They'd never allow any man or woman to set themselves up as gods."

She shrugged. "But you will be king."

"I'll be king if I get home alive." He shook his head. "King, but not pharaoh. The monarch of the Twin Kingdoms may lead, but never command. I am expected to uphold the old laws, respecting the rights of individual men and women."

"Women are valued in your country?"

"Yes, they are. A royal princess may inherit the throne if there are no worthy male candidates. Any freeborn woman may inherit property, buy and sell land, own as many businesses as she can manage, and retain control over her young children."

"Eire is much the same," she said. "Although a queen may not rule in her own name, her bloodline is considered sacred. Eire's daughters may not be forced into marriage without their consent, and they can divorce a bad husband and take back everything they brought to the union."

"In the Twin Kingdoms as well. Our laws are different from Egypt's. If I am crowned king, any farmer, cook, or mule driver, male or female, is guaranteed the right to approach me and speak his mind without fear of reprisal."

"So it is on my island," Kiara said. "A king leads only so long as he maintains the respect of his people. A coward or a despot is soon laughed from his throne."

"But all that will change if Paris reaches the Twin Kingdoms before I do. His intentions may be the best, or he could be plotting to overthrow my mother's army, assassinate her and my father, and seize Bactria and Sogdiana for himself or for Ptolemy."

"I thought your father was already dead. Is he not the great Alexander, brother to Ptolemy?"

"My sire, yes, but Alexander of Macedon died before I was born. My mother entrusted me to her distant cousin Kayan, the man who is now her husband. They had loved each other and intended to marry before my father conquered Persia and the Twin Kingdoms. She thought the political climate too dangerous for me, so she sent me away."

"To Prince Kayan?"

"Yes. My grandfather, Prince Oxyartes, adopted Kayan while my mother was a captive in Macedonia. Kayan raised me as his own son. He was both father and mother until I was eight, to me and to my brother Val, whom you know as Prince Paris of Egypt."

"A tangled web," she murmured, glancing up at him. "But you are fortunate still. Not many men can claim two fathers." Alexander's hair was covered in a dirty white turban, and he was swathed in folds of faded cloth so that none of his features other than his striking blue-gray eyes were visible. "I believe you were born under a lucky star."

"I don't believe in luck," he answered. "A man makes his own destiny."

She shook her head. "You're wrong. Life is full of mystery, and the creator's ways are often beyond our ken."

"A woman's fancy."

She sighed, wishing that things were different, that she didn't need him so much. Didn't have feelings for him that she had no right to feel. It was plain to see that Alexander regretted their bargain. So far he had respected her person and done all that she'd asked of him. He'd found them passage on this grain boat bound for Rhodes, and his stern presence had protected her from the attentions of both captain and crew. Soon they would be on the open sea and—if not beyond the reach of Pharaoh's vengeance—far safer than she'd felt for many years. "You do intend to keep your word to me, don't you? To take me home to Eire?"

Alexander's fingers closed on her shoulder. "I'm grateful to you, but I can't allow you to keep me from my duty."

Sparks of unease made her voice throaty. "You made me a promise," she reminded him.

"A promise I have kept and will keep. I'll find you a suitable escort back to your island. I'll pay whatever he demands, but I can't be that man. I have to get to Bactria before Paris."

"No!" Panic seized her. "No! It must be you."

"Spare me your tears. There are more important matters at stake than the needs of one woman, even a beautiful one."

Her throat constricted. "You can't do this."

"Can't I? What will you do to stop me?"

Chapter 19

"Mother!" Shahi rushed into the courtyard.

Roxanne stood ankle-deep in snow, embracing a tall chestnut stallion with a white patch on his forehead. A red-faced herd boy of about thirteen years of age waited a few feet away, the end of Shirzad's lead rope in his mittened hands.

"It's Shirzad?" Shahi cried. "You're certain?"

Roxanne pressed her face into the stallion's neck. The animal's hair was thick and tangled; clumps of ice matted his long mane and tail. "Yes, it's your father's horse. I'd know him anywhere."

"You found him like this?" Shahi demanded of the herd boy. "No saddle or bridle?"

"As you see, lady. He was with the mares this morning. Porchaji is the horse master in charge of the mares, and said that I should bring the animal to the head groom in the royal stables. He thought that someone might recognize the chestnut. The horse is well trained. He allowed me to slip a rope over his head and . . ."

The lad averted his eyes and kicked at the snow with a stout boot. "Porchaji said that I must tell the head groom that the stallion . . . that he . . ." His ruddy face glowed with embarrassment. "The head groom said that I must bring the horse here, that he thought he was Prince Kayan's stallion. Please, lady, intercede for me or I will lose my place. The stallion mounted two mares before I could catch him. Porchaji said that it was my duty to prevent the mares from being covered by stray stallions. Now the breeding charts will be ruined and—"

"You did right to bring him to the royal stables," Shahi said. "I will speak to Porchaji. You will not be punished."

"If I lose my place, I will have to go back to my father's farm. I hate sheep, gracious lady. I want to work with the horses. I swear that I won't—"

"Return to your mares," Shahi said. "I will take responsibility for Shirzad. Porchaji will have to mark the mares that you saw with Shirzad and count the days until they drop their foals. My father's stallion is a noble one. The bloodlines may be disarrayed, but not ruined. Go back to your tasks, and next time watch your charges more carefully." She scowled at him. "I will not be so lenient next time . . . What is your name?"

"I am Vohu, son of Buzargmeher and Ruhae, lady."

"Well, Vohu, remember that the mares are a great treasure. Be vigilant. Is your mother living?"

The boy nodded. "Yes, lady."

"And have your parents other sons to herd their sheep?"

"Three younger sons and five daughters."

Shahi removed her gold and ruby earrings and handed them to the boy. "Take these to your mother. Blessed by so many daughters, she will need to provide

234

dowries for them." Shahi took the lead rope. "Go," she ordered. "And let me hear only good about you from now on."

"That was well done," Roxanne said as the lad dashed away. Her eyes widened and she clasped her swollen belly.

"Are you all right?" Shahi dropped the lead rope and slipped an arm around her mother. "You should be in bed, not out in this weather."

"No, I'm fine." She smiled wanly. "It is your little brother. He kicks like a mule."

"But that's good, isn't it? They are supposed to move around, aren't they?"

"Yes, they are. He is." Roxanne patted the chestnut's nose. "There are a dozen reasons why Shirzad would come home without your father."

"If he had no saddle, that means he was loose when he wandered away," Shahi said quickly. But she knew the animal was devoted to her father and would never abandon him, and she could tell by the worry in her mother's eyes that Roxanne was thinking the same. "See, his right hoof is cracked," Shahi continued. "Father wouldn't have ridden him in that condition. He may have turned him loose."

"I was wrong to let them go." Roxanne's tone was low and controlled. "Especially Ava."

Shahi shook her head. "You could not have prevented it. My sister is as stubborn as Father. She would have just run off after him. They are both safe and well. Snows have been heavier than usual this winter. You'll hear from them soon."

Roxanne nodded. "It's foolish of me to worry so without reason. I don't know why I have this terrible feeling that something is wrong. They're probably holed up in some frontier outpost. When the snow melts, after the baby comes, we'll all laugh about this. Ava will have some fantastic tale of snow leopards and griffins—"

"She's safe with Papa. He'd never allow anything bad to happen to her. And he'd never put her in harm's way."

"It's just that I've had such disturbing dreams. We've heard nothing from Alexander, and now Shirzad appearing alone . . ." Roxanne straightened and studied her daughter from toe to head. "Your novice's robes . . . Today was the retreat in preparation for your initiation ceremony. Why are you dressed for a winter journey?"

Shahi swallowed. She'd known this wouldn't be easy. "I was coming to tell you. I've made the decision not to take my temple vows tomorrow. I'm going to put it off for another year."

"But you were so certain. Is this what you want? Or are you doing this for me?"

"For all of us," Shahi said. "As Father has reminded me often enough, if Alexander doesn't return, I'll be queen. Why take vows that I may have to renounce?"

"You didn't feel that way a week ago." Roxanne brushed a snowflake off the end of Shahi's nose. "I want you to be happy. If that means giving you to the temple, then so be it. You're old enough to decide these things yourself. No one will force you to be queen. There is always Ava."

"What are you always telling me about rank? I was born a princess of the Twin Kingdoms. I've enjoyed the privileges. Now I must earn them." She gripped Roxanne's arm. "Reports from the southern border are disturbing. The Greek force camped just beyond our territory is larger than it was in the autumn. Our troops are restless and eager to go home and be with their families. I need to ride south and see for myself if this is the start of a new invasion."

"You think the Greek general, Isandros, may have news we don't?"

"Possibly." Shahi grimaced. "I don't want to think that something bad has happened to Alexander—to any of them. But we should have heard from him. He knew we were waiting to crown him king as soon as he got home. What reason would he have for delay?"

"Some deception of Ptolemy's?"

"You said it yourself, Mother. Ptolemy is a snake. He's not to be trusted. If my brother wasn't so sure of himself, he might have—"

"Been here with us now. Instead of—" She broke off as a trainer and two grooms crossed the courtyard.

"Your majesty." The oldest man touched his fist to the spot over his heart. "Shall we take the stallion? The herd boy said—"

"Yes. Take him to the stables, rub him down, feed him well, and tend to that right front hoof. This is Prince Kayan's horse, and if any ill comes to him there will be repercussions."

The horse master grinned. "He will be taken of, highness. None would dare the prince's anger if his mount was neglected."

"Are my horses ready?" Shahi asked.

"As you ordered, Princess."

"Take Shirzad then," Shahi said. "I will be ready within the hour."

"Who rides with you?" the queen asked when they were again alone.

"A full company of archers." She quickly named the aides and officers she would command. "I forget nothing you've taught me."

"So it seems." Her mother nodded. "The Wise God keep you safe." She sighed. "Do one thing for me. Take Tiz with you."

"Tiz? He's older than the mountain."

"Yes, and he has fought in more battles than either of us put together will ever see. He will appreciate the opportunity to get away from his young wife and that bevy of children for a few months. Tiz is happiest when he is needed."

"All right." Shahi shrugged. "I'll take him, and I'll listen to his advice, but I won't promise to follow it. I know what I'm doing. And it's not as if I'm leading an army to attack Athens. I'll be safe enough inside our borders."

"You will be. I want to make certain of it. My job is to safely deliver this." She patted her protruding stomach. "And yours is to act in my stead."

"I'll send you a messenger every day."

"Write in your own hand," her mother instructed. "And if there is anything vital, use the leopard code. Only a handful know it, and all are loyal to our house."

"I promise." She kissed Roxanne's cheek. "I thought you'd be angry with me."

"What anger I feel is only toward myself. Do what you think is best." She pulled an emerald ring off her finger. "Take this. Whatever you command, you do so in my name."

"I won't let you down," Shahi said.

Her mother hugged her tightly. "I know you won't. You have too much of your father in you."

Sword in hand, Kayan rounded the burning yurt to where his man Abadi still battled a Scythian warrior. Arrows hissed over his head, and Kayan caught sight of a youth ducking down behind a fallen horse. He raced toward the hidden archer, dodged another feathered shaft, and sliced through the boy's bowstring before he could notch another arrow.

"Kayan!"

The prince raised his sword and the Scythian boy

fell backward, flipped onto hands and knees, and scurried away. The shout came again behind him, and Kayan turned to see his lieutenant riding up with a spare horse in tow. Kayan vaulted onto the animal's back, guided the shaggy bay to Abadi's side, and extended a hand. Abadi's foe was down, wounded, but still alive.

"Leave him!" Kayan called. Abadi's fingers closed around his own, and Kayan swept him up behind himself on the horse.

Together the three men galloped out of the Scythian camp onto the grasslands, where they were able to secure a Bactrian gelding with an empty saddle and trailing bridle leathers. Once Abadi was mounted, they swiftly rounded up a band of horses and drove them back at a run through the enemy camp.

Scythians scattered before the pounding onslaught. Trained to war, the Bactrian horses cut a swath of death among the enemy, killing and injuring more than Kayan could claim with his sword. Woman and children ran screaming from burning yurts, and Kayan had to rein his horse up so sharply to avoid running down a terrified little girl that the animal reared and Kayan nearly lost his seat.

A nomad in a pointed leather cap hurled a spear at him. Kayan threw himself onto his mount's withers to avoid being skewered, drew an arrow from his own quiver, and drove two feet of shaft through the Scythian's hip before he could take two strides. A woman ran shrieking to the fallen man and attempted to stop the blood running down his leg.

Kayan forced his horse down on all fours and lashed him across the rump, driving him between the yurts to the couple. He leaped out of the saddle, seized a fistful of the woman's thick hair, and dragged her off her wounded man. Bending the struggling woman's spine backward, he pressed the edge of his bloody sword to her throat. "I seek a Bactrian child! A girl! Where is she?" he demanded in Scythian.

His captive's eyes rolled back in her head and she wailed for mercy. "I don't know! I have seen no mountain child!"

"She was a prisoner! Taken on a raid inside Bactria. You must have heard of her!"

"No! No, I haven't," the woman cried. "Don't kill me! Please don't kill me!"

"Let her go, Kayan," Abadi shouted. "She hasn't seen Ava."

"Tell me!" Kayan roared at the man with the arrow through his thigh. "An eight-year-old girl with black hair! Tell me where she is or I'll slice her head from her shoulders!"

The Scythian's eyes rolled white. "There is no Bactrian child here," he babbled.

Black rage swept over Kayan. With a cry, he raised the sword to deliver the death blow.

A hand closed on his shoulder. "No, Kayan!"

He whirled, prepared to strike down the interloper.

"Kayan! It's me! Abadi! No!"

For the space of a heart's contraction, Kayan hesitated. Then the blood tide receded and his fury turned to grief. He flung the screaming woman down and turned away.

"Come, my prince," Abadi shouted. "We've killed enough. She isn't here."

"No." Kayan sucked icy air into his lungs. His eyes clouded. He shook his head. "No," he rasped. "She's not here."

"We have to go home," Abadi urged. "It's time. In spring we will return. Search again. Offer a reward for her safe return."

"No." Kayan struggled to control himself. "No reward. We cannot pay gold for one of our own."

"For a princess royal? Surely the law—"

"The law stands!" Kayan grabbed his mount's reins and swung into the saddle. "Free people do not pay for their own children! We cannot . . ."

Abadi vaulted onto his own horse. "In the spring," he repeated. He stood in the stirrups and motioned to the lieutenant and another of their troopers. "We'll take the mares," he said, "as retribution for our losses."

Kayan nodded.

"The steppes in winter are no place for the free people."

For an instant their gazes met. Abadi looked away.

"I must go home," Kayan said. "I must go home and tell the queen that I've lost our daughter."

"Not lost," Abadi answered. "Not dead."

"No," Kayan echoed. "Not dead. We will come again when the snows have melted. And I will have her back, or my bones will lie beside hers on these accursed grasslands."

"This is as far as we go together," Alexander said. "I've made arrangements for you to continue your journey, but I can't go with you. I'm needed at home."

Kiara didn't cry. She argued. She pleaded. She told Alexander that he was sending her to her death, but she refused to surrender to tears.

"You'll be all right," he assured her. "Demoleon can be trusted. He'll see you safely on your way."

"Believe that, and you'll believe that elephants aren't born from cow elephants," she flung back, "but spring half-grown out of vulture eggs. How can you be so stupid?"

"I'll forget you said that. I'm looking out for your

safety, Kiara. You have to trust that I know what's best for us both."

"You are a royal bastard!"

"I doubt it," Alexander said. "You'd have to know my mother."

"I wish I did. I wish I could tell her what a coward she raised for a son."

"Quiet, woman, before I show you exactly how much of a bastard I can be."

"Quiet? I should be quiet and let you send me back into slavery?"

"Calm yourself. You're being hysterical. I wish I could do as you want, but I can't, and there's an end to it. The sooner you stop fuming and get used to the idea, the better it will be for you."

Once they'd arrived on the island of Rhodes, Alexander had sought out the town's most respected merchant and spun him a tale of his sister's betrothal to a nobleman in the Tin Isles. He'd offered a great amount of money, in the form of gems pried from his sword hilt and funeral armor, and even insisted that the merchant bring a priest of Poseidon to witness the bargain.

"She must go untouched and unharmed to her husband," Alexander had insisted. "May your bowels rot and your soul be thrown into eternal torment if you break this agreement."

Kiara had watched from behind her veil as Alexander paid a fortune for her passage and for the services of a Nubian mercenary to guard her. Alexander also presented her with a bag of gold coins, which she presumed he'd gotten in trade for another of the rubies. But she knew it was all in vain. She would never be permitted to keep the money. And she would never leave Rhodes a free woman. All this arrogant, thickheaded, barbarian prince had done was to land her in slavery again.

"Have you so swiftly forgotten your own oath to

me?" she whispered as he embraced her in parting. "Have you so little care for your own mother's soul?"

"I gave you the choice of going with me to my own country," he reminded her. "You would have wanted for nothing there so long as you drew breath."

"You are a liar and a deceiver," she replied in as dulcet a voice as she could command. "And you will live to regret this. I promise you that."

"I'd take you if I could," he said. "You know that."

"I know only that the Twin Kingdoms will have a coward and a weakling for a king . . . If you ever make it alive to your land of scabrous goats and wild beasts."

Chapter 20

Wrapped in a cloak against the damp wind, Alexander stood squarely in the bow of a fishing boat bound for a small village on the coast of Lydia. His gaze was fixed on the blue horizon and his thoughts were troubled.

He was going home. Doing what he had to do. Fulfilling his obligation to his family and nation. So why did raw guilt gnaw at him? And why did the taunts of a green-eyed slave girl cause him shame?

She'd called him liar and coward to his face, words no man could utter and live to boast of it. Yet he'd held his temper and given her enough money to start a new life. Hadn't he done more than any other prince—any man—would do? He'd stripped himself of wealth to provide for her journey to her Misty Isles, and he'd passed her into responsible hands. Taking her to Eire, literally keeping his oath, would have been a noble gesture that could only end badly for both of them. Her island lay at the end of the world. His future waited in a mountain kingdom beyond the borders of

Persia. Not even Alexander the Great would have agreed to such folly.

He'd done nothing to be ashamed of. Hadn't he kept barely enough coin to buy himself a decent horse and supplies in Ephesus? Either he'd have to risk the dangerous trek alone or hire himself out as a mercenary to some caravan to get home.

Sane men traveled with a large armed force. One man on horseback, no matter how skilled at arms or familiar with the wastelands, could hardly hope to cross desert, mountains, bandit strongholds, and land ravaged by war, drought, and famine without coming to grief.

He'd left Sogdiana on his way to Alexandria with over two hundred crack cavalrymen, some of the finest fighting men in the world. Together they'd faced Greek armies, renegade Persian archers, a Syrian warlord, and the dubious hospitality of two Egyptian generals, not to mention fierce nomads, storms, and floods. Twice the wedding party had broken camp and fled for their lives from overwhelming numbers of unidentified soldiers.

He had no one now to rely on except himself. He couldn't afford to have his mind clouded with doubt. He'd made his decision—the same decision any sane man would make. He'd chosen his country over a shapely whore.

"You are a fool."

Alexander started and glanced around, wondering who had spoken to him in Parsi. But he saw no one. The fishermen were busy mending nets at the stern of the vessel, and he was the only passenger.

He rubbed his eyes. He'd had nothing more to drink than two mugs of weak ale. He'd eaten, and he felt fine. He wasn't feverish, and he hoped he was in full possession of his wits. Where had the voice come from?

It was a fluke. Nothing more. He'd been so wrapped up in his own thoughts that he'd spoken aloud without realizing it. Or he was dreaming. Men did dream and sleep on their feet.

Once, in the mountains near the Hindu Kush, his patrol had been shadowed by a party of Indian raiders. The running skirmish had continued unabated for four days. He'd not slept in all that time, not really slept, although he'd catnapped on horseback. He'd dreamed then, vivid dreams of the sea, of strange gray seals, and strangest of all, of massive stones standing in circles. The slabs had borne unfamiliar markings and he'd known, somehow, that the stones were the handiwork of men long vanished from the face of the earth.

"Alexander."

The hair stood up on his arms. This time there was no mistake. The voice hadn't come from the deck of the fishing boat or from the water. The speaker was here beside him, yet not.

Alexander was as religious as the next man. But he wasn't superstitious, and he took all tales of angels and demons appearing to men as wishful delusions. He remembered the voice he'd heard in the tomb—or thought he'd heard. But you couldn't count that as an actual visitation. He'd been drugged, and he'd gone without water and food for days. No one would account him mad for thinking he saw light or heard voices in his head when he'd been buried alive.

"Are you so lacking in wits that you can't see what you've thrown away?" This time the tone was not only mocking; it held anger and contempt.

"Who is it?" Alexander demanded. "Who's there?"

A hand tugged at his elbow. "Are you all right?"

He turned to find the boat's captain, a short, stocky man with sun-bleached hair, a weathered face, and shrewd eyes, behind him. "Did you see something in the water?"

Alexander shook his head. "No. Nothing. I was simply . . ."

"These waters are old, very old. Monsters rise from the sea here, and ships vanish. Sometimes sailors throw offerings overboard in this place to ensure good weather. Have you something of value to—"

"No. I need to go back. We need to go back. To Rhodes. Turn the boat around. I'll pay whatever—"

The seaman scoffed. "You've paid for your passage. I told you when you came to me that I am a fisherman. I said I would take you to my home village. And so I will. But we do not turn back. It is bad luck."

"Your luck will be worse if you don't do as I ask."

"No, swordsman. Here I give orders, not you. There are five of us. If I said the word, my men would throw you into the sea as an offering to Poseidon's daughters."

Alexander touched the hilt of his sword. "Five men are only flesh and bone. This blade is of harder stuff."

"Kill us," the captain said with a shrug. "Kill us and sail this boat back to Rhodes. If you can." He laughed. "You see your problem, stranger? You are bound for the mainland, whether you like it or not. And if you're lucky, you'll get there alive."

Kiara suspected she was in trouble when she saw coin pass between the rich merchant, Demoleon, and the Nubian mercenary, Yair, whom Alexander had paid to protect her. And she knew it when two of the merchant's house slaves came to strip her of her veil and clothing.

"Let's see what you will bring on the market, little chicken," Demoleon said. "I know you are young by your voice, but are your breasts ripe melons or shriveled dates? Do you have the face of an angel or a whiskered ewe?"

Better that she did have whiskers and the features of a sheep, she thought. An ugly slave might be pressed into service as a cook or a children's nurse. From the time she'd been stolen from the Island of the Stone Heads, her face and form had been her curse. The first few times she'd been violated, she'd fought. She'd scratched and bitten and kicked. She'd been strong, but still only a child without her full growth.

And determined men were always stronger.

She'd learned the hard way that it was easier to step away from her body, to return to the seals and the waves and the glittering beach. If she didn't fight, she was less likely to be injured, to lose an eye or to have her nose and mouth slit, like some of the other women she'd seen. In time, she'd even acted the role of a trained courtesan, laughed at the right time, pretended excitement, cried out in feigned ecstasy to please her partner.

She became the toy that men expected, but she never allowed herself to take more than the simplest physical pleasure, and she never made the mistake of seeking or expecting to find love in the many acts of copulation.

Kiara had long believed that she was past shame. Thus the waves of heat that enveloped her and the nausea in the pit of her stomach that came when the men undressed her were an unpleasant surprise. The shame shocked her and moved her to the brink of tears.

The merchant gave an order, and the Nubian grasped her arms from behind. Demoleon caught her chin and lifted her head so that he could stare into her face. He was a short, middle-aged man, not much taller than she was, and wiry. His cropped hair had once been black. Now both head and chin whiskers were sparse and yellow-gray. Clumps of hair sprouted from his ears, and he had a black mole on his lower lip.

"Lovely. Striking eyes," Demoleon said. "I've never seen a woman with eyes this color."

She winced as he thrust fingers between her thighs, roughly probing her inner folds. "Fresh, but no virgin." He grunted. "You would bring more if you'd not whored with your brother."

She gazed back at him through tear-glazed eyes, but she did not see his face. Instead she saw the prow of a hide curragh and foaming water so green that herds of sea horses must graze in its lush fields.

The merchant pinched her breast, twisting the flesh between thumb and finger. She felt the pain, but it was far away, as if it were another woman who was being hurt and she was only a seabird watching.

"Are you lacking in wit, girl?" Demoleon demanded. He leaned closer, covering her mouth with wet lips and thrusting his tongue between her teeth.

He tasted of jellied eel and rotting teeth.

Kiara looked into the swirling water and saw a giant stone face staring back. The image was that of a kind woman with a straight nose and full, curving lips. Bubbles rose from the sand at the base of the chin. Fish darted amid the stands of feathery seaweed.

"Hold her," Demoleon said. "We'll see if she's made of wood or honey." He fumbled with his tunic and withdrew a discolored, uncircumcised phallus. "Down!" He laughed. "See how you like the taste of this, Green Eyes."

Kiara chuckled as a young seal thrust its head up from the waves with a fish dangling by the tail from its mouth. The seal was a speckled one with large, luminous eyes. It was so close that she could almost touch it. The wind was off the sea, and the cold salt spray stung her face. White-winged black terns swooped over the surface of the water, startling a bright-beaked puffin.

Nails bit into her shoulders, forcing her to her knees.

She focused on the little seal, his big eyes, the drops of water on his fur, the wiggling fish. . . .

Not a fish. Something . . . Mist shadowed the sea, a demanding male voice rasped, drowning the cries of the terns. The merchant stood over her, his tumescent member only inches from her lips, ordering her to do what was suddenly inconceivable.

"No!" Kiara screamed. "No!" She wrenched free of her captors and lunged forward and up, driving her head into the merchant's hairy groin, knocking him backward onto the red-and-blue-striped rug. Naked, she plunged past him, through the archway, into the central courtyard.

Geese scattered with a great hissing and flapping of wings. Maidservants shrieked and fled. A tame bird flapped and screeched. A dog leaped up and began to bark as the two men who had held her burst into the courtyard. Kiara dodged around a weaving frame and shoved it backward, striking Yair. The Nubian yelped in pain.

Kiara didn't look back. Instead she ran through a curtained doorway, shoved aside a wide-eyed woman, and fled back through the house. The men pounded after her, their sandaled feet slapping on the stone floor. She darted into the kitchen and made for an open half door, but a stout cook rose from the bench where he'd been scaling a fish and barred her way with a filleting knife.

"Stop her!" shouted Demoleon. "I'll teach her who—"

Kiara went for the knife. The cook slashed at her.

Kiara ducked and stuck out her leg to trip him. The force of the fat man's charge sent him crashing to the floor. The knife clattered across the stone. Kiara dove for it.

Knife in hand, she whirled to run through the doorway, but the delay had cost her. One of the men stood in the opening. He snatched up a three-legged stool, wielding it like a bat, while Yair advanced on her.

She backed into a corner and raised the tip of the knife to her throat. She pressed it against the spot where blood pulsed heaviest through her veins and began to utter the prayer of finality in her native tongue.

Smoke from the central fire pit swirled. Through it she could see the ocean. If she listened hard enough, she could hear the seabirds calling her name. And beyond the kitchen, where the far wall had stood only seconds ago, rose the sheer cliffs of a green island. Home. She was going home.

Tears or salt spray wet her cheeks. Her heart swelled with joy. A familiar figure waved from halfway up the rocky path.

"Wait," Kiara murmured. "I'm coming."

She closed her eyes.

Shahi trudged down the slippery trail, leading her mare. Snow was falling, and wind whipped around the mountain, threatening to tear them from the narrow ledge. Shahi was tired. The night's camp near the summit had been cold, the ground beneath their bedrolls frozen.

She should hate playing the general and riding the borders in winter to extinguish fires of rebellion and give heart to her mother's troops. She, who loved to sleep between silk sheets and wear the finest gowns and jewelry, should have despised the long hours in the saddle, the rough camp food, and the constant danger. Oddly, the hardships had not produced those responses. Rather, they had made her feel empowered, exhilarated.

It was most puzzling.

Shahi had always considered herself a person of reason. She'd watched her friends trade their dreams for marriage and babies, and she'd always considered herself lucky that her parents allowed her to choose her own future. She'd wanted to be a priestess since she'd been Ava's age.

Great-granddaughter of an Amazon princess or not, she'd never wanted to sit the throne of the Twin Kingdoms or to be the warrior-prince her mother had been. She couldn't picture herself at the head of an army, conquering far lands. Neither could she see herself as a wife and mother, destined to spend her nights waiting for the man she loved to be killed in battle, or enemy raiders to burn her house and bash in her children's heads.

She had never known peace. All her life Sogdiana and Bactria had struggled to hold back the menacing armies of India, Greece, and Egypt. And it had amazed her that girls her age had willingly committed themselves to marriage and a family that might be ripped apart at any moment by mindless violence. It wasn't that she didn't love. She adored her father and brother, cherished her mother and sister despite all their differences, cared deeply for her friends, relatives, and pets. But only in the temple had she found sanctuary.

There, in the ordered worship of the creator, a priestess was expected to love all people, to feel compassion for all living things. And with so many to love, it stood to reason that the loss of a single dear one, or even a handful, couldn't hurt so much. Within the solid walls of the holy places, each day, each season followed a routine. A priestess devoted herself to prayer and also specialized in some aspect of the order. She might become an educator, a historian, a clairvoyant, or a healer. She would be free to travel to other cities or remain in her home temple, and she would never know want, loneliness, or despair. If she were ambitious, she could climb through the ranks of the order to achieve power equal to that of an oriental potentate.

And yet . . . Shahi breathed deeply of the icy mountain air. And yet she couldn't remember being happier in a long time. Worry still rode her shoulders, of course. She felt concern for the safety of her mother in her coming childbirth, for her father and Ava. But she didn't believe that anything bad had happened to them. Her father was too shrewd a general. He'd fought many battles against far more dangerous enemies. A few Scythian horse thieves couldn't best him. And he would guard Ava with his last drop of life's blood.

Shahi had to admit that she missed the little brat. No one could be quite as annoying as Ava. She, Shahi, was the best rider, the best archer among her friends. Yet Ava, at eight, was better. Shahi loved horses, thrilled to galloping across an open valley or splashing through a rocky stream. Ava, unchecked by wiser heads, would fling herself on a half-broken stallion's back and race pell-mell down a mountainside that would give a goat nightmares. She'd seen Ava urge her mount to leap a six-rail fence, then laugh about the punishment she received for her daring accomplishments. And she'd seen the child plunge into a dogfight with only a riding crop, separate the animals, and bandage their wounds without a moment's concern for her own safety.

Ava was fearless. She flung her arms wide and embraced life without anxiety or doubt, in ways that she,

Shahi, would never dare. Ava never lied. She never doubted herself or hesitated to try again and again if she failed at a challenge. She learned languages simply by hearing them spoken, and she had the voice of an angel. Ava should have been born male. She had all the qualities of a prince with the tender heart of a princess. She was the perfect daughter for Roxanne and Kayan of the Twin Kingdoms. Ava was bold enough to seize love and hold it close through war and childbirth and storm.

Shahi wished Ava were here with her now, riding beside her, chattering away, telling her silly jokes, and assuring her that tonight's camp would be snug and warm, and they would dine on roast mountain lamb and apple-honey cakes spiced with cinnamon.

The lead rider, Tiz, stopped and held up his hand. Word passed from man to man. "Part of the path has fallen. Keep close to the wall."

Shahi exhaled softly between her teeth, observing as her warm breath froze in the air. Turning back was not an option. It was not possible on the ledge. They must go forward or . . . She supposed that if the mountain trail vanished altogether, she might have to give the order to push the horses to their deaths and traverse the goat path on foot. Taking this route had been her decision. This track would lead them to a sheltered fort on an aerie overlooking the Greek camp. They carried much-needed supplies for the garrison and messages from home villages that would lift the spirits of her troops.

Reaching the stronghold would also give her a chance to speak to Lord Nekmard, who commanded this outpost. Her father had doubts about the nobleman's loyalty. Nekmard's father had turned traitor some years before, taking gold from the Greeks to allow them passage across his lands. When his perfidy had been discovered, Roxanne had ordered the traitor executed. Nekmard had pleaded innocence of his father's crime, and her mother had pardoned him. But Kayan was not so trusting or forgiving. He'd kept a close eye on Nekmard, an ambitious soldier who would never have been given this command if his superior officer hadn't been killed in last fall's fighting.

Her mother had instructed her to try to discover where Lord Nekmard's loyalty lay and to offer him rewards of gold and lands if she felt they would bind him firmly to his nation's cause. It was more responsibility than Shahi had ever been given, and she was determined to complete the task to her parent's satisfaction.

Tiz waved, and the line of men and horses edged along the precipice once more. Shahi hadn't believed that the horses could follow a path this narrow without pitching off into space. She was glad that heights didn't bother her. The only creatures safe at this altitude were eagles, hawks, and the great vultures with wingspans twice as wide as her outstretched arms.

She placed her feet carefully in the boot prints ahead of her and spoke soothingly to her horse. Ahead, the mountain curved sharply, turning back in on itself. Once the rump of the packhorse vanished around the bend, she had only the silence to prove that the others hadn't tumbled off to their deaths.

With a whispered prayer, she moved forward. *Think of Ava,* she told herself. Her little sister would consider traversing this ledge in the middle of a snowstorm great fun. "If she can do it, I can do it," Shahi said, and urged her horse onward.

Chapter 21

Kiara's scream drove Alexander past Demoleon's armed household guards and through the back door of the house. Sword in hand, he crashed into the low-ceilinged kitchen with its smoke-blackened beams and rough stone floor. Seeing Kiara naked—with a knife to her throat—he cut his way to her side through staff-wielding slaves, snapping dogs, and the red-faced cook. As he sprinted across the wide kitchen, he saw the Nubian, Yair, draw his scimitar and launch himself into the fray.

"No!" Alexander yanked the knife out of Kiara's hand and tucked it into his belt. For an instant before he twisted to face the mercenary's charge, he met her vacant gaze. He wanted to pull her into his arms, to tell her that he was her, that he would protect her, but there was no time.

Yair lunged at them, curved scimitar descending. Behind him Demoleon bounced from foot to foot and bellowed for reinforcements. "The city patrol! Call the patrol!"

Alexander's focus was riveted on the immediate

threat. Yair's right hand wielded the scimitar, his left a jeweled knife with a ten-inch blade. Protecting Kiara with his body, Alexander swept his own weapon up to block the scimitar's downward slash.

Bronze clashed with bronze, and the force of the blow jolted Alexander from skull to ankles. Yair was both taller and heavier than he was. And he was very good. Alexander had considered three other candidates before hiring him to protect Kiara. His own skill with weaponry was better, but here in this cramped space with only seconds to dispose of Yair before help arrived, he knew the fight could go either way.

Alexander continued the assault, attempting to drive the Nubian back with quick, strong blows, overturning benches and cooking pots and clay containers in the process. Each time the mercenary met the attack, retaliating with fierce strikes, refusing to give ground, following each encounter with quick jabs of his knife. They thrust and parried as Yair tried to get past him to reach Kiara. Seconds became minutes. The merchant continued to cry out for assistance, and his wail was echoed by servants and family crowding behind him.

Alexander gasped and staggered back, feigning weakness. Instantly Yair took the bait and rushed forward. Alexander brought the short sword up and back down in the classic figure-eight sword stroke that Kayan had taught him when he was nine.

Yair was fast, but not fast enough. The downward rush of Alexander's blade took his left arm off at the elbow and sliced deep into his right thigh. Screaming, the man collapsed in a tide of blood. Alexander leaped over his thrashing body, seized the merchant by the throat, and forced him to his knees.

"Spare me! Spare me!" Demoleon begged. "I'll pay! I'll pay!"

"What do you say, Kiara? Shall I cut his throat?"

Alexander glanced back at her, expecting to see her still cowering in the corner. To his surprise she was on the floor, seemingly oblivious to her nakedness, wrapping a length of twine around the Nubian's spurting arm to form a tourniquet.

"Hold him," she ordered the cook and the only one of the two slaves who was able to stand. Scooping fresh coals from the fire pit on a flat board used to cook bread, she pressed the contents onto Yair's bleeding stump.

Yair howled, high and shrill, before he fainted.

Kiara repeated the process with fresh coals, ignoring the cries of the onlookers and the stench of burning flesh. "Find spiderwebs and wrap the arm and the wound on his leg," she told the cook. "When the bleeding stops, apply honey fresh from the hive twice a day. And may your eyes rot from your head if you do not care for him as though he were your brother."

"Kiara," Alexander called. "We don't have a lot of time."

"We do," she said, coming to his side. "We have all we need." She stared into the merchant's terrified face. "Have one of your servants fetch me clothing, sandals, a cloak, and women's items suitable for a journey. At once. And have your slaves turn back the city guard."

"I can't stop them," Demoleon sputtered.

"Send them away. Tell them that your house guards killed the intruder. Tell them anything, but get rid of them or my brother will roast you alive with an apple in your mouth."

Alexander stared at Kiara in astonishment. He'd expected hysteria, tears, even rage, not cold logic.

Demoleon groaned. "This is a misunderstanding. Surely we can come to terms without—"

She tilted her face so that the merchant couldn't see her and winked. "He's too stupid to live," she said. "Kill him."

Alexander smiled. "Gladly."

"No! No! Take whatever you want!"

"First call off your dogs," Kiara said. "If we are to discuss terms, there is no need for armed slaves or for city guards, is there?"

"No, no," Demoleon blubbered.

Kiara turned to Alexander and raised a hand. "No, wait. I believe you paid him gold to transport me to my homeland. He has broken the agreement. He must return the full amount."

"Do whatever she asks," Alexander warned. "Or I'll slice your throat like a spring lamb."

The frightened man gave orders and servants scattered. Outside, Alexander could hear shouts and arguing. Kiara knelt beside Yair and searched his kilt until she found what she was looking for—a small, stained moneybag. She poured the silver out into her palm.

"How much did you pay him?" she asked. Alexander named the sum and she counted out the Greek coins. "This money is yours as well, I believe, my lord."

"Hold it for me," Alexander said. "I've got my hands full at the moment."

"As you wish." She tossed the money bag on Yair's chest. "Steal from him while he recovers," she warned the cook, "and your ballocks will shrivel and fall off." She frowned. "You don't believe me? You should. I'm the priestess of a powerful goddess. I am a sorceress, and I have the power to shrink your rod to the size of a babe's smallest toe."

The cook made Poseidon's sign to ward off evil as he threw up his hands and backed away. "I'm no thief," he insisted.

"Remember, Yair must be cared for until he is well," Kiara repeated. "The curse will work as well on any of you."

A whey-faced woman came with an armload of

clothing and a large bundle. "Here," she cried, dumping the items onto the stone floor and shrinking away. "From my mistress's own chest."

Kiara dressed quickly without revealing the slightest bit of embarrassment. When she was fully garbed in a sky-blue tunic, cape, and shoes, she took the time to fasten her loosened braids with a length of ribbon. Then she advanced on the merchant, saying to Alexander, "Hold him, my lord. We don't want him to have an accident and die before he produces your gold, do we?"

"The gold is coming," Demoleon said. "I sent Morys to get it."

"Kiara," Alexander said. "We should be out of—"

"It's all right," she said. "Demoleon is an important man. He will have a fine ship in the harbor to carry us to Zacynthus or even to Corcyra. Isn't that true, Demoleon?"

"Yes, yes, take the ship. Take whatever you want. Just go."

"We will go, never fear," she assured him. "And you will go with us." She touched the center of his forehead with her fingertips, leaned close, and whispered in his ear.

Beads of sweat blossomed on Demoleon's face. On the floor, Yair began to recover consciousness. Moaning, he writhed, sat up, and rocked back and forth, cradling his maimed arm. Kiara glanced at him. "Stay where you are or I will have him finish you," she said, then turned her attention to the merchant. "You, Demoleon, will send the city guards away. You will give my brother his gold, which you so treacherously sought to cheat him of, and you will come quietly with us to the harbor."

"Anything. Anything," Demoleon agreed. "Don't hurt me."

260

Kiara smiled. "You see? He is a reasonable man, an honorable man, a man who has no wish to die before his time. A man who doesn't want to see his business ruined, his family sold into slavery. And would rather not suffer the horrible tortures that I know you are eager to visit upon him."

"Please," Demoleon pleaded. "I meant no harm."

"Good," Kiara said. "Good intentions are always to be admired, even in a wart on the stinking butt of a hyena such as yourself. A misshapen growth with the most pitiful man-root I have ever laid eyes on."

From the hall came a stifled snicker. Then an elderly male servant pushed his way through the crowd and extended a heavy pouch to Kiara with trembling hands.

"Thank you," she said, and after swiftly counting the gold, tucked the bag into her sash. "It seems to be all here."

"All was not his," Demoleon whined. "Half of what is there is mine."

"No longer," Kiara said. "The balance I claim for the pleasure you took in my services. You called me a whore. Now you can pay a whore's fee."

"Now can we leave?" Alexander demanded. He pressed the blade to Demoleon's throat so hard that a thin trickle of blood ran down the blade.

She nodded. "Yes, but keep a tight grip on Master Demoleon, for it seems he is leery of our company and—given a choice—would not accompany us on our sea voyage."

"For the love of Hera, let him go!" a thin, pretty woman wailed from the doorway. "My husband is a good man. He sacrifices at the temple. He feeds the lepers. You can't murder him. I have five children. Would you orphan them? Cast them on the street to starve?"

"Hold your tongue, mistress," Kiara said. "If you

261

would have this lump of dog vomit back, care for the Nubian until his wounds are healed. And pray that Demoleon has the good sense not to anger a powerful sorceress or my brother. My magic is strong, but his temper, when aroused, is both fearsome and deadly. And I suspect that he is in bad sorts this evening and would like nothing more than to lop off Demoleon's head and use it for a chamber pot."

"You know we'll never reach your accursed island," Alexander said to her two days later, as Demoleon's ship sailed bravely on across the open Mediterranean. "If we reach Corcyra alive, the merchant will report us to the authorities. We'll be seized and hanged as pirates." He grimaced. "I'll be hanged. Demoleon and his crew will take you back with them as entertainment."

Kiara smiled and dipped her hand over the gunwale to touch the sea. "You worry too much, barbarian. You thought we would never get out of the tomb. And then Memphis. You see, all things are possible." She had washed her hair earlier with rainwater, combed it out with her fingers, and left it loose to dry in the wind. It blew around her face like a dark curtain, and it was all he could do not to catch it between his fingers and feel the texture.

Never since he'd been fifteen had he gone this long without a woman. His need made him irritable, as did sailing so far from the sight of land. He was a man for solid earth under his feet, and his distrust of boats was as great as his distrust of this surly crew.

He glanced to where Demoleon sat a few yards away, propped against the mast, arms and legs bound. A cloth secured his mouth to prevent him from talking. "These men would kill us as quick as look at us," Alexander grumbled.

"They might like to," she said softly, "but they will

not, not so long as we hold their master prisoner. He owns the ship and pays their wages. There is no need for anyone to die attempting to play the hero. Once we arrive in the land of the Etruscans—"

"Etruscans?" He stared at her in disbelief. "You said we were going to—"

"Ah, my lord. Did I? Forgive my foolishness. It was but a small error, and if you remember, our future was not so certain at the moment I said it. It has come to mind that the Greeks would gladly hand you over to Ptolemy. We left Demoleon's household alive. The slaves will talk, and the kidnapping of a wealthy merchant will be the talk of Rhodes. How long before Pharaoh's soldiers start asking questions? A faster ship might reach those harbors before we do, and we might be sailing into a trap. No, it is definitely safer for us to go farther before we touch land, beyond the reach of your uncle."

"This leaking crate will never take us that far," Alexander said. There was truth in what she said, but he'd allowed her to have her way too long. When he thought of it, he'd risked his life to save her from Demoleon, and she'd immediately taken control and started giving him and everyone in the merchant's household commands. He'd agreed only because her suggestions suited him, and he couldn't come up with a better idea. But his patience was at an end. It was time she remembered who was the prince and who the little pleasure girl.

He scowled at her. "Don't you think you should have discussed our destination with me before you made a decision?"

"We are discussing it, my lord. At this instant."

She had a tongue as glib as Ava's. And she was as imperious. But he was no merchant in fear for his life. He didn't believe her wild tales of being a witch or a priestess. And for all her supposed powers, she hadn't been doing so well when he'd arrived in Demoleon's kitchen.

"What difference does it make where the ship takes us, so long as it is in the direction of the Misty Isles and Eire?" she continued. "We need to find a real sailing ship. My sea is not this little goose pond. Wait until you lay eyes on real waves. I have seen them higher than the top of this mast."

Alexander shook his head. "The captain will never agree to take us to the land of the Etruscans. The crew will mutiny. They believe that the world ends out there somewhere." He motioned toward the horizon. The waters pour over the edge of—"

She laughed merrily. "Do you think that?"

"Me? No, I don't believe it. I was taught by Chin and Persian scholars, but these are ignorant sailors. They—"

Her eyes widened in astonishment. "You are like all princes. You think the rest of us are stupid. Perhaps your goatherders think the world ends in Poseidon's cauldron, but not sailors. They may not know what is out there. None of us do, but the monsters in the sea are no worse than those that rule in high places. I have already spoken to the captain. He will take us to an Etruscan seaport. And from there, he tells me that I can find a Phoenician ship and crew to take us west."

"And if they can't find your island? If your sea is so vast, one island might be difficult to—"

She sighed and touched his hand. "Prince Alexander. You know your mountain country, do you not?"

"Of course."

"And it is far from the Nile."

"Yes, but—"

"Exactly. You know the way to your homeland. You could find your path over desert, rivers, even mountains. Understand that I am the same. I was little more than a child when I was stolen from my people, but I know the direction we sailed. I remember the many ports we touched before I was sold, first in Crete, and again in Alexandria. I will find Eire. Trust me."

"You ask too much of me."

She flashed a smile at him that tugged at his soul. "You had your chance. You were on a boat, sailing from Rhodes. Yet you came back for me."

"I may live to regret that choice. It nearly got me killed. I had to fight four men on that fishing boat. They threatened to throw me overboard."

She laughed. "I prayed for you. I prayed and you came."

"You didn't look as though you were praying when I got there. You looked as though you—"

"I told you. I will never be a slave again. I will die first. I had a moment of weakness. I lost faith and thought you had abandoned me, and so I was going to take the easy way—"

"Easy? To cut your own throat?"

"Life is always harder than death."

He looked at her thoughtfully. "My mother once said almost exactly the same thing."

"Then she is indeed wise and we would probably get on well together. Oh, look," she cried. "Dolphins! There and there! Luck is with us."

He gazed out at the waves. At first he saw nothing, but then a gray body leaped out of the sea. A second followed, and a third. He was captured by their beauty, by the wild enthusiasm they displayed.

"You see," Kiara murmured. "They show us the path. They are the souls of the drowned and they will guide and protect us."

"Souls of the drowned," he muttered. The days at sea had tinted her cheeks a rosy hue. Now drops of spray sparkled on her lashes and lips. Her face was thinner than it had been when he'd first laid eyes on her in his uncle's palace, but if anything, she was even lovelier than she had been.

For a short space of time, he wished they hadn't stopped at Rhodes. If he'd forced her to go with him, they could have been in Miletus or even Ephesis. He could have made her his concubine, and no one in the Twin Kingdoms would know or care what she had done before reaching Bactria. As future king, he needed a queen of noble birth, one who would bring wealth and bonds of kinship between nations. He could not offer Kiara his name, but he could protect her and secure her future. She would have status, and any children they might have would not be scorned because they were born out of wedlock.

Kiara could not expect him to marry her. Royalty rarely found romance with a mate. Dynasties were cemented by political power.

True, his mother had chosen Kayan for love and they had been happy together, but they were an exception to the rule. By all accounts, she'd been forced into her first union with his sire. Affection and respect had come later.

Had his marriage to Mereret gone as planned, they might have followed the same pattern. In time they might have suited each other, or perhaps not. She might have hated Bactria and pined for her old life in Alexandria, and he might have tired of her, as couples often did. He'd found her physically desirable, and as the daughter of Pharaoh she would have given him sons worthy to sit his throne. They both would have filled the role that life had laid out for them.

"What will happen when and if we reach your Eire?" he demanded gruffly of Kiara.

"Once I am home, I will release you from your vow," she answered. "You will be free to return to your mountains."

"To return by the same vessel that carries us. Alone. Without you?"

"Of course, without me. My place is with my people. Have I led you to believe otherwise, my lord?"

"No." He stood and flexed his shoulders. "I wanted to make certain that you had no other secret agendas. Some small change in our bargain that you'd neglected to tell me about."

She smiled guilelessly. "For my part, I have never strayed from my promise. I rescued you from the tomb, and I expect you to take me home to Eire." She pressed her palms together and uttered a small sound of excitement. "See the dolphins! Two have calves. Look, there. The small black one. Aren't they magnificent?"

"Let's hope they've come to guide us, rather than to collect more drowned souls," Alexander said.

"I told you, they bring good fortune. You'll see."

"If this is what you call good luck, I'd hate to see bad," Alexander shouted over his shoulder to Kiara. It was two days after they had first sighted the dolphins, and midafternoon, although the clouds and driving rain made the sky almost as dark as night. Alexander's sword was unsheathed, and he stood unsteadily on the pitching deck, blocking the path of the captain and four angry sailors.

Sullen skies the evening before had given way to gusts of rain and an ever-rising wind. For the last two hours cold raindrops had driven needlelike against their exposed skin, drenching their clothing and chilling them to the bone. Whitecaps boiled, waves rose higher and higher, crashing over the sides of the boat. The crew had furled the sail, lest it be torn to shreds, leaving them helpless after the storm passed.

None aboard had slept much during the night, and all were tired and hungry, the crew most of all. Sometime after midnight, Kiara had removed Demoleon's gag and covered him with a spare length of sail, but that had quickly soaked through, leaving him as miserable as the rest of them. Now it seemed that her mercy had been ill placed. Demoleon's wicked tongue had caused trouble.

"Cut me loose," the merchant begged for the tenth time. "If the ship goes down, I'll drown."

"Don't talk of such things," the captain said. "Bad enough we have a woman aboard without tempting the gods to destroy us."

"Woman nothing," Demoleon answered. "She's no woman. She's a witch. She admitted as much in my house. She's called up this storm."

"Offer her to Poseidon!" a sailor cried. "We'll all die if she stays aboard."

"If you must offer someone to your bloodthirsty god, let it be the merchant," Alexander said. "Or whoever comes in range of my blade first."

"Give us the woman," another shouted from the rear of the pack. His voice was nearly drowned in the screech of the gale.

"Who wants to be first?" Alexander offered.

The boat plunged bow first into a trough, struggled gallantly, and then fought her way up with timbers creaking. But the force of the rushing water was too great for the mast. It splintered at midpoint and fell onto the deck, shattering a cask of fresh water.

A bolt of lightning illuminated the sky, sending blue flames skittering along the waves and dancing over the stump of the mast. Thunder cracked and rolled overhead. Demoleon screamed and the captain cut him free. The merchant fell to the deck on hands and knees and called out to Poseidon to save them.

The captain staggered forward and shouted to Alexander, "Give us the witch and we'll let you live."

He lifted his sword. "You'll not lay a hand on her."

"Wait," Kiara said, laying her hand on Alexander's arm. "Shed no more blood for me. Tell them that I'll calm the tempest."

"Are you mad?"

"No madder than you to think you can solve all the world's woes by killing everyone. Ask them to let me try. What harm can it do?"

"If you don't do it, they'll try to throw you overboard."

"It looks like that's what they're attempting to do now."

"Leave this to me!" Alexander took a step forward. "They'll calm down once I—"

"I am a sorceress!" Kiara cried. "I will ask my God to spare us."

"It's a trick," Demoleon warned.

"You said she was a witch," one of the sailors reminded him. "Save us, woman! For mercy's sake, save us."

"Kiara!" Alexander seized her arm.

"No," she said softly. "Let me do this. But warn them it may take time." Turning her back to him, she dropped to her knees, held out her arms, palms up, and began to speak in her own language.

A deafening peal of thunder crashed as another spear of lightning pierced the clouds. The stench of sulfur filled Alexander's head, and he could taste ashes on his tongue. Rain came down in sheets. The boat bobbed and pitched, but Kiara remained where she was, no longer speaking, but singing into the wind.

Minutes passed. The storm showed no signs of weakening, and the sailors began to mutter again.

"Throw her to Poseidon, I say," Demoleon shouted.

"No." The captain waved his men back. "She said it would take time. Even a witch cannot command the gods at will. Let her speak for us."

Another quarter of an hour slipped by, and it

seemed to Alexander that the waves were not quite so high nor the wind so vicious. He hoped he wouldn't have to kill any of them. He could take them down one by one until only he and Kiara remained alive, but then who would sail the boat? Silently he added his own prayers to hers.

"There!" the captain said. "Look there."

A dolphin surfaced, flashed his fin, and vanished beneath the storm-laced waves.

"Poseidon," a sailor said.

Thunder rumbled farther away to the west, and in the east the black sky took on a purple-gray hue.

"The storm passes," the captain pronounced. "Our thanks, witch. We owe you our lives."

Kiara raised her head and looked at him. "Not to me," she said. "To the One I serve. She has pardoned you and saved us."

Demoleon scowled. "I say she brought the storm."

"Say no more," the captain admonished. "Speak against her again, and owner or not, you will never see dry land again." He looked up at Alexander. "Put away your sword, soldier. We will do no harm to her or to you. Poseidon favors you, and you need have no fear of us."

Alexander turned to Kiara. As she stood, he slipped an arm around her shoulders to steady her. "Is it possible? Are you a sorceress?" he murmured. "Do you have such power?"

"No," she whispered.

"Then how—"

The corners of her mouth turned up mischievously. "What did I have to lose by stalling for time?"

Chapter 22

Following Tiz's instructions, Shahi crept forward on her hands and knees through the cold slush to the brink of the overlook. She'd been mildly annoyed when her mother had sent the old campaigner along to advise her, but she'd blessed his presence a dozen times since. Tiz was rough-spoken, irreverent, shrewd, and tough as old leather. He treated her as a favored and slightly mischievous grandchild, rather than a royal princess, and he didn't hesitate to admonish her when he thought she was making a mistake.

This had the makings of a rotten day. Her trousers, coat, and boots were wet; her fingers were numb with cold. She'd left her fur mittens in her saddle pack because they'd only slow her down if she had to shoot her bow or use a sword. And here on the border, action against the enemy was a regular occurrence.

Farther down in the valley, lush spring grass had already replaced the ice and melting snow, but here on the heights it was still winter. Behind her rose the peak of a rugged mountain. Below lay a steep and twisting

271

pass, so narrow that men on horseback had to ride single-file, one of the few trails that led from the border country to the fertile farmlands and open pastures that were the natural treasures of her kingdom. It was these treacherous corridors that an enemy had to traverse to reach the heart of Bactria; protecting them was worth the lives of generations of gallant men and women.

All the combined armies of the Twin Kingdoms could not equal a portion of the troops that the greedy Greek invaders, the Persians, the Egyptians, and the Indians could mass against them. Only the courage of citizens willing to die to protect their land and the ruggedness of these high mountains kept out the human predators.

Shahi had wanted to be home by now. She was worried about her family. Her mother was due to give birth in another month, and the last dispatch had carried no news of her father and sister, or of Alexander. She could only imagine how Roxanne had suffered, unable to do anything but wait. Shahi had never expected her stint on the border to last so long, and she'd still not completed her mission—to discover if Nekmard was a patriot or a traitor.

True liegeman or deceiver, Nekmard was smart, and many of the soldiers under his command were of his blood and owed their loyalty to him rather than the monarchy. As long as she wasn't certain if Nekmard could be trusted, Shahi wasn't willing to return to the central palace and leave the nobleman to guard the passes against the Greek general Isandros and his army. On the other hand, removing him from his post without proof that he was unfaithful might bring on civil war at a time when the throne was held by a pregnant woman who might not survive the ordeal of childbirth.

A hawk shrieked and Shahi glanced up, expecting to see the bird soaring overhead. But the blue sky was cloudless and empty. The call came again, and she grimaced. *Tiz.* He was a few hundred yards away, out of sight behind an upthrust of sheer rock. His birdcall was a signal that he'd seen something and wanted to alert her.

She'd not expected to hear a hawk's cry. Yesterday it had been a mountain goat, and last week he'd chattered like a ground squirrel. The one-eyed veteran could imitate any creature that flew, ran, or crawled in these mountains. He was old, but still able to run all day and half the night with a heavy pack, and he still beat his comrades out of a month's pay at dice before dawn. On horseback, Tiz was one of the finest riders she'd ever seen. She'd match him against any Scythian, no matter how young and strong.

Shahi shaded her eyes against the glare of the snow and strained to see movement in the pass below. Nothing. She listened, but Tiz didn't repeat the hawk's cry. What she did hear was a faint snap, as if a careless trooper had broken a twig underfoot. There was an outcropping of low bare bushes behind her, but nothing that would hide a man. And none of her men were supposed to be behind her.

Four others were on patrol with her and Tiz. Two were farther down the pass; one, hardly more than a boy, remained with the horses where the goat trail ended, perhaps a quarter of a mile below. The last man was supposed to work his way down a steep chasm to look for enemy footprints in the snow. Wild creatures also followed the gully to the trail below, and Tiz had instructed the warrior to watch for game. Fresh meat would be a welcome addition to their larder. Last night they'd had to satisfy their appetites with bread, cheese, and melted snow.

Shahi rubbed her eyes. She'd been cursed with weak vision. She could see fine close up, but making out details of a rider far off was a strain. Everything beyond bowshot became a blur. Was that a horse coming below? Yes, it definitely was, and the sun glinted off the rider's head and chest, meaning that he must be wearing a helmet and armor. Greek, more likely than not. One of General Isandros's scouts. Behind him came two more men on horseback. She wondered at their stupidity. This pass had been guarded all winter. Surely the Greeks weren't stupid enough to think scouts could sneak through in broad daylight.

She slipped an arrow from her quiver and nocked it on her bowstring. Helmets and cuirasses offered protection, but a warrior's neck was exposed, as were his thighs. She'd learned where her shafts would do the most damage. She was an excellent shot at close range, but the problem was, the riders were still at some distance. And downward shots were always tricky.

Her muscles tensed. She forgot that she was cold, forgot that she had never wanted to lead fighting men, or that her temple studies had taught love and nonviolence. Today she was Roxanne's daughter, a guardian of her people who would take whatever steps she must to protect the innocent. The Greek invaders had chosen to put themselves in harm's way when they'd crossed the border, and they would pay the price.

The sound of a man's scream on the mountain behind her cut through her concentration. She whirled, angry, wondering who had dared to break the silence. The quick movement saved her when an arrow slammed into the rock where she'd lain only a heartbeat before.

Without thinking, Shahi rolled, leaped to her feet, and ran for the nearest shelter, a boulder about ten yards away. A second iron arrowhead clanged on stone behind her, but she reached her goal unharmed.

Heart in her throat, she looked around, seeking movement, listening, hoping she could hear her assailant approach.

Another cry came from the right. A man's agonized scream of pain faded to a moan. Next came the unmistakable clash of metal on metal. She knew it could only be swordplay, but between whom, and where? Sounds echoed off the rocks and the exact location was difficult to pinpoint.

She couldn't tell what was happening. Had her own patrol turned on her, or had the Greeks somehow managed to surround them and strike first? And where was Tiz? She hadn't heard anything unusual from the direction where he'd been last, but she couldn't be certain that he was unharmed. Tiz had the disturbing habit of appearing where she least expected him. He could have circled behind her and been hurt or killed.

If her men had been ambushed, it wouldn't be safe to return to where they'd left the horses down at the tree line. She was three miles as the eagle flew from the outpost. It would take her hours to cover the ground on foot. She'd never make it by dark. The temperature would drop dramatically as soon as the sun went down, and her bedroll and fire kit were in the saddle pack on her mount.

The hawk whistled again, not along the rim, but behind and to her left. Ducking low, presenting as small a target as possible, she crept along the cliff face toward the source of the signal. Keeping her bow ready, she moved as her mother had taught her, stepping lightly, using all her senses.

There! Just ahead, crouched behind a stunted pine, she could make out the shape of a man. It couldn't be Tiz. He'd been wearing a mottled-white sheepskin coat that blended perfectly with the patchy snow. This figure wore brown. She tried to remember what the other members of the patrol had been clad in. As she watched, the man cupped his hands to his mouth and imitated a hawk calling to his mate.

Sun gleamed off a helmet. None of her companions owned a helmet. She pulled her bowstring back to full draw, taking careful aim. "Drop your weapons or die!" she shouted in as deep a voice as she could summon.

The stranger turned toward her and raised his own bow. She heard the twang as he launched a feathered shaft toward her. She released her own bolt, aiming for the man's chest. His arrow missed her by two feet. Hers struck true.

A groan came from behind her. As she pulled another arrow from her quiver, she glanced back over her shoulder and saw Nekmard a few yards away. He was on his knees, blood spilling down his chin and throat. His sword lay on the ground, and he clutched at the arrow in his chest.

Shahi cursed, twisted, and loosed her second shaft at the Greek. The force of the impact drove him staggering back. Drawing her sword, she raced uphill over the rocks toward him. The Greek yanked his own blade from his sheath and braced himself to meet her attack.

"Murdering Greek bastard!" she shouted.

Blood ran down his bare leg in two thick streams. In the instant before her sword met his, she saw that her second arrow had taken him in the thigh. She'd been certain her first arrow had been a killing shot, but she saw the snapped shaft protruding from his chest over his heart. She didn't know how he was still on his feet, but there was no time to think.

"Wait! I'm not a Greek!" He blocked her sword blow.

"Liar!" She recovered and thrust low, aiming for his groin.

He countered, deflecting her swing and jabbing chest-high. "I tell you, I'm a Sogdian."

"You'll be a dead one!" Shahi dodged and circled, counting on his injuries to slow him.

He held his ground, defending, but not attacking. "You've made a mistake," he panted. "Take me to Prince Kayan or the queen. She'll tell you—"

"Liar! I'll take her your head!"

"Damn you, woman! Listen to reason!"

His arms were longer, his sword heavier, but blood loss was making him slow. She rushed in, blade flashing.

"No! You've got to listen to me." He sidestepped and nearly disarmed her with a smashing overhand blow.

She stopped, shaken, arm throbbing, just out of range. Deliberately she reached down and drew the dagger out of her boot sheath. Tiz had taught her to kill rats with a throwing knife, and this vermin was well within range.

His eyes widened and he threw up a hand in protest. "Don't! Listen to me! I'm Alexander's friend!"

Shahi drew back her arm to throw, but before she could complete the motion, a powerful hand closed around her wrist.

"No, Shahi!" Tiz shouted.

She tried to pull free, but it was impossible. Shaking with anger and fear, she cried out. "Let me finish him off! He shot—"

"He shot the traitor who ambushed and killed three of our patrol. Another instant and Nekmard would have taken off your head. That one . . ." He pointed at the Greek. "He saved your life."

"No! You're wrong. I saw him—"

Tiz yanked her against his chest and pinned both of

her arms. "Hush, my little tigress, before you make a greater fool of yourself than you've already done. You're wrong. This is no Greek. This is your brother you've nearly killed. This is Kayan's adopted son, Prince Val."

Shahi stared at him. "You're wrong. You must be. He's a Greek. Look at him."

Tiz laughed. "Wrong? Me? Not likely. You heard him giving the hawk's cry, didn't you? I taught him when he was younger than Princess Ava." He released her and went to the stranger. "How bad are you hit?"

"There were Greek scouts in the pass. I saw—"

"Dead Greeks now if Hermes did his part," Val said. He slid slowly to the ground. "You're a good shot, little sister." He was breathing hard now, deep breaths, and his face was gray. "Lucky for me that I wore my cuirass under my vest. Your first shot . . ." He blinked. "Tiz, can you do something for . . ."

Shahi ran to his side and examined the leg wound. The arrow had passed through the fleshy part of his thigh, and dark blood oozed out around the shaft. "You're lucky," she said. "It missed the bone. You'll walk again if you don't die of infection."

Val glanced at Tiz. "Did you make her like this, or was she always so tenderhearted?"

The old soldier crouched beside Shahi and looked at the injury. "Alexander spoiled her. Her father as well."

"I would appreciate it if the two of you wouldn't talk of me as though I weren't here," Shahi said. "I've never seen this man before. We were under attack. Assuming he was one of Isandros's scouts was the natural—"

"How many men do you have with you?" Tiz asked.

"Thirty-seven. Most were Alexander's."

"You bring news of him from Egypt?" Shahi asked.

Val averted his eyes. "It can wait. Do something about this leg if you want me to last until morning."

278

"You're certain Nekmard . . ." She motioned to the dead man. "You didn't make a mistake when you killed him?"

"He killed a boy farther down the mountain, or some of his friends did. He was in Isandros's camp last night. We saw Nekmard and twenty riders leaving."

"The others?" Shahi said. "Tiz, did—"

"Two of our patrol dead, plus the horse boy." He shook his head. "I don't know about the fourth man. I saw Nekmard put an arrow through Khodo back along the ridge. I couldn't get close enough to get a clear shot, or I would have killed Nekmard myself. He meant to wipe us out and send whatever report pleased him back to the queen."

"The queen? What of Kayan?" Val demanded. "He's still alive, isn't he?"

"Of course he's alive," Shahi answered. "He's on the Scythian border, chasing bandits. Has been all winter." She touched Val's thigh. "I think the best thing to do would be to cut the shaft above and below. We should wait to take it out until we can properly stanch the bleeding."

A birdcall rang out just above their position, near the head of the chasm that led down to the pass. Val attempted to return the signal, but could manage only a dry squeak. "Tiz . . ."

Tiz replied with an exact imitation of the whistle, and in less than a minute a young man strode into sight. Val waved. "Here."

"Jahan?" Shahi stood up as she recognized the young man. "Did you see the Greeks in the pass? Are they . . . ?"

The youth hurried toward them. "Princess." He looked at Val. "Hermes wanted you to know that we were successful."

"All dead?" Val asked.

Jahan nodded. "Yes, lord, and we've sent men to bury the bodies in a crevice. Isandros won't know what happened to them." He touched his chest with his fist and nodded to her. "Lady."

She gazed at him. Jahan was Alexander's squire. He'd been in and out of the palace all her life and had almost become one of the family. She was shocked at how much he'd changed in a year's time. He looked not simply older, but tougher, sadder. "Where's my brother?" She glanced at Val and shook her head. "No, not him. Alexander. Where's Alexander? Is he with you? He's not come to harm, has he?"

Jahan's eyes widened and he looked at Val. "I don't . . ." he began.

"No," Val said. His mouth grew firm and he nodded. "Tell her, lad. She has a right to know."

"The prince . . ." Jahan fought for words. "I'm sorry, princess. There was nothing we could do. Ptolemy . . ."

Shahi felt panic blossom in her chest. "What? What's happened to him? Tell me."

"Ptolemy murdered him. Prince Alexander is dead."

It was ten days before Val was fit enough to mount a horse, and another two weeks before they reached the palace. Once they arrived, Shahi called for the physicians to see to his leg. Tiz had remained behind at the fort in command of the remains of Alexander's cavalry unit, replacing those traitors who had died with Nekmard or fled after his death. All the Bactrians and Sogdians who had returned from Egypt with Prince Val either knew Prince Kayan's lieutenant personally or had heard of his legendary exploits. They would serve Tiz loyally until the queen could send troops to man the vital outpost.

"Remember, you are to say nothing to my mother—to our mother—about Alexander's death until after she is delivered of the child," Shahi warned Val as they rode into the palace courtyard.

Although she was grateful that this so-called half brother had arrived in time to save her and Tiz from Nekmard's treachery, she didn't trust Val completely. The disjointed tale that he'd related about Alexander's death didn't satisfy her. All seemed hearsay and rumor rather than fact.

Shahi couldn't accept the loss of Alexander. He was too strong, too vital to the future of the Twin Kingdoms. Her mother's hopes rested with him. He was to have been king; he should have been the man to lead her country to victory over their enemies. All her parents had done for their entire lives was to prepare the way for Alexander.

Now he was gone, if she were to believe this Egyptian upstart, and she wasn't about to trade a beloved brother for Ptolemy's son. Yes, he'd killed a few Greek scouts and prevented General Isandros from overrunning the border, but who was to say that it wasn't a trick—that Ptolemy hadn't sent his son to lull the royal family into accepting him and trying to steal the throne for himself?

He was no Alexander. Paris or Val or whatever he chose to call himself might be a fair enough sword fighter and leader of troops, but he couldn't fill her true brother's shadow. She, for one, would never call Val *brother*. He might have deceived Tiz, an old man who remembered the boy Val had once been, but he couldn't fool her. How had Val returned alive and Alexander not?

She had never wanted to be queen after her mother's death. The throne was a heavy burden. To accept such a responsibility would mean giving up her own dreams and hopes to put the welfare of the Twin Kingdoms first. If Val had any intention of claiming

JUDITH E. FRENCH

the crown himself, he would have to murder both her and Ava.

"What will I tell the queen?" Val demanded, breaking through her musing and yanking her back to the moment she'd dreaded—when she must shatter her mother's heart. "When she learns the truth, and she will, Roxanne will never forgive me for keeping Alexander's death from her. You must know that."

She forced herself to look into his gray eyes. "Do you have any genuine affection for my mother?"

"I did years ago. She was the only mother I've ever known. She wasn't with me long, but she treated me like . . ." Val's tanned and rugged countenance lost some of its self-assurance, and for a moment she thought she read longing in his gaze. "Yes. Yes, I do feel affection for the queen. She was good to me when I was a child."

"Then lie to her," Shahi said. "Mother's pregnancy has been a difficult one. The physicians say she may not survive the birth of this child. If it is meant for her to pass to the next world, my brother will be waiting to catch her in his arms. No need to give her sorrow in her time of danger."

"And Kayan? Do you want me to lie to him too?"

"No, of course not. But Papa hasn't returned from the Scythian borders yet." Her father's absence weighed heavy on her heart. He never should have left, she now realized. Regardless of his anger about her mother's pregnancy, it was wrong of him to stay away when her life and that of the child were at risk.

Shahi wouldn't allow herself to consider that he and her sister might not ever come back—that they could be dead as well. Her mother was strong, but human flesh and spirit could survive only so many blows. "I'll tell her that you've come home. It should cheer her," Shahi said to Val as household guards helped him to

282

dismount from his horse. "You rest. Let the physicians work their magic on—"

"On the wounds you gave me?"

Shahi scowled at him. "You're healing well enough."

"Am I? What if I carry this limp to my grave?" he teased.

"Then we may hope that there's no need to start digging the hole anytime soon." She swung down out of her saddle and tossed the reins to a groom. "Go with Mani." She pointed to a plump and smiling maid with an ample bosom. "She'll install you in a comfortable chamber, and I'll prepare Mother."

"Prepare me for what?" Roxanne called from the doorway of the lower hall. She carefully descended the wide stone steps and, despite the obvious bulk of her pregnancy, walked quickly toward them. "Shahi! Darling, I was worried sick. We've had no word in weeks. And who is this—" She stopped and stared. "Sweet breath of God . . ."

Chapter 23

Trembling, all color drained from her face so that she was as pale as an ivory carving, Roxanne raised a hand to her lips. "Can it be you?"

"Mother." Shahi went to embrace her, but Roxanne kept gazing wide-eyed at Val.

"Is it you?" she murmured. "My lost son? After so long?"

Val waved away the guards and limped toward the two of them. He touched his fist to his chest, directly over his heart, in the traditional salute. "It's been a long time, your highness, but you are as beautiful as I remember you."

"Highness?" She bit her lower lip as tears welled up in her eyes and overflowed. "Why not *Mother?* I've always considered you my son, regardless of who bore you. And you are as great a liar as your father. Sweet lies to a woman's ears, but the truth is, time has aged me as it has you."

"You will never grow old. You're still the loveliest woman in Persia."

"Yes." Her eyes sparkled. "But we aren't in Persia, are we?" She chuckled. "You can't know how happy this makes me. Kayan will be overjoyed at your return. We'd hoped that Alexander might tempt you home, but we feared that . . ." She threw her arms around Val and hugged him tightly. "Welcome home, son."

Val put his arms around her stiffly. "It's been too many years."

"Years without knowing if you were dead or alive." Roxanne released him and stepped back, so overcome with emotion that her voice cracked. "Shahi." She kissed her and gave her a squeeze. "My prayers have been answered. I feared for you."

"You didn't think I was up to the assignment?"

"I knew you were. It was just a foolish woman's concerns for a beloved child."

"Not a child any longer."

"No, you're right. You aren't. I'm very proud of you. It's just that I remember how dangerous the mountains can be in winter, not to mention the Greeks, or troops that may not remain loyal. I want a full report."

"You'll have it. But not out here."

"Yes." Her mother shivered. "It's a raw day. Did you have problems with the men?"

"No." She smiled sheepishly. "I think Tiz knocked sense into those who showed less respect than he thought I was due. You were right to send him with me. I didn't want him, but he proved his worth a dozen times over." She touched her mother's cheek. "How is your health?"

"As well as . . ." Roxanne turned her attention to Val again. "I just can't believe it. Your features are more evenly formed than Ptolemy's, and your eyes have remained gray, but they have the shape of your mother's. You're the best of two words, East and West, as is Alexander. May the Wise God bless you. How did—" She inhaled sharply. "You're hurt, aren't you?"

"It was my fault," Shahi admitted. "I took him for a Greek and put an arrow through his thigh."

Val grinned. "Two arrows, actually. I'd forgotten how deadly the women of the Twin Kingdoms can be. Your advice saved me, lady. I remember you insisted that Kayan wear his cuirass that day we came upon the nomad bandits. It saved his life when the armor deflected the arrowhead. And now—"

"Twenty years I've not laid eyes on you, and you let your little sister nearly kill you?" Roxanne wrung her hands, crying and laughing at the same time. "You are the best news. You don't know how happy this makes me. Where's Alexander? Is he coming with his bride? Trust a man to forget what needs to be done to welcome a new daughter-in-law. Shahi, you should have sent a courier. Alexander—"

"He's not here," Shahi said.

Val shrugged. "I'm sorry, your highness. Alexander isn't with us."

"Not here?" Roxanne's smile faded.

"He remained in Egypt," Shahi said quickly. "Just for a while. Can we go inside? It's too cold out here for you, Mother. You don't even have a cloak on."

Her mother hugged her again. Shahi slipped her arms around her and felt her stiffen.

"You mustn't worry," Shahi said hurriedly. "The princess Mereret . . . her mother, the queen . . . She couldn't bear for Mereret to leave Egypt yet. Alexander decided to stay a few months more, but he sent Val back to let you know that all was well."

"Yes," Val agreed. "He did."

Roxanne swayed slightly. "Come here," she said. "Let me touch you to make certain you're not a mirage. It's been so . . ." She gasped and laid her hands on her greatly swollen belly. "Oh, my. Sorry it's not much of a homecoming, but I think . . ."

"Here you are, your majesty." A physician hurried down the stairs, followed by several ladies-in-waiting. He motioned, and a tall noblewoman draped a fur cloak around Roxanne's shoulders. "Your women told me that you had come down to meet the princess." He shook his head. "Princess Shahi, she should not be on her feet. I have ordered her to bed."

"Are you unwell again, Mother?" Shahi demanded. "Why didn't you say?"

Roxanne took her arm and leaned close to whisper, "Boys are ever impatient, darling. This little one is determined to be born. My waters broke early this morning." She glanced back at Val and forced a smile. "I fear your sister will have to see to your proper homecoming, my son. I'll be unavoidably occupied for the next few hours."

Shahi's stomach turned over. "You can't be having the baby. It's too soon."

Roxanne's skin blanched to gray, and she bit her lower lip again. "It seems that this one will be as difficult as all my children. None of them are obedient, and none can bring themselves to do what is reasonably expected."

Hours later, Shahi paced the corridor outside her mother's palace chamber. She held a packet that a rider had just delivered; it was directed to the queen and marked with her father's seal. She knew that Roxanne would want to see the letter immediately, but her mother was in active labor. Shahi was afraid that whatever the message said would only disturb Roxanne more, and delivering a child safely was enough for any woman.

And even if she'd wanted to give the message to Roxanne, the queen had forbidden anyone to allow Shahi to enter the room.

"This is no place for you," Roxanne had admonished earlier, delivering her decision with a hug and a kiss to Shahi's forehead. "Childbirth is a difficult and messy business. Husbands, sons, and unmarried daughters are best kept away."

"You need me with you," Shahi had argued.

"I will need you more after the child is born." Her mother had gripped her hand hard enough to cause Shahi to wince. "Promise me that if I die, you will care for this babe as though he were yours. I must have your solemn oath."

"You aren't going to die." She'd wiped the sweat from her mother's brow with a soft cloth.

"Not if I can help it." Roxanne's voice came low and strained. "But I must know that the baby will be all right, no matter what. If I die, your father will take it badly. He may not consider the needs of the infant in his grief. A child must know love from the time he first opens his eyes."

"Why did you insist on having it?" Shahi had asked her. "If you hadn't . . . If you hadn't . . ." She couldn't finish, couldn't tell her mother that she wished the child were dead, that nothing was as important as Roxanne's life.

"Swear to me!"

"I swear it. I will care for the baby as my own."

"Now go," her mother had said. "Go and pray."

She should have argued, should have insisted that she remain with the queen. Instead she had fled the overheated room, coward that she was. She'd gone and remained outside the door.

Until now. Until this missive forced her to reconsider. Her father didn't know that her mother was in childbed. He might still be angry; perhaps he'd said things in the letter that he shouldn't. In which case, it would better that Roxanne not read it until afterward.

THE WARRIOR

If the packet had been sealed with her father's mark, it must have come from him. So he was well. That was all her mother needed to know, that her father was alive and that he and Ava would be coming home.

She tore open the seal, removed a thin strip of tanned goatskin, and held the message under the torchlight so that she could read what it said.

To Roxanne, queen of Bactria and Sogdiana, from her devoted husband, Kayan,

I hope that you and the child you carry are well. I want to be with you, but I cannot. The words I have to say are bitter. Our daughter Ava is a captive of the Scythians. We hunted for her all winter and returned to the fort when the snows became too heavy. Now a Skoloti trader has come claiming that the Pestici hold a Bactrian girl child. I go to find her. If I do not come home, know that I have followed her footprints over the star path to the next world. Remember always that no man ever loved a woman more.

The letter ended with the brand of her father's signet ring, heated and pressed into the soft leather. Shahi held it to her cheek and wept. She couldn't give this message to her mother. She would tell her that Kayan and Ava were safe but delayed. As Alexander had been *delayed . . .*

Would her mother believe it? And what would she do when she found out the truth? Shahi had lied the first time to protect her mother. And now, so soon, she must lie again.

She could not imagine Ava among the savage Scythians, masters of rape, butchery, and torture. Some were said to devour the flesh of their enemies and feast on their own dead. It was monstous to think of little Ava in their clutches. How could her father have allowed it?

"I heard that you'd had a message from Kayan."

Shahi started. In the shadow of a marble effigy she saw Val. "Do you make a habit of creeping up on women?" she snapped. "This is no place for you. My mother is having a baby."

Ignoring her tirade, he said, "You opened it, didn't you?" He came closer. "The packet was for the queen, not you. The courier said that it must be placed in her hands alone."

"Who are you to say what I can and can't do?"

"Kayan raised me. I have a duty to—"

"A duty to what? To come back and try to steal Alexander's throne?"

He laughed. "You sound like the spoiled child he spoke of, not the sensible woman I saw in the mountains. Which are you, little sister? Brat or princess?"

"Don't call me sister. You have no right."

"I have every right. According to the laws of the Twin Kingdoms, I am Kayan's son, as he was Oxyartes's adopted son. Do you question the old laws?"

"No." She looked away. "I'm sorry. I shouldn't have said that."

"No, you shouldn't. I've given you no reason to accuse me of trying to steal the crown."

She closed her eyes and gathered her wits. "Forgive me. My remark was insulting and uncalled-for. You saved me from Nekmard's treachery, and you stopped the Greek patrol, something I should have done. I am grateful. It's just that . . . that you're a stranger to me, and you brought such terrible news. It's hard for me to accept you in Alexander's place." She held out the letter. "I'm not in the habit of prying into my mother's affairs. Into anyone's. I opened this to make certain it wasn't bad news."

"And?"

She sighed. "My sister has been stolen by Scythians and my father has gone to bring her back. He isn't coming now. And if he doesn't find her . . ."

"You don't want your mother to know."

"How can I tell her that? Now, of all times? How can I tell her that they both may be dead and—"

"You don't think that the queen's suspected it?" He moved closer and lowered his voice. "How is she? Is the birth progressing normally?"

"How do I know? She doesn't want me in there, and the women tell me nothing. I've never had a baby, never been near one being born."

"Nor have I."

"I'm at least female. You have no business here."

He made a sound of amusement. "You are a prickly one, aren't you? Alexander said that you had your mother's temper without her sense of humor."

Shahi's mouth gaped. "That's so unfair. I do have a sense of—"

A woman's cry split the hush of the stone passageway.

"Mama!" Shahi thrust the leather pouch into Val's hands and rushed into the royal bedchamber.

Eire, green and mysterious, appeared, faded into the mist, then reappeared before Alexander's eyes. "What magic is this?" he demanded of Kiara. "Is it real or sorcery?"

Kiara laughed and clasped his hand. "I told you, didn't I? I told you!" She pointed. "See that rock rising from the sea? That's the island where I was taken years ago. You've done it!" she cried in excitement to the sturdy Phoenician at the tiller of the high-prowed vessel. "You've found the right spot."

"I took your coin, didn't I?" Hamilcar answered. The little man's eyes twinkled. He was as brown and bald as the deck of the ship, and—despite the cool temperature—wore nothing more than a length of canvas tied around his loins. "I'd be a poor captain if I couldn't find an island the size of Eire, wouldn't I?"

"Don't know," one of the crew quipped. "Seems to me that I remember a trip to Carthage where we missed the port by—"

"What would you know about that, Plalaris?" Hamilcar taunted. "You were so drunk on plum wine that Sidon had to tie you to the mast to keep you from falling overboard."

The others in the crew laughed and added colorful insults to the brew. It had been a good voyage from the islands off the Roman boot. Not only was the *Dawn Flyer* a stout and seaworthy ship, but the captain had earned his hire many times over. He'd remained cheerful through storm and hardship, knowing how to outrun pirates, seek shallow water to avoid boarding by Greek and Egyptian warships, and keep his crew content when the wind failed and food stores grew scarce.

Weeks at sea had become months, and Alexander had begun to believe they would never find Eire, that they would go on sailing day after day for eternity. Then, suddenly, without warning, Kiara had shouted with glee and pointed out land in the morning mist.

"Now what?" Alexander asked.

"Now we anchor off the coast and wait," Hamilcar said. "I'd not set foot on that island for all the gold in Crete. The tribes here are fierce. I've heard they collect heads."

"We do not take heads," Kiara corrected him. "Some of the more primitive tribes do, but not my people. We are descended from the red-hairs of Atlantis. We're civilized."

"That's all well and good," Hamilcar said, "but the prow of the *Dawn Flyer* doesn't touch the beach.

You're free to use the dingy, but if we're attacked, I have to look to the safety of my ship and men. I've no wish to add my head to their heathen displays."

"You are a follower of Astarte, aren't you?" Kiara teased. "We worship a lady, too."

"Not my lady," Hamilcar replied, touching the small token of Astarte that he wore on a thong around his neck. "Due respect to all local deities, but mine is a jealous woman and frowns on her people paying too much attention to other goddesses."

"Sounds like most women I've known," Alexander agreed. He glanced down at Kiara, who stood at his side. In all the time they'd spent together, there had been no opportunity to be intimate. Life on the deck of the *Dawn Flyer* was lived within arm's length of other men, and Kiara had made it clear that she had no intention of sharing sexual pleasures with him.

He couldn't understand why.

She was the most desirable woman he'd ever known. Her hair, the shape of her lips and eyes, her ripe body were all exceptional, but it was her essence that lured him more than all of the rest. Her mind was never still; she had a tender heart and a merry spirit. Kiara was above all a mystery, one that he could not solve. He couldn't claim her as his own, yet he wasn't willing to let her go.

Or was he?

How many times had he reminded himself of what she was, what she had been to so many other men? How often had he wondered if possessing her would release him from her spell? Yet he was no rapist. If she would not, he could not.

Surely she owed him something for bringing her halfway across the known world to this misty bit of land in an endless ocean. He had paid good gold for her sake. She had saved him, yes, but that had been an act of mercy, one that any true priest or brave lad might have done.

Liar. No one else had come, not his brother Val, not any holy man. No one had come to bring him from darkness to light but one gentle woman, Kiara.

Alexander stroked the silken braid of her hair. It hung below her waist to bounce tantalizingly against her sweet backside. He toyed with her plait now, tugging it, tickling her with the soft brush at the end.

She placed a hand on his chest and caressed his bare skin, easily brushing aside the opening of his sleeveless leather vest. Beneath he wore nothing. A thigh-length kilt and high, soft-soled boots were his only concession to the raw winds that swept down from the north. Kiara's palm and fingers were warm. Her touch sent heady sensations racing through his body, but he forced himself to pretend indifference.

"All may not be as you remember," Alexander warned. "You've been away many years. Your tribe may have moved to a new spot, or they—" He bit back his words as he saw movement along a narrow beach.

Twenty—no, forty men appeared. They approached a heap of green and began to throw off camouflaged nets, revealing two hidden boats. As he watched, the men launched the craft into the surf and scrambled over the sides. The open boats were perhaps thirty feet in length and the spread of a big man's arms in width. The freeboards were high, and both stem and stern rose up in a tall, graceful curve.

As the men of Eire began to paddle out toward the Phoenician ship, Hamilcar ordered his sailors to run a white sheepskin with a red hand painted on it to the top of the mast. "It's a sign that we come in peace," the captain explained to Alexander. "That we're honest men seeking trade and not pirates or slavers."

The lead boat grew closer, and Alexander noted that

it was covered in animal hide. The men at the oars were tall and muscular, mostly dark-haired, and heavily armed with spears, bows, war clubs, and swords.

"There! There in the second boat," Kiara cried. "That's my cousin, Bran." She pointed to a red-bearded giant.

"Off the starboard," Hamilcar said. "Looks like we're getting a royal welcome."

Three more boats came around a bend in the coastline.

"Show no weapons," Hamilcar advised his men. "Hold out your hands to show that they are empty."

"Cian!" Kiara shouted. "There's Cian!" She leaped barefooted onto a rower's seat.

"Careful!" Alexander warned. He grabbed for her but she was too quick. She yanked her tunic over her head and dove naked over the side. "Kiara!" He prepared to leap into the cold sea after her, but Hamilcar seized his arm.

"Stay where you are!" the Phoenician said. "You go after her, and they'll think you're trying to prevent—"

"The sea's too rough! She'll drown."

A second sailor grabbed Alexander's other arm. "Let go of me," he shouted.

"Wait," Hamilcar said. He pointed at the dark head bobbing above the waves. "Does she look like she's drowning? Swims like a seal, your woman." He laughed. "Yes, she's a selkie, a magical seal woman. I knew there was something special about her. No wonder we had such a good passage through the Straits of Hercules. We were carrying a sea witch on the *Dawn Flyer.*"

Chapter 24

Two days later, on Eire's mainland, Kiara stood in a torchlit cave surrounded by a circle of six women. Her eyes were blindfolded so that she saw nothing but darkness, yet she felt no fear. She could smell the pungent scents of cedar, pine, and oak moss, hear the familiar chants, and feel a gentle hand holding hers. Flames crackled from an outer circle of fires, taking the chill from the underground cavern.

Some of the voices that caressed and enveloped her were thin and cracked, others rich and full. At least one was high and sweet, that of a young initiate. Pipes played the ancient melodies along with drum, rattle, and the deep, echoing notes of a purple whelk shell. Most of the singers she would recognize if she could see them.

Soft yet strong, a pair of hands found hers; other fingers removed the woven crown of pine boughs and her garments. Naked as when she was born, she walked down a flight of steps so old and worn by human feet that none could say whether they had been carved by men or by the sea. The stairs led down to a tidal pool that entered the cave through a long underground passage from the ocean.

Kiara took a deep breath and tried not to panic when those same loving hands pushed her under. Seconds passed. Water swirled around her. She could smell the sea, but she was cold, very cold. Her chest pounded. How long could she go without breathing?

The pressure was released and she was pulled up, out of the water. She exhaled the remaining air in her lungs and took another breath. Again she was thrust under. This time it seemed as though she stayed under longer, because she began to see shadows behind her eyes. When her sisters drew her out, she gasped and choked, but she made no protest when they forced her under the surface of the pool a third and final time.

Kiara endured, going far longer without a breath than she would have believed possible. This time when the shadows appeared, she didn't fight them. She allowed her spirit to flow with them, and to her surprise an image formed, the head and shoulders of a speckled seal. The sacred animal's eyes were large and liquid, full of compassion. Kiara felt a weight being lifted from her, almost as though the seal had taken all her burdens so that her heart leaped with joy. She no longer had any wish to leave the tidal pool. Instead she wanted to swim out and away with the seal, to be one with the sea and sky.

"Kiara!" A voice cut through her waking dream. "Kiara! The cleansing ritual is over. All your sins are washed away."

"Open your eyes, child," an old woman commanded.

Kiara drew in a deep breath and began to choke up water.

"It's all right," another said. "You're safe now."

Kiara coughed again, and water ran from her nose and mouth. The blindfold was gone, and she blinked against the brightness of the firelight. "I saw a seal," she stammered. "She was there. Under the water."

Excited whispers.

"A blessing. You have received a blessing from the One," a girl said.

"I saw it. It was real," Kiara insisted, "so beautiful." She was so cold that her teeth were chattering, but her friends ushered her to one of the fires, wrapped her in snow-white furs, and gave her warmed honey-water to drink.

Once she had recovered from the ordeal, she was led through a circle of willow boughs. Laughter, a shower of flower petals, and joyous embraces waited on the other side. Everyone began talking at the same time, asking questions about the far lands she had seen, filling her in on family additions and marriages, surrounding her with the love and affection she'd missed so badly.

Only one question the Sisterhood of the Seven Shields did not ask: no one mentioned the bad things that had happened to her in the years since she'd been kidnapped from her homeland. Those experiences no longer existed. Magic and the glad hearts of those who had remained behind had taken the evil away. Spirit and body, she was once more a holy virgin, chosen priestess of the Lady.

Alexander sat at the high table in the great hall, where he was welcomed with all manner of food and drink. He could not understand a word of his hosts' language, nor they of his, but sharing needed no common tongue. His companion and guide, the red-haired giant that Kiara had pointed out as her cousin Bran, sat beside him, making certain that nothing was left out that might make Alexander comfortable.

The people of Eire offered everything but what he wanted most: he needed to know what had happened to

Kiara. She'd not swum to one of the boats, as he'd expected when she'd jumped off Hamilcar's vessel. Instead she'd struck out for land, swimming strongly through the waves. He'd watched her, his heart in his throat, expecting at every moment to see her vanish beneath the surf. But she hadn't drowned. She'd run up the beach and disappeared behind an outcropping of rock that looked like a giant's head. He'd not seen her since.

Alexander glanced around the great hall, marveling at the huge wooden columns that held up the high timber-framed roof, taking in the carved wainscoting and the colorful woolen tapestries stitched with brightly colored sea creatures. It seemed that every square inch of wood in the building was carved with elaborate designs, some geometric, such as spirals and knotwork, others stylized birds and animals.

Three fire pits ran down the center of the chamber, each large enough to roast an ox. The massive double doors were wooden, carved as skillfully as the upright beams, and inlaid with glittering seashell seascapes and beaten-gold dolphins, fish, and whales.

Richly dressed men and women sat side by side at the long wooden tables. Children, obviously cherished, climbed on adults' laps, chased each other up and down the aisles, and gathered in giggling flocks at the hearths. Proud parents passed babies from hand to hand, dandled them on shoulders, and cuddled them in the crooks of strong arms.

As with the warriors he'd first seen in the boats, Alexander observed that most of Kiara's kinsmen seemed to be dark-haired and handsome, with only a spattering of blonds and redheads among the throng. The women were adorned with fine jewelry, modestly but elegantly dressed in woven, sleeved tunics that revealed little skin between calf and throat. The men wore less clothing, displaying their muscled bodies openly, and were weighed down with heavy gold torques around their necks, both gold and copper armbands, earrings and ornate ornaments for their hair fashioned of gold and silver.

The leader, one of the rare red-haired Eires, sat in a cushioned, black stone chair with a scene of leaping dolphins carved into the high back. Beside him was a freckle-faced woman with a golden circlet on her head. Bran gave the young chieftain's name as Cian. Although he was not as tall or heavy as Bran, Cian was an equally fine specimen who seemed popular with his companions. Alexander wished that Kiara were here to translate or that he had some knowledge of their language, so that he could join in the spirited conversation.

Kiara had mentioned the chieftain's name before she dove into the sea. Bran she had identified as her cousin. Alexander wondered what the red-haired leader was to Kiara—a relative, or something more? This Cian could hardly be a lover, since as far as he could fathom, Kiara had been stolen when she was still a child.

"Kiara?" he asked Bran for the third time. "Where is Kiara?"

Bran looked at him. Alexander repeated Kiara's name, but Bran only shook his head and reached for his mug of fermented honey-beer. If he understood what Alexander was asking, Kiara's cousin was a consummate actor. Was it possible that her real name was something other than Kiara?

Another course followed the second one of meat and bread. This time young men carried in great platters of seafood displayed on beds of seaweed: crabs, lobsters, shrimp, fish, mussels, and clams cooked and served in their shells. Alexander tasted a little of everything and found it all delicious, but he couldn't stop wondering about Kiara.

Her people had shown none of the warlike tendencies that had gained them a dangerous reputation among the Phoenicians, but weapons were apparent everywhere. The knives and swords that the men displayed were not merely for show; the blades were too sharp, and the defenses of this town too well thought out for a peaceful farming community.

Earlier, Bran had led Alexander around the town, which was built on a flat-topped hill that overlooked lush green fields and grasslands. It was a site Alexander would have picked for a fortress, since it commanded the territory for miles around. The road leading up snaked back and forth, passing through high gates before it reached the summit. There, a wooden bridge led over a moat guarded by a palisade of tree trunks sharpened to points, a wall of earth, and a second wooden palisade.

Inside the walls, houses stood along hard-packed streets that intersected like the spokes of a wheel. Around the outer section of the wheel were paddocks where cattle and small horses grazed. The horses, he noticed, were smaller than those of the Scythians, too small to carry a man into battle. But the excellent condition of the animals, the chariots standing nearby, and the many carts and wagons proved that the shaggy beasts were used as more than children's pets.

The solid one- and two-story houses, each boasting a kitchen garden, were built of stone and wood with steeply pitched thatched roofs. Wide thoroughfares led to stables and larger buildings, and at the heart of the ring, another enclosure of stone. Inside this wall stood the great hall surrounded by dozens of round-topped, freestanding granaries.

Compared to the great cities in Egypt and Greece, Eire was a primitive place, but here on the fringes of the world, it seemed a prosperous and well-ordered land that drew its strength from fertile farmlands, mighty forests, and the ever-present sea. Alexander wished he could stay here long enough to learn the customs and history of the race, but his own people needed him. If he didn't return, the future of the Twin Kingdoms would rest in Shahi's slender hands, and he feared that his sister lacked their mother's strength.

A nubile young woman with dark brown hair and blue eyes came to wiggle in beside Alexander on the bench. Bran introduced her as Tatiana.

She smiled coyly at Alexander, and he smiled back. Bran nodded, motioned to Tatiana, and clasped his hands suggestively.

Alexander shook his head. "Kiara?" he asked again. But Bran only shrugged, and Tatiana leaned close, chose a choice shrimp from Alexander's plate, and held it teasingly to his lips.

He ate the tidbit rather than insult the lady, but he wasn't in the mood for a playmate. He couldn't stop thinking about Kiara. Why had she left him alone, knowing he couldn't speak to anyone here or be understood? He worried that she might be in danger.

When he'd left Hamilcar on the boat and gone with Bran, the Phoenician captain had held up three fingers. "Three days," the little man had said. "On dawn of the fourth day, I sail for warmer waters. If you are here, I will take you. If not, may the blessings of Astarte shower you for the remainder of your days—which, I fear, may not be long."

Three days wasn't long, but Alexander wondered what he would do if he hadn't heard from Kiara in that time. Would he just leave with Hamilcar and never know what had happened to her, or would he stay, not knowing when he could find another vessel to take him to the Mediterranean?

Young women carried in the next course: raw greens, vegetables, a type of onion, and what seemed to be stewed seaweed. Accompanying the women were entertainers, singers, dancers, and musicians. An old man in a blue kilt, wearing deer antlers on his head, recited what must have been a story poem. The performance was long, but even the children remained silent during the bard's delivery, and when he was finished his audience clapped, cheered, and threw lumps of raw gold at his feet.

Children brought in bowls of nuts and dried fruit. Youths served containers of the honey-spirits. Men rose from the tables and danced, and then separately, women did so to different music. Men showed off their skills at knife and ax throwing, and an arm wrestler took on all comers.

Finally, Cian, his wife, and the assortment of red-haired and freckled boys and girls, who could only be his children, bestowed costly presents of gold, weapons, jewelry, household goods, linen, furniture, and personal items such as combs and clothing to every guest. A small tot of no more than four struggled under an armload of treasures for Alexander, including golden armbands, a torque of the same precious metal, iron fishhooks, a flute of shiny black wood set with pearls, and three golden rings.

Shortly after the last gift was given, the chief and his family left the hall. The drinking, eating, and merrymaking continued, but one by one the rest of the Eires began to drift away, presumably to their own homes. The beer must have been stronger than Alexander had thought, because he suddenly realized that Bran had left the table unnoticed, and he was alone with Tatiana.

She tugged at his hand and spoke softly to him.

"I don't understand," he said.

She beckoned. Bewildered, he followed her from the hall, out across the common space and through the streets to a small house near the inner palisade. She led him inside through the smaller hall to a sleeping chamber. Indicating that he should sit on the bed, Tatiana extinguished the rush light, then left the room momentarily. When she returned, the room was so dark he could barely see her figure.

"Tatiana," he said hesitantly. "I don't . . ." He started to stand, but the bed platform seemed to sway under him.

"Shh." Soft hands pushed him back against clean linen.

"Tatiana, no," he said as she joined him on the bed.

The beer had clouded his thinking, but not so much that he did not realize there was something different about the woman now.

Her fingers massaged his temple, his eye sockets, and the tense area in front of his ears. "Shh," she repeated.

Her lips pressed against his, and he inhaled the scent of wild violets and pine. A scent he would recognize anywhere. She moved her head so that her unbound hair flowed across his face like waves of black water.

Alexander groaned with sudden, overwhelming desire.

Her fingers were back, stroking his cheeks and his lips, making small tight circles down his neck to his collarbone. He sucked in a breath of air and held it as she kissed the pulse at his throat.

Two can play at this game, Kiara, he thought. He forced himself to lie motionless, suppressing the urge to throw her down and drive his throbbing erection between her thighs. He moaned as she continued to caress him, rubbing and kissing, moving ever lower over chest and midriff, teasing him with the tip of her moist tongue.

A small fire glowed in the central pit, but the coals cast no light on the bed or on the woman who seemed determined to pleasure him. He was breathing heavily now. Sweat sheened his skin.

It had been so long.

He felt her warm breath on the tight curls at his groin. She lingered there, nestling her face, murmuring wordless endearments, before moving lower to the source of his need. He shuddered as she kissed his swollen phallus, nipping lightly with sharp teeth, laving and suckling gently at the tip of his rod.

He locked his fists against his sides as tears squeezed between his tightly closed eyelids. He tossed his head from side to side. He felt the mattress sag as she knelt on it.

By all that was holy! How far would Kiara take this game, pretending to be a woman she was not? She was kneeling over him. He could feel the heat of her body, hear the whisper of her breathing, sense the pulsing throb of her own desire. She lowered her naked breasts against him and covered his mouth with hers.

He opened his mouth, taking in her wet, thrusting tongue, tasting the sweetness of her. And then she arched her back and pressed her heat against his.

He would turn the tables on her, he decided, let her see how it felt to be played for a fool. Drawing away slightly, he exclaimed, "Forget Kiara, woman. You're all I need tonight."

"What?" Kiara screamed in his ear. "You prefer Tatiana? That hussy?" She struck him over the left eye with a balled fist, and drew it back to deliver another blow.

Alexander was nearly helpless with laughter. Gasping for breath, he caught a handful of her hair and brought her head down to kiss her again. "Just when were you planning to reveal your real identity?" he demanded.

Cursing him in five languages, Kiara hit him in the nose with her other fist and struggled to get off him. "Demon!" she cried. "Worse than a demon. You are more despicable than any other man I've had."

Still laughing, he wrapped his long legs around hers, rolled on top of her, and pinned her wrists to the bed. "I was worried about you," he said. "I love you, you little hellion. I don't care if you slept with a hundred men, I—"

"A thousand!" she declared. "All better endowed than you."

He caught her lower lip between his teeth and sucked at it gently, then slipped his tongue into her mouth. He found a breast and teased the nipple to a hard nub before moving his head to kiss it. "I love you," he said. "I don't care what you did or with whom. I want you, Kiara, only you."

"As your whore," she accused. "Your fourth concubine."

"Wait," he teased, savoring the curve of her breast and the feel of her wriggling body under his. "Could I have an hour? If you please me, I might consider moving you up to third concubine."

"Heartless barbarian. I hate you. I wouldn't go with you if you promised me your crown. Not if you begged me on bended knee to become your queen."

"On bended knee." He chuckled. "And how would that look, the son of the great Alexander on his knees before a seal-witch? That's what Hamilcar thinks you are, you know. He was quite impressed. A seal-woman on his boat."

"Go! Go back to your camels and your mountains. Take a goat to wife, for all I care. Fornicate with sheep, as many as you like. A dozen a night."

He nibbled her other nipple and laved it with his tongue. She felt as he knew she would feel, hot and ready for him. "A sheep?" he whispered into her ear. "I never thought of a sheep. I've loved camels, but never a—"

"Liar! Liar. You don't love me. It's what men say when they want—"

"This?" He chuckled wickedly. "And this." He caressed her belly and slipped long fingers between her damp thighs. "It seems to me that I remember the taste of—"

"Hush," she scolded him. "Will you stop tormenting me?"

"Will you marry me?"

"Marry you? I'd sooner wed Hamilcar."

He found her mouth again, kissing her with all the pent-up passion that he'd hoarded in the long days and nights of the sea journey from Egypt. "Have pity on me, Kiara. I am a stupid barbarian. It's taken me too long to realize what a treasure I had in my arms."

"A treasure? I am a treasure?"

"Yes, yes." He trailed damp kisses down her face and throat. "Come back with me."

"And be fourth concubine?"

"Second," he teased.

"Stay here with me in Eire. I'll teach you to launch a curragh in the surf and I'll show you where the fairies dance under the full moon."

"Kiara, heart of my heart. Ask me anything but that."

"Shh," she said. "No more words. If you love me, prove it. Let me taste your love."

With a groan he thrust deep into her secret folds, forgetting everything but the need that threatened to rob him of sanity, withdrawing and plunging between her thighs again and again. She rose to meet him, crying out with a wild joy, welcoming his lust with equal ardor until at last he could contain himself no longer, and he felt the hot rush of seed fill her womb. Her climax came quickly after, and for long moments they held each other, whispering sweet nothings until desire again drew them into heated writhing.

Three times in the night Alexander made love to her, and during the last interlude neither spoke. At last, exhausted, spent and fulfilled, he slept.

When he awoke at daybreak and reached for her, she was gone. "Kiara!" he called. "Kiara, where are you?"

But the only answer was the drumming of a woodpecker on the ridgepole of the house. He was alone except for a single dark lock of hair tied with a length of seaweed lying on the empty bed beside him.

"I believe you should think about the Bactrian prince's offer," Ashkuzi said. "A man doesn't offer a hundred horses for a worthless girl child every day."

Targitaos grabbed the older man by the throat. "You've not told him that we have such a girl, have you?"

"No, great chief, no. I would not betray your trust in such a manner." Targitaos released his grip. Ashkuzi coughed and rubbed his neck. "I have told him nothing."

Targitaos scowled and looked suspiciously around the yurt as if Bactrians were hiding behind his wife's skinning platform. "What's in it for you?"

"Twenty mares, good ones, at least half in foal."

"And if I refuse? What will the Bactrian pay you then?"

"Ten. No more. Ten for arranging the meeting and asking if you have seen the captive."

"Umm." Targitaos grunted. He lifted his horn of koumiss and drank deeply. "There was a girl like that.

I traded her to a man for an iron pot and two bulls. I heard that she died in the winter."

Ashkuzi nodded. "Such things happen. A shame that you took another offer. The Bactrian says that the girl was his daughter. They put much store by their women, these mountain folk."

"Nevertheless, the girl is dead, and there's an end to it. A pity you will gain only ten horses. This Bactrian, where did you say he is camped?"

The older man stroked the sparse hair on his chin. "Near the bend in the river, at the place men call Old Woman Crossing. You know it?"

Targitaos nodded. "I used that route last fall. The footing there is tricky. Sometimes a horse will sink into sand without a bottom." He considered the coals in the fire pit. "He has these hundred horses with him, this Bactrian prince?"

Ashkuzi grinned. "Yes. But he is not alone. Two score horsemen ride with him, hard men, men who have known the face of war."

"But then the grass is dry, is it not? If something happened to drive off these hundred mares and a spark should accidentally set off a fire . . ."

"One hundred and twenty mares," the guest reminded him.

"You say you have men with you?"

"Not so many. Nine, including my grandson. He is twelve."

"Nine men. Enough to start a small fire in the night, I believe."

"And if my people were to start this fire, would there be others to call upon to help us drive these mares to safety?"

Targitaos reached for a hunk of roasted flesh. "Your twenty, most assuredly, would be safe. We ride to the

309

great gathering in another month. There the Pestici will pick a khan. It would not be amiss if I had Bactrian mares to give to some of the leaders, would it?"

"Not amiss at all, my friend." Ashkuzi chuckled. "Not at all."

Later, after the stranger had left the camp, Jun climbed naked into her husband's bed. "Why not trade the girl for the horses?" she asked. "It is a great price."

Targitaos kneed her hard in the belly. "Hold your flapping tongue," he said. "Who are you to advise me?"

She whimpered. "I'm sorry. I had no right to speak. It was just that you can always find another slave girl, and this one eats so much."

"She belongs to Papai."

"Yes, lord, so you have said. But she is young. She will not have her woman's blood for many seasons. Is it worthwhile to keep her so long when another would do?"

"Not so long," Targitaos said. "Only until the next crescent moon. We go to the gathering. There I will make a gift of her pain to Papai."

"Will the supreme god want such a skinny girl without breasts?"

"What does it matter? Papai can wait as well as I. On the crescent moon, the Bactrian whelp will burn. And her screams will be music to his ears."

"Ah," Jun said. "You know best, husband."

"I do."

On the far side of the yurt, Ava drew her knees up and bit down on her hand to keep from crying out in fear. Her father was so close, but she'd never live to see him. She was going to die. They would marry her to their wicked god in fire and ash. And there was nothing she could do to prevent it.

Chapter 25

Shahi sat in one of the smaller family rooms, holding her new sister, Asha, in her arms. The infant was small and perfectly formed, with rosebud lips and a dimpled chin. "She's beautiful, don't you think?" Shahi demanded of Val. "Have you ever seen anything so precious?"

"She's a baby," Val murmured from his bench near the central fire pit, "the littlest one I've ever seen." He concentrated on the sword he'd been sharpening by the light of an oil lamp. Two shaggy wolf dogs lay at his feet. At a table in the far corner, Jahan, Alexander's former squire, and now Val's, pored over a scroll describing Alexander the Great's victory over the Indian kings along the Indus River. No one else was in the room.

"Would you like to hold her?" Shahi stood beside him, holding out the baby.

Val dropped the sharpening stone so quickly that he nearly sliced off a finger on the edge of the blade. "No." He held up a hand in protest. "No, thank you." He shook his head and retrieved his stone. "Babies are definitely outside my area of expertise. I might squeeze her too hard and crush her bones or—"

"Nonsense. She's a baby, not an alabaster goblet." Shahi pushed back the blanket and kissed the red-gold fuzz on top of Asha's head. "Just support her neck. Like this." Shahi regarded Val with suspicion. "You're afraid, aren't you? You're afraid to hold a baby."

"I'm not afraid." Val put his hands behind his back. "It's not seemly for a prince to—"

She scoffed. "You are afraid. It's simple. Just use reasonable care and Asha will be fine."

"You never give up, do you? You're like a mosquito, buzzing, buzzing, until you get your stinger in a man."

Across the room, Jahan flushed to the roots of his hair and coughed, obviously trying to hide his amusement at the exchange and to remind the two combatants that he was still present.

Shahi sighed in exasperation. "You're being obstinate, Val. Put down the sword and take her, just for a minute. Jahan!"

"Yes, lady?" He looked up, wide-eyed, as if he'd been engrossed in his studies, rather than listening to every word.

"You've been staring at that same page for half an hour. I know you aren't studying. Come and get the prince's weapon. If he sharpens it any longer, it will be too thin to cut through anything tougher than cheese." She smiled, transforming her finely drawn features from those of a pretty girl to a stunning one.

Val stifled his thoughts. Shahi was Kayan's blood daughter. It was wrong for him to think of her as an alluring woman. She was his younger stepsister, an annoying, spoiled member of the royal family, nothing more.

"If you're not afraid, prove it," she needled him.

She was worse than annoying. She was a demon incarnate. He scowled at her, but when Shahi began to snicker, he handed the sword to Jahan and awkwardly took the squirming bundle. "Are you satisfied?"

Shahi was blessedly silent.

The infant was heavier than he'd expected. She was warm as a roasted nut, and she didn't smell of sour milk and pee, as he'd expected. She smelled like a new-hatched duckling. Holding a baby was an unfamiliar, yet not unpleasant sensation, and despite his annoyance with Shahi, he found himself smiling at the tiny female. As he stared down at her, she opened black button eyes and gurgled in contentment.

"Her eyes are dark, aren't they?" he ventured. "I thought they were gray, but they are as black and shiny as olives."

Shahi smiled. "Her name is Asha. It won't hurt to say her name. And you see, she won't bite, not until she grows teeth, anyway. If Papa were here, he'd hold her. I remember that he used to carry Ava around all the time. Once he took her to the barracks. She wasn't much older than this little one. The officers were playing at dice, and she so captivated them that they contributed all their winnings to buy her a pony."

"A pony?" he scoffed. "A pony could eat her in one bite." Hastily he handed her back. "I'll hold her when she's older." He could still feel Asha's warmth, and it made him feel oddly happy.

"You'll have to hold her and bounce her on your knee when she learns to sit up. Without Alexander or Papa, it will be your responsibility to teach her to ride and to shoot a bow."

"If I remember, your mother is the best rider in the country. I'm certain she can manage to instruct the child, if you can't." His eyes narrowed. "You give too many orders for a woman. Even for the heir to the throne."

"She does, doesn't she?" Roxanne agreed, coming

into the chamber. "But she's right. We'll expect you to teach her those skills, and not just Asha. What of her twin sister? Is Arzu to be neglected simply because she's second-born?"

Shahi laughed. "I doubt she'll let anyone neglect her. She's quick enough to protest if she doesn't get what she wants."

"In Egypt the women of the royal family content themselves with palace matters," Val observed.

"This isn't Egypt," Shahi said. "Our girls have always been taught to defend themselves and to be self-sufficient. Even merchants' daughters learn to ride, almost before they can walk."

"I find no fault with your riding," Val said.

"Good. I'm glad to learn that there is something about me of which you approve."

"Be nice, children." Roxanne crossed to the divan and sat down. A nursemaid placed Arzu in the queen's arms. Roxanne smiled down at the sleeping baby. "This one reminds me of you when you were small, Shahi."

"Is she bad-tempered?" Val asked.

Shahi frowned at him.

"How can you tell which is which?" he said. "They're as alike as two arrows in a quiver. Both golden-haired and black-eyed with a little blob of dough for a nose. And neither, so far as I can tell, is a boy. You did tell Shahi and everyone who would listen that—"

"That I was carrying the next prince. Yes," Roxanne admitted with a smile. "I was wrong. The strapping boy who kept me awake for nine months with his kicking and squirming turned out to be two very small girls."

"Which probably saved your life. And theirs," Shahi said. "Are you sorry, Mama? Would you trade them for sons?"

"No, I wouldn't. I'm properly chastised." Roxanne cradled Arzu against her breast. "The Wise God knows more even than mother's instinct. Girls are much easier." She glanced at Shahi. "Some girls."

"You are right that they have different personalities, and I have no trouble telling them apart," Shahi said.

"I heard you say that Asha's eyes reminded you of black olives," Roxanne said to Val. "I'm certain she'll appreciate that when she's old enough to take an interest in boys."

He stood. "I've got a lot to do, highness. I'll be leaving before dawn. Are you certain you want me to lead Alexander's personal cavalry unit?"

Roxanne kissed the baby and passed her back to the nurse. "Take them to bed, but be certain that a woman remains with them and stays awake at all times. The Wise God help her if one of these little ones comes to harm through her fault." She glanced at her oldest daughter. "Give her up, Shahi. Her tummy is full, her swaddling clothes are fresh, and it's time she joined her twin."

Shahi handed Asha to the second nurse. "She likes to lie on her stomach," she admonished the middle-aged woman. "And be certain that you don't put too many blankets on her. She doesn't like to be overheated."

"You sound more like a nursemaid than a general," Roxanne said. "Perhaps you should remain at the palace, and I should join Val on the border."

"Don't even suggest it, Mama," Shahi said. "And I'm not a general. I'll be there to observe, to keep you informed of what's happening, and to make decisions if I have to. You can't think of climbing on a horse yet. We came too close to losing you."

The queen waved away Shahi's arguments. "I've no intention of riding to war tomorrow morning. For now, Tiz, Val, and my nobles can command the troops defending our borders. But I depend on you to tell me everything that's happening. Tiz would rather put out

315

his remaining eye than dictate a letter, and some of my officers aren't much better. If Ptolemy's army is on the march and your father doesn't return, I'll have to come. But that shouldn't be for weeks, perhaps months."

"You won't have to," Shahi said. "Papa will return soon. Just because we haven't heard anything else doesn't mean that we should think the worst. You know how difficult it is to track Scythians on the steppes."

"I know from experience what Scythians are," Roxanne replied. "That's what worries me. The truth may be that your father's been killed or captured himself." She turned to Val. "If you hadn't returned from Egypt, we would have done what was necessary, but I want you to know how glad I am to have you here." She put out a hand. "Don't be offended, but there is something I must ask. Can you lead troops against your sire— against Ptolemy?"

Val ran a hand down his dark green doeskin trousers, unconsciously massaging the newly healed wound on his thigh where he'd been shot by Shahi's arrow. "I've asked myself that question, my lady. The truth is that I don't know. I fought Ptolemy's archers in the streets of Alexandria, but that wasn't all-out war. Many of the soldiers I'd be fighting in this campaign, I've served with, even led."

"Exactly my point," Shahi interjected. "How can we trust him with Alexander's cavalry if he's not sure he'll be willing to throw them against the Egyptians?"

"If you can't fight Ptolemy, no one will hold it against you," Roxanne said. "There are other places you can be effective. I can send you against the Greeks or to guard the Scythian borders."

"I'll never betray the Twin Kingdoms," he promised. "Or you and the girls. If I can't do my duty, I'll step down, let my second-in-command lead my men."

"Easy to say now," Shahi said. "But I wouldn't give

you the chance to switch sides when we need you most."

"Enough of your squabbling," Roxanne said. "I am still queen here, and I trust him."

"As you say, Mother. It is your decision."

"The two of you are like fighting cocks. Whatever one says, the other contests it. You're brother and sister and must learn to—"

"No, lady," Val insisted. "I may be your foster son, but—"

"My *son*," Roxanne said. "My husband's *son*. Thus, you are Shahi, Ava, and the twins' brother."

"I don't consider him my brother, Mother," Shahi said sharply. "I won't. Maybe if we'd grown up together, it would be different, but when I look at him, I see—"

"Ptolemy's son?" Val demanded. "An Egyptian? What?"

Shahi averted her eyes. "A warrior," she said. "A stranger. You frighten me, if you want the truth. I can't decide if you're a friend or an enemy."

"Ah," Roxanne said, "so that's the way of it. Val disturbs you."

"Exactly," Shahi agreed. "I don't contest his intelligence or his fighting ability. It's . . ." She flung up her hands. "As you say, your word is law." With an angry toss of her head, Shahi stalked from the chamber.

Roxanne motioned to Jahan. "It's late. You may want to return those to the library before you turn in," she said softly.

"Yes, Majesty, but . . ."

"What is it?"

"I was wondering." He straightened his shoulders. "I want to fight with the troops."

"How old are you?" Roxanne asked.

"Seventeen this summer, lady."

The queen toyed with the end of her thick braid.

Val noticed that her hair was still as bright and glossy as he remembered. "He has served bravely," Val said, "but . . ."

Roxanne nodded. "I appreciate how faithfully you served Prince Alexander, but the decision isn't mine to make. You are in the service of my son Val." She glanced back at Val.

"Another six months," he said. "You're too valuable to me as my aide, and you've not completed your education. In the fall, you'll have your first promotion."

"But the Greeks are here at our gates now," Jahan said. "And if the Egyptians come—"

"I promise you that there will always be enemies for you to fight," Roxanne said. "And if we have none, perhaps Prince Val can send you to Chin or India as second officer with a caravan escort. The hill bandits are certain to provide you with enough action to satisfy you."

"Autumn," Val said. "Providing you don't disgrace yourself before that."

"I won't," Jahan said with a grin. Gathering the scrolls, he hurried out.

Roxanne looked at Val. "The young are always anxious for battle."

"You could say that about Shahi, as well," he answered.

"She has her father's temper. What can I say?"

He moved toward her, but did not sit. "She has your temper, I think, highness. As I remember my father, he had a great deal more patience."

The queen looked thoughtful. "This tension between you troubles me. I know you've only returned to us a short time, and Shahi is taking Alexander's death hard. It's been difficult—"

"More difficult for you, lady."

Roxanne's brown eyes glistened with moisture. "It is unnatural for a mother to lose a child. I have seen two go before me, and it is—" She broke off. "Hard."

"Shahi blames me."

"For Alexander's death."

"Yes."

"And you? Do you blame yourself?"

He nodded. "Some, yes. But I tried to reason with him, tried to tell him what Egypt was. He wouldn't—"

"Alexander wouldn't listen," Roxanne finished. "You tried, as I did. He went his own way, like his father before him. Once either of them was set on a thing, rational or not, it was as if their will were carved in stone."

"I should have done more, should have gone with him into the temple—"

Roxanne rose and embraced him. "No," she murmured. "It was not your fault that Ptolemy had your brother murdered. He has always craved the riches of Bactria and Sogdiana. Sometimes I think it would have been better for my country if I had allowed her to become part of Greece."

He hugged her, and then stepped away. "You don't really believe that, do you?"

"No." She shook her head. "No, I don't, but I weary of the endless fighting. We need peace; and since Alexander isn't here to help me secure it, you must take his place. Can you do that? Can you be the prince that the Twin Kingdoms need so desperately?"

"I'm not Alexander."

She smiled up at him, and he saw a single tear dampen her cheek. "Do you think me so foolish to believe that one child can replace another? Long ago, Kayan and I lost a small daughter to fever. It tore away a piece of my heart, but I went on, as I must, as every woman must. Now the Wise God has given me two more daughters. They cannot take the place of . . . of Ava or of . . . Oh, Val." She covered her face with her hands and gave in to the tears.

He stood helpless, not knowing what to do to ease her pain. "Ava's not lost yet, or Kayan."

"If I knew for certain that they were dead, it might be easier to bear. It is the endless waiting. It is hoping, when you wake in the night with despair choking off your breath. When the blackness threatens to crush all—"

"Hope is a good thing. Without it, where would any of us be? I came here hoping that there might be a place for me. Not to take my brother's place . . . not to seek his throne, no matter what Shahi might think."

"You came because you could no longer live under Ptolemy's deceit, because, despite everything, your true father was here. Isn't that it?"

"Yes. Maybe it is. I knew I couldn't serve a king who would murder his own nephew for gain."

"Kayan should have been here for you. He would have, if I hadn't insisted on having my own way. Maybe Shahi is more like me than I realized."

"I'm thinking none of us expect any real fighting until midsummer. What if I went to the frontier where Kayan wintered? I should be able to find out something of his whereabouts. Some of his men must know if he's been lost or is simply hunting for Ava."

"That might be the wisest thing to do. Knowing that he isn't coming back will make it easier to make plans for the succession. Don't think that because I speak of these things, I don't love him. I do, more than my own life."

"And he you. I remember his face when he learned you hadn't died in Macedonia."

"My love for Kayan is different from what I felt for the great Alexander. Just as fierce, but different. Kayan has given me more happiness than I ever knew as wife of the conqueror, and if he is lost, I will mourn him forever. But as queen my thoughts must be for the good of my people. Shahi is heir to the throne, as you know, but she can't rule alone."

"You'll be queen for many years yet."

"Perhaps. But a crown is a heavy burden."

"Ptolemy said the same thing."

Roxanne sighed. "In that, we agree, but on little else, it seems. He was once my friend, your sire. Among Alexander's Greek companions, he was my only friend, and for that I remain grateful."

"There is good in him, but I fear his wisdom is hampered by his greed."

"A failing that many rulers share," Roxanne said.

"Which is why I never want a throne. I prefer myself as I am, a soldier, not as Ptolemy. I don't want to find out if I'd become as he is, given the chance."

"I admire a man who knows himself, and I respect your decision. Go and see what you can find out about Kayan." She hugged him. "And be careful. I could not stand to lose you."

He saluted her and started to walk away.

"One more thing, Val."

"Yes?" He glanced back at her.

"She doesn't hate you." Roxanne smiled. "Believe me, if she did, you'd know it."

On the isle of Eire, Alexander had no more luck in locating Kiara the morning after they'd made love than he had the day before. Although Tatiana had returned to the house to lead him to a river to bathe and had then offered him food and new clothing, she couldn't answer any of his questions.

Bran came for him at midmorning and led him back to the central square, where hundreds of people were gathering. The big man escorted him to a woven mat and seated him among what seemed to be an elite group of Eire warriors. Again Bran took a place beside him. More and more men and women crowded into the public space. Children found perches on rooftops and men's shoulders, and women jostled good-naturedly for places.

"What is this?" Alexander demanded of Bran. Again the big redhead only shrugged. Patience fast wearing thin, Alexander settled on the rug to wait.

The sun climbed higher. It was not so warm on his face as in Egypt or in the high mountains, but it felt good. If this was to be his public execution, or Kiara's, the spectators seemed in the best of moods.

Now came dancers and musicians, some of whom he recognized from the night before in the great hall. Drums, rattles, pipes, and a strange stringed instrument that produced sounds not unlike a lyre gave forth joyous melodies. This time no one rose to dance.

Groups of young women, with flowers in their hair and robed in pristine white, shuffle-danced through the rows of onlookers, raising their hands to the sky and singing. A small freckle-faced boy in a forest-green kilt led other similarly garbed children in a circle dance.

At last, when the sun was high, a procession of warriors appeared. Naked, armed with ritual weapons faced with gold, they circled the assembly three times before forming ranks in the center of the square. The drums hushed as citizens cried out, as if asking a question. A single pipe trilled a high, sad reply. The drums boomed again and grew silent as the people repeated their entreaty. A chorus of pipes blew a sweet, hopeful reply.

In unison, the entire audience rose and turned to look at the road running from the gates of the citadel to the sea. There, to the accompaniment of clashing cymbals and a flurry of pipes, came seven barefoot women, all in hooded blue robes with strange blue patterns painted on their faces. Alexander recognized Kiara foremost in the group.

They were smiling they came, and all the onlookers cheered. As the women passed where Alexander stood, Kiara flashed him a mischievous smile. The hooded band proceeded to the spot where the golden warriors waited. Three took places on one side, three on the other. Kiara stood in the center, and together men and women called out the same question that the audience had cried earlier.

Immediately Cian strode from the crowd, walked to where Kiara waited, and dropped to his knees. Alexander looked at Bran.

"Kiara. Cian. Brother," Bran said in badly accented Phoenician. "Kiara . . ." He touched his brow, then pointed back at the scene unfolding before them.

Kiara held high a crown of gold, fashioned to look like a circle of dolphins rising from the waves. The audience watched in complete silence. Not even a baby cried. Kiara placed the diadem on Cian's head, and the Eires shouted and screamed their approval.

"Kiara priest," Bran exclaimed above the din. "Kiara make king."

"She crowned him king?" Alexander asked in the same language.

"She." Bran nodded vigorously. "She, not . . . not other."

"Only Kiara could crown her brother. Is that what you're trying to say?"

Bran threw his massive arms around Alexander and squeezed him. "Kiara," he repeated. "Only Kiara."

Cian stood and one of the warriors brought a sheathed sword and strapped it over his chest and shoulder. Another handed the new king a ceremonial ax that glittered in the noonday sun. The woman and children who had joined Cian at the head table the night before came forth to stand with him as each noble stepped forward to kneel and offer homage to their new lord.

As the line moved and men continued to pledge their fealty, Alexander glanced at Bran. What was he supposed to do when it came his turn? He could hardly offer his loyalty to a foreign king. To do so would be to commit the armies of the Twin Kingdoms to support Cian in time of war.

Bran walked to the king and knelt. Hundreds of eyes turned to Alexander. The drums boomed. Alexander stood unmoving.

Kiara came to his side, inclined her head, and reached for his hand. Together they approached Cian. The new king didn't hesitate; he came to meet them, offering both hands in friendship. Alexander clasped his hands, and side by side he, Kiara, and Cian turned to face the assembly.

Again, the hilltop rang with approval.

Kiara leaned close to Alexander. "No one could crown him king but me," she whispered. "I am the first of the Seven Shields."

He looked at her, still not comprehending what she meant.

"The seven priestesses," she explained. "We are all of royal blood, but only I could make my brother king. I had to return or my people faced civil war and a breakdown of the law that has stretched through the years since the first Orion."

"And now?" he asked.

She smiled at him. "Now," she said, "my vow is fulfilled, and I am free to follow my heart."

Chapter 26

Ava wiggled out of her blankets, held her breath, and listened for any sound that Targitaos, Jun, or Targitaos's new bride, Ushu, were awake. The yurt was quiet, or as quiet as a tent with six people and two dogs sleeping side by side could be. Ava thought that the Pestici had a lot to learn about communal living. Targitaos and one of the curs snored, and Jun's son sucked his thumb. Between the fleas, the dogs, Targitaos's incessant worrying of his two wives, and Ku's whining, it was difficult for anyone to get much rest.

Tonight Ava was concerned with sleep, but theirs, not hers. She'd heard most of what Targitaos had said to his visitor, and she was determined to get out of the tent without being seen. Somehow she had to sneak out of camp, steal a horse, and find the Old Woman Crossing the stranger had mentioned. If she got there before any of the Scythians, she could warn her father of the Pestici treachery.

No one had mentioned Prince Kayan, but if a Bactrian prince was offering a reward of a hundred prime horses to buy back a captive, it had to be he. A Scythian could hardly be expected to know that her father was Sodgian by birth. She remembered the fire that had started so much chaos in the village, and she wondered if she could set fire to the yurt and use the confusion to get away. But that plan would be too dangerous. Targitaos might catch her. Besides, she didn't want to hurt these people; she just wanted to get away from them.

She had to find a way out of the yurt. Using the entrance wasn't practical. Jun had laced the door flap shut and tied the knot in the sinew tightly. Both dogs lay in front of the door, and Ava knew from the bites and scratches on her arms and legs that the animals hated her. That left digging under the outer wall of the tent or slicing through the willow frame and double layer of hides that formed the skin.

It might be possible to cut through the thick hide wall if she had a knife—but she didn't. She knew where Jun kept her butchering blades. They were under her bed skins so that the new wife couldn't steal them. Ushu was younger and not as smart as Jun. Ava hoped that Ushu had carelessly left a knife lying out, but searching for it in the dark yurt without being discovered might be chancy. She decided to pull aside the mats and dig under the wall. It was spring, and the ground had thawed. She might just be able to burrow out without making much noise.

The hole was about ten inches deep when Ave heard an owl hoot just outside the tent. She froze. She wanted to imitate the noise, to see if it was a real bird or a signal, but if she made any sound at all, she might wake someone in the yurt. Papa's owl call sounded exactly like that. He'd taught her the same trick that Tiz had shown him. But there were at least fifty yurts. If it was Papa outside and not an owl, how would he know which tent she was in?

Ave chewed her lower lip and waited. Nothing. What if she'd imagined it? What if her father had been there, and when she didn't answer he'd gone away? There were owls in the woods here, but they weren't common. What if she misjudged the situation and got Papa killed?

She couldn't stand it. She tapped very softly on the wall, three taps, then two, then three again. She was so frightened, and yet so excited. If her father was there on the other side of the wall, if Papa had come with his warriors, then she would be rescued.

She began to whisper a silent prayer. "Great and Wise God, creator of Earth. Forget what I said before about going to war with the men. Just get me to my papa, and I promise I'll bathe every day. I'll even wash my hair and do my lessons without complaining. And forgive me if I was rude to my sister."

Three distinct taps came from the other side of the wall.

Ava wanted to scream. To shout. Instead she gave three answering raps, raps so small that even she could hardly hear them. The wait was terrible. She didn't know what she was supposed to do, so she squatted and waited . . . waited until she heard a soft shuffling, then thudding. She knew what it was at once. Papa was digging.

But he was digging in the wrong place! Quickly she tapped twice. The shuffling stopped. She moved her hand to a spot over her hole and tapped once. And when the digging started again, it was in exactly the right spot.

Minutes or hours later, Ava wiggled through the tunnel and up into her Papa's arms. For an instant he held her against him so close that she could feel the thudding of his heart.

"My girl," he whispered into her ear. "I've got you."

"How did you find me?" she asked once they slipped away from the camp.

"Later."

She was crying now, silent tears that made no sound, tears of happiness, but she didn't care. Papa wouldn't think she was a coward. No one could. She had survived being captured by the Scythians and lived to tell about it. She didn't know anyone but Mama who could say that without telling a lie.

"Are you hurt?"

"No."

"Are you sure? I can go back and kill them if—"

"I'm all right," she insisted. "But how? How did you know which yurt I was in?"

"That greedy weasel told me which yurt belonged to Targitaos. He wanted a hundred and twenty horses instead of a hundred, so one trickster betrayed another."

"Will you pay the horses?"

"What do you think?"

It was all Ava could do not to giggle at the thought of how mad Targitaos would be in the morning when he woke and found her gone. "You kept looking for me," she said, clasping his big, calloused hand. "You didn't leave me with the Pestici."

He crouched next to her in the tall spring grass. "Did you think I would face your mother without you?"

"No, I knew you'd come for me. I just didn't know if you'd find me in time."

"Neither did I, kitten. Neither did I."

She could hardly see Papa in the light of the waning moon. He wore nothing but a black loincloth, and his face and arms were smeared with ashes. "You really are an owl," she said, flinging herself into his arms again. "You're almost invisible, and you hunt at night."

* * *

Two hours before dawn, Val passed through the kitchens on his way out of the palace. Already roasts sizzled on the spits and bakers were raking hot coals out of the oven in preparation for making the morning's bread and meat pastics. Val stopped to slice off a piece of meat to break his own fast.

"Prince Paris, you're earlier than I'd expected." Hori, his charioteer, pushed aside a hanging and stepped into the room. The dwarf wore a heavy vest, Persian trousers, and knee-high boots. A bow and two quivers of arrows were slung over his back. He held a double-headed ax in one hand and half a mutton-and-cheese pie in the other.

"Did I call for my chariot? And it's not Paris here; it's Prince Val, my friend. Best get used to my new name if you want to make friends among the mountain—"

"Wait, Hormasji," a woman called. "You've forgotten your hat." She hurried out of the adjacent storeroom and shoved a fur hat at him. "You're just like my first husband. He'd forget his—" Her mouth gaped and her eyes widened when she caught sight of Val. "Begging your pardon, sir. I didn't realize that—"

"Hormasji?" Val grinned. "So I'm not alone. You've taken a new name too?"

"No," Hori said. "It's just this foolish woman. She can't pronounce my name properly, so I—"

"Speak a decent tongue, can't you," the woman chided in Parsi. "Lord, I am Delafruz," she said cheerfully. She was a short woman, hardly more than a head taller than the charioteer, and twice as wide. "No person of loose morals am I, but an honest widow. Third cook. None can whip up an oxtail soup as good as mine." She nudged Hori. "Did you ask him?"

Hori busied himself with the pie.

"We are to be wed, this Egyptian driver of war chariots and me. Begging your approval, sir," she added hastily.

Val's eyes narrowed. "Is this true? Did you promise marriage to this good woman?"

"Indeed he did," she supplied. "I'm no doxy to give myself without such a promise."

"Hori?" Val pretended a stern and regal manner, one he hoped would impress the bride-to-be with Hori's status.

Hori grinned, not in the least subdued. "It's a cold land, and little else for a man to do in winter."

"Then I give my approval. Wed you shall be." He slipped off a gold ring stamped with the mark of Anubis. "To pay for the wedding supper." Val pressed the ring into Delafruz's hand.

"I could buy a good house in Alexandria, two farms on the river, and slaves to work it for the price of that bauble," Hori grumbled. He reached for another pie, but Delafruz stepped between him and the platter.

"Then it will purchase land and houses here in Bactria," Val said. "And you should consider yourself lucky to find such a prosperous and clever wife."

"We're going to war. It's dangerous," Hori said. "I could get killed, and then you'd have given her gold for nothing."

Delafruz looked anxious. "Is it true, lord? He goes into great danger?"

Val nodded. "Yes, he goes into danger. But not for the first time. He is an able warrior, for all his honeyed talk, and a man you can trust to look out for his own skin."

"There's not so much of it," Hori said. "If I don't watch out for it, who will?"

"You're right," Val said. He pursed his lips. "You might not come back. Best you and the lady search out a priest and have him seal the marriage now, before we ride."

Hori groaned. "You are a wicked man, my prince, and the gods will surely judge you harshly when you come to the great weighing of souls."

Val folded his arms. "Married this morning, you shall be, my bold friend, so that if you do come to harm, you will leave this good woman to mourn your bravery without dishonor."

Torches shone from the royal stables. Men cursed and shouted; horses stamped and pawed the ground as the military units made ready to defend the border. Val looked for Shahi but didn't see her. He wished he were accompanying her instead of heading onto the steppes. This struggle against the Greeks and Egyptians was no place for a young woman who'd been trained in the temple, regardless of her skill with a sword. He wouldn't have considered searching for Kayan now, but he was certain that he'd be back long before Ptolemy's army arrived.

Couriers had come from Tyre and Babylon with messages for the queen, telling of the huge Egyptian army that marched toward Bactria. Pharaoh was publicly claiming his right to take the throne of the Two Kingdoms in the name of Princess Mereret and Alexander's unborn grandchild. A letter from a merchant in Alexandria with blood ties to Bactria said that Ptolemy had made a pact, giving General Isandros Sogdian land, gold, livestock, and slaves in exchange for his support.

Val knew that if he could find Kayan, it would be a tremendous morale boost to the warriors of the Twin Kingdoms. Outnumbered as they would be, they needed their prince more than ever, and his presence—not to mention his experience—would be invaluable.

A boy in a hooded cloak came out of the shadows leading a dapple-gray stallion. The horse Val had named Horus was sixteen hands, spirited, and obviously giving the groom a hard time. "Here," Val said. "Give me that lead rope. He's a warhorse and too much for an inexperienced youth to . . ." His words died in his throat as he caught a whiff of perfume. No boy, then, but a woman. "Who are—"

"I'll match my horsemanship against yours any day," Shahi said, handing over the rope. "This animal has a nasty disposition. He nipped at me. You should teach him better manners."

"Your highness." He drew the hood back to reveal Shahi's face. "I'm leaving. Can't we at least be civil to each other? I won't see you for weeks, and the Scythians may well hack off my head and stick it on a pole."

"It's true? You're going to search for Papa?"

He nodded. "Take care of yourself, little sister. It's not safe where you're going, either. If Isandros gets his hands on you, he may throw you to his men." The stallion sidled restlessly and bared his teeth at another horse.

"See? He's trouble. You should have him gelded if you want to make a trustworthy mount out of him."

"He'll be fine once I'm in the saddle." Val jerked the halter rope. "Settle down, Horus."

"Why would you go to hunt for Papa if you are spying for Ptolemy?" she said. "I've thought about that, and I've decided that it would be foolish. You've been telling the truth, haven't you? All the things I've said . . . the things I've thought about you. You really did come back to be one of us, didn't you?"

"Shahi . . ." The horse laid his ears back and moved closer, and Val slapped him on the neck and shoved him back. "Behave yourself!"

"Me or the stallion?" Shahi laughed. "Why couldn't

it be easy? I wanted to hate you, to blame you for Alexander . . ." She laid a hand on his arm.

"For his death. I knew you thought—"

"No, listen. Don't say anything, just listen. Please," she said. "Not just his murder. I wanted to blame you for Alexander's selfishness in abandoning us when we needed him most. We needed him here to take his crown, to unite his people." She shook her head. "You still don't understand, do you? Since the time of the great Alexander, the Twin Kingdoms have been torn by war. We need peace."

"All nations need peace."

"Strange talk for a man who's made a life of fighting."

"Because I had to, Shahi, not because I love killing."

An archer led a paint gelding past, keeping a safe distance from Horus's hind feet. Ears twitching, head tossing, the stallion watched the strange horse. Val wrapped the lead several times around his hand. "Hold still," he said, losing his patience with the horse. "I'm sorry, Shahi. This isn't the best place or time to talk."

"It might be the only time we have," she insisted. "The Greek invasions have robbed us of our greatest strength. Two generations of our young men have left their farms and mountains. Sons and daughters grow up without fathers. Women grow old too soon because they have no men to help shoulder the burdens."

He nodded. What she said was the truth, and he had no way to soften it.

"Alexander was Mother's hope. He left us to go marching across the world, to see Egypt, to claim Pharaoh's daughter. That wasn't the way it was supposed to be. Ptolemy's a better king for Egypt than my brother's been for Bactria and Sogdiana."

A rider crossed the courtyard on another stallion and the dapple gray snorted and tried to rear. Val wrapped his arms around the animal's neck. "Easy, boy. Easy, Horus."

"What did I say? Geld him or turn him out for breeding. He has good legs, and I like the shape of his head, but his disposition is nasty."

"He was Alexander's. The horse master told me that my brother was working with him before he left for Egypt. Alexander believed Horus would make a fine warhorse. I guess I thought I could work the kinks out of him."

"Something else he left for us to finish."

"He meant to come back. He would have, if he'd lived."

"Meant to?" Her small, heart-shaped face grew fierce. "What good are intentions when the prize is lost?"

"You'll be queen now. You have your mother's fire— her love for her country. You could unite the Twin Kingdoms."

She shook her head. "You've seen me fight. I'm good, for a woman. But you could have bested me if you'd tried. My father had a plan. Using his new saddles with stirrups, he built the best cavalry that's ever been mounted, better even than Alexander the Great's Macedonians. Papa wanted to make treaties with the Scythians, join with the nomads to drive the Greeks back to their homeland for good."

"I know that," Val replied. "I was a boy when Kayan formed his first units, when he trained the soldiers."

"The Scythians, the horse people, have no focus. They'd rather fight among themselves than join with us for a greater cause. Father's plan was a great one, brilliant, but it was left for Alexander to take that dream and make it reality. Father is a great prince, one of the finest generals who ever lived, but he is no king. What king would leave his country in time of war to hunt for a missing daughter?"

"And you think that makes him less of a warrior?"

"No. Papa is Papa. I love him, but he's no king. And without a great king, our nation is doomed. Sooner or later one invading army or another will finish the destruction the Macedonian's army started."

The stallion pawed restlessly, and Val looped a section of the rope around his nose and knotted it. "There, that should hold you." He looked back at Shahi. "You are a pessimist for one so young."

"Not so young. No woman in these times can afford to be innocent."

"If you believe it's such a lost cause, then why go to the front? Why fight for the Twin Kingdoms at all?"

She shrugged. "Because I'm as much a hopeless romantic as my father. I keep hoping that something may happen to save us. Ptolemy may die. The Greeks may go to war with one another. Or you just might make a fair commander-in-chief after all." She rose on tiptoe and kissed his cheek. "Take care of yourself," she said. "Don't let that beast toss you off a mountainside. And . . ." She smiled. "I'm not your sister."

"No?" He dropped his stallion's lead, took hold of Shahi's shoulders, and kissed her on the lips. He hadn't known what he'd expected, hadn't thought past the impulse. But their lips fit together perfectly.

She tasted as good as ripe mountain berries on a hot day.

Hastily he released her and stepped back, snatching up Horus's lead before the horse could bolt away. "I shouldn't have done that. I'm sorry."

"Are you?" She smiled at him again. "I'm not." She touched her mouth with two fingertips. "Maybe Mother was right. Maybe I wouldn't be happy in the temple."

"Shahi?"

"Find Papa, Val, and hold on to your head." Laughing, she darted away into the shadows.

JUDITH E. FRENCH

* * *

Alexander propped himself on one elbow and looked
down at Kiara. Her cheeks were infused with blood,
her hair tumbled around her face like some barnyard
trollop, and her beautiful dark eyes were sleepy with
satiated pleasure. Neither had slept this last night together, and they had spoken little. Instead they had
given and taken joy in each other without reservation.
Now all the fears that had been extinguished in their
passion returned to haunt them.

"What do you mean that you won't marry me?" he
demanded. "You told me that you were free—that you
could follow your heart."

"Mine, not yours," she whispered, tracing the line of
his jaw and the curve of his upper lip with a fingertip.
"It is your dream to be king. Why would I want to leave
all that I know to go with you to the far ends of the
earth to be fourth concubine to a conqueror's son?"

"There's no time for this. Hamilcar sails tomorrow."
He lowered his head and kissed her. Her lips parted
easily to welcome his tongue, to let him drink deep of
her and his soul touch hers.

"It's already tomorrow for us, Alexander," she said,
when at last they broke the kiss to draw breath. "Our
bargain is fulfilled.

And you are free to do what you were born for."

He nuzzled her breast, filling his head with her scent
and drawing strength from her pliant body. "Do you
know how beautiful you are?" he asked her. "How perfect this breast is?"

She smiled and stretched, letting her head fall back
so that the mass of her hair tumbled over the edge of
the bed to the floor. "And the other? Is it so ugly?" she
teased.

"It is more beautiful." He kissed that nipple to prove
its perfection. "A queen's breast." He drew in a deep

336

breath. "You know I would make you my wife," he reminded her. "My only wife."

"A whore?"

Rage turned his muscles rigid. "Never say that again!"

She did not flinch from his anger. "It is what I was, what I was forced to be from the time I was eleven."

"But no more," he muttered from between clenched teeth. "That is done. It was never by choice. What sin is there in actions forced upon you?"

She pushed at his chest and sat up, making no effort to cover her nakedness. "What sin there was, mine or another's, was washed away in the pool of eternal blessings. I am free, not only of my duty to crown my brother but of all the evil."

"Then why are we having this conversation? You will come with me, Kiara. I won't go without you. By all that's holy, if I have to fight my way to the beach with you across my shoulder, then—"

"No! No more. I've had enough of doing what I am told by men. And if I do not choose to go with you, then you and all of Ptolemy's armies can't take me."

"You think I couldn't get you on that boat?"

Her eyes narrowed. "You say that you want to marry me, and in the same breath you threaten to take me against my will. What am I to you? A conquest? A pretty woman to take to bed at your leisure? How long would it be before you began to regret your decision to place a woman with a shadowed past on your throne?"

"It wouldn't be like that. I love you, Kiara. I've never said that before."

"And I love you. But I must not let my heart's desire drown logic. Here I have my family, my Sisters of the Shield, and all that I hold dear . . . except for you. If I choose you, Alexander, if I go to far-off Bactria and leave all else behind, I could end my life alone and unwanted."

"Trust me, it won't be like that."

"As ruler, you will need heirs. What if I can't have children? What if the harm that was done to me so young has made me barren? Will you set me aside for another?"

"I tell you that I won't. I have two sisters. If I have no son, I'll raise one of theirs to follow me on the throne." He touched her face. "Aren't you the sorceress who calmed the storm? Can't you look in your magic pool and see that I'll never break faith with you?"

She laughed. "It doesn't work that way. Whatever gifts were given to me at birth, I can't use them for my own purposes. I'm as human as you and as likely to make foolish decisions."

"I don't believe it. I saw what you did on the ship—"

She silenced him with a kiss. "You saw what I wanted you to believe. That's what every woman does. We spin cloth of hopes and dreams."

He rose from the bed. "You deny you have powers beyond those of mortal—"

"I have the power to crown kings, Alexander. And no king crowned by a priestess of the Seven Shields has ever fallen in battle."

"Then come with me. Please. Add your strength to mine. Make me what my people expect: a man to match my father."

For a long moment, perhaps two, she did not answer. And then she smiled and offered him her hand. "I will come with you, my love, and I will crown you high king of your Two Kingdoms. But I will not be your wife. I will remain what I am, what I pray I will always be—mistress of your heart."

Roxanne was in the armory when a barefoot boy galloped up with news. "Your majesty," he shouted. "The prince! Prince Kayan and the princess! They're coming up the mountain road!"

338

Roxanne dropped the short sword she'd been holding, ran past the messenger, and swung up onto his mount.

"My lady—" he cried.

Roxanne didn't hear his last words. She'd already kicked the gelding into a gallop and reined him toward a five-foot pasture fence. They sailed over with inches to spare, and crossed the yearling compound. A groom saw her coming and swung open the gate onto the mountain road.

"Kayan!" she shouted when she first caught sight of him. He was alive. Her husband and daughter were alive. She prayed that this wasn't a dream, that he was as solid as the road beneath her horse's hooves.

"Mama! Mama!" Ava lashed her horse and tore past Kayan.

Roxanne reined in and dismounted. She'd waited so long. Surely she could wait a few more seconds. She sank to her knees and held out her arms.

"Mama!" Ava threw herself out of the saddle.

"My darling, my darling." Roxanne held her against her breast. "You're skin and bones. Did those savages never feed you?" She rained kisses on Ava's face and hair until a baby's angry wail broke through their frenzied reunion.

"What's that?" Ava demanded. "What have you got . . . oh."

Laughing, Roxanne slipped the sling off her back and deposited it into Ava's arms. "Someone wants to meet you. This is Arzu."

Ava stared down at the red face. "Arzu? Who names a boy Arzu?"

"A girl?" Kayan dismounted. "Is it . . . ours?"

"Of course it's ours, you great lump!" Roxanne threw her arms around his neck and kissed him.

Stunned, he embraced her. "Our daughter?" he asked disbelievingly. "We have a daughter?" He pushed Roxanne away and looked at her. "You're all right? The baby's all right?"

She kissed him again, touching his face to see if he was real, taking in the lines around his eyes, the new strands of gray in his dark hair.

"Roxanne . . ."

"Are you disappointed that I didn't give you a son?" Her heart was as fragile as an eggshell. If he was still angry with her, she couldn't bear it. "Oh, Kayan, you are, aren't you?"

"No, no. You . . . I told you that I'd rather have daughters." He lifted her off the ground and swung her around. "Woman, woman. I was afraid that . . . You'll be the death of me. Without you . . . You and the girls are my reason for living."

"I hope you're not disappointed. Isn't she a beautiful baby? Healthy and strong."

"Our Ava's grown a foot, hasn't she?"

"Yes, she has," Roxanne said, "but her hair smells like a midden. She's not . . . She wasn't . . ." She shook her head. "It doesn't matter, nothing matters but having the two of you safely home."

"I'm fine, Mama," Ava said. "I almost had to get married, but Papa dug a hole under the yurt and pulled me out."

The baby had stopped crying and was peering up at Ava.

"I think she likes me. Can I help take care of her?"

"What about me?" Kayan said, reaching for Arzu. "Let me take a look at this little mite."

"Our Val's come home," Roxanne said, not wanting to tell him about Alexander, not wanting to make his death real by saying the words. As long as Kayan didn't know, their son was still alive for him. "Val went looking for you and—"

"He found us at the last outpost. I know." He swallowed, and for an instant his eyes clouded with sorrow. "We know about Alexander." Kayan's deep voice grew thick. "How are you?"

"I'm all right," Roxanne said. "I think I had a premonition. I cry for him when I'm alone, but then I go on. What else is there to do?"

Kayan nodded. "Still, it's hard."

"Yes."

"Val turned back to join Shahi and Tiz on the border," he said. "I'll leave tomorrow for—"

"A week," Roxanne said. "I'll have you a week before you go back to war."

"Three days," he countered. "He told us about Ptolemy's army."

"Four," she answered. "Four nights in our bed before I let you get away again." She laid her head on his arm. "I was wrong, Kayan. I shouldn't have—"

"No," he said. "I took my anger out on you. I left when you needed me most. It's I who owe you an apology." He cradled Arzu in his arm. "Pretty, she's pretty. She looks like you did, Ava, when you were just born. But she's smaller. She is smaller, isn't she, Roxanne? I know it's been a while, but I don't remember Ava being—"

"Ah, yes," Roxanne agreed. "Arzu's perfectly healthy, but she is tiny."

"Why is that?"

Roxanne laughed. "Wait until you get back to the palace."

"Is it a surprise, Mama?" Ava asked.

"You could say that. And your papa . . ." She hugged Kayan again and chuckled. "I think your father will be very surprised."

Chapter 27

In late summer, Alexander, Kiara, and nine warriors from the Island of Eire reached the seaport of Tyre aboard the *Dawn Flyer*. The return journey had been blessed with fair weather and no hostile encounters. Hamilcar swore that the seal-woman had brought him luck and refused to accept payment for the additional passengers. "The lady's taming of the waves is such a good tale that men will buy me free drinks for the rest of my life," he said.

Others had not been so pleased at Kiara's taking ship again. When she broke the news to her brother that she was going to Bactria with Alexander, Bran, Cian, and all his subjects had blackened their faces with soot, extinguished all household fires, and mourned her for nine days. Surprisingly, Cian agreed with Kiara's decision to refuse Alexander's marriage proposal. "A wife may belong to her husband," he said, "but a free woman controls her own life." In token of his love for his sister, Cian appointed nine of his bravest warriors to accompany and protect her. His final gift to the two of them was gold, so much that Alexander feared it would be too heavy a cargo for the *Dawn Flyer*.

In Tyre, Alexander and Kiara bade farewell to the Phoenicians and sought out the home of Tahm of Gaza, son of a man who'd once given aid to Kayan and Roxanne. As Alexander had hoped, Tahm welcomed them into his home.

"Stay as long as you wish," Tahm declared after his wife had shown Roxanne to the guest quarters and he and Alexander were alone. "You'll not reach the Twin Kingdoms before the snow flies. And not at all by way of Babylon or Herat." The merchant shook his head. "Haven't you heard of the great war? Twelve thousand Greeks are camped on the borders of Bactria. Another ten thousand Egyptians left Sidon to join them in midsummer. So many chariots that it took a day for them to pass the city walls. Pharaoh himself was said to have led them."

"So it's begun," Alexander said. "I'd planned to join a caravan, but it's too late for that. I must get home as quickly as possible. Can you help me locate Bactrian racing camels? They are faster than any horse, and with their thick coats, they can survive the high-country snow and low temperatures. Also, I'll need to hire mercenaries. The nine warriors I have aren't enough."

"The camels, yes, I know a dealer. He has the finest stock, but they won't come cheap. Trustworthy men who know their trade won't be easy. If you were willing to take older veterans . . ."

"Find me what you can."

"War is not your only problem, lord. Plague has come to Persia. The skies over Babylon and Susa are black from the smoke of burning Egyptian bodies. It traveled as far as Alexandria. Queen Artakama took ill and her daughter died of it."

"Plague . . ." Alexander mused. "Poor Mereret. My father died in Babylon of a fever. Ptolemy should have known that summers there were bad for sickness."

Alexander entered their chamber as Kiara stepped from a sunken bath. He waved the maid away and lifted a towel from a reed basket. "I love to see you like this," he said to Kiara, "wet and dripping, as though you'd just risen from the sea on the morning of creation."

He held out the towel, and when she reached for it he snatched it out of her grasp and kissed her bare shoulder. She laughed and grabbed for the cloth again. "If you want it, you must pay a forfeit."

"You should not say such things." She bent and wrung the water out of her thick, dark hair, pulling it over her face like a veil. "Your words are music. Most men content themselves with less elegant phrases: 'Here, wench' and 'On your knees, girl.' "

He parted her long hair, revealing her breasts, flat belly, and the dark triangle below. "I'm crushed. I open my heart to the love of my life, and I'm rewarded with cynicism."

Kiara snatched the towel and wrapped it around her hips. "On the contrary, I'm impressed. Very impressed."

He bent and kissed one of her breasts, her throat, and then her mouth. She skimmed her fingertips over his shoulders and tilted her head back to deepen the kiss. Her swollen nipples brushed his chest, and he felt himself grow hard as he ran his hands down the curve of her back and over her womanly hips.

She trembled at his touch, and his pulse raced. Hot desire flared in the pit of his stomach. He wanted her once more before he told her that they couldn't rest here in Tyre as he'd promised, that he was leading her into a land ravaged by plague and war. The thought that her life would be in danger cut like a knife, but he'd promised never to leave her again. "Impressed with my honeyed words," he said thickly, "or my feats of prodigious—"

She giggled and shoved him playfully. "A gentleman doesn't boast of his performance between the sheets."

"What lady dares brag of her experiences with other men?"

She laughed. "You'll be surprised at what I dare." She moistened her lips with the tip of her tongue and kissed him again. "If I had to rate you," she teased, "I would say . . ."

"What? What would you say?" He snatched her up in his arms and threw her back across the wide bed. "Let me have another try at it before you start awarding prizes." He stripped away his kilt and vest, knelt on the bed, and sought her sweet mouth again. Their limbs entwined as the scent of her clean hair and body inflamed him. "Kiara." His breath came in shudders.

He could not get enough of her . . . of her womanly smell, the softness of her skin, the taste of her nipples, or the hot, wet depths between her thighs. Their mating was quick and fierce, and she gave as good as she got, crying out with pleasure when they climaxed.

"Would that I could stay with you like this all day," he whispered as they lay together, damp and satiated. "I have to buy camels and men." He kissed her on the tip of her nose. "Don't move from this spot until I get back. I want to think of you here . . . just like this." He drew her lower lip between his teeth and nipped it lightly. "Words said by a priest mean nothing to us. You are mine, now and forever . . . as much mine as any wife. And if I lose you, there will never be another for me."

She sighed and nestled her head in the crook of his throat. "Tell me, Alexander, tell me what's wrong?"

"What makes you think—"

"Shh." She touched his mouth with her finger. "No lies between us, ever. Tell me what troubles you so that I can share your burden."

Six weeks later, in the great palace of Bactria, Ava woke in a cold sweat. Her leopard, sensing her unease, rumbled and pushed her great black head against the girl's shoulder. "No, Banu," Ava said as the cat ran a raspy tongue down her arm. "No." Still shaking, she leaped up from her bed, ran barefoot across the cold stone floors with the leopard bounding behind her, and fled down the corridor to her parents' apartments.

"Something terrible has happened!" Ava cried, flinging herself into Roxanne's arms and beginning to sob. "Shahi . . . Shahi . . ."

"Hush, you can't know that. You're just worried about her and your papa because of the war." Her mother cradled her against her breast. "You're as cold as ice," she said, pulling a fur blanket around Ava's shoulders. "Nothing has happened to Shahi. Tiz is with her. You've had a bad dream."

"I saw it," Ava whispered hoarsely. "It wasn't a dream. I saw snow falling, and I heard the sounds of battle. Blood—the snow was red with blood. I smelled the smoke." She clutched her mother. "I still smell it."

Her mother gripped her shoulders. "You're certain? Not just a bad dream?"

Ava shook her head. "Different. Real. I heard horses screaming. . . ."

Roxanne nodded. "All right. I believe you." She rose. "I'm going to find Shahi."

"Tonight? Now? Can I come—"

"No, if you've had a vision—if Shahi is injured

346

or . . . dead—you're the heir to the throne. You must remain here in the palace."

"Mama, no! Take me with you. I can—"

"You are a princess, Ava. It's not what you want. It's what's best for our people. If the Greeks overrun our lines, you must take your little sisters and their wet nurses and ride north into Sogdiana by Green Pass. Take the household guard and go to your grandmother in Marakanda. No heroics. No attempts to defend the palace. Do you understand?"

"Don't leave me, Mama. I can fight. I want to go—"

"No, Ava. I leave you in command. The safety of the babies and of the Twin Kingdoms may rest with you. Have courage. You are the great-granddaughter of an Amazon."

"I don't want to be brave. I'm only eight."

Roxanne hugged her tightly. "None of us do, darling. But it is the price we pay for living."

The citadel fell in the hour before dawn. Fire arrows arched through the early morning darkness as Isandros's Greek swordsmen swarmed over the walls, outnumbering the defenders and cutting them down one by one. Shahi released her last arrow into the enemy charge and scrambled over the rear wall after Tiz, hand over hand down a knotted rope.

"Drop," he ordered when she reached the end of the rope.

Inside, fire had reached the stables, and Shahi could hear the frightened screams of the horses. The snow was knee-deep. Clouds of smoke drifted from the burning palisade, making it hard for Shahi to breathe. "I've no arrows left."

"I've three." Tiz grabbed her arm. "This way. We must reach Kayan before he closes the pass."

She dug into the bag at her belt and pulled out her

sheepskin mittens. If her bow was useless, there was no sense in freezing her fingers off. Around them, a few stragglers plunged through the rocks. The snow was coming down harder now, driven by a biting wind off the mountain.

Here in the high country, winter came early. Drifts made the walking hard, but there was no help for it. They'd held out for most of the night, firing down at the invaders as they attempted to storm the walls with ladders, but the Greeks were relentless. Tiz had sent two men for reinforcements sometime before midnight, but it was impossible to tell if they'd survived or whether they'd been able to locate Val's patrol.

Her father was hours away on the far side of the mountain. Since the heavy snows had begun, he and his company of mountaineers had used the elements to close the passes by activating snow slides and avalanches. Val had been on patrol for three days and was expected back by midafternoon, but that would be too late to help the fortress survivors. Even now the Greeks had spread out around the perimeter, hunting down the wounded and murdering them where they lay.

Shahi knelt in the snow beside a fallen soldier. "Can you walk?" she asked him. It was too dark to see his face. She didn't know who he was, only that the man was one of her countrymen.

"Leave him," Tiz said brusquely.

"We can't—"

"You will," he insisted, grabbing her shoulder. "We've got to keep moving. When the sun comes up they will track us." The wounded Sogdian moaned, and Tiz cursed. He leaned down and ran his fingers down the arrow shaft that protruded from the injured man's midsection. "Shot through the gut," Tiz said. "No chance." His hand went to his sheath.

"No!" Shahi protested. Tiz drew his knife across the

dying Sogdian's throat. Shahi gasped. "You killed him. One of our own. You killed him."

"I'll kill more if you don't get moving. You're what's important. Your father would roast me over a hot fire if I let harm come to you."

Tears mingled with the melting snow on Shahi's cheeks as she stumbled away, the sweet scent of the dead soldier's blood filling her head.

"He was dead already, girl. I'd want someone do the same for me if I were gut-shot."

She heard a cry behind her and turned to see a Greek running after them.

"Go!" Tiz ordered.

She fled, uphill and away, running until she could run no more; she leaned, panting, in the shelter of a boulder. Gray, muddy half-light spilled over the peaks. But where was the sun? She needed to find the sun's position to keep moving in the right direction. Here there were no paths, only goat tracks, and they were buried beneath drifts. She knew she must reach the pass where Nckmard had died before her father buried it in snow. If that happened, she'd be trapped on the wrong side of the mountains. If she didn't freeze to death, she'd be fair game for the Greeks or what was left of Ptolemy's army.

A hawk burst up from the small clump of stunted trees, alerting Shahi that someone was coming. She drew her sword and pressed her back against the stone. To her left was a sheer drop of forty feet or more, to her right an upthrust of rock no human could scale. She could run straight ahead, but it meant moving across open ground, and a man with longer legs than hers could overtake her before she reached the next cover.

Her stalker's boots crunched in the snow. She could hear his heavy breathing. She prayed it was Tiz, but she could wait no longer or she'd lose the element of surprise. She leaped into her own tracks, face-to-face with a tall hooded figure holding a drawn sword.

"Shahi! It's me."

She gave a tiny sigh of relief. "Val? Have you seen Tiz?"

"Coming behind me." His voice grew serious. "He's losing blood, but he's still on his feet. Hori's with him. My charioteer."

"They came over the walls before dawn—" she began.

"I know. We were beyond them, in the trees, but I'd only four men left. Joining the fight would have been suicide. We took out a patrol of Egyptians last night, but the cost was high."

"You killed Egyptians?"

He looked at her with resolute eyes. "I guess I made that decision without knowing I had. There's dissension among Pharaoh's nobles. Plague killed half of those who marched from Alexandria. Two of the generals want to turn back and try again next spring."

"How do you know?"

Val's lips tightened. "Hori can be very persuasive."

"Torture? That's for Greeks. We don't do that."

He looked away. "Wake up, Princess. This isn't a game. What Hori learned from that archer might make the difference between the Twin Kingdoms' falling to the invaders or holding fast. Without Ptolemy's army, Isandros may find winter fighting too bitter for his tastes."

"Then they'll just come again next year and the year after that. There will never be an end to it. We can't win, Val. There are too many of them."

"No, that's not true. What Kayan has done has made a tremendous difference. He's blocked the passes. The enemy can't take an army over the mountains."

"Yes, for now. But in the spring, when the snow melts—"

"That's just it. In spring the earth is saturated with water. It's unstable. When Alexander and I were kids, we nearly missed getting buried alive when half a mountain slid away. The Twin Kingdoms are surrounded by mountains. If we could use rock and earth to bury the passes, no one could reach us from the outside."

"Never again," she murmured. "Yes, yes, that could work. But why hasn't Papa done it before? Why didn't my grandfather or—"

"It doesn't matter," Val said. "What matters is that if we can do it now, we can stop the invasions, protect our homeland from the west."

"We'll tell Papa as soon as we reach him—if we can reach him."

"Before he blocks the passes," Val said. "Yes, there is that worry. In any case, we've got to get out of here. Over two hundred of Isandros's men are heading up this mountain and—"

A hawk's whistle sliced the air.

"Tiz," Shahi said. "There, just coming out of the trees."

Two men emerged, the shorter one obviously aiding the second. Val went back to help carry Tiz.

"I told him to leave me."

Hori grinned. A sword cut across his brow was seeping blood, and one pant leg was slashed and bore a dark growing stain. "I told you that this was an uncivilized country, my prince. Throwing him into my chariot would have been a lot easier than carrying him straight up a mountain." He tossed two quivers of arrows into the snow. "Thought these might come in handy."

"Take Shahi and get out of here," Tiz growled. "They're right behind us. There's a path over that ridge." His left arm hung unnaturally, and blood soaked the front of his vest. "There's a drop off the

351

edge, but the path below is wide enough to drive one of Hori's cursed chariots. It will take you straight as the hawk flies to the pass." He scooped up a handful of snow and pressed it against his wounded shoulder. "You'll miss it if you don't look sharp. You can't see it unless you lean over the cliff."

"If I remember, there used to be a spot where there was no trail," Val said, taking a half dozen arrows and passing them to Shahi. "Three logs side by side spanned the gap."

"Still there," Tiz said. "A man strong enough could cross the bridge and roll those logs into thin air."

Val glanced at Shahi. "You take her," he said. "I'll hold off Isandros's men long enough for you to reach that bridge. And Hori can make certain that there's no pursuit past that point."

Shahi's eyes widened. "No, we'll go together or not at all."

Val grabbed her shoulders, jerked her close, and kissed her. "You have to get to Kayan, little sister. But none of us will get there if the Greeks pick us off on that ledge."

Shahi struggled against him. "No, Val. No! I love you!"

Tiz swore. "No! I'm the one to stay. Not you."

"I am the master archer!" Hori said. "I serve you. I will remain and kill the Greeks. I have made a life's career out of killing Greeks."

"Tiz knows the trail, but he's not strong enough to tear up the bridge. And neither am I." Val opened his cloak to show a gaping wound in his lower side. "Get her out of here, or I'll put an arrow through both of you and save the Greeks the trouble!"

"Val, I won't let you die for me," Shahi wailed as Hori dragged her away.

"I'll gladly give my life for you, my love, and for my

country," he said, but the words were too soft for her to hear.

Hori, Tiz, and Shahi had barely reached the cliff edge when two of Isandros's mercenaries charged up the slope, followed by a third man wearing officer's colors. Val took out the lead warrior, a big man with dark hair. He put an arrow through the second's throat and sent the captain tumbling downhill with an arrow protruding from his chest.

The cries of the dying officer drew two more Greeks. The first he caught in the thigh. The man staggered but kept coming, and Val had to put two more shafts into him before he realized that he was dead. His companion blocked two shots with his shield before a third pierced his knee. Once he was flat on his stomach, he made an easier target.

The next wave was harder for Val to beat back. Arrows rained around him. Two found their mark. He stifled a groan as he took one through his calf and a second skimmed his throat, cutting a deep gash.

Snow fell harder. Wind whipped the flakes into his eyes and threatened to spoil his aim. He was cold, very cold, and the wound in his side made him stiff. He shrugged off the hooded cloak. He'd always thought that when he reached this moment, he'd think of something meaningful to say, some last thought to fill his head until he woke in paradise, but he could think of nothing but Shahi, Tiz, and Hori, treading an icy, snow-covered path. He could still taste Shahi's lips, hear her weeping as his friends dragged her away.

He beat back another assault, but his quivers were fast growing empty. His arm was tired; he drew deep, ragged breaths of biting mountain air. He wondered if Alexander was waiting for him, watching even now, laughing. Alexander . . . his brother . . .

Vaguely, he saw more figures storming up the rise.

He heard their battle cries, heard one soldier's death scream as his arrow struck him. Val reached for another arrow and found none. Laughing, he pulled his sword and raised it high.

Val never felt the four arrows that felled him.

Roxanne lashed her horse up the snowy rise, then threw herself from the saddle and ran the last few hundred yards to where her husband stood. "Stop!" she cried. "Don't trigger the snow slide."

"Woman! What are you doing here?" He caught her in his arms. "We have to. There's a large patrol of Greeks on racing camels halfway through the pass." He looked down into her face. "Why have you come?"

"Shahi! Ava had a dream. More than a dream—a vision. Shahi's in trouble. You can't close the pass. She and Val are at the citadel. This is the last road open. You'll cut them off from—"

"It's too late," he said. "I couldn't stop it if I wanted to. The men are up there." He pointed to the far side of the pass. "On the rim. There's no way to—"

"You must," Roxanne insisted. "Let the Greeks through. We'll fight them. I've brought soldiers. Surely—"

"Ava's a child. There's no reason to believe the citadel's fallen because of a child's bad dream."

Roxanne paled. "But what if she's right and we destroy Shahi's only escape route?"

"Below us, Prince Kayan!" a soldier cried. "The first of the Greeks!"

Kiara yanked hard on the camel's bridle, and the shaggy beast groaned and began to cough. "Alexander!" Kiara cried. "There, above us!"

Ahead, a steep gully cut through the side of the mountain. Coming down it, sliding and scrambling

354

through the deep snow, were three figures. The first man was small, hardly more than a youth, Alexander decided. Behind him came a sturdy child supporting a taller Bactrian. Farther behind raced a party of Greeks, swords drawn.

"Ride!" Alexander yelled. He slipped his bow off his shoulder and slapped it across Kiara's camel's rump. The beast lunged forward and began to lope down the narrow passageway between the high rock walls.

Kiara wrapped her fingers into the camel's long hair and held on as tightly as she could. The dromedary's sudden burst of speed sent them flying ahead, past her cousin Fiacaid, who'd been riding point, into the front of the column. The animal's powerful legs plowed through the snow, sending up feathery plumes. Kiara's hood flew off, and her hair came loose and trailed behind her.

Alexander's mount drew level with the steep gully just as the boy tumbled onto the lower trail. Tossing his bow to his other hand, Alexander leaned down and caught the lad's extended hand, dragging him up in front of him on the camel.

"Alexander?"

"Shahi? How—" Alexander seated her firmly in front of him and glanced back to see her companions still twenty yards from the road, their pursuers gaining with every step.

Shahi cried. "It's Tiz! You've got to help him!"

Alexander pulled hard on the camel's bridle, spinning the animal in a tight circle. "Get the other two!" he shouted to the Eire warriors behind him.

Seeing Alexander and his followers at the bottom of the pass, the Greeks began to fire on them. One arrow struck a camel. The animal squealed in pain and went down. Its rider leaped free, bow in hand, and fired back, catching one of the Greek mercenaries in the chest before another of Kiara's guards pulled him up behind him.

Tiz slipped and fell.

"Come!" one of the rescuers cried to the dwarf.

Hori looked at the Greeks bearing down on them, slung Tiz across his broad shoulders, and ran to the waiting camels as an earth-shaking rumble far above them drowned out the war cries of the mercenaries.

Alexander saw the mountain begin to move and lashed his camel into a run. Within seconds the Eire men had snatched up Hori and Tiz and were riding for their lives as thousands of tons of snow and rock roared down on them.

Carrying double, Alexander's mount raced ahead, while he clung to Shahi and concentrated on staying in the saddle. The others thundered after him, as the camels, seeming to understand the danger, ran like startled does.

Ahead, at the mouth of the pass, Kayan waited, bow drawn to shoot the first of the invaders to come into range. As the rider on the camel neared, his muscles tensed, and he took aim at the blue figure's chest. "There's one we won't have to fight again," he said.

"Wait!" Roxanne shouted. "That's a woman! Don't shoot! It's Shahi! See her dark hair! That's our Shahi!"

Kayan hesitated and lowered his bow just as the avalanche began to rumble and tear away the mountainside. Roxanne put her hands over her ears. Kayan stared at the pass as three more riders galloped from the mouth of the canyon. By the time the pass was sealed and the snow had stopped falling, Roxanne was already running for her horse.

Alexander caught up with Kiara and circled his mount to slow its mad pace. "Are you all right?" he shouted to Kiara. "Are you hurt?"

She shook her head. She signaled to her camel, and

when it dropped to its knees, she slid off and opened her arms to Alexander. He and Shahi were already on the ground. He crushed both of them against him.

"Shahi, Kiara of the Seven Shields, my Kiara. Kiara, my oldest sister, Shahi."

"We thought you were dead," Shahi said. "Val said—"

"Val? He's here? You've seen him, talked to him? Is he with Ptolemy's army or—"

"No," Shahi said, tears in her eyes. "Later, I'll tell you later."

"My Eiresmen?" Kiara looked back to see eight camels, three carrying double. "Did they come safe through the pass?"

Alexander kissed the crown of her head. "All of your men are safe."

"You're supposed to be dead," Shahi repeated. "Mother will be . . . Wait." She pointed toward the group of riders galloping toward them on horseback. "She'll want a good explanation. And unless my eyesight is failing me, that's her gray mare in the lead."

Kiara took a step back. Tears welled in her green eyes.

"What's wrong?" Alexander asked her. "We made it. We're here. You've nothing more to fear."

Kiara shook her head.

"What then?"

"Your mother, the queen. I think she'll not be pleased to have me here."

Alexander drew her into his arms and kissed her. "She'll love you," he said. "You're two of a kind. Mother fights with a sword, but you have other weapons, just as deadly."

Shahi looked at Alexander. "Do you love this woman, brother?"

"With all my heart and soul," he answered.

"Are you married to another?" she asked Kiara.

357

"No. My heart is pledged to him alone."

"And there's no reason why you can't give him a quiverful of strong sons?"

"I don't think there is," Kiara said, smiling through her tears. She touched her belly lightly. "I hope to give him sons and daughters."

"Then Mama will adore you on sight," Shahi promised. She touched Alexander's arm, just to make certain he was solid and real. "I have a plan for you and Papa," she said, "a plan to make Bactria and Sogdiana safe for a long time, but that can wait."

The riders were now close enough that both Alexander and Shahi could make out their mother racing neck and neck with Kayan.

Alexander took Kiara's hand in his. "Now will you agree to marry me and be my queen?"

She shook her head. "I told you that I would crown you king."

"I want you beside me, as wife and queen."

"Ask me later."

"How much later?"

She smiled up at him. "That, my lord, will depend entirely on your future good behavior."

The Conqueror

JUDITH E. FRENCH

For two long years her father's tiny mountain kingdom had withstood the conqueror's sweeping forces, but now the barbarians storm the mile-high citadel and the women cower in fear. All but the one called *Little Star*. Famed as the most beautiful woman in all Persia, Roxanne has the courage of a fierce warrior and the training of a prince of her people. When she learns that slavery is not to be her lot, but a brilliant political alliance, she vows to await her bridegroom with her snarling leopard at her side and silken seduction at her fingertips. For she is no plaything, but more than a match for any man, even Alexander the Great.
